DEBBIE MACOMBER

On A Snowy Night

First Published 2002
First Australian Paperback Edition 2004
ISBN 1 741 16175 4

THE CHRISTMAS BASKET © 2002 by Debbie Macomber
THE SNOW BRIDE © 2003 by Debbie Macomber
Philippine Copyright 2002
Australian Copyright 2002
New Zealand Copyright 2002

Published by
Mira Books
3 Gibbes Street
CHATSWOOD NSW 2067
AUSTRALIA

Printed and bound in Australia by
McPherson's Printing Group

CONTENTS

Dear Friends,

I'm big on tradition, and I've established several in my writing life. One is a small hardcover novel each winter; another is a letter to my readers in every book. I have to admit that I envision you, my readers, grabbing the book off the bookseller's shelf and immediately flipping to the page with my letter, in which I talk about the origin of the story or relate an anecdote concerning my grandchildren or update you on my husband and his pygmy goats. (Yes, really! Maybe the goats will turn up in a book one of these days.)

In this letter I'm going to tell you that my youngest son, Dale, has just married his sweetheart (and she *is* a sweetheart), Laurie Kalcso, and they're starting their life together. (Wayne and I are hoping for a new grandchild a few years down the road!) This book is dedicated to them with a heart full of love and pride. Dale and Laurie, may God grant you a long and happy life together and may you always be as much in love as you are now.

And you, my friends and readers... I wish you and your families much happiness, and I hope my story brings you pleasure this Christmas.

Debbie Macomber

P.S. I love hearing from you! Drop me a line at P.O. Box 1458, Port Orchard, Washington 98366, or log on to my Web site at www.debbiemacomber.com.

The Christmas Basket

To
Mr. and Mrs. Dale Macomber
(my son and Laurie)
Merry Christmas
Your first as husband and wife

NOELLE McDOWELL'S JOURNAL

December 1

I did it. I broke down and actually booked the flight to Rose. I have a ticket for December 18—Dallas to San Francisco to Portland and then the commuter flight to Rose.

All my excuses are used up. I always figured there was no going back, and yet that's exactly what I'm doing. I'm going home when I swore I never would. Not after what happened... Not after Thom Sutton betrayed me. I know, I know, I've always been dramatic. I can't help that—it's part of my nature.

When I was a teenager I made this vow never to return. I spoke it in the heat of passion, and no one believed me. For that matter, I didn't believe me, not really. But it proved to be so easy to stay away.... I hardly had to invent excuses. While I was in college I had an opportunity to travel to Europe two years in a row. Then in my junior year I had a summer job and was a bridesmaid in a Christmas wedding. And when my senior year rolled around, I was working as an intern for the software company, and it was impossible to get time off. After that...well, it was just simpler to stay away. Without meaning to, my family made it convenient. I didn't need to visit them; they seemed willing enough to come to Dallas.

All of that is about to end. I'm prepared to face my past. I joined Weight Watchers. If I happen to see Thom Sutton, I want him to know exactly what he's missing. I've already lost five of the ten pounds I need to get rid of, and by next week he'll hardly recognize me—if we even run into each other. We won't, of course, but just on the off chance, I plan to be prepared.

Good ol' Thom Sutton. I wonder what he's doing now. Naturally I could ask, but no one dares mention the name Sutton to my family. It's the Hatfields and McCoys or the Montagues and Capulets all over again. Except that it's our mothers who started this ridiculous feud.

If I really wanted to know about Thom, I could ask Megan or Stephanie. They're the only two girls out of my entire high school class who still live in Rose. But I wouldn't do that. Inquiring about Thom would only invite questions from them about what happened between the two of us. As far as I'm concerned, the fewer people who know, the better.

He's bound to be married, anyway. Good. I want him to be happy.

No, I don't.

If I can't be honest in my journal, then I shouldn't keep one. Okay, I admit it—what I really want is for him to have suffered guilt and regret all these years. He should have pined for me. His life should be a bleak series of endless days filled with haunting memories of me. It's what he deserves.

On a brighter note, I'm thrilled for Kristen. I'll return home, help her plan her wedding, hold my head high and pray that Thom Sutton has the opportunity to see me from afar, gorgeous and thin. Then I want him to agonize over all the might-have-beens.

Chapter One

It would be the wedding of the year. No—the wedding of the century.

Sarah McDowell intended to create the most exquisite event possible, a wedding worthy of *Vogue* Magazine (or at least a two-page spread in the Rose, Oregon, *Gazette*). The entire town would talk about her daughter's wedding.

The foundation for Sarah's plans rested squarely on booking the Women's Century Club for the reception. It was why she'd maintained her association with the club after *that* woman had been granted membership. She was outraged that such a fine institution would lower itself to welcome the likes of Mary Sutton.

Sarah refused to dwell on the sordid details. She couldn't allow herself to get upset over something that had happened almost twenty years ago. Although it didn't hurt any to imagine Mary hearing—second- or third-hand, of course— about Kristen's wedding. As Sarah understood it, Mary's daughter had eloped. Eloped, mind you, with some riffraff hazelnut farmer. Sarah didn't know that for sure because it was her Christian duty not to gossip or think ill of others. However, sometimes information just happened to come one's way....

Pulling into the parking lot of the Women's Century Club, Sarah surveyed the grounds. Even this late in the year, the rose garden was breathtaking. Many of the carefully tended bushes still wore their blooms, and next June, when the wedding was scheduled, the garden would be stunning. The antique roses with their intoxicating scents and the more recent hybrids with their gorgeous shapes and colors would make a fitting backdrop for the beautiful bride and her handsome groom. It would be *perfect,* she thought with satisfaction. Absolutely perfect.

Sarah had stopped attending the Women's Century Club meetings three years ago. Well, there wasn't any need to obsess over the membership committee's sorry lapse in judgment. For many years Sarah had chaired that committee herself. The instant she stepped down, Mary Sutton had applied for membership to the prestigious club—and received it. Now the only social event Sarah participated in was the annual Christmas Dance. Mary Sutton had robbed her of so much already, but Sarah wasn't letting her ruin that, too.

Sarah did continue to meet with other friends from the club and managed to keep up with the news. She understood that Mary had become quite active in the association. Fine. Good for her. It gave the woman something to write about in her column for the weekly *Rose Gazette.* Not that Sarah read "About Town." Someone had told her it was fairly popular, though. Which didn't bother her in the least. Mary was a good writer; Sarah would acknowledge that much. But then, what one lacked in certain areas was often compensated in others. And Mary was definitely lacking in the areas of generosity, fairness, ethics…. She could go on.

With a click of her key chain, Sarah locked her car and headed toward the large, two-story stone structure. There was a cold wind blowing in from the ocean, and she hurried up the steps of the large veranda that surrounded the house. A blast of warm air greeted her as she walked inside. Immediately in front of her was the curved stairway leading to the ballroom on the second floor. She could already picture Kristen moving elegantly down those stairs, her dress sweeping grandly behind her. Today, evergreen garlands were hung along the mahogany railing, with huge red velvet bows tied at regular intervals. Gigantic potted poinsettias lined both sides of the stairway. The effect was both festive and tasteful.

"Oh, how lovely," she said to Melody Darrington, the club's longtime secretary.

"Yes, we're very pleased with this year's Christmas decorations." Melody glanced up from her desk behind the half wall that overlooked the entry. The door to the office was open and Sarah heard the fax machine humming behind her. "Are you here to pick up your tickets for the Christmas dance?"

"I am," Sarah confirmed. "And I'd like to book the club for June seventh for a reception." She paused dramatically. "Kristen's getting married."

"Sarah, that's just wonderful!"

"Yes, Jake and I are pleased." This seriously understated her emotions. Kristen was the first of her three daughters to marry, and Sarah felt as if the wedding was the culmination of all her years as a caring, involved mother. She highly approved of Kristen's fiancé. Jonathan Clark was not only a charming and considerate young man, he held a promising position at an investment firm and had a degree in business. His parents were college professors who lived in Eugene; he was their only son. Whenever she'd spoken with Jonathan's mother, Louise Clark had sounded equally delighted.

Melody flipped the pages of the appointment book to June. "It's a good idea to book the club early."

Holding her breath, Sarah leaned over the half wall and stared down at the schedule. She relaxed the instant she saw that particular Saturday was free. The wedding date could remain unchanged.

"It looks like June seventh is open," Melody said.

"Fabulous." Sarah's cell phone rang, and she reached inside her purse to retrieve it. She sold real estate, but since entering her fifties, she'd scaled back her hours on the job. Jake, who was head of the X-ray department at Rose Hospital, enjoyed traveling. Sarah no longer had the energy to accompany Jake and also maintain her status as a top-selling agent. The number displayed on her phone was that of her husband's office. She'd call him back shortly. He was probably asking about the time of their eldest daughter's flight. Jake and Sarah were going to meet Noelle at the small commuter airport later in the day. What a joy it would be to have all three of their girls home for Christmas, not to mention Noelle's birthday, which was December twenty-fifth. This would be the first time in ten years that Noelle had returned to celebrate *anything* with her family. Sarah blamed Mary Sutton and her son for that, too.

"Should I give you a deposit now?" she asked, removing her checkbook.

"Since you're a member of the club, that won't be necessary."

"Great. Then that's settled and I can get busy with my day. I've got a couple of houses to show. Plus Jake and I are driving to the airport this afternoon to pick up Noelle. You remember our daughter Noelle, don't you?"

"Of course."

"She's living in Dallas these days, and has a high-powered job with one of the big computer companies." What Sarah didn't add was the Noelle had become a workaholic. Getting her twenty-eight-year-old daughter to take time off work was nearly impossible. Sarah and Jake made a point of visiting her once a year and sometimes twice, but this couldn't go on. Noelle had to get over her phobia about returning to Rose—and the risk of seeing Thom Sutton. Oh, yes, those Suttons had done a lot of damage to the McDowells.

With Kristen announcing her engagement and inviting the Clarks to share their Christmas festivities, Sarah had strongly urged Noelle to come home for the celebration. This was an important year for their family, and it was absolutely necessary that Noelle be there with them. After some back-and-forth discussion, she'd finally capitulated.

"Before you leave, there's something you should know," Melody said hesitantly. "There's been a rule change about members using the building."

"Yes?" Sarah tensed, anticipating a roadblock.

"The new rule states that only members who have completed a minimum of ten hours' community service approved by the club will be permitted to lease our facilities."

"But I'm an active part of our community already," Sarah complained. She provided plenty of services to others.

"I realize that. Unfortunately, the service project in question must be determined by the club and it must be completed by the end of December to qualify for the following year."

Sarah gaped at her. "Do you mean to say that in addition to everything else I'm doing in the next two weeks, I have to complete some club project?"

"You haven't been reading the newsletters, have you?" Melody asked, frowning.

Obviously not. Sarah refused to read about Mary Sutton, whose name seemed to appear in every issue these days.

"If you attended the meetings, you'd know it, too." Melody added insult to injury by pointing out Sarah's intentional absence.

Despite her irritation, Sarah managed a weak smile. "All right," she muttered. "What can I do?"

"Actually, you've come at an opportune moment. We need someone who's willing to pitch in on the Christmas baskets."

Sarah was trying to figure out how she could squeeze in one more task before the holidays. "Exactly what would that entail?"

"Oh, it'll be great fun. The ladies pooled the money they raised from the cookbook sale to buy gifts for these baskets. They've made up lists, and what you'd need to do is get everything on your list, arrange all the stuff inside the baskets and then deliver them to the Salvation Army by December twenty-third."

That didn't sound unreasonable. "I think I can do that."

"Wonderful." A smile lit up Melody's face. "The woman who's heading up the project will be grateful for some help."

"The woman?" That sounded better already. At least she wouldn't be stuck doing this alone.

"Mary Sutton."

Sarah felt as though Melody had punched her. "Excuse me. For a moment I thought you said *Mary Sutton*."

"I did."

"I don't mean to be catty here, but Mary and I have…a history."

"I'm sure you'll be able to work something out. You're both adults."

Sarah was stunned by the woman's lack of sensitivity. She wanted to argue, to explain that this was unacceptable, but she couldn't think of exactly what to say.

"You did want the club for June seventh, didn't you?"

"Well, yes, of course, but—"

"Then be here tomorrow morning at ten to meet with Mary."

Numb and speechless, Sarah slowly turned and trudged toward the door.

"Sarah," Melody called. "Don't forget the dance tickets."

Dance. How could she think about the dance when she was being forced to confront a woman who detested her? The feeling might be mutual but that didn't make it any less awkward.

One across. A four-letter word for fragrant flower. Rose, naturally. Noelle McDowell penciled in the answer and moved to the next clue. A prickly feeling crawled up her spine and she raised her head. She disliked the short commuter flights. This one, out of Portland, carried twenty-four passengers. It saved having to rent a vehicle or asking her parents to make the long drive into the big city to pick her up.

The feeling persisted and she glanced over her shoulder. She instantly jerked back and slid down in her seat as far as the constraints of the seat belt allowed. It couldn't be. *No, please,* she muttered, closing her eyes. *Not Thom.* Not after all these years. Not now. But it was, it had to be. No one else would look at her with such complete, unadulterated antagonism. He had some nerve after what he'd done to her.

Long before she was ready, the pilot announced that the plane was preparing to land in Rose. On these flights, no carry-on bags were permitted, and Noelle hadn't taken anything more than her purse on board. Her magazines would normally go in her briefcase, but that didn't fit in the compact space beneath her seat, so the flight attendant had stowed it. She had a *Weight Watchers* magazine and a crossword puzzle book marked *EASY* in large letters across the top. She wasn't going to let Thom see her with either and stuffed them in the outside pocket of her purse, folding one magazine over the other.

Her pulse thundered like crazy. The man who'd broken her heart sat only two rows behind her, looking as sophisticated as if he'd stepped off the pages of *GQ*. He'd always been tall, dark and handsome—like a twenty-first century Cary Grant. Classic features that were just rugged enough to be interesting and very, very masculine. Dark eyes, glossy dark hair. An impeccable sense of style. Surely he was married. But finding out would mean asking her sister or one of her friends who still lived in Rose. Coward that she was, Noelle didn't want to know. Okay, she did, but not if it meant having to ask.

The plane touched down and Noelle braced herself against the jolt of the wheels bouncing on tarmac. As soon as they'd coasted to a stop, the Unfasten Seat Belt sign went off, and the people around her instantly leaped to their feet. Noelle took her time. Her hair was a fright. Up at three that morning to catch the 6:00 a.m. out of Dallas/Ft. Worth, she'd run a brush through the dark tangles, forgoing the usual routine of fussing with mousse. As a result, large ringlets fell like bedsprings

about her face. Normally, her hair was shaped and controlled and co-
erced into gentle waves. But today she had the misfortune of looking
like Shirley Temple in one of her 1930s movies—and in front of Thom
Sutton, no less.

When it was her turn to leave her seat, she stood, looking staunchly
ahead. If luck was with her, she could slip away unnoticed and pretend she hadn't seen him. Luck, however, was on vacation and the instant she stepped into the aisle, the handle of her purse caught on the
seat arm. Both magazines popped out of the outside pocket and flew
into the air, only to be caught by none other than Thom Sutton. The
crossword puzzle magazine tumbled to the floor and he was left holding the *Weight Watchers'* December issue. As his gaze slid over her,
she immediately sucked in her stomach.

"I read it for the fiction," she announced, then added, "Don't I know
you?" She tried to sound indifferent—and to look thin. "It's Tim, isn't
it?" she asked, frowning as though she couldn't quite place him.

"Thom," he corrected. "Good to see you again, Nadine."

"Noelle," she said bitterly.

He glared at her until someone from the back of the line called,
"Would you two mind having your reunion when you get off the plane?"

"Sorry," Thom said over his shoulder.

"I barely know this man." Noelle wanted her fellow passengers to
hear the truth. "I once thought I did, but I was wrong," she explained,
walking backward toward the exit.

"Whatever," the guy behind them said loudly.

"You're a fine one to talk," Thom said. His eyes were as dark and
cold as those of the snowman they'd built in Lions' Park their senior
year of high school—like glittering chips of coal.

"You have your nerve," she muttered, whirling around just in time
to avoid crashing into the open cockpit. She smiled sweetly at the pilot.
"Thank you for a most pleasant flight."

He returned the smile. "I hope you'll fly with us again."

"I will."

"Good to see you, Thom," the pilot said next.

Placing her hand on the railing of the steep stairs that led to the
ground, Noelle did her best to keep her head high, her shoulders
square—and her eyes front. The last thing she wanted to do was trip
and make an even worse fool of herself by falling flat on her face.

She was shocked by a blast of cold air. After living in Texas for the last ten years, she'd forgotten how cold it could get in the Pacific Northwest. Her thin cashmere wrap was completely inadequate.

"One would think you'd know better than to wear a sweater here in December," Thom said, coming down the steps directly behind her.

"I forgot."

"If you came home more often, you'd have remembered."

"You keep track of my visits?" She scowled at him. A thick strand of curly hair slapped her in the face and she tossed it back with a jerk of her head. Unfortunately she nearly put out her neck in the process.

"No, I don't keep track of your visits. Frankly, I couldn't care less."

"That's fine by me." Having the last word was important, no matter how inane it was.

The luggage cart came around and she grabbed her briefcase from the top and made for the interior of the small airport. Her flight had landed early, which meant that her parents probably hadn't arrived yet. At least her luck was consistent—all bad. One thing was certain: the instant Thom caught sight of her mother and father, he'd make himself scarce.

He removed his own briefcase and started into the terminal less than two feet behind her. Because of his long legs, he quickly outdistanced her. Refusing to let him pass her, Noelle hurried ahead, practically trotting.

"Don't you think you're being a little silly?" he asked.

"About what?" She blinked, hoping to convey a look of innocence.

"Never mind." He smiled, which infuriated her further.

"No, I'm serious," she insisted. "What do you mean?"

He simply shook his head and turned toward the baggage claim area. They were the first passengers to get there. Noelle stood on one side of the conveyor belt and Thom on the other. He ignored her and she tried to pretend he'd never been born.

That proved to be impossible because ten years ago Thom Sutton had ripped her heart right out.

For most of their senior year of high school, Thom and Noelle had been in love; they'd also managed to hide that fact from their parents. Sneaking out of her room at night, meeting him after school and passing notes to each other had worked quite effectively.

Then they'd argued about their mothers and the ongoing feud between Sarah and Mary. They'd soon made up, however, realizing that what really mattered was their love. Because they were both eighteen and legally entitled to marry without parental consent, they'd decided to elope. It'd been Thom's suggestion. According to him, it was the only way they could get married, since the parents on both sides would oppose their wishes and try to put obstacles in their path. But once they were married, he said, they could bring their families together.

Noelle felt mortified now to remember how much she'd trusted Thom. But their whole "engagement" had turned out to be a ploy to humiliate and embarrass her. It seemed Thom was his mother's son, after all.

She'd been proud of her love for Thom, and before she left to meet him that fateful evening, she'd boldly announced her intentions to her family. Her stomach twisted at the memory. Her parents were shocked as well as appalled; she and Thom had kept their secret well. Her mother had burst into tears, her father had shouted and her two younger sisters had wailed in protest. Undeterred, Noelle had marched out the door, suitcase in hand, to meet the man she loved. The man she'd defied her family to marry. Except that he didn't show up.

At first she'd assumed it was a misunderstanding—that she'd mistaken the agreed-upon time. Then, throwing caution to the winds, she'd phoned his house and asked to speak to him, only to learn that Thom had gone bowling.

He'd gone *bowling?* Apparently some friends from school had phoned and off he'd gone, leaving her to wait in doubt and misery. The parking lot at the bowling alley confirmed his father's words. There was Thom's car—and inside the Bowlerama was Thom, carousing with his friends. Noelle had peered through the window and seen the waitress sitting on his lap and the other guys gathered around, joking and teasing. Before she went home, Noelle had placed a nasty note on his windshield, in which she described him as a scum-of-the-earth bastard. Their supposed elopement, their so-called love had all been a fraud, a cruel joke. She figured it was revenge what for her mother had done, losing Thom's grandmother's precious tea service. Not *losing* it, actually. She'd borrowed it to display at an open house for another real estate agent—and someone had taken it. That was how the feud started and it had escalated steadily after that.

To make matters worse, she'd had to return home in humiliation and admit that Thom had stood her up. Like the heroine of an old-fashioned melodrama, she'd been jilted, abandoned and forsaken.

For days she'd moped around the house, weeping and miserable. Thom hadn't phoned or contacted her again. It was difficult to believe he could be so heartless, but she had all the evidence she needed. She hadn't seen or talked to him since. For ten years she'd avoided returning to the scene of her shame.

The grinding sound of the conveyor belt gearing up broke Noelle from her reverie. Luggage started to roll out from the black hole behind the rubber curtain. Thom stepped forward, in a hurry to claim his suitcase and leave, or so it seemed. Noelle was no less eager to escape. She'd rather wait in the damp cold outside the terminal than stand five feet across from Thomas Sutton.

The very attractive Thomas Sutton. Even better-looking than he'd been ten years ago. Life just wasn't fair.

"I would've thought your wife would be here to pick you up," she said without looking at him. She shouldn't have spoken at all, but suddenly she had to know.

"Is that your unsubtle way of asking if I'm married?"

She ground her teeth. "Stood up any other girls in the last ten years?" she asked.

His eyes narrowed. "Don't do it, Noelle."

"You're the one who shouldn't have done it."

The man from the back of the plane waltzed past Noelle and reached for his suitcase. "Why don't you two just kiss and make up," he suggested, winking at Thom.

"I don't think so," Noelle said, sending Thom a contemptuous glare. She was astonished to see his anger, as though *he* had something to be angry about. *She* was the injured party here.

"On that I'll agree with you," Thom said. He caught hold of a suitcase and yanked it off the belt with enough force to topple a second suitcase. Without another word, he turned and walked out the door.

No sooner had he disappeared than the glass doors opened and in walked Noelle's parents.

Noelle's youngest sister held a special place in her heart. Carley Sue was an unexpected surprise, born when Noelle was fifteen and

Kristen twelve. She'd only been three when Noelle left for college. Nevertheless, all three sisters remained close. Or as close as e-mail, phone calls and the occasional visit to Dallas allowed.

Sitting on Noelle's bed, Carley rested her chin on one hand as Noelle unpacked her suitcase. "You don't mind that I have your old room, do you?" she asked anxiously.

"Heavens, no. It's only right that you do."

Some of the worry disappeared from Carley's eyes. "Are you really going to be home for two whole weeks?"

"I am." Noelle had tentatively planned a discounted cruise with a couple of friends. Instead, she was vacationing with her parents, planning her sister's wedding and trying not to think about Thom Sutton.

"You're going to the Christmas dance, aren't you?"

"Not if I can get out of it." Her mother was the one who insisted on these social outings, but Noelle would live the rest of her life content if she never attended another dance. They reminded her to much of those long-ago evenings with Thom....

"Mom says you're going."

Noelle sat down on the end of the bed and sighed. "I'll tell her I don't have anything to wear."

"Don't do that," Carley advised. "She'll buy you a pink dress. Mom loves pink. Not just any old pink, either, but something that looks exactly like Pepto-Bismol. She actually wanted Kristen to choose pink for her wedding colors." She grimaced. Reaching down for her feet, Carley curled her fingers over her bare toes and nodded vigorously. "You'd better come to the dance."

This was one of the reasons Noelle found excuse after excuse to stay away from Rose. Admittedly it wasn't the primary reason— Thom Sutton and his mother were responsible for that. But as much as she loved her family, she dreaded being dragged from one social event to the next. She could see her mother putting her on display— in Pepto-Bismol pink, according to Carley. If that wasn't bad enough, Sarah had an embarrassing tendency to speak as though Noelle wasn't in the room, bragging outrageously over every little accomplishment.

"Hey, you want to go to the movies tomorrow?" Noelle asked her sister.

Carley's eyes brightened. "Sure! I was hoping we'd get to do things together."

The doorbell chimed and Carley rolled onto her stomach. "That's Kristen. She's coming over without Jonathan tonight."

"You like Jonathan?" Noelle asked.

"Yeah." Carley grinned happily. "He danced with me once and no one asked him to or anything."

This was encouraging. Maybe he'd dance with her, too.

"Noelle!" Kristen called from the far end of the hallway. She burst into the room, full of energy and spirit. Instantly Noelle was wrapped in a tight embrace. "I can't believe you're here—oh Sis, it's so good to see you."

Noelle hugged her back. She missed the chats they used to have; discussions over the phone just weren't the same as hugs and smiles. "Guess who I ran into on the plane?" Noelle had been dying to talk about the chance encounter with Thom.

Some of the excitement faded from Kristen's eyes. "Don't tell me. Thom Sutton?"

Noelle nodded.

"Who's Thom Sutton?" Carley asked, glancing from one sister to the other.

"A guy I once dated."

"Were you lovers?"

"Carley!"

"Just curious." She shrugged as if this was information she was somehow entitled to.

"Where?" Kristen demanded.

"He was on the same flight as me."

"He still lives here, you know. He's some kind of executive for a mail-order company that's really taken off in the last few years. Apparently he does a lot of traveling."

"How'd you know that?" They'd always avoided the topic of Thom Sutton in their telephone and e-mail communications.

"Jon told me about him. I think Thom might be one of his clients."

"Oh." Not only was Thom Sutton gorgeous, he was successful, too. "I suppose he's engaged to someone stunningly beautiful." That was to be expected.

"I hear—again from Jon—that he dates quite a bit, but there's no one serious."

Noelle shouldn't be pleased, but she couldn't help it. She didn't want to examine that reaction too closely.

"I want to know what happened," Carley demanded, rising to her knees. "I'm not a kid anymore. Tell me!"

"He was Noelle's high school sweetheart," Kirsten explained.

"The guy who left you at the altar?"

"Who told you that?" Noelle asked, although the answer was obvious. "And he didn't leave me at the altar." *Just being accurate,* she told herself. *I'm not defending him.*

"Mom told me 'cause she wants me to keep away from those Suttons. When I asked her why, she said you learned your lesson the hard way. She said a Sutton broke your heart and jilted you."

"There's more to it than that," Kristen told her.

"I want to know *everything,*" Carley pleaded. "How can I hate them if I don't know what they did that was so awful?"

"You shouldn't hate anyone."

"I don't, not really, but if our family doesn't like their family, then I should know why."

"It's a long story."

Carley sat back on her heels. "That's what Mom said."

"God help me," Kristen murmured, covering her eyes with one hand. "Don't tell me I already sound like Mom. I didn't think this would happen until I turned thirty."

Noelle laughed, although she wasn't sure how funny it was, since she herself was only days from her twenty-ninth birthday.

"Did you love him terribly?" Carley asked with a faraway look in her eyes.

Noelle wasn't sure how to respond. She felt a distant and remembered pain but refused to let it take hold. "I thought I did."

"It was wildly romantic," Kristen added. "They were madly in love, but then they had a falling-out—"

"That's one way to put it," Noelle said, interrupting her sister. Thom had apparently fallen out of love with her. He'd certainly fallen out of their plans to elope.

"This is all so sad," Carley said with an exaggerated sigh.

"Our parents not getting along is what started this in the first place."

"At least you and Thom didn't kill yourselves, like Romeo and Juliet—"

"No." Noelle shook her head. "I've always been the sane, sensible sister. Remember?" But even as she spoke, she recognized her words for the lie they were. Staying away for ten years was a pretty extreme and hardly "sensible" reaction. Even she knew that. The fact was, though, something that had begun as a protest had simply become habit.

"Oh, sure," Kristen teased. "Very sensible. You work too hard, you don't date nearly enough and you avoid Rose as though we've got an epidemic of the plague."

"Guilty, guilty, not guilty." She wasn't *purposely* avoiding Rose, she told herself, at least not anymore and not to the extent that Kristen implied. Noelle's job was demanding and it was difficult to take off four or five days in a row.

"I've never met Thom, and already I don't like him," Carley announced. "Anyone who broke your heart is a dweeb. Besides, if he married you the way he said he would, you'd be living in Rose now and I could see you anytime I wanted."

"Well put, little sister," Kristen said. She shrugged off her coat, then joined Carley at the foot of the bed.

Noelle smiled at her two sisters and realized with a pang how much she missed them. Back in Texas it was all too easy to let work consume her life—to relegate these important relationships to fifteen-minute conversations on the phone.

"Look," Kristen said and stretched out her arm so Noelle could see her engagement ring. It was a solitaire diamond, virtually flawless, in a classic setting. A perfect choice for Kristen. "Jon and I shopped for weeks. He wanted the highest-quality stone for the best price." Her eyes softened as she studied the ring.

"It's beautiful," Noelle whispered, overcome for a moment by the sheer joy she saw in her sister's face.

"You'll be my maid of honor, won't you?"

"As long as I don't have to wear a dress the color of Pepto-Bismol."

"You're safe on that account."

"If you ask me to be the flower girl, I think I'll scream," Carley muttered. "Why won't anyone believe me when I tell them I'm not a little kid anymore? I'm almost fourteen!"

"Not for ten months," Noelle reminded her.

"But, I'm *going* to be fourteen."

Kristen brushed the hair away from Carley's face. "Actually, I intended to ask you to be a bridesmaid."

"You did?" Carley shrieked with happiness. "Well, then, I'll tell you what I overheard Mom tell Dad." Her voice dropped to a whisper as she detailed a conversation between their parents regarding Christmas baskets.

"Mom's meeting with *Mrs. Sutton* tomorrow morning?" Noelle repeated incredulously.

"That's what she said. She didn't sound happy about it, either."

"I'll just bet she didn't."

"This should be interesting," Kristen murmured.

Yes, it should, Noelle silently agreed. *It should be very interesting, indeed.*

NOELLE McDOWELL'S JOURNAL

December 19
(2:00 a.m.)

So I saw him before I even got back to town. Of all the flights I could've taken...

Seeing Thom after all these years was probably the most humbling experience of my life, except for the last time I was with him. Correction. Wasn't with him. Why did this have to happen to me? Or did I bring it on myself because of my obsession over seeing him again?

Okay, the thing to do is look at the positive aspect of this. It's over. I saw him, it was worse than I could have imagined, but now I don't need to worry about it anymore. Thom made it clear that he wasn't any happier to see me than I was about running into him. At least the feeling's mutual. Although I'm kind of confused by that, since I'm the offended one. He jilted me. Unfortunately, after this latest run-in, he doesn't have any reason to regret that. I behaved like an idiot.

On a brighter note—and I'm always looking for brighter notes!—it's good to be home. I shouldn't have stayed away for ten years. That was foolish and I'm sorry about it. I walked all through the house, stopping in each room. After a while, I got all teary as I looked around. Nothing's really changed and yet everything's different. I didn't realize how much I've missed my home. Mom's got the house all decorated for Christmas, including those funny-looking cotton-ball snowmen I made at camp a thousand years ago. When I commented on that, she told me it was tradition. She puts them out every Christmas. She got all choked up and I did, too. We hugged, and I promised I'd never stay away this long again. And I won't.

Carley Sue (she hates it when I use her middle name) is so much fun. Seeing her here, in her own space (even if it is my old room), is like discovering an entirely different side of her. She's freer, more relaxed, and so eager to share the camaraderie between me and Kristen.

Speaking of Kristen—she's on cloud nine. We sat up and talked for hours, and she told me all about meeting and falling in love with Jonathan. I'd heard it before, but the story felt brand-new as I listened to her tell it in person. It's so romantic, meeting her future husband in a flower shop when he's there to pick up a dozen red roses for another woman. I give him credit, though; Jonathan knew a real flower when he saw one. It was Kristen who walked out with those roses.

Carley warned me that Mom's going to be looking for company when she has to meet Mrs. Sutton in the morning. We've already thwarted her. We sisters have our ways....

Chapter Two

Sarah would have preferred a root canal to meeting with Mary Sutton. A root canal without anaesthetic.

Her husband lingered over his morning coffee before leaving for the hospital. "You're really stressed about this, aren't you?"

"Yes!" Sarah wasn't afraid to admit it. "The last time I spoke to Mary was the day she wrote that dreadful article about me in her column."

"You think that article was only about you," Jake said. "But it could've been about any real estate agent. Maybe even a bunch of different ones." His voice drifted off.

Sarah didn't understand why her husband was arguing when they both knew the entire dreadful piece titled, *The Nightmare Real Estate Agent,* was directed solely at *her.* Although she hadn't committed any of sins Mary had described, she'd been guilty of the one crime Mary hadn't mentioned. Never once had she misrepresented a home or hidden a defect. Nor had she ever low-balled a client. But Sarah had borrowed something she couldn't return.

"Was that *before* or *after* you planted the *OPEN HOUSE* sign in her front yard?" Jake asked.

"Before, and she deserved it."

Her husband chuckled. "Go on, meet with her and don't for a moment let her know you're upset."

"You sound like a commercial for deodorant."

"Yes, dear." He kissed her cheek and headed out the door to work.

Tightening the belt of her housecoat, Sarah gazed out the front window as he drove away. *Meet with her...* Easy for him to say. He wasn't the one coming face-to-face with Mary after all these years.

Yawning, Noelle wandered into the kitchen and poured a cup of coffee. Sarah's spirits lifted immediately. It was so good to have her daughter home—and even better that she'd arrived at such an opportune moment. Noelle could act as a buffer between her and that demented newspaper writer who'd once been her friend. True, there was the business with the Sutton boy, but if nothing else, that unfortunate bit of history would distract them all from this current awkwardness. She felt a twinge of guilt at the idea of involving her daughter. Still, she needed reinforcements, and surely Noelle was long over her infatuation with Thom.

"Good morning, dear," Sarah said, mustering a cheerful greeting. "I was wondering if you'd like to come with me this morning." Try as she might, she couldn't keep the plea out of her voice.

Her daughter leaned against the kitchen counter, holding the mug with both hands. "I promised to take Carley shopping and to the movies."

"Oh. That won't be until later, will it?"

"Mom," Noelle said, sighing loudly. "I'm *not* going to let you use me as a buffer when you meet Mrs. Sutton."

"Who told you I was meeting..." She didn't bother to finish the question, since the answer was obvious. Jake! Dumping the rest of her coffee down the sink, she reluctantly went to her room to dress. She'd be entering the lion's den alone, so she wanted to look her best.

"I don't think she's nearly the monster you make her out to be," Noelle called after her.

That her own daughter, her oldest child—the very one who'd been jilted by Thom Sutton—could say such a thing was beyond Sarah. As far as she was concerned, there was too much forgiveness going on here. And if Noelle thought Mary was so wonderful, then she should be willing to come along.

Didn't Noelle grasp the unpleasantness of this situation? Clearly not. Even Jake didn't take it seriously. He seemed to think this was some kind of joke! Well, she, for one, wasn't laughing.

Despite her bad feelings about the meeting with Mary Sutton, Sarah arrived at the Women's Century Club twenty minutes early. This was the way she'd planned it. As she recalled, Mary possessed a number of irritating habits, one of which was an inability to ever show up on time. Therefore, Sarah considered it advantageous to be early, as though that would highlight Mary's lack of responsibility and basic courtesy.

"Good morning, Melody," she said as she stepped briskly into the entry.

"Morning," came Melody's reply. The phone rang just then, and she reached for it, still standing in front of the copy machine.

While she waited, Sarah checked her appearance in the lobby rest room. She'd taken an inordinate amount of time with her makeup that morning. Her hair was impeccably styled, if she did say so herself, and her clothes looked both businesslike and feminine. Choosing the right outfit was of the utmost importance; in the end, after three complete changes, she'd chosen navy-blue wool slacks, a white cashmere sweater and a silk scarf with a pattern of holly and red berries.

Melody finished with the phone. "Sorry, it's crazy around here this morning. Everyone's getting ready for the dance."

Of course. In her dread, she'd nearly forgotten about the annual dance.

The door opened, and with a dramatic flair—all swirling scarves and large gestures—Mary Sutton entered the building. Did the woman think she was on stage, for heaven's sake? "Hello Melody," she said, her voice light and breezy. Then—as if she'd only now noticed Sarah—she turned in her direction, frowned slightly and then acknowledged her with a curt nod.

"Good to see you, too," Sarah muttered.

"I'm here for the list. The Christmas basket list," Mary said, walking over to the half wall behind which Melody stood.

"That's why I'm here," Sarah said and forced herself into the space between Mary and the wall.

The two jockeyed for position, elbowing each other until Melody stared at them aghast. "What's *wrong* with you two?" she asked.

"As I explained earlier, we have a *history,*" Sarah said, as though that should account for everything.

"A very long and *difficult* history," Mary added.

"You'll have to work together on this." Melody frowned at them both. "I'd hate to see these needy families deprived because you two can't get along." The phone rang again and Melody scooped up the receiver.

"You're impossible to work with," Mary said, practically shoving Sarah aside.

"I won't stand here and be insulted by the likes of you," Sarah insisted. Talk about impossible!

"This isn't going to work."

"You're telling me!" She was ready to walk out the door. But then she realized that was exactly what Mary wanted her to do. She'd been provoking Sarah from the moment she'd made that stagy entrance. This was a low, underhanded attempt to prevent her from holding Kristen's wedding reception at the club. Somehow Mary had found out about the wedding and hoped to thwart the McDowells' plans. That had to be it. But Sarah refused to let a Sutton—especially *this* Sutton—manipulate her.

"There are ways of doing what needs to be done without tripping over each other's feet," Sarah murmured, trying to sound conciliatory. She could only hope that Kristen truly appreciated the sacrifice she was making on her behalf. If it wasn't for the wedding, she wouldn't be caught dead working on a project with Mary Sutton, charity or not!

"What do you mean?"

"There *must* be a way." She personally didn't have any ideas, but perhaps the club secretary could think of something. "Melody?"

Another line rang, and Melody put the first caller on hold in order to answer the second. She placed her palm over the mouthpiece and said, "Why don't you two go talk this out in the lobby?" She waved them impatiently away. "I'll be with you as soon as I can."

Sarah took a few steps back, unwilling to voluntarily give up hard-won territory. This was more of a problem than she'd expected. For her part, she was willing to make the best of it, but she could already tell that Mary had her own agenda.

"The Christmas decorations are lovely this year, aren't they?" Sarah said, making an effort to start again. After all, she was stuck with the woman.

"Yes," came Mary's stilted reply. "I'm the chair of the decorating committee."

"Oh." She studied the staircase again and noticed a number of flaws apparent on closer inspection. Walking to the bottom step, she straightened a bow.

"Leave my bows alone!"

"A little possessive, are we?" Sarah murmured.

"You would be, too, if you'd spent twenty minutes making each of those velvet bows."

"I could have done it in ten."

"Next year, I'll let you." Then, as if she was bored with the subject, Mary said, "I understand Noelle's in town."

"Yes, and I'd appreciate if you'd keep your son away from her."

"My son!" Mary cried. "You don't need to worry about *that*. Thom learned his lesson as far as your daughter's concerned a long time ago."

"On the contrary, I believe your son broke my daughter's heart."

"Ladies!" Melody came out from behind the counter, shaking her head. "I thought we were discussing ways you two can work together to fill those Christmas baskets."

"I don't think I *can* work with her," Mary said, crossing her arms. She presented Sarah with a view of her back.

"Then divide the list," Melody suggested. "One of you can shop for the gifts and the other can buy the groceries. Arrange a day to meet and assemble the baskets, and then you'll be done with it."

Sarah didn't know why she hadn't thought of that earlier. It made perfect sense and would allow them to maintain a healthy distance from each other.

"Divide the list," Mary instructed with a dramatic wave of her hand.

"By all means, divide the list," Sarah said and mimicked Mary's gesture.

"All right," Melody said. She went back to her office, with the two women following, and slipped the list into the photocopier. The phone rang again, and she answered it, holding the receiver between her shoulder and ear. Melody retrieved the original and the copy, reached for the scissors and cut both lists in two. Still talking, she dropped the papers, then picked them up and handed half of the original list to Mary and half to Sarah. The copies of each woman's list went into a file on her desk.

Sarah glanced over her list and tucked it inside her purse. "When do you suggest we meet to assemble the baskets?"

"The twenty-third before noon. That way, we'll be able to drop them off at the Salvation Army in plenty of time. They'll distribute the baskets on Christmas Eve."

"Fine." That settled, Sarah charged out the door without a backward glance. This wasn't the best solution, but it was manageable. She'd do her share of the work, and she wasn't about to let anyone suggest otherwise.

"This is so cool," Carley said as they left the mall late Thursday afternoon, their arms loaded with bags and packages. Noelle smiled fondly at her youngest sister. That summer, Carley had spent two weeks with her in Texas while their parents were on a cruise. She'd matured noticeably in the six months since then.

"Mom's not selling much real estate anymore," her sister told her as they climbed into the car. "I think she's bored with it, but she won't admit it."

"Really?"

"She's totally involved in Kristen's wedding. It's all she thinks about. She's read a whole bunch of books and magazine articles and has everything set in her mind. Just the other day, she said that what this town really needs is a wedding planner."

"And you think Mom would enjoy that?"

"Are you kidding?" Carley said. "She'd *love* it."

Their mother was extremely sociable, which was one of the reasons she was such a successful real estate agent, Noelle mused. Sarah knew nearly everyone in town and had wonderful connections. Perhaps Carley was right.

"The Admiral really hasn't changed," Noelle murmured. She'd spent a lot of time at the old downtown theater, back in high school. It was there, in the balcony, that Thom had first kissed her. To this day—as much as she wanted to forget it—she remembered the thrill of that kiss.

The Admiral was a classic theater built sixty years earlier. The screen was huge and the second-floor balcony held the plush loge seats—always Noelle's favorite place to sit.

They purchased the tickets, a large bucket of popcorn and drinks.

"Do you want to go up to the balcony?" Carley asked.

"Where else would we sit?" Noelle was already halfway up the winding stair that led to the second floor. She went straight to the front row and plopped down on a cushioned seat. Carley plopped down beside her. The main feature was a Christmas release, an animated film starring the voices of Billy Crystal and Nathan Lane.

"I'm not a kid anymore, but I'm glad you wanted to see this movie, too," her sister confided.

Noelle placed the bucket of popcorn between them. "Thanks for giving me the excuse." She leaned forward and looked at the audience below. The theater was only half-full and she wondered if she'd recognize anyone.

"Oh, my goodness," she whispered. This couldn't be happening! Thom Sutton sat almost directly below her. If that wasn't bad enough, a blonde sat in the seat beside him and—to Noelle's disgust—had her hands all over him.

"What?" Carley demanded.

"It's Thom." Heaven help her, Noelle couldn't keep from watching. The blonde's hand lingered at the base of his neck; she was stroking his hair with all the tenderness of a longtime lover.

"Not Thom Sutton? The son of the enemy?" Carley asked.

Noelle nodded. Sad and shocking though it was, he obviously still had the power to hurt her. No, not hurt her—infuriate her!

Carley reached for a kernel of popcorn and tossed it down.

Noelle gasped, grabbing her sister's hand. The last thing she wanted was to call attention to the balcony. "Don't do that!"

"Why not? He jilted you and now he's here with another woman." She hurled another kernel in his direction.

Noelle glanced down and saw the blonde nibbling on his earlobe. That did it. She scooped out a handful of popcorn and threw it over the balcony railing. Noelle and her sister leaned back and smothered their giggles. A few minutes later, unable to resist, Noelle looked down again.

"Oh, no," Carley muttered under her breath as she sent a fresh shower of popcorn over the edge. She jerked back instantly.

"What?" Noelle asked.

"I think we're in trouble. He just turned around and looked up here and I don't think he's pleased."

Fine, the management could throw her out of the theater if he complained. Noelle didn't care.

"I want to know about you and him," Carley said. "I wasn't even born when his mom and our mom had their big fight."

Noelle was reluctant to describe all this old history, but she supposed her sister had a right to know. "Well, Mom had just started selling real estate and was making new friends. She claims Mary was jealous of those friends, especially one whose name was Cheryl. Cheryl had been working at the agency for a while and was kind of showing Mom the ropes. She was holding an open house and wanted something elegant to set off the dining room. Mom knew that Mary had this exquisite silver tea service—the perfect thing. But Mom also knew that if she asked Mary to lend it to Cheryl, Mrs. Sutton would turn her down. Instead, Mom asked to borrow it for herself, which was a fib."

Carley frowned. "So that's why Mrs. Sutton blamed Mom? Because Mom lied—I mean fibbed—and then the expensive silver tea service got stolen? Oh, I bet Mom was just sick about it."

"She felt awful. According to Mrs. Sutton, the tea service had belonged to her grandmother and was a family heirloom. It was irreplaceable."

"What did Mom do?"

"She called the police and offered a reward for its return, but the tea service didn't turn up. She went to every antique store in the area, looking for something similar. Finally there was nothing more she could do. She tried to repair the damage to the friendship, but Mrs. Sutton was angry—and really, you can't blame her. She was hurt because Mom had misled her. They got into this big argument about it and everything escalated from there. Mrs. Sutton did some petty things and Mom retaliated. Next thing you know, a grudge developed that's gone on to this day."

"Retaliated?" Carley asked. "How?"

"When it became clear that Mrs. Sutton wasn't going to forgive and forget, Mom tried another tactic. She thought she'd be funny." Noelle smiled at the memory. "Mrs. Sutton got her hair cut, and Mom sent her flowers and a sympathy card. Then Mrs. Sutton ordered pizza with double anchovies and had it delivered to Mom. You know how Mom hates anchovies—and furthermore she had to pay for it." She shook her head. "It's sad, isn't it? That a good friendship should fall apart for such a silly reason."

"Yeah," Carley agreed. "They acted pretty childish."

"And my relationship with Thom was one of the casualties."

"When did you fall in love with him?" Carley wanted to know.

"We became good friends when we were kids. For a long time, our families got along really well. We often went on picnics and outings together. Thom and I were the closest in age, and we were constant companions—until the argument."

"What happened after the argument?"

"Mrs. Sutton sent Thom and his older sister to a private school, and I didn't see him again for about six years. He came back to public school when we were sophomores. We didn't have a lot in common anymore and hardly had anything to do with each other until we both were assigned to the same English class in our senior year."

"That was when you fell in love?" Carley's voice rose wistfully.

Noelle nodded, and the familiar pain tightened her stomach. "Apparently I fell harder than Thom."

Noelle carefully glanced down again. Talking about Thom and her romance—especially while she was sitting in this theater—brought up memories she'd prefer to forget. Why wouldn't the stupid movie start? It was two minutes past the scheduled time.

The boy who'd rung up the popcorn order marched down the side aisle toward Noelle and Carley. He wore a bored but determined look. "There's been a complaint from the people down below about you throwing popcorn," he said accusingly.

Noelle could feel the heat build up in her cheeks. "I'm sorry—that was, uh, an accident."

The kid's expression said he'd heard it all before. "Make sure it doesn't happen again, okay?"

"It won't," Noelle promised him.

"Sorry," Carley said in a small voice as the boy left.

"It was my fault. I encouraged you."

"But I started it."

"You think you're the one who invented throwing popcorn? Hey, I've got fifteen years on you."

"I want to fall in love one day, too," Carley said, leaning back in her seat, which rocked slightly.

"You will," Noelle said, hoping her sister had better luck in that department than she'd had.

The lights dimmed then and with a grand, sweeping motion the huge velvet curtain hanging over the screen slowly parted. Soon, they were watching previews for upcoming features. Noelle absently nibbled on popcorn and let her mind wander.

Thom had changed if the blonde down below was the type of woman he found attractive. That shouldn't surprise her, though. Time changed a lot of things in life. Some days, when she felt lonely and especially sorry for herself, she tried to imagine what would've happened if she *had* married Thom all those years ago. Getting married that young rarely worked out. They might've been divorced, she might've ended up a single mother, she might never have completed her education.... All kinds of difficult outcomes were possible. In all honesty, she told herself, it was for the best that they hadn't run off together.

Carley slid forward and peeked over the railing. Almost immediately she flopped back. "You wouldn't *believe* what they're doing now."

"Probably not."

"They're—"

Noelle gripped her sister's elbow. "I don't want to know."

Carley's eyes were huge. "You don't want me to tell you?"

"No."

Her sister stared at her in utter amazement. "You really don't care?"

Noelle shook her head. That wasn't the whole truth—or even part of it. But she didn't want to know if Thom had his arm around the blonde or if he was kissing her—or anything else. It was a lot less painful to keep her head buried in a popcorn bucket. Forget Weight Watchers. Sometimes fat grams were the only source of comfort.

"Are you going to confront him after the movie?" Carley asked excitedly.

Noelle snickered. "Hardly."

"Why not?"

"Just watch the movie," she advised.

Carley settled in her seat and and began to rock back and forth. Another time, the action might have annoyed Noelle, but just then she found it oddly comforting. She wanted a special someone to put his arm around her and gently rock her. To create a private world for the two of them, the way Thom had once done in this very theater, on this very balcony. He'd kissed her here and claimed her heart. It'd been a pivotal moment in their fledgling romance. From that point onward, they knew—or at least Noelle had known. She was in love and willing to make whatever sacrifices love demanded.

All too soon, the feature had ended and the lights came back on. "That was great," Carley announced.

Caught up in wistful memories, Noelle got to her feet, gathering her coat and purse. She took pains not to glance below, although her curiosity was almost overwhelming.

"We meet again," an all-too-familiar voice said from behind her.

"Thom?" She turned to see him two rows back, with a four- or five-year-old boy at his side.

Noelle's reaction was instantaneous. She looked below and discovered the blond beauty with her male friend, who just happened *not* to be Thom Sutton. "I thought—"

"*You're* Thom?" Carley asked, glowering with righteous indignation.

"Don't tell me you're Carley," he returned, ignoring the girl's outrage. "My goodness, you've grown into a regular beauty."

Carley's anger died a quick death. "Do you really think so?"

"I sure do. Oh, this is my nephew Cameron."

"Hello, Cameron," Noelle said. "Did you enjoy the movie?"

The boy nodded. "Yeah, but the best part was when the man came up and told you not to throw any more popcorn. Uncle Thom said you got in trouble." The kid sounded far too smug for Noelle's liking.

So Thom had heard and seen the whole thing.

Oh, great.

Friday morning, Sarah dressed for her Christmas basket shopping adventure. She felt as though she was suiting up for an ordeal, some test or rite of passage. The hordes of shoppers were definitely going to try her patience; she'd finished her own shopping months ago and failed to see why people waited until the very last week. Well, the sooner she purchased the things on her half of the list, the better. With Christmas only five days away, she didn't have a minute to waste.

She wasn't getting any help from her family—not that she'd really expected it. Jake was at work, and Noelle was driving Carley to her friend's house and then meeting Kristen for lunch.

She was on her own.

Wanting to get the most for her buying dollar, Sarah drove to the biggest discount store in Rose. The Value-X parking lot was already filled. After driving around repeatedly, she finally found a space. She locked her car and hunched her shoulders against the wind as she hurried toward the building. The sound of the Salvation Army bell-ringer guided her to the front entrance. She paused long enough to stick a dollar bill in his bucket, then walked into the store.

Sarah grabbed a cart and used the booster seat to prop up her purse. The list was in the side pocket of her bag, and she searched for the paper as she walked. She hadn't gone more than a few feet from the entrance when she nearly collided with another woman obtaining a cart.

"I'm sorry," she said automatically. "I—" The words froze on her lips.

"I should've known anyone that rude must be you," Mary Sutton muttered sarcastically.

Although her heart was pounding, Sarah made a relatively dignified escape and steered the cart around Mary. With purpose filling every step, she pushed her cart toward the toy department. Her list was gifts, which meant Mary had the grocery half. Hmph. It didn't surprise her that Mary Sutton bought her family's Christmas gifts at a discount store—or that she waited until the last minute.

The first part of the list directed her to purchase gifts for two girls, ages six and seven. The younger girl had requested a doll. Having raised three daughters, Sarah knew that every little girl loved Barbie. This late in the season, she'd be fortunate to find the current Barbie.

Almost right away she saw that the supplies were depleted, just as she'd suspected. But one lone Firefighter Barbie stood on the once-crowded shelf. Sarah reached for it at the precise moment someone else did.

"I believe I was first," she insisted. Far be it from her to allow some other person to deprive a poor little girl longing for a Barbie on Christmas morning.

"I believe you're wrong."

Mary Sutton. Sarah glared at her with such intensity that Mary must have realized she was not about to be dissuaded.

"Fine," Mary said after a moment and released her death grip on the Barbie.

"Thank you." Sarah could be gracious when called upon.

With her nose so high in the air she was in danger of hitting a light fixture, Mary stomped off in the opposite direction. Feeling satisfied with herself, Sarah studied the list again and noticed the name of a three-year-old boy. A small riding toy would do nicely, she decided and headed for that section of the department.

As she turned the corner she ran into Mary Sutton a third time. Mary stopped abruptly, her eyes narrowed. "Are you following me?" she demanded.

"Following *you?*" Sarah faked a short, derisive laugh. "You've got to be joking. I have no desire to be within ten feet of you."

"Then I suggest you vacate this aisle."

"You can't tell me where to shop or in what aisle!"

"Wanna bet?" Mary leaned forward and, intentionally or not, her cart rammed Sarah's.

Refusing to allow such an outrage to go unanswered, Sarah retaliated by banging her cart into Mary's.

Mary pulled back and hit her again, harder this time.

Soon they were throwing stuffed French poodles at each other, hurling them off the shelves. A German Shepherd sailed over Sarah's head. That was when she reached for the Golden Retriever, the largest of the stuffed animals.

"Ladies, ladies." A man in a red jacket hurried toward them, his arms outstretched. His name badge read Michael and identified him as the store manager.

"I'm so sorry, Michael," Sarah said, pretending to recognize him. "This little, uh, misunderstanding got completely out of hand."

"You're telling me!" Mary yelled.

"This woman is following me."

"Oh, puh-leeze." Mary groaned audibly. "This woman followed *me.*"

"I don't think it's important to know who followed whom," the manager said in a conciliatory voice. "But we need to—"

"She took the last Barbie," Mary broke in, pointing an accusing finger at Sarah. "I got it first—the doll was *mine.* Any jury in the land would rule in my favor. But I kindly offered it to her."

"Kindly, nothing. I had that Barbie and you know it!"

"Ladies, please…" The manager stood between them in an effort to keep them apart.

"There's only so much of this I can take," Mary said, sounding close to tears. "I'm here—"

"It isn't important why you're here," Sarah interrupted. She wasn't about to let Mary Sutton come off looking like the injured party. The woman had purposely rammed her cart. "She assaulted me."

"I most certainly did not!"

"You should check the front of my cart for damage, and if there is any, I suggest that you, as manager, charge this woman," Sarah said.

Two security officers arrived then, dressed in blue uniforms.

"Officer, officer…"

Mary turned soft and gentle. "Thank you for coming."

"Oh, give me a break," Sarah muttered. "Is it within your power to arrest this woman?" she demanded.

"Ladies," the manager said, trying once more, it seemed, to appeal to their better natures. "This is the season of goodwill toward men— and women. Would it be possible for you to apologize to each other and go about your business?"

Mary crossed her arms and looked away.

Sarah gestured toward the other woman as if to say Mary's action spoke for itself. "I believe you have your answer."

"Then you leave me no choice," the manager said. "Officers, please escort these two ladies from the store."

"What?" Mary cried.

"I beg your pardon?" Sarah said, hands on hips. "What is this about?"

The larger of the two security guards answered. "You're being kicked out of the store."

Sarah's mouth fell open.

The only person more shocked was Mary Sutton. "You're evicting me from Value-X?"

"You heard the manager, lady," the second officer said. "Now, come this way."

"Could I pay for the Barbie doll first?" Sarah asked, clutching the package to her chest. "It's for a little girl and it's all she wants for Christmas."

"You should've thought of that before you threw the first poodle," the manager said.

"But—"

Dramatically, he pointed toward the front doors. "Out."

Mortified to the marrow of her bones, Sarah turned, taking her cart with her. One wheel was now loose and it squeaked and squealed. Just when she figured things couldn't get any worse, she discovered that a crowd had gathered in the aisle to witness her humiliation.

"Merry Christmas," she said with as much bravado as she could manage.

The officer at her side raised his hand. "We're asking that everyone return to their shopping. What happened here is over."

With her dignity intact but her pride in shreds, Sarah made her way to the parking lot, still accompanied by the officer.

She could see the "About Town" headline already. *Manager Expels Sarah McDowell From Value-X After Cat Fight.* Although technically, she supposed, it should be Dog Fight.

She had no doubt that Mary Sutton would use the power of the press to complete her embarrassment.

NOELLE McDOWELL'S JOURNAL

December 19 11:30 p.m.

I can't believe it! Even now, when it's long past time for bed, I'm wide-awake and so furious, any chance of falling asleep is impossible. I doubt if anyone could do a better job of looking like a world-class idiot. Right there in the theater, with my little sister at my side, I behaved like a juvenile.

I've worked hard to be a positive influence on Carley. I take my role as oldest sister very seriously. Then I go and pull a stunt like this. Adding insult to injury is the fact that I then had to face Thom, knowing he was completely aware of what a fool I'd made of myself.

Speaking of Thom...no, I don't want to think about him. First the airplane and now this! I'd sincerely hoped he'd be married with a passel of kids. I wanted him to be so completely out of the picture that I'd never need to think about him again. Instead—just my luck—he's single, eligible and drop-dead handsome. Life can be brutally unfair.

One good thing that came from all this is the long conversation I had with Carley after the movie. She's young and idealistic, much the same way I was at her age. We talked some more about Mom and Mrs. Sutton. It's really a very sad feud. I told her what good friends our two families used to be. The telling brought up a lot of memories. At one time, our families did everything together.

Thom was the first boy ever to kiss me. We were both sixteen. Wow! I still remember how good it felt. I don't remember what movie was playing and I doubt Thom does, either. That kiss was really something, even though we had no idea what we were doing. There was a purity to it, an innocence. His lips stayed on mine for mere seconds, but somehow we knew. I certainly did, and I thought Thom did, too.

It's funny how much it hurts to think about the way he deceived me. I try not to dwell on it. But I can't help myself, especially now....

Chapter Three

"I've never been so humiliated in my life!" Thom's mother sagged into the chair across from his desk as if she were experiencing a fainting spell. The back of her hand went to her forehead and she closed her eyes. "I'll never be able to look those people in the eye again," she wailed. "Never!"

"Mother, I'm sure no one recognized you," Thom said, hoping to calm her down before she caused a second scene by retelling the first. He hadn't really appreciated his mother's flair for drama until now. This was quite a performance, and he could only imagine the show she'd put on at the store.

"Of *course* I was recognized," Mary insisted, springing to life. "My picture's right there by my news column each and every week. Why, I could be fired from the newspaper once the editor gets wind of this." She swooned again and slumped back in the chair. "Where's your father, anyway? He should've known something like this was bound to happen. It seems every time I need him, he's conveniently in court." Greg Sutton was the senior partner in a local law firm.

Thom managed to hold back a smile. As far as he was concerned, his father possessed impeccable timing. Unfortunately, that meant his mother had sought solace from him.

"I'll sue Sarah McDowell," his mother said, as if she'd suddenly come to that decision. "Assault and besmirching my reputation and…and—"

"Mother," Thom pleaded. He stood and leaned forward, his hands on the edge of his desk. "Take a couple of deep breaths and try to calm down." Dragging a lawyer—most likely someone from his father's firm—into the middle of this feud would only complicate things.

"Do you believe it's remotely possible to calm down after this kind of humiliation?"

Perhaps she was right. "Why don't I take you to lunch and we can talk about it," Thom suggested. It was the Friday before Christmas and he could spare the time.

"The Rose Garden?" His mother raised pleading eyes to him. The Rose Garden was the most elegant dining room in town.

"If you like." It was more a "ladies who lunch" kind of place, but if that was what it took to make his mother listen to reason, then he'd go there.

"At least the day won't be completely ruined," she mumbled, opening her purse. "Let me put on some lipstick and I'll be ready to go." She took out her compact and gasped when she saw her reflection in the mirror.

"What?" Thom asked.

"My hair." Her fingers worked feverishly to repair the damage. "Why didn't you say something?"

Mainly because he hadn't been able to get a word in edgewise from the moment she'd stormed into his office. At first, Thom had assumed she'd been in some kind of accident. His mother had spoken so fast it was hard to understand what she was saying—other than the fact that she'd been kicked out of the Value-X because of Sarah McDowell.

"This must have happened when she hurled a French poodle at me."

"Mrs. McDowell threw a dog at you?" He gazed at her in horror.

"A stuffed one," she qualified. "It hit me on the head." Her hand went back to her hair, which she'd more or less managed to straighten.

Thom could picture the scene—two grown women acting like five-year-olds fighting in a schoolyard. Once again, he struggled to hide his amusement. His mother had tried to give him the impression that she was an innocent victim in all this, but he strongly suspected she'd played an equal role.

"I think I might be getting a bruise on my cheek," she said, peering closely into the small compact mirror. She lowered it and angled her face for him to get a better look.

"I don't see anything," he told her.

"Look harder," she said.

To appease her, he did but saw nothing. "Sorry," he said and reached for his overcoat. "Ready for lunch?"

"I'm starving," his mother told him. "You know how hungry I get when I'm angry."

He didn't, and felt this was information he could live without. The Rose Garden was only a block from his office, so they decided to walk. His mother chattered the whole way, reliving the incident and her outrage all over again, embellishing it in the retelling. Thom listened politely and wondered what Noelle would think when she heard *her* mother's version of the incident. He quickly pulled himself up. He didn't want to think about Noelle; that was something his self-esteem could do without.

As he'd expected, The Rose Garden bustled with activity. Christmas was only a few days away, and shoppers taking a welcome lunch break now filled the restaurant. Thom glanced about the room as they were waiting to be seated. He recognized a few associates, who acknowledged him with nods. Two women sitting by the window gave him an appreciative glance and he warmed to the attention. That was when he caught sight of another pair of women.

Noelle and her younger sister, Kristen. Wouldn't you know it? He nearly groaned aloud. He hadn't seen or heard from her in ten years and yet in the last three days she seemed to turn up every place he went.

This wasn't good. In fact, if his mother were to see them, she might very well consider it her duty to create a scene and walk out of the restaurant. Worse yet, she might find it necessary to make some loud and slanderous comment about their mother. Staring in their direction was a dead giveaway, but for the life of him, he couldn't stop. Noelle. The years had matured her beauty. He'd been in love with her as a teenager and she'd become the greatest source of pain in his life. For a long time, he'd convinced himself that he hated her. Eventually he'd realized it wasn't true. If anything, he was as strongly drawn to her now as he had been back then. More so, and he detested his own weakness. The woman had damn near destroyed him. In spite of that, he couldn't look away.

"I can seat you now," the hostess said.

Thom hesitated.

"Thom," his mother said, nudging him, "we can be seated now."

"Yes, sorry." He could only hope it wouldn't be anywhere close to Noelle.

The hostess escorted them to a table by the window. He pulled out his mother's chair, making sure her back was to Noelle and Kristen. Unfortunately, that meant *he* was facing them. Kristen had her back to him, which left him with an excellent view of Noelle. She apparently noticed him for the first time because her fork froze halfway to her mouth. For the longest moment, she stared at him, then caught herself and averted her eyes.

"Do you see someone you know, dear?" his mother asked, scrutinizing the menu.

"Yes...no," he corrected. He lifted the rather large menu and pretended to read over the offerings. The strategy of entertaining his mother in order to get her mind off the events of that morning was about to backfire.

In the years since Noelle, Thom had been in several relationships, two of which had grown serious. Both times he'd come close to suggesting marriage and then panicked. It was little wonder after what Noelle had done to him, but he couldn't blame her entirely.

When the moment came to make a commitment, he couldn't. He simply couldn't. And he knew why—although the reason baffled and frustrated him. He didn't love either Caroline or Brenda with the same intensity he'd loved Noelle. Perhaps it was impossible to recapture the emotional passion of that youthful episode; he didn't know. What he did know was that the feelings he'd had for other women hadn't been enough. He'd found them attractive, enjoyed their company...but he needed more than that.

He needed what he'd had with Noelle.

As he thought about the scene at the theater, he started to grin. It couldn't have worked out better had he planned it. Just thinking about her tossing popcorn at some poor, unsuspecting moviegoer's head was enough to keep him laughing for years. He'd listened in while she talked about their mothers—and about them. But the most priceless part of all was the astonished look on her face when she'd realized he was sitting right behind her and had heard every word.

"What is so amusing?" his mother asked.

"Oh, I was just thinking about something that happened recently."

"What? Trust me, after the morning I've had, I could use a good laugh."

Thom shook his head. "It'll lose something in the translation."

"Oh." She sounded disappointed, then sighed. "I do feel better. This was an excellent idea."

The waitress came by and his mother ordered a glass of wine. "For my nerves," she explained to the woman. "Ordinarily I don't drink during the day, but…well, suffice it to say I've had a very difficult morning."

"I understand," the waitress told her in a sympathetic voice. She glanced at Thom and gave him a small coy smile.

"What a nice young woman," his mother commented as the waitress walked off.

"I suppose so," he said with little interest. He looked up, straight into Noelle's steady gaze.

"Perhaps now isn't the right moment to broach the subject, but both your father and I think it's time you considered settling down."

She was right; the timing could be better. However, a little appeasement seemed in order. "I've been thinking the same thing myself," he said, forcing himself to focus on his mother.

"Really?" Her face lit up. "Is there someone special?"

"Not yet." Involuntarily he stared at Noelle again. As if against her will, her eyes met his and held. Then she looked away—but she quickly looked back.

Kristen turned around and glanced at him over her shoulder.

"Did you know Kristen McDowell is getting married?" his mother said.

Thom nearly choked on his glass of water. "Now that you mention it, I remember hearing something about that." It also explained why his mother had brought up the subject of his settling down. She didn't want Sarah McDowell to outdo her in the married children department.

"Now," his mother said, eagerly leaning forward, "tell me about your lady friend."

"What lady friend?"

"The one you're going to propose to."

"Propose?" He'd only proposed to one woman, the one watching him from two tables away. "I told you already—I'm not seeing anyone."

"You were never able to keep a secret from me, Thomas. I'm your mother."

He stared at her blankly, not knowing how to respond. "What makes you think I've met someone?"

"It isn't *think,* Thom, I know. I told your father, too. Ask him if you don't believe me. I noticed it the day you came home from your business trip to California. It was the sparkle in your eyes."

"California?" Thom tried to recall the trip. It had been a quick one, and strictly business. But on the return flight, he'd bumped into Noelle McDowell.

Noelle got home after lunch with Kristen to discover her mother sitting in the family room, stocking feet propped up on the ottoman. She leaned back against the sofa cushion and held an icepack to her forehead.

"Mom?" Noelle whispered. "Are you ill?"

"Thank goodness someone's finally home," her mother said, lowering the bag of ice.

"What's wrong?"

"Never in all your life could you guess the kind of morning I had." She clutched Noelle's arm as she spoke.

"What happened?"

Sarah closed her eyes. "I can't even tell you about it. I have never been more humiliated."

"Does this have something to do with Mrs. Sutton?"

Her mother's eyes sprang open in sheer terror. "You heard about it? Who told you?"

"Ah…"

"She's going to report it in the newspaper, I just know she is. I wouldn't put it past her to use her news column to smear my good name. It was *her* fault, you know. She followed me, and then purposely rammed her cart into mine. And that was only the beginning."

An ugly picture began to take shape in Noelle's mind. A Sutton/McDowell confrontation would explain the fierce looks Thom had sent her way during lunch. The fact that he'd showed up at The Rose Garden—with his mother in tow—was a coincidence she could have done without.

Kristen had invited her to lunch, and then after a few minutes of small talk, her sister had immediately turned to the subject that happened to be on Noelle's mind: Thom Sutton. Noelle had described the disaster at the movies the day before and reluctantly confessed her part. To her consternation, Kristen had thought the incident downright hilarious. Noelle, however, had yet to recover from the embarrassment of knowing that Thom had seen her resort to such childish behavior.

Now their mother had been involved in another confrontation with Mary Sutton. If her present state of mind was anything to go by, Sarah had come out of it badly. Judging by what Noelle had seen of Mrs. Sutton at the restaurant, *she* wasn't the least bit disturbed.

"The police took down our names and—"

"The *police?*"

"Value-X Security, but they wear those cute blue uniforms and look just like regular policemen."

"They took your names? What for?"

Her mother covered her face with both hands. "I can't talk about it."

The door off the garage opened and in walked Noelle's father. "Dad," she said, hoping to prepare him. "Something happened to Mom this morning."

"Oh, Jake…" Her mother languished in her seat as though she lacked the energy to even lift her head.

"Sarah?"

"Apparently Mom and Mrs. Sutton tangled with security at the Value-X this morning."

"We more than tangled," her mother insisted, her voice rising, "we were…banished. The officer who escorted me out told me I won't be allowed inside the store for three months." She bit her lip and swallowed a loud sob. "I don't know if I misunderstood him, but I think I might be permanently banned from all blue-light specials."

"No!" Her father feigned outrage.

"Jake, this is serious."

"Of course it is," he agreed. "I take it this is Mary's doing?"

Her mother's fist hit the sofa arm. "I swear to you she started it!"

"You don't need to tell me what happened," Jake said. "I can guess." So could Noelle.

"From here on out, I absolutely refuse to be in the same room as that woman." She sat straighter, jaw firm, head back. "For years I've had to deal with her…her malice, and I won't put up with it anymore!"

Jake reached for Sarah's hand and gently patted it. "You're absolutely right—you shouldn't."

Her mother's eyes narrowed suspiciously. "How do you mean? Are you being sarcastic?"

"Of course not, dear," he said reassuringly. "But there's no need to rehash old history, is there?"

"No-o-o." Noelle heard her mother's hesitation.

"Not going to the Christmas dance will show Mary Sutton that she won't have you to kick around anymore."

As far as Noelle was concerned, missing the Century Club Christmas dance was far from a tragedy. The only reason she'd agreed to attend was to placate her mother. This mysterious incident at the Value-X was a blessing in disguise; it seemed her father saw it in the same light. She just hoped he hadn't overplayed his hand with that last ringing pronouncement.

"Who said anything about not going to the dance?" her mother demanded.

"You did." Her father turned to Noelle for agreement, which she offered with a solemn nod.

"Yes, Mom, you just said you won't be in the same room with that woman ever again."

"I did?"

"Yes, sweetheart," Noelle's father said. "And I agree wholeheartedly. Missing the dance is a small price to pay if it means protecting your peace of mind."

"We aren't going to the dance?" Carley asked, entering the room. She looked disappointed, but then Noelle's little sister was too young to understand what a lucky escape she'd just had.

"No," Jake said. "We're going to skip the dance this year, and perhaps every year from now on. We won't let Mary Sutton hurt your mother's feelings or her reputation again!"

"We're going," her mother insisted.

"But sweetheart—"

"You're absolutely right, Jake, Mary Sutton's done enough to me. I refuse to allow her to ruin my Christmas—and Noelle's birthday— too. We're going to show up at the dance and hold our heads high. We have nothing to be ashamed of."

"But…" Her father cleared his throat. "What if Mary mentions the incident at the Value-X?" He lowered his voice, sounding as though that would be a horrible embarrassment to them all. Noelle had to give her father credit; he was good at this.

"She won't say a word," her mother said with complete confi- dence. "Mary wouldn't dare bring up the subject, seeing that she was tossed out on her ear, right along with me."

Her resolve clearly renewed, Sarah stood and placed her hands on her hips. Nothing would thwart her now. "We're attending the dance tomorrow night, and that's all there is to it."

Her father made a small protesting noise that echoed Noelle's senti- ments. She was stuck going to this dance when it was the very last thing she wanted.

Dressed in a floor-length pink formal that had once been worn by Kristen in high school, Noelle felt like last year's prom queen. Her enthusiasm for this dance was on a par with filing her income tax re- turn.

"You look positively lovely," her mother told her as they headed out the door.

How Noelle looked had little to do with how she felt. Her father brought the car out of the garage and held open the doors for Noelle and Carley, then helped their mother into the front seat beside him.

"How did I get so lucky—escorting three beautiful women to the biggest dance of the year?"

"Clean living," Noelle's mother said with authority. "And a clear conscience." Noelle didn't know whether to laugh at that remark or shrug in bewilderment. Leaning forward in order to look out the front window, Sarah added, "I think it's going to snow."

Hearing "Jingle Bells" on the car radio, Noelle suspected her mother was being influenced by the words of the song.

"We're more prone to ice storms than snow this time of year," her father said mildly.

Noelle had forgotten about the treacherous storms, although she'd experienced a number of them during the years she'd lived in Rose. They created astonishing beauty—and terrible dangers.

"Kristen and Jonathan are meeting us at the dance, aren't they?" Carley asked.

"That's what she said," Noelle answered. Carley was dressed in a full-length pale blue dress with cap sleeves and she wore matching low-heeled shoes. She looked lovely and so mature it was all Noelle could do not to cry. Her baby sister was growing up.

"Do you think *she'll* be there?" her mother asked, lowering her voice.

"Mrs. Sutton's probably asking the same thing about you," Noelle said.

Her mother gave an exaggerated sigh. "I'll say one thing about Mary Sutton—she never did lack nerve."

The Century Club was festive, with Christmas music and evergreen swags and large red bows. The ballroom was on the second floor, the cloakroom, a bar and buffet on the first. Couples lingered on the wide staircase, chatting and sipping champagne.

Noelle glanced toward the upstairs, and her stomach tensed. Thom was there. She didn't need to see him to feel his presence. Why did he have to show up everywhere she did? Was this some kind of cosmic joke?

"Kristen!" her mother called. "Yoo hoo!" Anyone might think it'd been weeks since she'd last spoken to her daughter. "Hello, Jonathan." She hugged her soon-to-be son-in-law.

"Hi, Mom. Hi, Dad." Kristen paused in front of Carley, feigning shock. "This isn't my little sister, is it? It can't be."

Carley rolled her eyes, but couldn't hide her pleasure. "Of course it's me. Don't be ridiculous."

"Shall we go upstairs?" her mother suggested.

Noelle recognized the order disguised as a request. They were to mount the stairs on guard, as a family, in case they ran into the dreaded Mary Sutton.

Kristen cozied up to Noelle. "He's here," she whispered in her ear.

"I know."

"Who told you?"

"No one." She couldn't explain how she'd recognized Thom's presence. She just did. Like it or not.

The ballroom was crowded, and although this wasn't the kind of social activity Noelle would have attended on her own, she couldn't help getting caught up in the spirit of the evening. A six-piece orchestra was playing a waltz, the chandeliers glittered and she saw that it had indeed begun to snow; flakes drifted gently past the dark windows. On the polished dance floor, the women in their long shimmery gowns whirled around in the arms of their dashing partners. The scene reminded her of a Victorian Christmas card.

"Would you care to dance?" Jonathan asked.

Surprised, Noelle nodded. She'd only spoken once or twice to this man who was marrying her sister, and was anxious to know him better. "Thank you. That would be very nice."

Just as Noelle and Jonathan stepped onto the dance floor, Kristen's gaze met her fiancé's. Noelle could have sworn some unspoken message passed between them. She didn't have time to question her sister before Jonathan loosely wrapped her in his arms.

"I assume you heard what happened at the Value-X store," she said, searching for a subject of conversation.

"Did you have as much trouble not laughing as I did?"

"More," Noelle confessed with a grin.

"I've done business with the Suttons. They're good people."

"This feud between our mothers is ridiculous." Out of the corner of her eye, she noticed Kristen, who was dancing, too—her partner none other than Thom Sutton. It didn't take a genius to put two and two together, especially when she noticed that Kristen was steering Thom in her direction. Noelle marveled at her sister's courage in asking Thom to dance with her. And of course she had. Thom would never have sought Kristen out, especially for a dance in the Women's Century Club Ballroom with both mothers present.

The two couples made their way toward the center of the polished floor. When they were side by side, Jonathan stopped.

"I believe you're dancing with the wrong partner," he said.

Noelle didn't need to look over her shoulder to guess Jonathan was speaking to Thom.

"I believe you're with the wrong woman," Noelle heard Kristen tell her partner.

Jonathan released Noelle, and Kristen stepped out of Thom's embrace and sailed into her fiancé's waiting arms, leaving Thom and Noelle standing alone in the middle of the crowded dance floor.

Slowly, dread dictating every move, Noelle turned and came face-to-face with Thom. He didn't look any happier than she felt at this sudden turn of events. "I didn't plan this," she said in clear, even tones.

His expression implied that he didn't consider her comment worthy of a response.

"Are you two going to dance or are you just going to stand there and stare at each other all night?" Jonathan asked.

Thom shrugged, implying that he could do this if he had to. Reluctantly Noelle stepped into his arms. She wasn't sure what to expect. Actually, she hadn't expected to feel anything, certainly not this immediate deluge of emotion. He kept her at arm's length and gazed into the distance.

To Noelle's horror, tears filled her eyes as all the old feelings came flooding back. She was about to turn and walk off the dance floor when his fingers dug into her upper arms.

"You're not running away from me again."

"Me?" she cried, furious at the accusation.

"Yes, you."

His words made no sense, she thought grimly, but said nothing. The dance would be over soon and she could leave him behind. Or try to. Kristen would answer for this.

No, she decided, she had only herself to blame. Over lunch, Noelle had confided in her sister. Kristen, being idealistic and in love, had plotted to bring Noelle and Thom back together. She didn't understand that reconciliation wasn't always possible.

"I'd like to ask you a question," she said when she could tolerate the silence no longer.

"Fine."

"Why'd you do it? Did you want revenge for your mother so badly it was worth using me to get it?"

He stopped dancing and frowned at her. "What?"

"You heard me." She couldn't keep the pain out of her voice.

He continued to frown, as if he still didn't understand the question.

"Don't give me that injured look," she said, clenching her jaw. "Too many years have passed for me to be taken in by that."

"You were the one who stood *me* up."

"Yeah, right," she said with a mocking laugh. "After I made an idiot of myself in front of my parents, too. That must've given you a real kick."

"I don't know what you're talking about."

"Thom, I waited in that park for two miserable hours and you didn't show."

Not an inch separated them now as his icy glare cut into her. Dancing couples swirled around them, but Noelle was barely conscious of anyone else. For all she knew or cared, they were alone on the dance floor.

"I waited hours for you, too."

His lying to her now was almost more than she could stand. "I beg to differ," she said stiffly.

"Noelle, listen to me! I was there."

"You most certainly were not." Then, to prove that she wasn't going to accept a lie, no matter how convenient, she added, "You think I just waited around? I was sure something had gone wrong, sure there was some misunderstanding, so I phoned your home."

"I wasn't there because I was waiting for you!"

He persisted with the lie and that irritated her even more.

"You were gone, all right," she said, spitting out the words. "You were with your buddies bowling."

His eyes narrowed and he began to speak.

But the music stopped just then, which was all the excuse Noelle needed to get away from him. He reached for her hand and pulled her back. "We need to talk."

"No. It happened years ago. Some things are better left alone."

"Not this time," he insisted, unwilling to budge.

"What do you hope to accomplish by going through all of this now? It's too late." They'd gain nothing more than the pain of opening old wounds. Any discussion was futile. It'd been a mistake to let herself get drawn into this silly drama—just one very big mistake.

"I'm not hoping to accomplish one damn thing," he told her coldly.

"I didn't think so."

Thom released her hand. "Just a minute," he said as she turned from him.

Noelle hesitated.

"I *was* there. I stood there for two hours and waited. You were the one who never showed."

"That's not true!"

They stood glowering at each other, both refusing to give in. Noelle wasn't going to let him lie his way out of this, though—not after what his deception had cost her.

"Hey, you two, this is Christmas," someone called out.

The voice ended Noelle's resolve. Whatever had happened in the past didn't matter anymore. Certainly not after all these years.

"If you find comfort in believing a lie, then do so," he said, "but don't involve me." He walked away, his face hard and impassive.

Left alone in the middle of the dance floor, Noelle stared at him in amazement. Of all the nerve! He'd stopped her from leaving and now *he'd* taken off!

Picking up her skirt, she raced after him. "All right! You want to talk this out, then we will."

"When?" He continued walking, tossing the question over his shoulder.

With Christmas so close, her time was booked solid. "I…soon."

"Tonight."

"All right." She swallowed hard. "When and where?"

"After the dance. In the park, same place as before."

That seemed fitting, since it was where they were originally going to meet the day they'd planned to elope.

"What time is the dance over?"

"Midnight." He glanced at his watch. "So make it one."

"I'll be there."

He shot her a look. "That was what you said the *last* time."

NOELLE McDOWELL'S JOURNAL

December 21 5:00 p.m.

Everyone's getting ready for the big dance, but my head's still spinning and I've learned that it helps me sort through my emotions if I write everything down. I ran into Thom again. It's as though we're being drawn together, as though we're trapped in some magnetic field and are being pulled toward each other from opposite directions. I can tell he doesn't like it any better than I do.

It happened yesterday when I met Kristen for lunch at The Rose Garden. No sooner had our order arrived when in walked Thom and his mother.

Try as I might, I couldn't keep my eyes off him. He apparently suffered from the same malady. Every time I glanced up, he was staring at me—and frowning. His mother was with him and I could see that he was trying to keep her distracted so she wouldn't notice Kristen and me. I didn't completely understand why until we arrived home and discovered that Mom and Mrs. Sutton had had another run-in while shopping for the Christmas baskets. That must have been something to see, although I'm grateful I didn't!

After we left the restaurant, Kristen and I had a long talk about Thom. I told her far more than I meant to. I don't think I've thought or talked this much about Thom in years, and I found myself experiencing all those pathetic emotions all over again. Kristen confessed that she's been hurt and upset with me for staying away, and now that I'm home, I can understand her disappointment. It's ironic, because after I told her how devastated I was when Thom and I broke up, she said she could understand why I'd stayed away. She even said she'd probably have done the same thing.

When I got back to the house, Mom was in quite a state. For a moment I thought she might have talked herself out of attending the dance, but our hopes were quickly dashed. Dad and I should've realized Mom has far too much pride to let Mary Sutton get the upper hand.

This Christmas-basket project is driving her nuts, but Mom's determined to make Kristen's wedding one this town will long remember, and she's willing to make whatever sacrifice is necessary. I do admire her determination.

It's time to get ready for the dance. Wouldn't you know it? Mom came up with a dress, and just as Carley predicted, it's pink. Pepto-Bismol pink. I can only hope Thom doesn't show up, but at the rate my luck is running...

Chapter Four

The rest of the Christmas dance passed in a blur for Noelle. She danced with a constant stream of attractive men. She greeted longtime family friends and socialized the evening away, but not once did she stop thinking about Thom. They were finally going to settle this. Only she wasn't a naive eighteen-year-old anymore and she wouldn't allow his lies to go unchallenged. Thom claimed he'd been waiting for her in the park, but she knew otherwise.

At the end of the evening, the families trooped down the wide sweeping staircase. Noelle, Carley and their mother waited while Jake stood in line to collect their coats. No more than three feet away from them was Mary Sutton, who also appeared to be waiting for her coat. Noelle had to hand it to the woman; she did a marvelous job of pretending not to see them.

"Good evening, Mrs. Sutton," Noelle greeted her, refusing to ignore Thom's mother.

Sarah's onetime friend opened and then closed her mouth, as if she didn't know how to respond.

"Noelle." Her mother elbowed her sharply in the ribs. "What's the matter with you?"

"Nothing. I'm greeting an old family friend."

"*Former* friend," her mother insisted. "We haven't been friends in almost twenty years."

"But you once were."

Her mother sighed wearily. "I was younger then, and I didn't have the discretion I have now. You see, back then I took friendship at face value. I trusted in goodwill and forgiveness."

"Hello, Noelle," Mary Sutton said, moving closer. "I, too, was once young and I, too, believed in the power of friendship. But I was taught a painful lesson when the woman I assumed was my dearest friend lied and deceived me and entrusted a priceless family heirloom to another. But that was a very long time ago. Tell me," she said, turning a cold shoulder to Noelle's mother. "How are *you?*"

"Very well, thank you."

Her mother clasped Carley's arm and stepped back as though to protect her youngest daughter.

"You're looking lovely," Thom's mother said, and her eyes were kind.

"Thank you," Noelle said, although she could feel her mother's gaze burning into her back.

Mary Sutton lowered her voice. "I couldn't help overhearing your mother's comments just now about friendship. I probably should've stayed out of it—but I couldn't."

"It's so sad that the two of you have allowed this nonsense to go on for all these years."

"Let me assure you, my grandmother's tea service is not nonsense. It was all I had to remind me of her. Your mother lied to me about using it, and then lost it forever." Her downcast eyes clearly said that the loss of her grandmother's legacy still caused her pain. "You're right, though. It's unfortunate this has dragged on as long as it has."

That sounded encouraging, and Noelle was ready to leap on what she considered a gesture of peace.

"However," Mrs. Sutton continued, "there are certain things no friendship can overcome, and I fear your mother has crossed that line too many times to count. Regrettably, our friendship is unsalvageable."

"But—"

"Another thing," Mrs. Sutton said, cutting Noelle off. "I saw you dancing with Thom this evening. You two were once sweet on each other, but you hurt him badly. I hope for both your sakes that you're not thinking of renewing your acquaintance."

"I...I..." Noelle faltered, not knowing how to answer.

Noelle's mother stepped forward. "I suggest your son stay away from our daughter."

"Mom, keep out of this, please," Noelle cried, afraid of what would happen if the two women started in on each other—particularly after the Value-X incident. This was the town's biggest social event of the year, and a scene was the last thing either family needed.

Mr. Sutton returned with the coats, and Noelle's father followed shortly afterward. The McDowells headed immediately for the parking lot, careful to avoid any and all Suttons. Everyone was silent on the drive home, but Noelle knew she'd upset her mother.

Fifteen minutes later as they walked into the house, she decided she should be the one to compromise. "Mom, I wish now that I hadn't spoken to Mrs. Sutton," she said quietly. And she meant it; she should have restricted her remarks to "Hello" and maybe "Merry Christmas."

"I do, too," her mother said. "I know your intentions were good, but it's best to leave things as they are. I tried for a long time to make up with her, but she refused to accept a replacement set and she refused my apology." Sadness crept into her voice. "Mary did make one good point, though."

Noelle mentally reviewed the conversation.

"She said it's a good idea for you to stay away from Thom, and she's right." She sighed, then briefly placed her palm against Noelle's cheek. Her eyes were warm with love. "The two of you have a history you can't escape."

"Mom, it isn't like that. We—"

"Sweetheart, listen please. I know you once had strong feelings for that young man, and it hurt me deeply."

"It hurt *you?*"

Her mother nodded. "Very much so, because I knew you'd be forced to make a choice between your family and Thom. I couldn't bear the thought of you married to him or sharing my grandchildren with Mary Sutton. You saw for yourself how she feels about me. There's no forgiveness in her. Really, is this the kind of woman you want in your life and the lives of your children? That's the history I mean." She kissed Noelle on the cheek and headed down the hallway to her room. "Good night now."

Noelle shut her eyes and sagged against the wall. She'd been just a moment away from explaining that she was going to meet Thom in order to talk things out. Her mother sounded as though she'd consider it a personal affront if Noelle so much as looked at him. It was like high school all over again.

The only thing left to do now was sneak out the same way she had as a teenager. She couldn't leave him waiting in the cold, that was unthinkable. Besides, this might be her one and only chance to sort out what had really happened, and she wasn't going to throw it away. She didn't intend any disrespect toward her mother or his, but she *had* to be there. If she didn't show up, she'd confirm every negative belief he already had about her.

Carley was in bed asleep as Noelle passed her room. She went in to drop a kiss on her sister's forehead, then softly closed the door. Noelle changed out of her party dress, choosing wool slacks and a thick sweater to wear to the park. Sitting on the edge of the bed, she waited for the minutes to tick past. With luck, her parents would be exhausted and both go directly to bed. Then Noelle could slip away undetected.

Finally the house was dark and quiet. The only illumination came from the flashing Christmas lights that decorated the roofline.

Opening her bedroom door, Noelle was horrified by the way it creaked. On tiptoe, she carefully, silently crept down the narrow corridor.

"Jake." Her mother was instantly awake. "I heard something."

"Go to sleep, honey."

"There's someone in the house," her mother insisted.

Noelle froze. She could hardly breathe. Just imagining what her mother would say was enough to paralyze her.

"Jake, I'm serious."

"I don't hear anything," her father mumbled.

"I did. We could all be murdered in our beds."

"Sarah, for the love of heaven."

"Think of the children."

Noelle nearly groaned aloud. She was trapped. She'd have to pass her parents' bedroom in order to steal back into her own. They were sure to see her. She couldn't go forward and she couldn't go back.

"All right, all right," her father muttered as he climbed out of bed.

"Take something with you," her mother hissed.

"Like what?"

"Here, take a wooden hanger."

"So I can hang him out to dry if I happen on a burglar?"

"Just do it, Jake."

"Yes, dear."

Noelle had made it safely into the kitchen by the time her father came upon her. "Dad," she whispered, hiding in the shadows, "it's me."

"Why didn't you say so?" he whispered back.

"I couldn't. I'm sneaking out of the house."

"This late? Where are you going?"

He wouldn't like the answer, but she refused to lie. "I'm meeting Thom Sutton in the park. We're going to talk."

Her father didn't say anything for a long moment. Then it sounded as if he was weeping.

Noelle felt dreadful. "Dad? I'm sorry if this upsets you."

"Upsets me?" he repeated. "I think it's hilarious."

"You...do?"

"Go ahead and meet your young man and talk all you want. This thing is between Sarah and Mary. Greg and I have been friends for years."

This was news to Noelle. "You're still friends?"

"Of course. He's the best golfing partner I ever had."

"You and Mr. Sutton are golf partners?" Noelle thought perhaps she'd slipped into another dimension.

"Shhh." Her father raised a finger to his lips. "Your mother doesn't know."

"Mom doesn't know." This was more unbelievable by the moment.

"Scoot," her father ordered, and reaching for the keys on the peg outside the garage door, he said, "Here, take my car. It's parked on the street."

Noelle clutched the set of keys and leaned forward to kiss his cheek. "Thanks, Dad."

He coughed loudly as she opened the back door. "You're hearing things, Sarah," he called out. "There's nothing." He gave her a small wave and turned back toward the hallway.

As soon as she was out the door, Noelle sprinted toward her dad's car. It took her a moment to figure out which key she needed and then another to adjust the mirror and the seat. When she glanced at her watch, she was shocked to see the time. It was already ten minutes past one.

Thom would assume she wasn't coming. He'd think she'd stood him up…when nothing could be further from the truth.

Thom expelled his breath into the cold, and it came out looking like the snort of a cartoon bull. An *angry* cartoon bull. That was exactly how he felt. Once again, he'd allowed his heart to rule his head and he'd fallen prey to Noelle McDowell.

He should have known better. Everything he'd learned about heartache, Noelle had taught him. And now, fool that he was, he'd set himself up to be taken again. Noelle McDowell was untrustworthy. He knew it and yet he'd still risked disappointment and worse.

Slapping his hands against his upper arms to ward off the cold, he paced the area beneath the trees across from the pool at Lions' Park. This had been their special meeting place. It was here that Thom had kissed Noelle for the second time. Here, they'd met and talked and shared their secrets. Here, he'd first confessed his love.

A car door slammed in the distance. Probably the police coming to check out his vehicle, which was parked in a lot that was closed to the public at this time of night. He deserved to get a ticket for being enough of an idiot to trust Noelle.

He didn't know why he'd hung around as long as he had. Looking at his watch he saw that it was twenty after one. She'd kept him waiting nineteen minutes too long. Her non-appearance was all the proof he'd ever need.

"Thom…Thom!" Noelle called out as she ran across the lawn.

Angry and defiant, he stepped out from beneath the shadow of the fifty-foot cedar tree.

"Thank goodness you're still here," she cried and to her credit, she did sound relieved. She was breathless when she reached him. "I had to sneak out of the house."

"Sneak out? You're almost thirty years old!"

"I know, I know. Listen, I'm so sorry." She pushed back the sleeve of her coat and squinted at her watch. "You waited—I can't believe you stayed for twenty extra minutes. I prayed you would, but I wouldn't have blamed you if you'd left."

The anger that had burned in him moments earlier evaporated so fast it shocked him.

"When did they turn Walnut into a dead-end street?"

"Years ago." Of course she'd drive down the same street they'd used as teenagers. He'd forgotten the changes made over the last decade; it hadn't occurred to him that she wouldn't know. "You're here now."

"Yes…listen, I know I shouldn't do this, but I can't help myself." Having said that, she slipped her arms around his waist and hugged him hard. His own arms went around her, too, tentatively and then with greater strength.

Closing his eyes and savoring the feel of her was a mistake, the first of many he knew he'd be making. She smelled like Christmas, somehow, and her warmth wrapped itself around him.

"Why'd you do that?" he asked gruffly as she released him and took a step back. He was trying to hide how damn good it'd felt to hold her.

"It's the only way I could think of to thank you for staying, for believing in me enough to wait."

"I wasn't exactly enumerating your good points while I stood here freezing."

"I know, I wouldn't either—I mean, well, you know what I mean."

He did.

Clearing off a space on the picnic table, Noelle climbed up and sat there just as she had when they were teenagers. "All right," she said, drawing in a deep breath. "Let's talk. Since you were the one to suggest we do this, you should go first."

So she'd become a take-charge sort of woman. That didn't surprise him. She'd displayed leadership qualities in high school, as well, serving on the student council and as president of the French Club. "All right, that's fair enough." She might be able to sit, but Thom couldn't. He had ten years of anger stored inside and that made it impossible to stand still for long. "We argued, remember?"

"Of course I do. The argument had to do with our mothers. You said something derogatory about mine and I defended her."

"As I recall, you had a less-than-flattering attitude toward *my* mother."

"But you were the first…" She paused. "None of that's important now. What we should be discussing is what happened afterward."

Once again she was right. "We made up, or so I thought."

"We made up because we refused to allow the ongoing feud between our mothers to come between us. Later that day, you wrote me a note and suggested we elope."

Her voice caught just a little. He wanted so badly to believe her. It was a struggle not to. "I loved you, Noelle."

She smiled, but he saw pain in her eyes and it shook him. For years he'd assumed that she'd used his love against him. That she'd stood him up just to hurt him. To humiliate him. He'd never really understood why. Was it vindication on behalf of her mother?

"We were going to confront our parents, remember?" Noelle said.

"Yes. I made a big stand, claiming how much I loved you and how I refused to let either of our mothers interfere in our lives. You should've heard me."

"I did, too!" she declared. "I spilled out my guts to them. Can you imagine how humiliating it was to have to go back and confess that you'd tricked me—that you'd jilted me?"

"Me!" he shouted. "You were the one—"

Noelle held up both hands and he let his anger fade. "Something happened. It must have." She pressed one hand to her heart. "I swear by all I consider holy that I've never lied to you."

"You're assuming I did?" he challenged.

"Yes. I mean no," she cried, confused now. "Something *did* happen, but what?"

"I don't know," he said. "I was here at three, just like I wrote you in the note."

She frowned, and he wondered if she was going to try to tell him she hadn't gotten his note. He knew otherwise because he'd personally seen Kristen hand it to her at school.

"The note said eight."

"Three," he insisted. Now it was his turn to look perplexed. "I wrote down three o'clock."

"The note said..." She brought her hand to her mouth. "No, I refuse to believe it."

"You think Kristen changed the time?"

"She wouldn't do that." She shook her head. "I know my sister, and she'd never hurt me like that."

"How do you explain the discrepancy then?"

"I have no idea." She squeezed her eyes shut. "I remember it vividly. You'd sent it to me after your math class."

His defenses were down. Time rolled back, and the events of that day were starting to focus in his mind. The fog of his pain dissipated. Finally he was able to look at the events with a clear head and an analytical eye.

"Kristen spilled soda on it," Noelle said thoughtfully. "Do you think that might have smudged the number?"

"It might explain part of it—but not the nasty note you left on my windshield."

She had the grace to blush at the reminder. "After waiting until after ten o'clock, I didn't know what to do. It was pretty dark by then, and I couldn't believe you'd just abandon me. I was positive something must've happened, so I phoned your house."

He nodded, encouraging her to go on.

"Your father said you were out with your friends bowling. I went to the alley to see for myself." Her voice tightened. "Sure enough, you were in there, boozing it up with your buddies."

"Don't tell me you actually thought I was having a good time?"

"Looked like it to me."

"Noelle, I was practically crying in my beer. I felt...I felt as if I'd just learned about some tragedy that was going to change my whole life."

"Why didn't you call me? How could you believe I'd stand you up? If you loved me as much as you said, wouldn't you make some effort to find out what happened?"

"I did." To be fair, it'd taken him a day, but he had to know, had to discover how he could've been so mistaken about Noelle. "I waited until the following afternoon. Your mother answered the phone and said I'd already done enough damage. She hung up on me."

"She never told me," Noelle whispered. "She never said a word."

"Why would she?" Thom murmured. "Your mother assumed I'd done you wrong, just the way everyone else in your family did."

"I left that horrible note on your car and you still phoned me?"

He nodded.

"I can only imagine what you must have thought."

"And you," he said.

They both grew quiet.

"I'm so sorry, Thom," she finally said. "So very sorry."

"So am I." He was afraid to touch her, afraid of what would happen if she came into his arms.

Noelle brushed the hair back from her face and when he glanced at her, he saw tears glistening in her eyes.

"It all worked out for the best, though, don't you think?" he asked. He had to say *something.*

She nodded. Then after a moment she spoke in a voice so low he had to lean closer to hear. "Do you really believe that?"

"No." He reached for her then, crushing her in his arms, lifting her from the picnic table and holding her as if his very life depended on keeping her close to his heart.

His mouth found hers, and her lips were moist and soft, her body melting against his. Their kisses were filled with hunger and passion, with mingled joy and discovery. This sense of *rightness* was what had been missing from every relationship he'd had since his breakup with Noelle. Nothing had felt right with any other woman. He loved Noelle. He'd always loved her.

She buried her face in his shoulder and he kissed the top of her head. Her arms circled his neck and he ran his fingers through her hair, gathering it in his hands as he closed his eyes and let his emotions run free—from anger to joy. From joy to fear. From fear to relief.

"What happens now?" he asked. They didn't seem to have many options. Each had made a life without the other.

She didn't answer him for a long time, but he knew she'd heard the question.

"Noelle," he said as she raised her head. "What do we do now?"

She blinked back tears. "Do we have to decide this minute? Can't you just kiss me again?"

He smiled and lowered his mouth to hers. "I think that could be arranged."

Fresh from Sunday services—where she'd been inspired by a sermon on giving—Mary Sutton drove to the local Wal-Mart store. She refused to show up the following day and not have the items on her list. No doubt Sarah McDowell assumed she'd arrive at the club empty-handed, but Mary fully intended to prove otherwise.

As soon as Greg had settled in front of the television set watching the Seahawks' play-off game, she was out the door. Shopping this close to Christmas went against every dictate of common sense. Usually she was the organized one. Christmas gifts had been purchased, wrapped and tucked away soon after Thanksgiving. But, with these six Christmas baskets, she had no choice. She had to resort to last-minute shopping.

The parking lot at Wal-Mart was packed. Finding a space at the very rear of the lot, Mary trudged toward the busy store. She dreaded dealing with the mob of shoppers inside. On the off-chance she might have a repeat of that horrible scene in Value-X, she surveyed the lot—looking up one row and down the next—in search of Sarah's vehicle. She sighed with relief when she didn't see the other woman's car.

List in hand, Mary grabbed a cart and headed straight for the toy section. She hoped the store would have Barbie dolls left on the shelf. She hated the thought of a single child being disappointed on Christmas morning. Fortunately, the shelves appeared to have been recently restocked.

Reaching for a Firefighter Barbie doll, she set it inside her basket. With a sense of accomplishment, she wheeled the cart around the corner to the riding toys. To her horror and dismay, she discovered Sarah McDowell reading the label on a toddler-sized car. This was her worst nightmare.

"No," she muttered, not realizing Sarah would hear her.

Her bitterest enemy turned and their eyes locked. "What are *you* doing here?" Sarah demanded.

"The same thing you are."

Sarah gripped her cart with both hands, as if she was prepared to engage in a second ramming session. Frankly, Mary had suffered all the humiliation she could stand and had no desire to go a second round.

"Can't you buy your grandson's gifts some other time?"

"How dare you tell me when I can or cannot shop." Mary couldn't believe the gall. She would shop when and where she pleased without any guidance from the likes of Sarah McDowell.

"Mary, hello."

Mary wanted to groan out loud. Janice Newhouse, the pastor's wife, was easing her cart toward them. "This must be Sarah McDowell. I've seen your photo on a real estate brochure." She smiled warmly at the woman who had caused Mary so much pain. "I'm Janice Newhouse."

"Hello." Sarah's return greeting was stiff.

"I've heard so much about you," Janice said, apparently oblivious to the tension between the two women.

"I'll just bet you have." Sarah said this as though to suggest that Mary was a gossipmonger, when nothing could be further from the truth. For years, she'd quietly refused to get drawn into any discussion involving Sarah. It wouldn't do either of them any good. The same could not be said for Sarah McDowell. She'd taken delight in blackballing Mary's membership in the Women's Century Club. She'd dragged Mary's name and reputation through the mud. Mary, on the other hand, had chosen the higher ground—with the exception, perhaps, of that newspaper column on the perfidy of real estate agents, and that certainly hadn't been a personal attack.

"I understand the Willis family bought their home through you," Janice said, making polite conversation.

"You know the Willises?"

"Yes, they're members of our church. So are Mary and her husband." Sarah's expression was glacial. "Oh."

"Sarah and I are buying gifts for the charity baskets," Mary said.

"We divided the list and now we're each getting half," Sarah went on to explain. "Tomorrow we're assembling the baskets and taking them to Salvation Army headquarters."

That was much more than Janice needed to know, Mary thought irritably. Sarah was just showing off.

"That's wonderfully charitable of you both," Janice murmured.

"Thank you." Sarah added a pull toy to her basket.

Mary reached for one herself.

Next Sarah took down a board game; Mary took two.

Sarah grabbed a skateboard.

"How generous you are," Janice commented, eyes widening as she observed their behavior. "Both of you appear to be very...zealous."

"I believe in giving back to the community," Mary said.

"As do I," Sarah insisted. By now her cart was so full she couldn't possibly cram anything else into it.

"Leave something for me to buy," Mary challenged, doing her best to keep the smile on her face from turning into a scowl.

"I'm the one who has the little girl who wants a Firefighter Barbie on my list," Sarah said, staring pointedly at the doll in Mary's cart.

"*I'm* the one with the gift list," Mary countered. "Besides, there are plenty of Barbie dolls."

"You aren't even supposed to be buying toys. That was *my* job." Sarah's eyes narrowed menacingly.

"Ladies, I don't think there's any reason to squabble here." Janice raised both hands in a calming gesture. "Let me look at your lists."

"Fine," Sarah snapped.

"Good idea," Mary added in a far more congenial tone. She opened her purse and dug out the list Melody Darrington had given her.

Janice examined both pages. She ran down Sarah's first and then Mary's. She frowned. "Here's the problem," she said, handing them back. "You have the same list."

"That's impossible," Mary protested.

"Let me see." Sarah snatched Mary's from her hand with such speed it was a wonder Mary didn't suffer a paper cut.

"That's what I think happened," Janice said. "You were accidentally given one list instead of two."

Sarah glanced over each page. "She's right."

Mary wanted to weep with frustration. "Do you mean to say we're actually working from the same list?" It made sense now that she thought about it. Melody had been so busy that morning. and the phone was ringing off the hook. It was no wonder the secretary had been distracted.

"You were supposed to pick up the grocery items," Mary said.

"I most certainly was not. That was *your* job."

If Sarah was trying to be obtuse and irritating, she was succeeding.

Janice glanced from one to the other. "Ladies, this is for the Christmas baskets, remember?"

Mary smiled benevolently at the pastor's wife, who was new to the area. Janice couldn't know. But then, a twenty-year-old feud wasn't something Mary was inclined to brag about.

"She's right," Sarah said again. "We're both behaving a bit childishly, don't you think?"

Mary was staying away from that question.

"I'll call Melody in the morning and pick up the second half of the list."

"No, you won't," Mary told her. "I'll do it."

"I said I would," Sarah said from between clenched teeth.

"You don't need to, I will."

"Would you ladies prefer that I do it?" Janice volunteered.

"No way," Sarah muttered.

"Thank you, but no," Mary said more politely.

Janice looked doubtful. "You're sure?"

"Yes."

"Yes." Sarah's voice blended with Mary's.

"All right, ladies, I'll leave you to your good works then."

Out of the corner of her eye, Mary watched Janice stroll away.

As soon as the pastor's wife was out of earshot, Sarah said, "You can pick up the list if you want." She made it sound as though she was making a big concession.

Naturally, she'd agree now. Mary sighed; this problem with the list complicated everything. "I'll need time to shop for the groceries."

"And your point is?"

"Shouldn't it be obvious?" Clearly it wasn't. "We'll need to meet on the morning of the twenty-fourth now."

"Christmas Eve?"

"Yes, the twenty-fourth is generally known as Christmas Eve," Mary told her a bit sarcastically.

"Fine. Let's meet at the club at nine and deliver the baskets to the Salvation Army from there."

"Fine."

"In the meantime," Sarah suggested, "let's do the sensible thing and divide up the toys on this list. Why don't I get the girls' stuff and you get the boys'?"

Wordlessly, they each returned half of their purchases. Mary hated to follow Sarah's lead, but for once the woman had come up with a reasonable idea. "I'll see you Tuesday morning at nine," she finally said.

Sarah gave a curt nod.

Mary wheeled her cart to the front of the store. All the cashiers were busy, so she found the shortest line and waited her turn. Not until a few moments later did she notice that Sarah stood in the line beside hers.

Mary took a magazine from the stand, leafed through it and tossed it into her cart.

Sarah placed two magazines in hers.

Mary decided to splurge and buy a candy bar. As she put it in the cart, she glanced at Sarah. The other woman grabbed one of every candy bar on the rack. Refusing to be outdone, Mary reached for two.

Sarah rolled her eyes and then emptied the entire container of candy into her cart.

Mary looked over and saw two men staring at them. A woman was whispering to her companion, pointing in her and Sarah's direction.

Once again, they'd managed to make spectacles of themselves.

December 22

I just got back from church, and it was lovely to attend services with Mom and Dad and Carley. The music was stirring and brought back so many memories of Christmases spent in Rose. I wish I'd paid closer attention to the sermon, but my mind refused to remain focused on the pastor's message. All I could think about was Thom.

Now that we've talked, I think we've actually created more problems than we've solved. We're going to get together again later in the day, but that's not until one. We both realize we can't leave things as they are, yet neither one of us knows where to go from here.

Still, it's wonderful to know my faith in him was justified. That makes this decision even harder, though. I'm afraid I'm falling in love with him again—if I ever stopped!—but there are so many complications. In fact, I wonder if our best choice would be simply to call it quits. But I'm not sure we can, because we made a mistake last night. We kissed.

If we hadn't done that, I might've found the courage to shake Thom's hand, claim there were no hard feelings and walk away. But we did kiss and now. . .well, now we're in a quandary. I wish his kisses didn't affect me, but they do. Big time. Oh boy, nothing's changed in that department. It's as if I was sixteen all over again, and frankly, that's a scary feeling.

I felt Thom's kisses all the way through me, from head to toe. Thom felt them, too, and I think he's just as confused as I am. Things got intense very quickly, and we both recognized we had to stop. Now it's decision time.

Thom withdrew from me, physically and emotionally, and I did from him, too. We both tried to play it cool—as if this was all very nice and it was good to clear the air. He acted as if we should just get on with our lives. I played along and was halfway back to the car when he stopped me. He wanted to know if we could meet at the mall today to talk again.

God help me, I jumped at the invitation. Maybe I should've been more nonchalant, but I couldn't do it. I was just happy for the chance to see him again.

Chapter Five

Shopping was the perfect excuse to get out of the house on Sunday afternoon, and Noelle used it. Her mother was gone, her father was absorbed in some televised football game and Carley was in her room checking "Buffy" Web sites on her computer.

"I'm going out for a while," Noelle said casually.

Her father's eyes didn't waver from the television screen. "Are you meeting Thom?"

"Ah…"

Her father raised his hand. "Say no more. What do you want me to tell your mother if she asks?"

"That I've gone shopping… We're meeting at the mall."

"That's all she needs to know."

Noelle kissed her father on the cheek. His eyes didn't leave the screen as he reached inside his pants pocket and handed her his car keys. "Why don't you take my car again?"

"Thanks, Dad."

"Don't mention it." Then her father did look away from the television and his gaze sought hers. "You have feelings for this young man?"

Noelle nodded. It was the truth, much as she hated to acknowledge it, even to herself.

Her father nodded, too. "I was afraid of that."

His words lingered in Noelle's mind as she drove to the Rose Mall on the west side of town. She'd lived for this moment ever since she and Thom had parted the night before. They'd resolved what both had considered a deception, but so many questions were still unanswered. They needed time to think, to consider the consequences of becoming involved a second time. Nothing had changed between their families—or more specifically, their mothers— but other things *were* different. Noelle wasn't the naive eighteen-year-old she'd been ten years ago; neither was Thom.

It took a good twenty minutes to find a parking space, and the mall was equally crowded. Carolers dressed in Victorian costumes stood in front of the JCPenney store, cheerfully singing "Silver Bells." Noelle wished she could listen for a while, but fearing she might be late, she paused only a moment to take in the sights and the sounds of the holiday season.

She hurried through the overheated mall and found Thom at a table in the food court, just the way they'd agreed. He stood as she approached.

"I haven't kept you waiting, have I?" she asked.

"No, no. It occurred to me that with Christmas this close we might have trouble finding a table so I grabbed one early."

He'd always been thoughtful. As he put down his coffee and pulled out her chair, she shrugged out of her coat and threw it on the back of the seat. "Would you like to get some lunch?"

She shook her head. "You should have something, though." Her stomach had been upset all morning.

"Are you ill?"

"No—it's guilt." He might as well know. She'd been anxious since last night, since their first moonlit kiss... All through church services and afterward, she'd repeatedly told herself how ridiculous it was to sneak around behind her mother's back. Her father had apparently been doing it for years, but secretive actions truly bothered Noelle.

"Guilt?"

"I don't like being dishonest."

"Then tell your mother." Thom made it sound so easy, but he didn't need an excuse every time he stepped out the front door. He didn't even live at home, and he wasn't visiting his family for Christmas the way she was. He wasn't accountable to his parents for every minute spent outside their presence.

"Did you let your parents know we were meeting?" she asked.

He half-grinned, looking sheepish. "No."

"That's what I thought."

"How about coffee?" he asked in an all-too-obvious effort to change the subject. "I could use a refill."

She gave a quick nod. She'd been counting the minutes until they could talk again. After their meeting in the park, she'd barely slept. She'd relived their conversation—and their kisses—over and over. It seemed a miracle that they'd finally learned what must have happened that day ten years ago. Truly a Christmas miracle. Now, if only their mothers would miraculously reconcile...

Thom left and returned a few minutes later with two steaming cups of coffee.

Noelle held her cup with both hands, letting the heat warm her palms. She hadn't felt chilled before, but she did now. "I—I don't know where to start."

"Why didn't you ever come home?" he asked bluntly. "Start by telling me that."

"It was just too painful to come back here. I made excuses at first and it got easier after a while. Plus, Mom and Dad and my sisters were always willing to visit Texas. It's beautiful in a way that's completely different from the Northwest. Oh, and the shopping is excellent."

He laughed. "Is there anyone special in your life?"

"I have a number of good friends."

"Male or female?"

She hesitated. "Female."

Thom visibly relaxed. "You don't date much, then?"

"Of course I date—I've gone out lots. Well, maybe not as much as I'd like, but I *was* engaged for a while. How about you?"

"I came close to getting engaged. Twice."

Without knowing a single detail, Noelle was instantly jealous. "Who?"

He seemed pleased by her reaction. He leaned back in his chair, stretched out his legs and crossed his ankles. "No one you know. Besides, I'm the one asking the questions here. You can drill me later."

"No way! In other words, you became some kind of ladies' man after you dumped me?"

His face suddenly grew serious and he reached across the table for her hand. "I didn't dump you, Noelle."

She'd meant to tease him but realized her remark was insensitive—not to mention plain wrong. "I know. I apologize. Chalk it up to a bad choice of words."

Thom squeezed her hand. "Do you think that's what happened with our mothers?" he asked. "A bad choice of words?"

"How do you mean?"

"Think about it. Just now, you reverted to your old thought pattern—your assumption that you'd been betrayed. It wasn't until after you spoke that you remembered what had really happened."

He was right. The words had slipped out easily, thoughtlessly.

"Our mothers are probably behaving in the same way. After all these years, they're caught in this pattern of disparaging each other, and they can't break the habit."

Noelle wasn't sure she agreed with him. For one thing, she knew her mother had desperately tried to end the feud. Every attempt had been rebuffed. "I don't think it's a good idea to discuss our mothers."

"Why not?"

"Because we argue. You want to defend your mother and I want to defend mine, and the two of us end up fighting. Besides, weren't we talking about the women in your life after I left Rose?"

He chuckled. "You make it sound like there were hordes of them."

"There weren't?" She pretended to be shocked.

He shook his head. "Not really. Two I considered marrying and a few others I saw for a while. What about you?"

"You keep asking. All right, I was serious once. Paul was a computer programmer, and we both worked for the same company, developing new software. It was an exciting time in the business and we got caught up in the thrill of it all." Paul was actually very sweet and very brilliant, but their romance wasn't meant to be. Noelle had been the first to realize it. She'd ended their brief engagement, and they'd parted on good terms, remaining friends to this day. "After the launch of Curtains, our new operating system, well…it was curtains for our marriage plans, too," she said, smiling at her own feeble pun.

"Just one guy?" Thom asked.

"Don't sound so disappointed." Noelle had told him far more than necessary. He hadn't said a word about either of the women he'd loved.

"Listen, what I said earlier regarding our mothers—I wonder if—"

"I don't want to discuss our mothers, Thom."

"We can't avoid it forever."

"Maybe not," she agreed, "but does it have to be the first thing we talk about?"

"It's not," he argued.

"Look at us," she said. "I haven't been with you fifteen minutes and already we're both on the defensive. This isn't going to work." She was ready to give up and go home, but Thom stopped her.

"Okay, we'll leave our mothers out of the conversation."

Now it seemed neither one had anything to say.

"I kept waiting to hear that you were married," she said after a silence. "But I refused to ask. That's silly I suppose." It was like waiting for the dentist's drill; when it happened there'd be pain and she hadn't been in a hurry to experience it.

"I assumed you'd get married first," he said.

Noelle grinned, shaking her head. "There's something else we need to talk about," she murmured. "What are we going to do now?" She began with the least palatable option—which was also the easiest. "I mean, we could shake hands and say it's great to have this cleared up, then just go back to our respective lives." She waited, watching for a response from him.

His face revealed none of his thoughts. "We could do that," he said. "Or..." He looked at her.

"Or we could renew our friendship."

Thom leaned back in his chair. "I like that option."

So did Noelle. "But, as you said, there's still the situation with our mothers." Now she was the one bringing it up, although she'd hoped to avoid any mention of their mothers' feud. It was futile, she realized. They *couldn't* avoid it, no matter how hard they tried.

"If your mother hadn't borrowed my great-grandmother's tea service," Thom began, "she—"

"My mother?" Noelle cried. "I agree she made a mistake, but she was the first to admit it. Your mother refused to forgive her, and that says a lot about the kind of person she is."

Thom's eyes were flinty with anger. "Don't paint *your* mother as the one who was wronged because—"

Noelle was unwilling to listen to any more. "Listen, Thom, this isn't going to solve anything. I think it'd be best if we dropped the subject entirely."

"That isn't the only thing you want to drop, is it?"

It was a question she didn't want to answer. A question that implied it would be best for all concerned if they simply walked away from each other right now. Their circumstances hadn't changed, not really; the business with their mothers would always be an obstacle between them. They could ignore it, but it would never disappear.

She stood and gathered her purse, pulled on her coat. This time Thom didn't try to stop her.

"So, you're walking away at the first sign of difficulty," he said.

"No. As a teenager my heart was open to you and your family, but I'm older now."

"What's that got to do with anything?" he demanded.

"This time, my eyes are open, too."

He looked as if he wanted to continue their argument. But she didn't have the heart for it. Obviously Thom didn't, either, because he let her go without another word.

"Help me carry everything in, Greg," Mary Sutton said as she stepped into the house. Her arms were loaded with plastic bags bursting at the seams.

Mary had never understood or appreciated football, and she didn't mind saying so. Her husband's gaze reluctantly left the television screen, where a bunch of men in tight pants and large helmets chased after an oddly shaped ball. As far as she was concerned, it was ridiculous the way they grunted and called out a few numbers now and then and groped their privates right on national television.

"Greg, are you going to help me or not?"

Her husband slowly stood up, his eyes still on the TV. "Honey, it's third down and inches."

He might as well be speaking Greek, but she wasn't going to argue with him. From the sudden reaction of the crowd, something had happened. Greg muttered, shaking his head in a disparaging manner. Mary pretended not to hear and walked back out to the car.

A moment later, he met her in the garage. "We're losing."

"Sorry, darling." She hoped she sounded sympathetic, but she didn't try very hard. Men and their football.

"What on earth did you buy?" he complained, lifting the last of the blue plastic bags from the car's trunk.

"Oh, various things," she said dismissively. "This Christmas basket project hasn't been a positive experience," she went on, following her husband into the house.

"Why not?"

Distressed and angry, she blurted out, "You won't believe this. Sarah McDowell was there!"

"At Wal-Mart?" Even Greg sounded surprised. "Don't tell me we've lost our shopping privileges there, too?"

"Very funny." The incident at the Value-X would haunt her forever.

"So you got along better?"

"I wouldn't say that, but I did discover the problem. We had the same list."

"For the Christmas baskets?"

"Yes." Mary set her load on top of the kitchen counter.

The football game ended, and Greg reached for the remote control to turn off the television set. He opened the first sack and seemed pleasantly surprised to find a stash of candy bars. "For me?" he asked. Without waiting for her to respond, he peeled the wrapper halfway down a Baby Ruth bar and took a bite.

"You can have them all." She threw herself onto the sofa.

Her husband walked into the family room and sat down. "You'd better tell me exactly what happened."

"What makes you think anything did?"

Greg chortled. "I haven't been married to you all these years without knowing when something's bothering you."

"Oh, Greg," she moaned. "I behaved like such an idiot." She longed to cover her face with her hands.

"What went wrong this time?"

She shook her head, unwilling to reveal how low she'd sunk. One thing she'd discovered years ago was still true: Sarah McDowell brought out the very worst in her. It never failed. Mary became another person whenever Sarah was around—a person she didn't like.

"Do you want to talk about it?"

"No. I want to crawl into bed and hide my head in shame." The most embarrassing part of all was that the pastor's wife had seen the whole thing.

"Tomorrow morning, I need to go back to the Club."

"For what?"

"I need the second half of the list."

"What's on the list?"

"I won't know until I see it, now will I?" She didn't mean to be short-tempered, but this afternoon hadn't been one of her best.

"I don't know if I want you driving. There's an ice storm forecast."

"Greg, I have to get that list. I told Sarah I'd take care of this. It's my responsibility."

"Then I'll drive you."

"You will?" Mary felt better already.

"Of course. Can't have you out on icy roads." Her husband finished off the candy bar and returned to the kitchen, where he rummaged through the bags on the counter. "You never did say why you bought all this candy."

Mary looked over at the ten plastic bags that lined her kitchen counter and shuddered. Half of them were filled with candy bars. "You don't want to know."

Greg didn't respond, but she caught him sneaking more Baby Ruth bars into his pockets and the sleeves of his sweater. He wasn't fooling her, but some things were best ignored.

On the other hand, certain things had to be faced. "Greg," she said thoughtfully. "I'm worried about Thom."

"Why?"

"Did you see him with Noelle last night? The two of them were dancing."

"Yes, dear, I saw them."

"Doesn't that concern you?" she asked.

"No." He added a couple of candy bars to his pants pockets, as though she wasn't going to see them protruding.

"Well, it should. Noelle is a sweet girl, but she's her mother's daughter. She's not to be trusted."

"Thom is an adult. He's fully capable of making his own decisions. My advice is to stay out of it."

Mary couldn't believe her husband would say such a thing to her. "You don't mean that! After what happened the last time—"

"You heard me. Stay out of it."

"But Thom is—"

Greg just shook his head. She wanted to say more but swallowed the words. Fathers weren't nearly as caring and concerned about matters of the heart; they lacked sensitivity. Greg hadn't spent time with Thomas the way she had that fateful summer ten years earlier. The McDowell girl had crushed him.

Her husband started toward the garage.

"Greg," she said.

"Yes, dear?"

"Put the candy bars back. I'm adding them to the charity baskets."

He muttered something under his breath, then said, "Yes, dear."

When Thom returned from the mall, he was suffering a full-blown case of the blues. His apartment had never seemed emptier. The small Christmas tree he'd purchased already decorated looked pitiful in the middle of his coffee table. Some Christmas this was turning out to be.

The light on his answering machine blinked, demanding his attention, and for half a heartbeat he thought it might be Noelle. But even as he pressed the Play button, he realized she wouldn't phone.

"Hey, Thom, this is Jonathan Clark," the message said. "Give me a call when you've got a moment."

Thom reached for the phone and punched in the number the investment broker had left. He knew Jonathan but didn't consider him a close friend. He was a business associate and Kristen McDowell's fiancé. This was the first time Jonathan had sought him out socially; Thom hoped it had something to do with Noelle.

After a brief conversation, they agreed to meet at a local pub. Jonathan didn't say why, but it didn't matter. The way Thom felt, he was grateful for any excuse to get out of the house. The walls were closing in around him. Some jovial guy-talk and loud music was exactly what he needed. Although Jonathan was about to marry into the other camp, Thom knew he'd be objective.

Jon was sitting at the bar nursing a dark ale when Thom joined him. The music in the background was Elvis Presley's "Blue Christmas"— appropriate under the circumstances. They exchanged pleasantries and then Jonathan got right to the point.

"I wanted to make sure there weren't any hard feelings about last night."

"You mean finagling it so I ended up dancing with Noelle? No problem."

"I didn't really want to do it, but Kristen seemed to think it was important."

Thom pulled out his wallet and paid for his beer when the bartender delivered it. "Like I said, it wasn't a big deal."

"So you and Kristen's sister were once an item?"

"Once."

"But no more?"

Thom took a deep swallow of the cold beer. "There's trouble between our families."

"Kristen told me about it."

"You're lucky, you know." Jonathan faced none of the challenges he did.

"Very," Jonathan agreed.

There was a pause, not an uncomfortable one. Jon seemed willing to discuss the situation further, but he wouldn't force it. He'd left it up to Thom.

"Noelle and I talked after the dance," he finally ventured.

Jonathan swiveled around on his stool in order to get a better look at Thom. "How'd it go?"

"Last night? Good." His blood warmed at the memory of their kisses. It'd taken every ounce of self-control he'd possessed to let her go. That was one of the reasons he'd suggested they meet at the mall today; it was neutral ground.

"Did you two work everything out?"

"We tried." He waited, half hoping Jonathan would question him about it. Jonathan didn't. Thom sighed, feeling a little discouraged. Now that he'd started, he wanted to talk. "I think we're both leery of getting involved a second time," he continued. "Her home's in Texas now and I live here."

"Right, got ya."

"But it's more than logistics." He tipped back the mug and took another swallow of beer. "We have…this situation. She wants to defend her mother. I want to defend mine."

"Only natural." Jonathan glanced at his watch.

Thom shut up. He had the feeling he was boring the other man. Perhaps he had someplace he needed to be.

Jonathan's next remark surprised him. "Kristen and I were making out our guest list and I put down your name. You'll come, won't you?"

"Sure," Thom answered almost flippantly, and then it occurred to him that if he accepted the invitation, he'd see Noelle again. He found himself eager for the opportunity. "Speaking of the wedding—" well, not really, but he didn't know how else to introduce the topic "—did Kristen ever mention her sister being involved with a guy named Paul?"

Jonathan considered it for a moment, then shook his head. "Not that I can remember. Why?"

"Just curious." And jealous. And worried. Noelle had said it was over between her and this Paul character, but Thom had to wonder. She seemed far too willing to walk away from their conversation this afternoon. Maybe the relationship with Paul wasn't as dead as she'd led him to believe.

"Paul," Jonathan repeated slowly. "Did she give you a surname?"

Thom shook his head.

The door to the pub opened, and Kristen McDowell walked inside. Jonathan glowed like a neon light, he was so pleased to see her. "Over here, sweetheart," he called, waving his hand.

Kristen walked to the bar and slipped her arm around her fiancé's waist. "Hello, Thom," she said as naturally as if they saw each other every day. "How's it going?"

"All right. I understand congratulations are in order."

Kristen smiled up at Jonathan and nodded.

Thom felt like an intruder. Reaching for his overcoat, he was getting ready to go when Kristen stopped him.

"There's no need to rush off."

He was about to pretend he had people to see, places to go, but then decided not to lie. "You sure?"

"Of course I'm sure."

Thom was eager to learn what he could about Noelle, so he lingered and ordered another beer. Jon did, too; Kristen had a glass of red wine.

Thom paid for the second round. The three of them sat on bar stools with Kristen in the middle, talking about Christmas plans for a few minutes. "She had me call you," Jonathan confessed suddenly.

Kristen elbowed her fiancé in the ribs. "You weren't supposed to tell him."

The second beer had loosened Thom's tongue. "She damn near knocked me off my feet when I first saw her."

"Kristen?" Jonathan asked, sounding worried.

"No, Noelle."

"Really?" This appeared to please Noelle's younger sister. "So you're still stuck on her, after all these years."

"Damned if I know," Thom muttered. He did know but he wasn't willing to admit it. "We decided it's not going to work."

"Why not?" Kristen sounded outraged.

"We met and talked this afternoon," Thom informed them both.

Jonathan frowned. "I thought you met last night after the dance."

"We did."

"So you've talked twice in the past twenty-four hours."

"Yeah, and like I said, we both realized there are too many complications."

Kristen raised her hand for the bartender. "We need another round."

"I think we've already done enough damage," Jonathan protested.

"Coffee here," she said, pointing at her fiancé. "Same as before over here." She made a sweeping gesture that included Thom.

The bartender did as requested. As soon as the wine and beer arrived, Kristen turned to face Thom. "I thought you loved my sister."

"I did once." He was still working on his second beer.

"But not now?"

Thom didn't want to answer her. Hell, the last time he'd admitted to loving Noelle he was just a kid. But he'd stood up to his parents and been willing to relinquish everything for Noelle. To say he'd loved her was an understatement. He'd been crazy about her.

"Well?" Kristen pressed. "Don't you have an answer?"

"I do," Thom said, picking up his beer. "I just don't happen to like it."

"What's that mean?" Jonathan asked Kristen.

"I think it means he still has feelings for Noelle." Then, as though she'd suddenly remembered, she said, "Hey! Her birthday's on Christmas Day, you know."

Like he needed a reminder. Not a Christmas passed that Thom forgot.

"She doesn't feel the same way about me," he murmured.

"Yeah, right," Kristen said, exaggerating the words. It took only two beers for him to bare his soul—and it was all for nothing because Noelle didn't love him anymore. It took only two beers to make him maudlin, he thought sourly.

"Yeah, right," Kristen said again.

"It's true," Thom argued. "Did you ask her?"

"Did you?" Kristen asked.

NOELLE McDOWELL'S JOURNAL

December 22 Afternoon

I blew it. I had the perfect chance to have a rational conversation with Thom. We had a chance to settle this once and for all without the angst and emotion. It didn't happen. Instead I let the opportunity slip through my fingers. Naturally I have a wealth of excuses, the first one being that I didn't sleep more than a couple of hours all night. This situation between Thom and me was on my mind and I couldn't seem to let it go. My feelings swung from happiness to dread and from joy to fear, and then the whole cycle repeated itself. I kept thinking about what I wanted to say when we saw each other again. Then I started worrying what would happen if he kissed me.

How is it that I can develop complicated software programs used all over the world, but when it comes to Thom Sutton I'm hopeless?

Mom's home from shopping, and when Carley asked if she'd gotten everything she needs for the Christmas baskets, it looked as if Mom was about to burst into tears. She said she had a headache, and went to bed. Apparently I wasn't the only one suffering from too little sleep. I have a feeling that something happened with Mrs. Sutton again, which is bad news all the way around.

Kristen wasn't home when I tried to phone, although she hadn't said she was going out. I'd hoped to discuss this with her, get her perspective. She's heard just about everything else that's gone on between Thom and me since I arrived. I could use a sympathetic ear and some sisterly advice.

Everything fell into place so naturally between her and Jonathan, but it sure hasn't been that way with me. I actually considered talking to Carley, which is a sign of how desperate I'm beginning to feel.

I'm not going to see Thom again. We left the mall and nothing more was said. It's over, even though I don't want it to be. It was within my power to change things, and I didn't have the courage to do it. I could've run after him and begged him not to let our relationship end this way, not after we'd come so far. But I didn't, and I'm afraid this is something I'm going to regret for a long time to come.

Chapter Six

"You don't need to worry about the dishes," Sarah McDowell protested.

Noelle continued to load the dishwasher. "Mom, quit treating me like a guest in my own home." The menial task gave her something to do. Furthermore, she hoped it would help take her mind off her disastrous meeting with Thom at the mall. She'd reviewed their conversation a dozen times and wished so badly it had taken a different course. Their second attempt at a relationship had staggered to a halt before it had really begun, she thought with regret as she rinsed off the dinner plates and methodically set them inside the dishwasher.

"Thank you, dear. This is a real treat," her mother said, walking into the family room to join her dad.

Sarah had returned from her shopping trip in a subdued mood. Noelle didn't ply her with questions, mainly because she wasn't in a talkative mood herself. Even Carley Sue seemed to be avoiding the rest of the family. Except for dinner, her sister had spent most of the day in her room, first on her computer, and then wrapping Christmas presents.

As Noelle finished wiping the counters, her youngest sister entered the kitchen. Carley glanced into the family room where her parents sat watching television. Their favorite courtroom drama was on, and they seemed to be absorbed in it.

"Wanna play a game of Yahtzee?" Noelle asked. It was one of Carley's favorites.

Her sister shook her head, then motioned for Noelle to come into her room. Carley nodded toward their parents, then pressed her finger to her lips.

"What's going on?" Noelle asked, drying her hands on a kitchen towel.

"Shh," Carley said, tiptoeing back toward her room.

"What?" Noelle asked impatiently.

Carley opened her bedroom door, grabbed Noelle's hand and pulled her into the bedroom. To her shock, Thom stood in the middle of the room, wearing his overcoat.

"Thom!"

"Shh," both Thom and Carley hissed at her.

"What are you *doing* here?" she whispered.

"When did you trade bedrooms with your sister?" he asked.

"A long time ago." She couldn't believe he was in her family's home. Years ago, he'd come to the house and tapped on her bedroom window, and she'd leaned out on the sill and they'd kissed. Amazingly, her parents hadn't heard—and the neighbors hadn't reported him. "Why are you here?"

"I came to see you."

Okay, that much was obvious. But she still didn't understand why he'd come.

"It was a bit of a surprise to bump into your little sister."

"I didn't mind," Carley said. "But he scared me like crazy when he knocked on the window."

"Sorry," Thom muttered.

"You said he broke your heart," Carley said, directing her remarks at Noelle. "We threw popcorn at him, remember? At least, we thought it was him, but then it wasn't."

Noelle didn't need any further reminders of that unfortunate incident. "I broke his heart, too. It was all a misunderstanding."

"Oh." Carley clasped her hands behind her back and leaned against the door, waiting. She was certainly in no hurry to leave and seemed immoderately interested in what Thom had to say.

Thom glanced at her sister, who refused to take the hint, and then said, "We need to talk."

"Now? Here?"

He nodded and touched her face in the gentlest way. "Listen, I'm sorry about this afternoon. We didn't even talk about what's most important—and that's you and me."

"I'm sorry, too." Unable to resist, Noelle slipped her arms around his waist and they clung to each other.

"This is *so-o-o* romantic," Carley whispered. "Why don't you two sit down and make yourselves comfortable. Can I get you anything to drink?"

Her little sister was as much of a hostess as their mother, Noelle thought with amusement. "No, but thanks."

Thom shrugged. "I should leave, but—"

"No, don't," Noelle pleaded with him. It might make more sense to meet Thom later, but she didn't want him out of her sight for another second.

Thom sat on the edge of the bed and Noelle sat beside him. He took both her hands in his. "I've been doing a lot of thinking about us."

"I have, too," she said hurriedly.

"I don't want it to end."

"Oh, Thom, I don't either! Not the way it did this afternoon—and for all the wrong reasons." Noelle was acutely aware of her sister, listening in on their conversation, but she didn't care.

"Noelle, I know what I want, and that's you back in my life."

"Oh, Thom." She bit her lower lip, suddenly on the verge of tears.

Carley sighed again. "This is better than any movie I've ever seen."

Noelle ignored her. "What are we going to do about our families?" They couldn't pretend their relationship wouldn't cause problems.

"I've been thinking about that, but I'm just not sure." Thom stroked the side of her face, and his hand lingered there.

"Oh, this *is* difficult," Carley agreed.

Her little sister was absorbing every word. Had Carley left the room, Noelle was sure Thom would be kissing her by now. Then they'd be lost in the kissing and oblivious to anything else.

"Is there a solution for us? One that doesn't involve alienating our families. Or our mothers, at any rate." Thom didn't look optimistic.

"What about the tea service?" Noelle said, mulling over an idea.

"You said there's no replacing it, but maybe if we found a similar one, your mother would be willing to accept it."

"I don't know," he said. "This wasn't just any tea service. It was a family heirloom that belonged to my great-grandmother. We'll never find one exactly like it."

"I know, but finding one even remotely similar would be a start toward rebuilding the relationship, don't you think?"

He didn't seem convinced. "Perhaps."

"Could you find out the style and type?"

Thom shook his head doubtfully. "I could try."

"Please, Thom. And see if there are any photos."

They hugged again and Noelle closed her eyes, savoring the feel of his strong arms around her, inhaling his clean, outdoorsy scent.

Everything had changed for her. The thought of returning to Texas and her life there held little appeal. For years, she'd stayed away from her hometown because it represented a past that had brought her grief, and now—now she knew this was where her future lay.

There was a knock on Carley's door.

Noelle and Thom flew apart and a look of panic came into Carley's eyes.

"The closet," Noelle whispered, quickly ushering Thom inside. No sooner had she shut the door than her little sister admitted their mother into the room.

Noelle figured they must look about as guilty as any two people could. Carley stared up at the bedroom ceiling and Noelle was tempted to hum a catchy Yuletide tune.

"I thought I'd turn in for the night," her mother said. She obviously hadn't noticed anything out of the ordinary.

"Good idea," Carley told her mother.

"You don't want to wear yourself out," Noelle added, letting her arms swing at her sides. "With Christmas and all…"

Her mother gave them a soft smile. "It does my heart good to see the two of you together. You were like a second mother to Carley when she was a baby."

"Mom!" her little sister wailed.

"I always thought you'd have a house full of your own children one day," she said nostalgically. "Don't you remember how you used to play with all your dolls?"

Noelle wanted to groan, knowing that Thom was listening in on the conversation.

"You'd make a wonderful mother."

"Thank you, Mom," she said. "'Night now. See you in the morning."

"'Night." She stepped out the door.

Noelle sighed with relief and so did Carley. She was about to open the closet when her mother stuck her head back inside the room. "Noelle, do you have plans for the morning?"

"No, why?" she asked, her voice higher than normal.

"I might need some help."

"I'll be glad to do what I can."

"Thank you, sweetheart." And with that she was gone. For good this time.

After a moment, Thom opened the closet door and peered out. "Is it safe?"

"I think so."

"Do you want me to keep watch?" Carley asked. "You know, so you guys can have some privacy." She smiled at Thom. "He's been wanting to kiss you ever since you got here." She lowered her voice. "I think he's kinda cute."

"So do I," Noelle confessed. "And yes, some privacy would be greatly appreciated."

Carley winked at Thom. "I think I'll go out and see what Dad's doing."

The instant the door closed, Thom took her in his arms and lowered his mouth to hers. Noelle groaned softly, welcoming him. Together, they created warm, moist kisses, increasing in intensity and desire. Other than the brief episode in the park, it'd been years since they'd kissed like this. Yet his touch felt so familiar....

"It's always been you," he whispered.

She heard the desperation in his voice. "I know—it's always been you," she echoed.

He kissed her again with a hunger and a need that reflected her own. "Oh, Thom, what are we going to do?"

"We're going to start with your suggestion and find a silver tea service," he said firmly. "Then we're going to give it to my mother and tell her it's time to mend fences."

"What if we *can't* find one?" She frowned. "Or what if we do and they still won't forgive each other?"

"You worry too much." He kissed the tip of her nose. "And you ask too many questions."

Sarah was sitting up in bed reading a brand-new and highly touted mystery when her husband entered their room.

"You've been quiet this evening," Jake commented as he unbuttoned his shirt.

"Have I?" She gazed at the novel, but her attention kept wandering. She'd read this paragraph at least six times and she couldn't remember what it said. Every word seemed to remind her of a friend she'd lost twenty years ago.

"You haven't been yourself since you got back from shopping."

Sarah decided to ignore his words. "I stopped in and said goodnight to the girls before I went to bed. Isn't it nice that Noelle and Carley get along so well?"

"You're changing the subject," Jake said. "And not very subtly."

Sarah set aside the book. In her present frame of mind, she was doing the author and herself a disservice. She reached for the light, but instead of flicking it off, she fell back against her pillows.

"I ran into Mary this afternoon," she told her husband.

"Again?"

"Again," she confirmed. "This meeting didn't go much better than the one at Value-X."

"That bad?"

"Almost. I can't even begin to tell you how horribly the two of us behaved."

Jake chuckled, shaking his head. "Does this have anything to do with the two hundred or so candy bars I found in the back of the big freezer?"

"You saw?"

He nodded. "What is it with you two?"

"Oh, honey, I wish I knew. I *hate* this. I've always hated this animosity. It would've been over years ago if Mary had listened to reason."

Her husband didn't respond.

"Everything was perfectly fine until we were forced to work on this Christmas project. Until then, she ignored me and I ignored her."

"Ignored her, did you?" he asked mildly.

Sarah pretended not to hear his question. "I think Melody Dar-rington might have planned this." The scheme took shape in her mind. "Melody *must* have."

"Isn't she the club secretary?"

"You know Melody," Sarah snapped. "She's the cute blonde who sold me the tickets to the dance."

"I wasn't there when you picked up the tickets," Jake reminded her as he climbed into bed.

"But you know who I mean."

"If you say so."

"You do. Now listen, because I think I'm on to something here. Melody's the one who told me we couldn't rent the hall for Kristen's wedding unless I performed a community service for the club."

"Yes, I remember, and that's how you got involved in the Christ-mas basket thing."

"Melody's also the one who assigned me to that project," she went on. "There had to be dozens of other projects I could've done. Plus, she insisted I had to fulfill those hours this year. That makes no sense whatsoever."

"Why would Melody do anything like that?"

"How would I know?"

Her husband looked skeptical. "I think you might be jumping to conclusions here."

"Melody gave us half of the same list, too." Outrage simmered just below the surface as Sarah sorted through the facts. She tossed aside the covers and leaped out of bed. Hands on hips, she glared at her hus-band. Of course. It all added up. Melody definitely had a role in this, and Sarah didn't like it.

"Hey, I didn't do anything," Jake protested.

"I'm not saying you did." Still not satisfied, she started pacing the area at the foot of the bed. "This is the lowest, dirtiest trick anyone's every played on me."

"Now, Sarah, you don't have any real proof."

"Of course I do! Why did Melody make a copy of that list, any-way? All she had to do was divide it."

"Sounds like an honest mistake to me. Didn't you tell me the of-fice was hectic that morning? Melody was dealing with you, the phones and everything else when she gave you and Mary the lists."

"Yes, but that's no excuse for what happened."

"You're angrier with yourself than Melody."

Sarah knew the truth when she heard it. The outrage vanished as quickly as it had come, and she climbed back into bed, next to her husband.

For a long time neither spoke. Finally Jake turned on their bedside radio and they listened to "Silent Night" sung by a children's choir. Their pure, sweet voices almost brought tears to Sarah's eyes.

"In two days, it'll be Christmas," she said in a soft voice.

"And Noelle's birthday." Her husband smiled. "Remember our first year? We could barely afford a Christmas tree, let alone gifts. Yet you managed to give me the most incredible present of all, our Noelle."

"Remember the next Christmas, when I'd just found out I was pregnant with Kristen?" she said fondly. "Our gift to each other was a second-hand washer." In the early years of their marriage, they'd struggled to make ends meet. Yet in many ways, those had been the very best.

Jake smiled. "We were poor as church mice."

"But happy."

"Very happy," he agreed, sliding his arm around her shoulders. "I thought it was clever of you to knit Christmas stockings for the girls the year Noelle turned four. Or was it five?"

"I didn't knit them," Sarah said sadly. "Mary did."

"Mary?"

"Don't you remember? She knit all the kids stockings, and I baked the cookies and we exchanged?"

"Ah, yes. You two had quite a barter system worked out."

"If we hadn't traded baby-sitting, none of us would've been able to afford an evening out." Once a month, they'd taken the girls over to their dearest friends' home for the night; Mary and Greg had done the same. It'd been a lifesaver in those early years. She and Jake had never been able to afford anything elaborate, but a night out, just the two of them, had been heaven. Mary and Greg had cherished their nights, as well.

"I miss her," Sarah admitted. "Even after all these years, I miss my friend."

"I know." Jake gently squeezed her shoulder.

"I'd give anything never to have borrowed the silver tea service."

"You were trying to help someone out."

"That's how it started, but I should've been honest with Mary. I should've told her the tea service wasn't for my open house, but for Cheryl's."

"Why didn't you?"

She'd had years to think about the answer to that question. "Because Mary didn't like Cheryl. I assumed she was jealous. Now...I don't know."

Sarah remembered the circumstances well. She'd recently begun selling real estate and Cheryl Carlson had given her suggestions and advice. Cheryl had wanted something to enhance the look of the dining room for her open house, and Sarah had volunteered to bring in the tea service. When she'd asked Mary, her friend had hesitated, but then agreed. Sarah had let Mary assume it was for her own open house.

"You were so upset when you found out the tea service had been stolen."

To this day her stomach knotted at the memory of having to face Mary and confess what had happened. Soon afterward, Cheryl had left the agency and hired on with another firm, and Sarah had lost touch with her.

"I'd always hoped that one day Mary would find it in her heart to forgive me."

"I did, too."

"I'm so sorry, sweetheart," Sarah whispered, resting her head against her husband's shoulder.

"Why are you apologizing to me?"

"Because you and Greg used to be good friends, too."

"Oh."

"Remember how you used to golf together."

"Yes."

"I wonder if Greg still plays."

"I see him out at the club every now and then," Jake told her.

"Does he speak to you?"

"Yes."

Sarah was comforted knowing that. "I'm glad."

"So am I," her husband said, then kissed her goodnight.

* * *

On December twenty-third, Thom's office was running on a skeleton crew. His secretary was in for half a day and he immediately handed her the assignment of locating every antique store in a hundred-mile radius.

He'd called his father before eight that morning. "Tell me what you know about Mom's old tea service."

"Tell you what I know?" he repeated. "It was stolen, remember?"

"I realize that," Thom said impatiently.

"What makes you ask?"

"I thought I'd buy her a replacement for Christmas."

"Don't you think you're leaving your shopping a little late?"

"Could be." Thom didn't feel comfortable sharing what this was really about, but he was going to do whatever he could to replace that damn tea service.

"I think we might have a picture of it somewhere."

Thom perked up.

"For years your mother looked for a replacement, you know. We hadn't actually taken a picture of the tea set, but it was in the background of another photograph."

Thom remembered now. His parents had the photo enlarged in order to get as much detail as possible.

"Do you still have the photograph? Or better yet, the enlargement?"

"I think it might be around here somewhere. I assume you need this ASAP."

"You got it."

"Well, I promised to drive your mother out to the Women's Century Club this morning and then to the grocery store. You're welcome to stop by the house and look."

"Where do you figure it might be?"

His father considered that for a moment. "Maybe the bottom drawer of my desk. There are a few old photographs there. That's my best suggestion."

"Anyplace else I should look?"

"Your mother's briefcase. Every once in a while she visits an antique store, but for the most part she's given up hope. She's still got her name in with several of the bigger places. If anything even vaguely similar comes in, the stores promised to give her a call."

"Has she gotten many calls?"

"Only two in all these years," his father told him. "Both of them excited her so much she could barely sleep until she'd checked them out. They turned out to be completely the wrong style."

Thom didn't know if he'd have any better success, but he had to try.

"Good luck, son."

"Thanks, Dad."

As soon as he hung up, Thom called Noelle's cell phone. She answered right away.

"Morning," he said, warming to the sound of her voice. "I hope you're free to do a bit of investigating."

"I am. I canceled out on Mom—told her I was meeting an old friend."

"Did she ask any questions?"

"No, but I could tell she was disappointed. I do so hope we're successful."

"Me, too. Listen, I've got news." Thom told her about the old photograph and what his father had said earlier. He hoped it would encourage Noelle, but she seemed disheartened when she spoke again.

"If your parents searched all these years, what are the chances of us finding a replacement now?"

"We'll just keep working on it. I'm not giving up, and I'm guessing you feel the same way."

"I do—of course."

"Good. How soon before we can meet?"

"Fifteen minutes."

"I'll wait for you at my parents' place."

On his way out the door, Thom grabbed the list Martha, his secretary, had compiled and when he read it over, he knew why he paid this woman top dollar. Not only had she given him the name and address of every store in the entire state, she'd also listed their Web sites and any other Internet information.

"Merry Christmas," he said, then gave her the rest of the day off with pay.

Noelle was already parked outside his parents' house when Thom arrived. She got out of her car and joined him as he pulled into the driveway.

"Hi," she said softly.

Thom leaned over and kissed her. "Hi." The key to the house was under a decorative rock. He unlocked the door and turned off the burglar alarm. Holding Noelle's hand, he led her into his parents' home.

Noelle stopped in the entryway and glanced around. It'd been many, many years since she'd walked into this house. It wasn't really familiar—everything had been redecorated and repainted since she was a little girl—but the place had a comfortable relaxed feel. Big furniture dominated the living room, hand-knit stockings hung on the fireplace and the mantel was decorated with holly. The scent of the fresh Christmas tree filled the air.

"Your mother has a wonderful eye for color and design," she commented, taking in the bright red bows on the tree and all the red ornaments.

Still holding her hand, Thom led her into his father's den. The oak rolltop desk sat in the corner, and Thom immediately started searching through the bottom drawer. He found the stack of photographs his father had mentioned and sorted through them with Noelle looking over his shoulder. She leaned against him, and he wondered if she realized how good it felt to have her pressed so close to him. Or how tempting it was to turn and kiss her...

"That's it," she cried triumphantly when he flipped past a black-and-white picture. She grabbed it before he had a chance to take a second look. Examining the print, she murmured, "It really was exquisite, wasn't it?" She passed it back to him.

"It *is* beautiful," he said, emphasizing the present tense. Thom wasn't sure why he insisted on being this optimistic about finding a replacement. He suspected that wanting it so badly had a lot to do with it.

Reaching into his coat pocket, he pulled out the list Martha had compiled for him.

"Now that we have a picture," Noelle said, "I'll go home and scan it into Carley's computer. Then I'll send it out to these addresses and see what comes back."

"Great. But before you do, I'll get a copy of this photograph and start contacting local dealers. They might be able to steer me in a different direction."

"Oh, Thom, it'd mean so much to me if we could bring our mothers back together."

They kissed, and it would've been the easiest thing in the world to become immersed in the wonder of having found each other again. Her mouth was warm, soft to the touch. She enticed him, fulfilled him and tempted him beyond any woman he'd ever known or loved. He didn't know much about her present life. They'd spoken very little of their accomplishments, their friends, their jobs. It wasn't necessary. Thom *knew* her. The girl he'd loved in high school had matured into a capable, beautiful and very desirable adult.

"It's hard to think about anything else when you kiss me," she whispered.

"It is for me, too."

Before leaving the Sutton home, Thom put everything back as it was, and remembered to reset the burglar alarm.

After making a photocopy at his office, Thom gave her the original, thinking that would scan best.

"I'll go back to the house now and plead with Carley to let me on the computer," she told him.

"Okay, and I'll see what a little old-fashioned footwork turns up."

Noelle started to get into her car, then paused. "What'll happen if we don't find a replacement before I return to Texas?"

Thom didn't want to think about that yet. "I don't know," he had to admit.

"Want to meet in the park at midnight?" she asked.

Thom chuckled. "I'm a little old to be sneaking around to meet my girlfriend."

"That didn't stop you from climbing in my bedroom window last night."

True, but his need to see her had overwhelmed his caution, not to mention his good sense.

"I love you, Noelle." There, he'd said it. He'd placed his heart in her hands, to accept or reject.

Tears glistened in her eyes. "I love you, too—I never stopped loving you."

"Even when you hated me?"

She laughed shakily. "Even then."

NOELLE McDOWELL'S JOURNAL

December 23
11:00 a.m.

I feel as if I'm on an emotional roller coaster. One moment I'm feeling as low as I can get, and the next I'm soaring into the clouds. Just now, I'm in the cloud phase. Thom found the picture of the tea set! We're determined to locate one as close to the original as possible. As I said to Thom, I'm hoping for a Christmas miracle. (I never knew I was such a romantic.) Normally I scoff at things like miracles, but that's what both Thom and I need. We've already had one miracle—we have each other back.

Before we parted this morning, Thom said he loved me. I love him, too. I've always loved Thom, and that's what made his deception—or what I believed was his deception—so terribly painful.

Now all we've got to do is keep our mothers out of the picture until we can replace the tea service. I know it's a challenging task, but we're up to it.

As of right now, we each have our assignments. Carley's using the computer for ten more minutes and then it's all mine. My job is to scan in the picture he found at his parents' house and send it to as many online antique dealers as I can. Thom is off checking local dealers and has some errands to run. We're going to meet up again later.

I had to cancel a lunch date with Kristen and Jonathan, but my sister understood. She's excited about Thom and me getting back together. Apparently she's had more of a hand in this than I realized. I really owe her.

Finding a tea service to replace the one that was stolen is turning out to be even harder than I expected—but we have to try. I believe in miracles. I was a doubter less than a week ago, but now I'm convinced.

Chapter Seven

"How many turkeys did you say we had to buy?"

"Six," Mary said, checking the list to make sure she was correct. December twenty-third, and the grocery store was a nightmare. The aisles were crowded, and many of the shelves needed restocking. The last thing Mary wanted to do was fight the Christmas rush, but that couldn't be helped. Next year, she'd leave the filling of these Christmas baskets to someone else.

"Get six bags of potatoes while you're at it," she told her husband as they rolled past a stack of ten-pound bags.

"Getting a little bossy, aren't you?" Greg muttered.

"Sorry, it's just that there are a hundred other things I'd rather be doing right now."

"Then you should've given the task to Sarah McDowell. Didn't you tell me she offered?"

Mary didn't want to hear the other woman's name. "I don't trust her to see that it's done properly."

"Don't you think you're being a little harsh?"

"No." That should be plain enough. The more she thought about her last encounter with Sarah McDowell, the more she realized how glad she'd be when they'd completed this project. "Being around

Sarah has dredged up a whole slew of bad memories," she informed her husband.

Greg dutifully loaded sixty pounds of potatoes into the cart. As soon as he'd finished, Mary headed down the next aisle.

"My Christmas has been ruined," she said through gritted teeth.

"How's that?"

"Greg, don't be obtuse." She reached for several cans of evaporated milk and added them to the food piled high in their cart. "I've had to deal with *her.*"

"Yes, but—"

"Never mind," Mary said, cutting him off. She didn't expect Greg to understand. Her husband had never really grasped the sense of loss she'd felt when Sarah destroyed their friendship with her deception. The silver tea service was irreplaceable; so was the friendship its disappearance had shattered.

"Hello, Mary." Jean Cummings, a friend who edited the society page, pulled her cart alongside Mary's. "Merry Christmas, Greg."

Her husband had the look of a deer caught in the headlights. He no more knew who Jean was than he would a stranger, although he'd attended numerous social functions with the woman.

"You remember Jean, don't you?" she said, hoping to prompt his memory.

"Of course," he lied. "Good to see you again."

"It looks like you're feeding a big crowd," Jean said, surveying the contents of Mary's cart.

Mary didn't bother to explain about the Christmas baskets. "Is your family coming for the holidays?" she asked.

"Oh, yes, and yours too, I imagine?"

"Of course." Mary was eager to get about her business. She didn't have time to dillydally. As soon as she was finished with the shopping, she could go back to planning her own family's Christmas dinner. Greg would need to order the fresh Dungeness crabs they always had on Christmas Eve; he could do that while they were here.

"Tell me," Jean said, leaning close to Mary and talking in a stage whisper. "Am I going to get the scoop on Thom?"

"Thom?" Mary didn't know what she was talking about.

"I saw him just now in Mendleson's."

It was well known that the jeweler specialized in engagement rings.

"Thom's one of the most eligible bachelors in town. I know plenty of hearts will be broken when he finally chooses a bride."

Mary was speechless. She'd had lunch with her son on Friday and although he'd hinted, he certainly hadn't said anything that suggested he was on the verge of proposing. She didn't even know who he was currently seeing.

"I'm sure Thom would prefer to do his own announcing," Greg said coolly, answering for Mary.

"Oh, drat," Jean muttered. "I was hoping you'd let the cat out of the bag."

"My lips are sealed," Mary said, recovering. "Have a wonderful Christmas."

"You, too." Jean pushed her cart past them.

As soon as the society page editor was out of earshot, Mary gripped her husband's forearm. "Has Thom spoken to you lately?"

"This morning," Greg told her. "But he didn't say anything about getting engaged."

"Who could it be?" Mary cried, aghast that she was so completely in the dark. As his mother, she should know these things.

"If he was serious about any woman, we'd know."

Mary wasn't buying it.

"Let's not leap to conclusions just because our son happened to walk into a certain jewelry store. I'm sure there's a perfectly logical reason Thom was in Mendleson's and I'll bet it hasn't got a thing to do with buying an engagement ring."

"This is all Sarah's fault," she murmured.

Her husband looked at her as though she were speaking in a foreign language.

"I mean it, Greg. I've been so preoccupied with the whole mess Sarah's created about these baskets, I haven't had time to pay attention to my son. Why, just on Friday when we had lunch..." Suddenly disheartened, Mary let her words fade.

"What's wrong?" Greg asked.

All the combativeness went out of her. "I can't blame Sarah entirely—I played a role in this, too."

"What role?"

Once again, she was amazed by her husband's obliviousness. "This business with Thom. Now that I think about it, I'm convinced he wanted to talk over his engagement with me, only I was so rattled by the Value-X incident I didn't give him a chance. Oh, Greg, how could I have been so self-absorbed?"

"What makes you think he was going to tell you he was getting engaged? Why don't we call and ask him when we get home?" Greg suggested.

"And let him think we're interfering in his life? We can't do that!"

"Why not?"

"We'd ruin his surprise, if indeed there is one."

Greg merely sighed as they wheeled the cart to the checkout counter.

Ten minutes later, once everything was safely inside the trunk, Mary turned to him. "I just don't know what I'll do if *she's* the one he's interested in. I couldn't stand it if he married into *that* family."

"I don't think we need to worry about it," he told her as they started back to the house. "There's no evidence whatsoever."

"He *danced* with Noelle McDowell!"

"He danced with lots of girls."

The engine made a coughing sound as they approached the first intersection. "What's that?" Mary asked.

"It's time for an oil change," her husband said. "I'll have the car looked at after the holidays."

She nodded. She trusted the upkeep of their vehicles to her husband and immediately put the thought out of her mind. Car troubles were minor in the greater scheme of things.

By the end of the day, when clouds thickened the sky and the cold swept in, fierce and chilling, Thom finally had to admit that replacing the silver tea service wasn't going to be easy.

He'd tried everything he could think of, called friends and associates who might know where he could find an antique dealer who specialized in silver—anyone who might lead him to his prize. Far more than a gift lay in the balance. It was possible that his and Noelle's entire future hinged on this.

At seven, after an exhaustive all-day search, he went home. The first thing he did was check his answering machine, hoping to hear from Noelle. Sure enough, the message light was flashing. Without waiting to remove his coat, he pushed the button and grabbed paper and a pen.

A female voice, high and excited, spilled out. "It's Carley Sue. Remember me? I'm Noelle's sister. Anyway, Noelle asked me to call you. She'd call you herself, but I asked if I could do it, 'cause it was my bedroom window you knocked on. And my computer Noelle used."

Thom laughed out loud, almost missing the second half of the message.

"Anyway, Noelle wanted to know if you could meet her at the park tomorrow morning. She said you should be there early. She said six o'clock 'cause you have to drive all the way to Portland. She said you'd know why, but she wouldn't tell me. When you see Noelle, please tell her it's not nice to keep secrets from her sister, will you?" She giggled. "Never mind, I could get it out of her if I really wanted to. Bye."

Thom smiled, feeling a surge of energy. Obviously Noelle had had better luck than he did.

A second message followed the first.

"Thom, it's me. I wasn't sure Carley got the entire message to you. When we meet at the park, come with a full tank of gas. If this conflicts with your Christmas Eve plans, call me on my cell phone." There was a short pause. "I don't want you to get your hopes up. I found a tea service that's not *exactly* like your grandmother's, but I'm looking for a Christmas miracle. We'll need to compare it to the picture. The dealer's only keeping his store open until noon, which is why we need to leave here so early. I'm sorry I can't see you tonight. I wish I could, but I've got family obligations. I know you understand."

He did understand—all too well. A third message started; he was certainly popular today. It was his mother and she sounded worried.

"It's Mom… I ran into a friend from the newspaper this morning and she mentioned seeing you at Mendleson Jewelers. Were you…buying an engagement ring? Thom, it isn't that McDowell girl, is it? Call me, will you? I need reassurance that you're not about to make a big mistake."

This was what happened when you lived in a small town. Everyone knew your business. So, his mother had heard, and even with the wrong facts, she'd put together the right answer. Yes, he'd been at Mendleson's. And yes, it *was* "that McDowell girl."

Thom decided he had to talk about all of this with someone who understood the situation and knew all the people involved. Someone discreet, who had his best interests at heart. Someone with no agenda, hidden or otherwise.

The one person he could trust was his older sister. Suzanne was three years his senior, married and living ten miles outside of town; she and her husband, Rob, owned a hazelnut orchard. Thom didn't see Suzanne often, but he was godfather to his five-year-old nephew, Cameron.

A brief phone call assured him that his sister was available and eager to see him. Off he went, grabbing a chunk of cheese and an apple to eat on the way. Maybe his sister would have some wisdom to share with him…. How quickly life can change, he mused, and never more so than at Christmas.

Suzanne had a mug of hot cider waiting when he arrived. Rob was out, dealing with some late deliveries. His family owned the orchard and leased it to him. Rob worked long hours making a success of their business, and so did Suzanne. Both his sister and brother-in-law were honest, hardworking people, and he trusted their advice.

"This is a surprise," Suzanne said, pulling out a chair at the large oak table in the center of her country kitchen.

"Cameron's in bed already?" Thom asked, disappointed to miss seeing his nephew.

"He thinks if he goes to bed early Santa will come sooner." She gave a shrug. "Never mind that this is only the twenty-third. I guess he's hoping he can make time speed up," she said with a smile. "By the way, he had a ridiculous tale about you and some woman at the movies the other day. Throwing popcorn was a big theme in this story."

"I don't know what he told you, but more than likely it's true. We bumped into Noelle McDowell and her little sister at the theater."

"Noelle. Oh, no." Suzanne was instantly sympathetic. "That must've been uncomfortable."

"Yes and no." He hesitated, wondering to what extent his sister's attitude was a reflection of their parents'. "It was difficult at first, because we didn't exactly part on the best of terms."

"At first?"

His sister had picked up on that fast enough. "We've talked since and resolved our difficulties."

"Resolved them, did you?" Suzanne raised her eyebrows.

"I love Noelle." There, he'd said it.

"Who's Noelle?" Rob asked as he walked in through the kitchen door, shedding hat, scarf and gloves.

"I'll explain later," Suzanne promised, ladling a cup of cider from the pot on the stove. "Here, honey."

"Our families don't get along," Thom explained.

"Do Mom and Dad know?" his sister asked.

"Not yet, but Mom got wind of me going to Mendleson's. She must have her suspicions, since she left a message on my machine practically begging me to tell her I'm not seeing Noelle."

"Did you buy a ring?"

"That's not the point."

"Okay," his sister said slowly. "What *do* you plan to tell Mom and Dad?"

"I don't know."

Suzanne sipped her cider, then put down the mug to focus on him. "You're going to wait until Christmas's over before you say anything, right?"

Thom didn't know if he could. His mother was already besieging him with questions and she'd keep at him until she got answers—preferably the answers she wanted. He needed an ally and he hoped he could count on Suzanne.

"Let me play devil's advocate here a moment," his sister suggested.

"Please."

"Put yourself in Mom's place. Noelle's family has hurt our family. And now you're asking Mom to welcome Noelle into our lives and our hearts."

"Noelle is already in my heart."

"I know," Suzanne told him, "but there's more than one person involved in this. How does her family feel about you, for instance?"

That was a question Thom didn't want to consider. This wouldn't be easy for Noelle, either. Kristen and Carley were obviously supportive, but Sarah McDowell—well, she was another matter.

"We were ready to defy everyone as teenagers," he said, reminding his sister of the difficult stand he'd taken at eighteen.

"You were a kid."

"I was in love with her then, and I'm still in love with her."

"Yes," Suzanne said, "but you're more responsible now."

"I can't live my life to suit everyone else," he said, frustrated by her response.

"He's got a point," Rob said. "I don't understand the family dynamics here, but I have a fairly good idea what you're talking about. I say if Thom feels this strongly about Noelle after all these years, he should go for it. He should live his own life."

Thom felt a rush of gratitude for his brother-in-law's enouragement.

"That's what you wanted to hear, isn't it?" Suzanne said, smiling. "For what it's worth, I agree with my husband."

"Thanks," Thom said. "That means a lot, you guys." He shook his head. "Noelle and I are well aware of the problems we face as a couple. We'd hoped to come to our parents with a solution."

"What kind of solution?"

"I've been pounding the pavement all day, checking out antique stores and jewelry stores for a replacement tea service. Noelle's been doing an Internet search."

His sister frowned. "I don't want to discourage you, but you're not going to find one."

She certainly had a way of cutting to the chase. "Thank you for that note of optimism. Anyway, how can you be so sure? Noelle thinks she might have a lead."

"Hey, that's good," Rob said. "It's worth trying to find...whatever this thing is that you're looking for."

"An antique silver tea service—I'll fill you in later, Rob." She turned to her brother. "I don't want to be pessimistic. It's just that Mom and Dad looked for years. They've given up now, but for a long time they left no stone unturned."

"If we find one, we'll consider it a Christmas miracle."

"Definitely," Suzanne agreed. "And I'd consider it a lucky omen, too."

"But you don't think we'll succeed."

"No," his sister told him. "I don't think so, but who knows?"

"If I ask Noelle to be part of my life, will you accept her?"

"Of course." Suzanne didn't hesitate. "But I'm not the one whose opinion matters. However, Rob's right, you've got to live your own life, and we'll support you in whatever choice you make."

He visited with his sister a while longer and assured her that no matter what he decided, he'd meet the family for the annual Christmas Eve dinner, followed by church services.

The next morning Noelle was waiting in the park at the appointed time and place when he got there. His heart reacted instantly to the sight of her. She looked like an angel in her long white wool coat and cashmere scarf. A Christmas angel. He smiled at the thought—even if he *was* getting sentimental in his old age.

"Merry Christmas," he said.

"Merry Christmas, Thom." Her eyes brightened as he approached.

Thom folded her in his arms and their kisses were deep and urgent. His mouth lingered on hers, gradually easing into gentler kisses. Finally he whispered, "Ready to go?"

"I hope this isn't a wild-goose chase," Noelle told him as she leaned her head against his shoulder.

"I do, too." But if it was, at least he'd be spending the day with her.

If they couldn't carry out their quest, they'd simply have to find some other way to persuade both mothers to accept the truth—that Thomas Sutton and Noelle McDowell were in love.

It was Christmas Eve, nine in the morning, and Sarah McDowell was eager to finish with the Christmas baskets. She'd skillfully wrapped each gift to transport to the Salvation Army.

"You're coming with me, aren't you?" she asked her husband.

Jake glanced up from the morning paper, frowning. "I can't."

"Why not?" Sarah didn't know if she could face Mary alone—not again. She'd assumed Jake would drive with her.

"I've got errands of my own. It's Christmas Eve."

"What about you, Carley?" she said, looking hopefully toward her daughter.

"Can't, Mom, sorry."

But not nearly sorry enough, Sarah thought. Her family was abandoning her in this hour of need. "Where's Noelle?" she asked. Surely she could count on Noelle.

"Out," Carley informed her.

"She's left already?"

Carley nodded.

Sarah thought she saw Jake wink at Carley. Apparently those two were involved in some sort of conspiracy against her.

At least Jake helped her load up the car, shifting his golf clubs to the back seat, but he disappeared soon afterward. Grumbling under her breath, Sarah drove out to the Women's Century Club.

Mary's car was already in the lot when she arrived. So, Mary Sutton was breaking a lifelong habit of tardiness in her eagerness to finish this charity project. For that, Sarah couldn't blame her. She, too, had reached her limit.

The cold air cut through her winter coat the instant she climbed out of the car. The radio station had mentioned the possibility of an ice storm later in the day. Sarah only hoped it wouldn't materialize.

"Merry Christmas," Melody called out as Sarah struggled through the front door, carrying the largest and most awkward of the boxes.

Sarah muttered a reply. Her Christmas Eve was *not* getting off to a good start.

"Mary's waiting for you," Melody told her. "I understand there was a mix-up with the lists. I'm so sorry. It was crazy that morning, wasn't it?"

Sarah wasn't fooled by the other woman's cheerful attitude. Melody Darrington had done her utmost to manipulate the two of them into working on this project together, and Sarah, for one, didn't take kindly to the interference. It was clear that Mary hadn't realized anything was amiss, but then Mary Sutton wasn't the most perceptive person in the world. Still, Sarah wasn't going to make a federal case of it, on the off-chance that it *had* all been an innocent mistake as Melody was implying.

Sarah made her way into the meeting room, where Mary had the six baskets set up on a long table, as well as six large boxes, already filled with the makings for Christmas dinner.

"Is that everything you've got?" Mary asked, peering into Sarah's carton. Her tone insinuated that Sarah had contributed less than required.

"Of course not," she snapped. "I have two more boxes in the car."

Neither woman leaped up to help her carry them inside, although Melody did make a halfhearted offer when Sarah headed out the front door.

"No thanks—you've already done enough," she said pointedly.

"You're sure you don't need the help?" Melody asked.

Shaking her head, Sarah brought in the second of the boxes and set it on the table.

"I thought you'd bring one of the girls with you," Mary said in that stiff way of hers.

"They're busy." She started back for the last of the cartons.

"Noelle isn't with Thom, is she?"

The question caught her off guard. No one had said where Noelle had gone, but it couldn't be to meet Thom Sutton. Could it? No, she wouldn't do that. Not her daughter.

"Absolutely not," Sarah insisted. Noelle had already learned her lesson when it came to the Suttons.

"Good," Mary said.

"Noelle's with friends," Sarah returned and then, because she had to know, she asked a question of her own. "What makes you ask?"

"Oh—no reason."

Sarah didn't believe that for a moment. "You tell your son Noelle's under no illusions about him. She won't be so easily fooled a second time."

"Now just one minute—"

"We both know what he did."

"You're wrong, Sarah—but then you often are."

Melody stepped into the meeting room and stopped abruptly. With a shocked look, she regarded both women. "Come on, you two! It's Christmas."

"And your point is?" Sarah asked.

"My point is that the least you can do is work together on this. These baskets need to get to the Salvation Army right away. They're late already, and my husband just phoned and said there's definitely an ice storm coming, so you shouldn't delay."

"I'll get them there in time," Mary promised. "If we could get the baskets filled…"

"Fine," Sarah said. "I'll bring in the last box."

"We wouldn't be this late if you'd—"

Sarah ignored her and hurried out the door, only to hear Melody mutter something about an ice storm developing right in this room.

She knew that the minute she left, Melody and Mary would talk about her. However, she didn't care. Right after Kristen's wedding, she was letting her membership in the Women's Century Club lapse.

Once the third box was safely inside, Sarah placed the gifts in the correct baskets. Then both women sorted through the family names by checking the tag on each present. Sarah had spent a lot of time wrapping her gifts, wanting to please the recipients…and, to be honest, impress Mary and Melody with her talents. Given the opportunity, she could have decorated the club house to match Mary's efforts. No, to exceed them.

"You did get that Firefighter Barbie doll, didn't you?" Mary asked.

"Of course I did," she answered scornfully.

They attached ribbons to each basket, then prepared everything—gifts and groceries—for transport.

"Would you like help loading up your car?" Sarah asked. Since Mary was driving and this was a joint project, she felt constrained to offer.

Mary seemed surprised, then shook her head. "I can manage. But…thanks."

Sarah had wanted to make a quick getaway, but Melody stopped her at the door, appointment book in hand.

"I have a few questions about Kristen's wedding."

"What do you need to know?"

Melody flipped open the book. "Will you require the use of our kitchen?"

"I'm not sure because we haven't picked the caterer yet, but we'll do that right after the first of the year."

"I have a list, if you'd like to look at it."

"I would." Sarah wanted to make her daughter's day as special as she could. But as she answered Melody's questions, her mind drifted to Noelle. Mary had brought up a frightening possibility. Noelle had been absent from the house quite a bit since the dance on Saturday night. She was at the mall on Sunday, and then on Monday—oh, yes, she'd worked on Carley's computer most of the day. Reassured now, Sarah relaxed. Mary's fears about her son and Noelle were unfounded.

She glanced around the lot; Mary's car was gone. She'd apparently left for the Salvation Army already. She must have moved her vehicle to the side entrance in order to load up the baskets and boxes more easily and Sarah hadn't seen her drive off. That was just fine. Maybe this was the last she needed to see of Mary Sutton.

Now she could enjoy Christmas.

"Merry Christmas, Melody," she said. "I'm sorry for the way I snapped at you earlier."

Melody accepted her apology. "I realize this was hard on both of you but what's important are the Christmas baskets."

"I couldn't agree with you more."

Sarah's spirits lifted considerably as she walked to her car or rather, Jake's. He'd insisted she take his SUV, and she was glad of it. If possible, it seemed even colder out; she drew her coat more closely around her and bent her head as she trudged toward the car.

As she turned out of the parking lot, she saw that the roads were icing over. The warning of an ice storm had become a reality, and even earlier than expected. This weather made her nervous, and Sarah drove carefully, hoping she wouldn't run into any problem.

She hadn't gone a mile when she noticed a car pulled off to the side of the road. She slowed down and was surprised to see Mary Sutton in the driver's seat. Mary was on her cell phone; she looked out the passenger window as Sarah slowed down. Mary's eyes met hers, and then she waved her on, declining help before Sarah could even offer it.

A NOTE FROM NOELLE McDOWELL

Christmas Eve

Dear Carley Sue,

Good morning. I'll be gone by the time you read this. I'm meeting Thom in the park and we're driving to an antique store outside Portland to check out a tea service. Kristen knows I'm with Thom, but not why.

I'm asking you to keep my whereabouts a secret for now. No, wait—you can mention it to Dad if you want. Mom's the only one who really can't know. I don't think she'll ask, because she's got a lot to do this morning delivering the Christmas baskets.

This whole mix-up with those baskets has really got her in a tizzy. I find it all rather humorous and I suspect Dad does, too.

I'm trusting you with this information, little sister. I figured you (and your romantic heart) would want to know.

Love,
Noelle

Chapter Eight

The car had made a grinding noise as soon as Mary started it—the same sound as the day before. Greg had said he'd look into it after the holidays, but she'd assumed it was safe to drive. Apparently not.

The car had slowed to a crawl, sputtered and then died. That was just great. The Salvation Army was waiting for these Christmas baskets which, according to Melody, were already late. If Mary didn't hurry up and deliver them to the organization's office before closing time, six needy families would miss out on Christmas. She couldn't let that happen.

Reaching for her cell phone, she punched in her home number and hoped Greg was home. She needed rescuing, and soon. Greg would know what to do. The phone had just begun to ring when Sarah McDowell drove past.

Mary bit her lip hard. Pride demanded that she wave her on. She didn't need that woman's help. Still, she felt Sarah should've stopped; it was no less than any decent human being would do.

Well, she should know better than to expect compassion or concern from Sarah McDowell. Good Christian that she professed to be, Sarah had shown not the slightest interest in Mary's safety.

Mary clenched her teeth in fury. So, fine, Sarah didn't care whether *she* froze the death, but what about the Christmas baskets? What about the families, the children, whose Christmas depended on them? The truth was, Sarah simply didn't care what happened to Mary *or* the Christmas baskets.

The phone was still ringing—where on earth was Greg? Suddenly an operator's tinny voice came on with a recorded message. "I'm sorry, but we are unable to connect your call at this time."

"*You're* sorry?" Mary cried. She punched in Thom's number and then Suzanne's and got the same response. She tossed the phone back in her purse and waited. The Women's Century Club was on the outskirts of Rose. On Christmas Eve, with an ice storm bearing down, the prospect of a good Samaritan was highly unlikely.

"Great," she muttered. She might be stuck here for God knows how long. Surely *someone* would realize she wasn't where she was supposed to be. Still, it might take hours before anyone came looking for her. And even more hours before she was found.

With the engine off, the heater wasn't working, and Mary was astonished by how quickly the cold seeped into the car's interior. She tried her cell phone again and got the same message. There was obviously trouble with the transmitters; maybe it would clear up soon. She struggled to remain optimistic, but another depressing thought overshadowed the first. How long could she last in this cold? She could imagine herself still sitting in the car days from now, frozen stiff, abandoned and forgotten on Christmas Eve.

Trying to ward off panic, she decided to stand on the side of the road to see if that would help her cell phone reception. That way, she'd also be ready to wave for assistance if someone drove by.

She retrieved her phone, climbed out of the car and immediately became aware of how much colder it was outside. Hands shaking, she tried the phone. Same recorded response. She tucked her hands inside her pockets and waited for what seemed like an eternity. Then she tried her cell phone again.

Nothing. Just that damned recording.

Resigned to waiting for a passerby, she huddled in her coat.

Five minutes passed. The icy wind made it feel more like five hours. The air was so frigid that after a few moments it hurt to breathe. Her teeth began to chatter, and her feet lost feeling, but that was what she got for wearing slip-on loafers instead of winter boots.

A car appeared in the distance and Mary was so happy she wanted to cry. Greg was definitely going to hear about this! Once she got safely home, of course.

Stepping into the middle of the road, she raised her hand and then groaned aloud. It wasn't some stranger coming to her rescue, but Sarah McDowell. Desperate though she was, Mary would rather have seen just about anyone else.

Sarah pulled up alongside her and rolled down the window. "What's wrong?"

"Wh-what does it l-look like? M-my car broke down." She wished she could control the chattering of her teeth.

"Is someone coming for you?"

"N-not yet...I c-can't get through on my cell phone."

"I'm here now. Would you like me to deliver the Christmas baskets?"

Mary hesitated. If the gifts were to get to the families in time, she didn't really have much choice. "M-maybe you should."

Sarah edged her vehicle closer to Mary's and with some difficulty they transferred the six heavy baskets and the boxes of groceries from one car to the next.

"Thanks," Mary said grudgingly.

Sarah nodded curtly. "Go ahead and call Greg again," she suggested.

"Okay." Mary punched out the number and waited, hoping against hope that the call would connect. Once again, she got the "I'm sorry" recording.

"Won't go through."

"Would you like to use my phone?" Sarah asked.

"I doubt your phone will work if mine doesn't." It was so irritating—Sarah always seemed to believe that whatever she had was better.

"It won't hurt to try."

"True," Mary admitted. She accepted Sarah's phone and tried again. It gave her no satisfaction to be right.

"Go ahead and deliver the baskets," Mary said, putting on a brave front.

"I'm not going to leave you here."

Mary hardened her resolve. "Someone will come by soon enough."

"Don't be ridiculous!" Sarah practically shouted.

"Oh, all right, you can drive me back to the Club. And then deliver the baskets."

Sarah glared at her. "Aren't you being a little stubborn? I could just as easily drive you home."

Mary didn't answer. She intended to make it clear that she preferred to wait for Greg to rescue her rather than ride to town with Sarah.

"Fine, if that's what you want," Sarah said coldly.

"I'm grateful you came back," Mary told her—and she was. "I don't know how long I could've stood out here."

This time Sarah didn't respond.

"What's most important is getting these baskets to the families."

"At least we can agree on that," Sarah told her.

Mary climbed into the passenger side of Sarah's SUV and nearly sighed aloud when Sarah started the engine. A blast of hot air hit her feet and she moaned in pleasure.

Sarah was right, she decided. She *was* being unnecessarily stubborn. "If you don't mind," she said tentatively. "I would appreciate a ride home."

Sarah glanced at her as she started down the winding country road. "That wasn't so hard, now was it?"

"What?" she asked, pretending not to understand.

Just then, Sarah hit a patch of ice and the vehicle slid scarily into the other lane. With almost no traction, Sarah did what she could to keep the car on the road. "Hold on!" she cried. She struggled to maintain control but the tires refused to grip the asphalt.

"Oh, no," Mary breathed. "We're going into the ditch!" At that instant the car slid sideways, then swerved and went front-first into the irrigation ditch.

Mary fell forward, bracing her hands against the console. The car sat there, nose down. A frozen turkey rolled out of its box and lodged in the space between the two bucket seats, tail pointed at the ceiling. Sarah's eyes were wide as she held the steering wheel in a death grip.

Neither spoke for several moments. Then in a slightly breathless voice, Sarah asked, "Are you hurt?"

"No, are you?"

"I'm okay, but I think I broke three nails clutching the steering wheel."

Mary couldn't keep from smiling. Sarah had always been vain about her fingernails.

"Do you think we should try to climb out of the car?" Sarah murmured.

"I don't know."

"One of us should."

"I will," Mary offered. After all, Sarah would've been home by now if she hadn't come back to help.

"No, I think I should," Sarah said. "You must be freezing."

"I've warmed up—some. Listen, I'll go get Melody."

"It's at least a mile to the club."

"I know how far it is," Mary snapped. Sarah argued about everything.

"Why can't you just accept my help?"

"I'm in your car, aren't I?" She resisted the urge to remind Sarah that she hadn't actually been much help. Now they were both stuck, a hundred feet from where she'd been stranded. The charity baskets were no closer to their destination, either.

"Maybe another car will come by."

"Don't count on it," Mary told her.

"Why not?"

"Think about it. We're in the middle of an ice storm. It's Christmas Eve. Anyone with half a brain is home in front of a warm fireplace."

"Oh. Yes."

"I'll walk to the club."

"No," Sarah insisted.

"Why not?"

Sarah didn't say anything for a moment. "I don't want to stay here alone," she finally admitted.

Mary pondered that confession and realized she wouldn't want to wait in the car by herself, either. "Okay," she said. "We'll both go."

"Tell me what you found out about the tea service," Thom said as they headed toward the freeway on-ramp.

"The Internet was great. Your secretary's list was a big help, too. I scanned in the photograph you gave me and got an immediate hit with the man we're going to see this morning."

"Hey, you did well."

"I have a good feeling about this." Noelle's voice rose with excitement.

Thom didn't entirely share her enthusiasm. "I don't think we should put too much stock in this," he said cautiously.

"Why not?"

"Don't forget, my mom and dad searched for years. It's unrealistic to think we can locate a replacement after just one day."

"But your parents didn't have the Internet."

She was right, but not all antique stores were on-line. Under the circumstances, it would be far too easy to build up their expectations only to face disappointment. "You said yourself this could be a wild-goose chase."

"I know." Noelle sounded discouraged now.

Thom reached out and gently clasped her fingers. "Don't worry— we're going to keep trying for as long as it takes." The road was icy, so he returned his hand to the steering wheel. "Looks like we're in for a spell of bad weather."

"I heard there's an ice storm on the way."

Thom nodded. The roads were growing treacherous, and he wondered if they should have risked the drive. However, they were on their way and at this point, he wanted to see it through as much as Noelle did.

What was normally a two-and-a-half-hour trip into Portland took almost four. Fortunately, the roads seemed to improve as they neared the city.

"I'm beginning to wonder if we should've come," Noelle said, echoing his thoughts as they passed an abandoned car angled off to the side of the road.

"We'll be fine." They were in Lake Oswego on the outskirts of Portland already—almost there.

"It's just that this is so important."

"I know."

"Maybe we should discuss what we're going to do if we don't find the tea service," Noelle said as they sought out the Lake Oswego business address.

"We'll deal with that when we have to, all right?"

She nodded.

The antique store was situated in a strip mall between a Thai restaurant and a beauty parlor. Thom parked the car. "You ready?" he asked, turning to her.

Noelle smiled encouragingly.

They held hands as they walked to the store. A bell above the door chimed merrily when they entered, and they found themselves in a long, narrow room crammed with glassware, china and polished wood furniture. Every conceivable space and surface had been put to use. A slightly moldy odor filled the air, competing with the piney scent of a small Christmas tree. Thom had to turn sideways to get past a quantity of comic books stacked on a chest of drawers next to the entrance. He led Noelle around the obstacles to the counter, where the cash register sat.

"Hello," Noelle called out. "Anyone here?"

"Be with you in a minute," a voice called back from a hidden location deep inside the store.

While Noelle examined the brooches, pins and old jewelry beneath the glass counter, Thom glanced around. A collection of women's hats filled a shelf to the right. He couldn't imagine his mother wearing anything with feathers, but if she'd lived in a different era...

He studied a pile of old games next, but they all seemed to be missing pieces. This looked less and less promising.

"Sorry to keep you waiting." A thin older man with a full crop of white hair ambled into the room. He was slightly stooped and brushed dust from his hands as he walked.

"Hello, my name is Noelle McDowell," she said. "We spoke yesterday."

"Ah, yes."

"Thom Sutton." Thom stepped forward and offered his hand.

"Peter Bright." His handshake was firm, belying his rather frail appearance. "I didn't know if you'd make it or not, with the storm and all."

"We're grateful you're open this close to Christmas," Noelle told him.

"I don't plan on staying open for long. But I wanted to escape the house for a few hours before Estelle found an excuse to put me to work in the kitchen." He chuckled. "Would you like to take a look at the tea service?"

"Please."

"I have it back here." He started slowly toward the rear of the store; Thom and Noelle followed him.

Noelle reached for Thom's hand again. Although he'd warned her against building up their expectations, he couldn't help feeling a wave of anticipation.

"Now, let me see..." Peter mumbled as he began shifting boxes around. "You know, a lot of people tell me they're coming in and then never show up." He smiled. "Like I said, I didn't really expect you to drive all the way from Rose in the middle of an ice storm." He removed an ancient Remington typewriter and set it aside, then lifted the lid of an army-green metal chest.

"I've had this tea service for maybe twenty years," Peter explained as he extracted a Navy sea bag.

"Do you remember how you came to get it?"

"Oh, sure. An English lady sold it to me. I displayed it for a while. People looked but no one bought."

"Why keep it in the chest now?" Noelle asked.

"I didn't like having to polish it," Peter said. "Folks have trouble seeing past the tarnish." He straightened and met Thom's gaze. "Same with people. Ever notice that?"

"I have," Thom said. Even on short acquaintance, he liked Peter Bright.

Nodding vigorously, Peter extracted a purple pouch from the duffel bag and peeled back the cloth to display a creamer. He set it on the green chest for their examination.

Noelle pulled the photograph from her purse and handed it to Thom, who studied the style. The picture wasn't particularly clear, so he found it impossible to tell if this was the same creamer, but there was definitely a similarity.

The sugar bowl was next. Peter set it out, waiting for Thom and Noelle's reaction. The photograph showed a slightly better view of that.

"This isn't the one," Noelle said. "But it's close, I think."

"Since you drove all this way, it won't hurt to look at all the pieces."

Thom agreed, but he already knew it had been a futile trip. He tried to hide his disappointment. Against all the odds, he'd held high hopes for this. Like Noelle, he'd been waiting for a Christmas miracle but apparently it wasn't going to happen.

Bending low, Peter thrust his arm inside the canvas bag and extracted two more objects. He carefully unwrapped the silver teapot and then the coffeepot and offered them a moment to scrutinize his wares.

The elaborate tray was last. Carefully arranging each piece on top of it, Peter stepped back to give them a full view of the service. "It's a magnificent find, don't you think?"

"It's lovely," Noelle said.

"But it's not the one we're looking for."

He accepted their news with good grace. "That's a shame."

"You see, this service—" she held out the picture "—was stolen years ago, and Thom and I are hoping to replace it with one that's exactly the same. Or as much like it as possible."

Peter reached for the photograph and studied it a moment. "I guess I should've looked closer and saved you folks the drive."

"No problem," Thom said. "Thanks for getting back to us."

"Yes, thank you for your trouble," Noelle said as they left the store. "It's a beautiful service."

"I'll give you a good price on it if you change your mind," the old man said, following them to the front door. "I'll be here another hour or so if you want to come back."

"Thank you," Thom said, but he didn't think there was much chance they'd be back. It wasn't the tea service they needed.

"How about lunch before we head home," he suggested. The Thai restaurant appeared to be open.

"Sure," Noelle agreed.

Thom shared her discouragement, but he was determined to maintain her optimism—and his own. "Hey, we've only started to look. It's too early to give up."

"I know. You're right, it was foolish of me to think we'd find it so quickly. It's just that…oh, I don't know, I guess I thought it *would* be easy because everything else fell into place for us."

They were the only customers in the restaurant. A charming waitress greeted them and escorted them to a table near the window.

Thom waited until they were seated before he spoke. "I guess this means we go to Plan B."

"What about Pad Thai and—" Noelle glanced up at him over the menu. "What exactly is Plan B?"

Thom reached inside his coat pocket and set the jeweler's box in the middle of the table.

"Thom?" Noelle put her menu down.

This wasn't the way he'd intended to propose, but—as the cliché had it—there was no time like the present. "I love you, Noelle, and I'm not going to let this feud stand between us. Our parents will have to understand that we're entitled to our own happiness."

Tears glistened in her eyes. "Oh, Thom."

"I'm asking you to be my wife."

She stretched her arm across the table and they joined hands. "And I'm telling you it would be the greatest honor of my life to accept. I have a request, though."

"Anything."

"I want to buy that tea service. Not you. Me."

Thom frowned. "Why?"

"I want to give it to your mother. From me to her. I can't replace the original, but maybe I can build a bridge between our families with this one."

Thom's fingers tightened around hers. "It's worth a try."

"I think so, too," she whispered.

"I'm going to try my phone again," Sarah said. Technology had betrayed them, but surely it would come to their rescue. Eventually. Walking a mile in the bitter cold was something she'd rather avoid.

"Go ahead," Mary urged. She didn't seem any more eager than Sarah to make the long trek.

Sarah got her phone and speed dialed her home number. Hope sprang up when the call instantly connected, but was dashed just as quickly when she heard the recording once again.

"Any luck?" Mary asked, her eyes bright and teary in the cold.

She shook her head.

"Damn," Mary muttered. "I guess that means there's no option but to hoof it."

"Appears that way."

"I think we should have a little fortification first, though," Sarah said. Her husband's golf bags were in the back seat, and she knew he often carried a flask.

"Fortification?"

"A little Scotch might save our lives."

Mary's look was skeptical. "I'm all for Scotch, but where are we going to find any out here?"

"Jake." She opened the back door and grabbed the golf bag. Sure enough, there was a flask.

"I don't remember you liking Scotch," Mary said.

"I don't, but at this point I can't be choosy."

"Right."

Sarah removed the top and tipped the flask, taking a sizable gulp. Wiping her mouth with the back of her hand, she swallowed, then shook her head briskly. "Oh my, that's strong." The liquor burned all the way down to her stomach, but as soon as it hit bottom, a welcoming warmth spread through her limbs.

"My turn," Mary said.

Sarah handed her the flask and watched as Mary rubbed the top, then tilted it back and took a deep swallow. She, too, closed her eyes and shook her head. Soon, however, she was smiling. "That wasn't so bad."

"It might ward off hypothermia."

"You're right. You'd better have another."

"You think?"

Mary nodded and after a moment, Sarah agreed. Luckily Jake had refilled the flask. The second swallow didn't taste nearly as nasty as the first. It didn't burn this time, either. Instead it enhanced the warm glow spreading through her system.

"How do you feel?"

"Better," Sarah said, giving Mary the flask.

Mary didn't need encouragement. She took her turn with the flask, then growled like a grizzly bear.

Sarah didn't know why she found that so amusing, but she did. She laughed uproariously. In fact, she laughed until she started to cough.

"What?" Mary asked, grinning broadly.

"Oh, dear." She coughed again. "I didn't know you did animal impressions."

"I do when I drink Scotch."

Then, as if they'd both become aware that they were having an actual conversation, they pulled back into themselves. Sarah noticed that Mary's expression suddenly grew dignified, as though she'd realized she was laughing and joking with her enemy.

"We should get moving, don't you think?" Mary said in a dispassionate voice.

"You're right." Sarah put the flask back in the golf bag and wrapped her scarf more tightly around her neck and face. Fortified in all respects, she was ready to face the storm. "It's a good thing we're walking together. Anything could happen on a day like this."

They'd gone about the length of a football field when Mary said, "I'm cold again."

"I am, too."

"You should've brought along the Scotch."

"We'll have to go back for it."

"I think we should," Mary agreed solemnly. "We could freeze to death before we reach the club."

"Yes. The Scotch might make the difference between survival and death."

Back at the car, they climbed in and shared the flask again. Soon, for no apparent reason, they were giggling.

"I think we're drunk," Mary said.

"Oh, hardly. I can hold my liquor better than this."

Mary burst into peals of laughter. "No, you can't. Don't you remember the night of our Halloween party?"

"That was—what?—twenty-two years ago!"

"I know, but I haven't forgotten how silly those margaritas made you."

"You were the one who kept filling my glass."

"You were the one who kept telling me how good they were."

Sarah nearly doubled over with hysterics. "Next thing I knew, I was standing on the coffee table singing 'Guantanamera' at the top of my lungs."

"You sounded fabulous, too. And then when you started to dance—"

"I *what?*" All Sarah recalled was the blinding headache she'd suffered the next morning. When she woke and could barely lift her head from the pillow without stabbing pain, she'd phoned her dearest, best friend in the world. Mary had dropped everything and rushed over. She'd mixed Sarah a tomato-juice concoction that had saved her life, or so she'd felt at the time.

Both women were silent. "I miss those days," Sarah whispered.

"I do, too," Mary said.

Sarah sniffled. It was the cold that made her eyes water. Digging through her purse, she couldn't find a single tissue. Mary gave her one.

"I've missed you," Sarah said and loudly blew her nose.

"I've missed you, too."

The cold must have intensified, because her eyes began to water even more. Using her coat sleeve, she wiped her nose.

"Here," she said to Mary, handing her the flask. "I want you to have this. Take the rest."

"The Scotch?"

Sarah nodded. "If we're not found until it's too late—I want you to have the liquor. It might keep you alive long enough for the rescue people to revive you."

Mary looked as though she was close to bursting into tears. "You'd die for—me?" She hiccuped on the last word.

Sarah nodded again.

"That's the most beautiful thing anyone's ever said to me."

"But before I die, I need to ask you something."

"Anything," Mary told her. "Anything at all."

Sarah sniffled and swallowed a sob. Leaning her forehead against the steering wheel, she whispered, "Forgive me."

Mary placed her hand on Sarah's shoulder. "I do forgive you, but first you have to forgive *me* for acting so badly. You were right—I *was* jealous of Cheryl. I thought you liked her better than me."

"Never. She's one of those people who move in and out of a person's life, but you—you're my...my soul sister. I've missed you so much."

"We're idiots." Mary returned the flask. "I can't accept this Scotch. If we freeze, we freeze together."

Sarah was feeling downright toasty at the moment. The world was spinning, but that was probably because she was drunker than a skunk. The thought made her giggle.

"What's so funny?" Mary wanted to know.

"We're drunk," she muttered. "Drunk as skunks. Drunk as skunks," she recited in a singsong voice.

"Isn't it wonderful?"

They laughed again.

"Jake always insists I eat something when I've had too much to drink."

"We have lots of food," Mary said, sitting up straight.

"Yes, but most of it's half-frozen by now."

Mary's eyes gleamed bright. "Not everything. I'm sure the families would want us to take what we need, don't you think?"

"I'm sure you're right," Sarah said as Mary climbed over the front seat and into the back, her coat flipping over her head.

Sarah laughed so hard she nearly peed her pants.

Women's Century Club
Rose, Oregon

December 24

Dear Mary and Sarah,

Just a note to let you know how much the Women's Century Club appreciates the effort that went into preparing these Christmas baskets. You two did a splendid job. I could see from the number of gifts filling the baskets that you went far beyond the items listed on the sheet I gave you. Both of you have been generous to a fault.

Sarah, I realize it was difficult to come into this project at the last minute, but you are to be commended for your cooperation.

Mary, you did a wonderful job making all the arrangements, and I'm confident the baskets will reach the Salvation Army in plenty of time to be distributed for the holidays.

If you're both willing to take up the task again next year, I'd be happy to recommend you for the job.

Sincerely,

Melody Darrington

Chapter Nine

Jake McDowell glanced at the kitchen clock and frowned. "What time did your mother say she'd be home?"

"I don't know." His youngest daughter was certainly a fount of information. Carley lay flat on her stomach in front of the Christmas tree, her arms outstretched as she examined a small package.

"She should be back by now, don't you think?" Jake asked, looking at the clock again.

"I suppose."

"When will Noelle be home?"

Unconcerned, Carley shrugged.

Jake decided he wasn't going to get any answers here and tried Sarah's cell for perhaps the fiftieth time. Whenever he punched in the number, he received the same irritating message. "I'm sorry. We are unable to connect your call...."

Not knowing what else to do, he phoned his golfing partner. Greg Sutton answered on the first ring.

"I thought you were Mary," he said, sounding as worried as Jake was.

"You haven't heard from Mary?"

"Not a word. Is Sarah back?"

"No," Jake said. "That's why I was calling you."

"What do you think happened?"

"No idea. I could understand if one of them was missing, but not both."

Greg didn't say anything for a moment. "Did you phone the Women's Century Club?"

"I did. Melody said they were there and left two hours ago. She told me the ice storm's pretty bad in her area. She's going to stay put until her husband can come and get her this afternoon."

"What did she say about Mary and Sarah?"

"Not much. Just that they got the baskets all sorted and loaded into Mary's vehicle. Melody did make some comment about Sarah and Mary being pretty hostile toward each other. According to her, they left at different times."

"That doesn't explain why they're both missing."

"What if one of them had an accident and the other stopped to help?" Greg suggested.

Jake hadn't considered that. "But wouldn't they have been back by now?"

"Unless they got stuck."

"Together?"

"I wouldn't know."

Jake laughed grimly. "If that's the case, God help us all."

"What do you think we should do?"

"We can't leave them out there."

"You're right," Greg said. "But I have to tell you the idea is some-what appealing. If they *are* stuck with each other for a while, they just might settle this mess."

"They could murder each other, too." Jake knew his wife far too well. When it came to Mary Sutton, she could be downright unrea-sonable. "I say we go after them—together."

Jake had no objection to that. Greg owned a large four-wheel drive truck that handled better on the ice than most vehicles. "You want to pick me up?"

"I'm on my way," Greg said.

Sarah reached for another Christmas cookie. "What did you call these again?" she asked, studying the package. Unfortunately, the let-ters wouldn't quite come into focus.

"Pfeffernusse."

"Try to say *that* three times when you're too drunk to stand up."

Mary giggled and helped herself to one of the glazed ginger cookies. "They're German. One family on the list had a German-sounding name and I thought they might be familiar with these cookies."

Sarah was touched. Tears filled her eyes. "You're so thoughtful."

"Not really," Mary said with a sob. "I…I was trying to outdo you." She was weeping in earnest now. "How could I have been so silly?"

"I did the same thing." Sarah wrapped her arm around Mary's shoulders. "I was the one who got us thrown out of Value-X."

Mary sniffled and dried her eyes. "I'm never going to let anything come between us again."

"I won't, either," Sarah vowed. "I think this has been the best Christmas of my life."

"Christmas!" Mary jerked upright. "Oh, Sarah, we've got to get these baskets to the Salvation Army!"

"But how? We can't carry all this stuff."

"True, but we can't just sit here, either." She looked into the distance, in the direction of the Women's Century Club. "We're going to have to walk, after all."

Her friend was right. They had to take matters into their own hands and work together. "We can do it."

"We can. We'll walk to the club and send someone to get the baskets. Then we'll call Triple A. See? We have a plan. A good plan. There isn't anything we can't do if we stick together."

Sarah felt the tears sting her eyes again. "Is there any Scotch left?"

"No," Mary said, sounding sad. "We're going to have to make it on our own."

Clambering out of the car, Sarah was astonished by how icy the road had become in the hour or so they'd dawdled over their comforting Scotch. Luckily, she was wearing her boots, whereas Mary wore loafers.

Her friend gave a small cry and then, arms flailing, struggled to regain her balance. "My goodness, it's slippery out here."

"How are we going to do this?" Sarah asked. "You can't walk on this ice."

"Sure I can," Mary assured her, straightening with resolve. But she soon lost her balance again and grabbed hold of the car door, just managing to save herself.

"It's like you said—we'll do it together," Sarah declared. "We have to, because I'm not leaving you behind."

With Mary's arm around Sarah's waist and Sarah's arm about Mary's shoulder, they started walking down the center of the road. The treacherous ice slowed them down, and their progress was halting, especially since both of them were drunk and weepy with emotion.

"I wonder how long it'll take Greg to realize I'm not home," Mary said. Her husband was in trouble as it was, leaving her a defective vehicle to drive.

"Probably a lot longer than Jake. I told him I wouldn't be more than an hour."

"I'm sure there's some football game on TV that Greg's busy staring at. He won't notice I'm not there until Suzanne and Thom arrive for dinner." Mary went strangely quiet.

"Are you okay?" Sarah asked, tightening her hold on her friend.

"Yes, but...Thom. I was thinking about Thom. He's in love with Noelle, you know."

"Noelle's been in love with Thom since she was sixteen. It broke her heart when he dumped her."

"Thom didn't dump her. She dumped him."

Sarah bristled. "She did not!"

"You mean to say something else happened?"

"It must have, because I know for a fact that Noelle's always loved Thom."

"And Thom feels the same about her."

"We have to do something," Sarah said. "We've got to find a way to get them back together."

"I think they might've been secretly seeing each other," Mary confessed.

Sarah shook her head, which made her feel slightly dizzy. "Noelle would've told me. We're this close." She attempted to cross two fingers, but couldn't manage it. Must be because of her gloves, she decided. Yes, that was it.

"We're drunk," Mary said. "Really and truly drunk. The cookies didn't help one bit."

"I don't care. We're best friends again and this time it's for life."

"For life," Mary vowed.

"We're on a mission."

"A mission," Mary repeated. She paused "What's our mission again?"

Sarah had to stop and think about it. "First, we need to deliver the Christmas baskets."

Mary slapped her hand against her forehead. "Right! How could I forget?"

"Then…"

"There's more?" Mary looked confused.

"Yes, lots more. Then we need to convince Noelle and Thom that they were meant to be together."

"Poor Thom," Mary said. "Oh no." She covered her mouth with her hand.

"What?"

"I left a message on his answering machine. I may not remember much right now, but I remember that. I told him I didn't think he should marry Noelle…."

"Why would you do that?"

"Well, because—oh dear, Sarah, I might have ruined everything."

"We'll deal with it as soon as we're home," Sarah said firmly.

A car sounded from behind them. "Someone's coming," Mary cried, her voice rising with excitement.

"We've got to hitch a ride." Sarah whirled around and held out her thumb as prominently as she could.

"That's not going to work," Mary insisted, thrusting out her leg. "Don't you remember that old Clark Gable movie?"

"Clark Gable got a ride by showing off his ankle?"

"No… Claudette Colbert did."

The truck turned the corner; Sarah wasn't willing to trust in either her thumb or Mary's leg, so she raised both hands above her head and waved frantically.

"It's Greg," Mary cried in relief.

"And Jake's with him." Thank God. Sarah had never been happier to see her husband.

To their shock and anger, the two men drove directly past them.

"Hey!" Mary shouted after her husband. "I am in no mood for games."

The truck stopped, and the driver and passenger doors opened at the same time. Greg climbed down and headed over to Mary, while Jake hurried toward Sarah.

"We're friends for life," Mary told her husband, throwing her arm around Sarah again.

"You're drunk," Greg said. "Just what have you been drinking?"

"I know exactly what I'm doing," she answered with offended dignity.

"Do *you?*" Jake asked Sarah.

"Of course I do."

"We're on a mission," Mary told the two men.

Jake frowned. "What happened to the car?"

"I'll tell you all about it later," Sarah promised, enunciating very carefully.

"What mission?" Jake asked.

Sarah exchanged an exasperated look with Mary. "Why do we have to explain everything?"

"Men," Mary said in a low voice. "Can't live with 'em, can't live without 'em."

Her friend was so wise.

The drive back to Rose took even longer than the trip into Portland. The roads seemed to get icier and more slippery with every mile. Keeping her eyes on the road, Noelle knew how tense Thom must be.

"Would you rather wait until after Christmas?" she asked as they neared her family's home. It might be better if they got through the holidays before making their announcement and throwing their families into chaos. Noelle hated the thought of dissension on Christmas Day.

"Wait? You mean to announce our engagement?" Thom clarified. "I don't think we should. You're going to marry me, and I want to tell the whole world. I refuse to keep this a secret simply because our mothers don't happen to get along. They'll just have to adjust."

"But—"

"I've waited all these years for you. I'm not waiting any longer. All right?"

"All right." Noelle was overwhelmed by contradictory emotions. Love for Thom—and love for her family. Excitement and nervousness. Happiness and guilt.

"Do you know what I like most about Christmas?" Thom asked, breaking into her thoughts.

"Tell me, and then I'll tell you what I like."

"Mom has a tradition she started when Suzanne entered high school. On Christmas Eve, she serves fresh Dungeness crab. We all love it. She has them cooked at the market because she can't bear to do it herself, then Dad brings them home. Mom's got the butter melted and the bibs ready and we sit around the table and start cracking."

"Oh, that sounds delicious."

"It is. Does your family have a Christmas Eve tradition?"

"Bingo."

"Bingo?"

"Christmas Bingo. We play after the Christmas Eve service at church. The prizes aren't worth more than five dollars, but Mom's so good at getting neat stuff. I haven't been home for Christmas in years, but Mom always makes up for it by mailing me three or four little Bingo gifts."

"My favorite carol is 'What Child Is This,'" he said next.

"Mine's 'Silent Night.'"

"What was your favorite gift as a kid?"

"Hmm, that's a toss-up," she said. "There was a Christmas Barbie I adored. Another year I got a set of classic Disney videos that I watched over and over."

Thom smiled. "As a little boy, I loved my Matchbox car garage. I got it for Christmas when I was ten. Mom's kept it all these years. She has Dad drag it out every year and tells me she's saving it to give to my son one day."

She sighed, at peace with herself and this man she loved. "I want to have your babies, Thom," she said in a soft voice.

His eyes left the street to meet hers. The sky had darkened and he looked quickly back at the road. "You make it hard to concentrate on driving."

"Tell me some of the other things you love about Christmas. It makes me feel good to hear them."

"It's your turn," he said.

"The orange in the bottom of my stocking. Every year there's one in the toe. It's supposed to commemorate the Christmases my great-grandparents had—an orange was a pretty special thing back then."

"I like Christmas cookies. Especially meringue star ones."

"Mexican tea cakes for me," she said. "I'll ask your mother for the recipe for star cookies and bake you a batch every Christmas."

"That sounds like a very wifely thing to do."

"I want to be a good wife to my husband." Noelle suddenly realized that she was genuinely grateful they hadn't married so young. Yes, the years had brought pain, but they'd brought wisdom and perspective, too. The love she and Thom felt for each other would deepen with time. They were so much more capable now of valuing what they had together.

"What's it like to be born on Christmas Day?" Thom asked.

"It's not so bad," Noelle said. "First, I share a birthday with Jesus— that's the good part. The not-so-good is having the two biggest celebrations of the year fall on the same day. When I was a kid, Mom used to throw me a party in June to celebrate my half-year birthday."

"I remember that."

"Do you remember teasing me by saying it really wasn't my birthday so you didn't need to bring a gift?"

Thom chuckled. "What I remember is getting my ears boxed for saying it."

Twenty minutes later, they were almost at her family's house. They'd decided to confront her parents first. Their laughter, which had filled the car seconds earlier, immediately faded.

"You ready?" Thom asked as he stopped in front of the house.

Noelle nodded and swallowed hard. "No matter what happens, I want you to remember I love you."

His hand squeezed hers.

Glancing at her family's home, Noelle noticed a truck parked outside. "Looks like we have company." She didn't know whether to feel relief or disappointment.

"Oh, no." Thom's voice was barely above a whisper.

"What is it?"

"That's my parents' truck."

Dread slipped over her. "They must've found out that we spent the day together. That's my fault—I left a note for Carley telling her I was with you." Noelle could imagine what was taking place inside. Her mother would be shouting at Thom's, and their fathers would be trying to keep the two women apart.

"Should we wait?" Noelle asked, just as she had earlier.

"For another time?" His jaw tensed. "No, we face them here and now, for better or worse. Agreed?"

Noelle nodded. "Okay…just promise me you won't let them change your mind."

He snorted inelegantly. "I'd like to see them try."

Thom parked behind the truck and turned off the engine. Together, holding hands, they approached the house. Never had Noelle been more nervous. If this encounter went wrong, she might alienate her mother, and that was something she didn't want to do. In high school, she'd self-righteously cast her family aside in the name of love. But if the years in Dallas had taught her independence, they'd also taught her the importance of home and family. Her self-imposed exile was over now, and she'd learned from it. Listening to Thom talk about his Christmas traditions, she'd realized that he'd find it equally hard to turn his back on his parents.

He was about to ring the doorbell when she stopped him. "Remember how I said I was looking for a Christmas miracle?"

Thom nodded. "You mean finding a tea service similar to my grandmother's?"

"Yes. But if I could be granted only one miracle this Christmas, it wouldn't be that. I'd want our families to rekindle the love and friendship they once had."

"That would be my wish, too." Thom gathered her in his arms and kissed her with a passion that readily found a matching fire in her. The kiss was a reminder of their love, and it sealed their bargain. No matter what happened once they entered the house, they would face it together.

"Actually, this is a blessing in disguise," Thom said. "We can confront both families at the same time and be done with it." He reached for the doorbell again, and again Noelle stopped him.

"This is my home. We don't need to ring the bell." Stepping forward, she opened the door.

Noelle wasn't sure what she expected, but certainly not the scene that greeted her. Her parents and two sisters, plus Thom's entire family, sat around the dining room table. Her mother and Mrs. Sutton, both wearing aprons, stood in the background, while her father and Thom's dished up whole Dungeness crabs, with Jonathan pouring wine.

"Thom!" his mother shouted joyfully. "It's about time you got here."

"What took you so long?" Sarah asked Noelle.

Stunned, Thom and Noelle looked at each other for an explanation.

"There's room here," Carley called out, motioning to the empty chairs beside her.

Noelle couldn't do anything other than stare.

"What...happened?" Thom asked.

"It's a long story. Sit down. We'll explain everything later."

"But..."

Thom put his arm around Noelle's shoulder. "Before we sit down, I want everyone to know that I've asked Noelle to be my wife and she's accepted."

"Nothing you say or do will make us change our minds," Noelle said quickly, before anyone else could react.

"Why would we want to change your minds?" her father asked. "We're absolutely delighted."

"You can fight and argue, threaten and yell, and it won't make any difference," Thom added. "We're getting married!"

"Glad to hear it," his father said.

A round of cheers followed his announcement.

Thom's mother and Noelle's mother embraced in joy.

"One thing this family refuses to tolerate anymore is fighting," his mother declared.

"Absolutely," her own mother agreed.

Both Thom and Noelle stared back at them, shocked into speechlessness.

"There's no reason to stand there like a couple of strangers," her mother said. "Sit down. You wouldn't believe the day we had."

Sarah and Mary put their arms around each other's shoulders. "At least the Christmas baskets got delivered on time," Mary said with a satisfied nod.

"And no one mentioned that the two of us smelled like Scotch when we got there," her mother pointed out.

They both giggled.

"What happened?" Noelle asked.

Her father waved aside her question. "You don't want to know," he groaned.

"I'll tell you later," her mother promised.

Thom leaned close to her and whispered, "Either we just walked into the middle of an *X-Files* episode or we got our Christmas miracle."

Noelle slipped an arm around his waist. "I think you must be right."

Sarah McDowell

9 Orchard Lane Rose, Oregon

December 26

Dear Melody,

Mary and I found your note when we delivered the baskets on Christmas Eve. We did have a wonderful time, and Mary has agreed to head up the committee next year. I promised I'd be her cochair.

Now, about using the club for Kristen's wedding reception...Well, it seems there's going to be another wedding in the family, and fairly soon. Mary and I will be in touch with you about that right after New Year's.

Sincerely,

Sarah McDowell

Dear Reader,

I love romantic comedies. My favorite books and movies have always been the ones that make me laugh and sigh and fall in love all over again. There just don't seem to be enough of them, especially romantic comedies that involve Christmas. So, my friends, I've taken it upon myself to create one of my own.

Choosing to set the book in Alaska was a natural. I've been to Alaska. Some years ago I wrote six books that took place in the fictional town of Hard Luck, and while doing research for the series I spent two weeks in that incredible state. My husband, Wayne, and I had the opportunity to explore the tundra. At one point we flew over the Arctic Circle in a four-passenger bush plane. It was an experience I will long remember, crammed as I was in that tiny plane, holding the U.S. mail in my lap and landing in a tundra community with a population of less than twenty.

I hope you enjoy *The Snow Bride.* I promise you a chuckle now and then, and a sigh, too, but mostly I hope you'll fall in love.

Have a wonderful holiday season!

Debbie Macomber

P.S. Be sure to check out my Web page at www.debbiemacomber.com. I love to hear from my readers. If you aren't online, I can be reached at P.O. Box 1458, Port Orchard, WA 98366.

The Snow Bride

To
Renelle Wilson
For thirty-five years of friendship
Merry Christmas, my friend

Chapter One

"Alaska, Jen? This is crazy! You have no idea what you're letting yourself in for." Her mother swerved from one lane of the Los Angeles freeway to the next without bothering to glance in her rearview mirror. A car horn blared angrily from somewhere behind them, but Chloe Lyman was unconcerned; she'd never observed the rules of the road any more than she'd lived a conventional life.

Jenna Campbell swallowed a gasp and clung to her purse. When her mother was in this frame of mind, it was far better to agree with her and let her temper take its natural course. "Yes, Mom."

"Don't be so damned agreeable, either."

"Whatever you say, Mom."

"Asking me to drive you to the airport is just adding insult to injury."

"I know, I'm sorry, but—"

"Didn't I tell you to stop agreeing with everything I say?"

"Yes, Mom."

"I can't believe any daughter of mine is so…so mealymouthed. How on earth could you even think about something as ridiculous as becoming a mail-order bride? Haven't I taught you anything?"

"I didn't say I was *marrying* Dalton—"

"That's another thing. What kind of name is Dalton, anyway? And Alaska...*Alaska?* Have you lost your mind? This is the kind of thing *I'd* do, not you!"

"Mom..."

Chloe Lyman veered sharply across two lanes of traffic, going twenty miles above the speed limit as she did so, and nearly collided with the concrete wall dividing the freeway. "I don't like it."

"Dalton's name?" Jenna asked, purposely obtuse.

Chloe muttered something probably best left to the imagination, then added in a more audible voice, "I don't like anything about this. You find some man on the Internet and the next thing I know, you're quitting a job any woman would love. You give up a beautiful apartment. You uproot your entire life and take off for Alaska to marry this character you've never even met."

"I'm an executive assistant, which is a glorified way of saying *secretary,* and I'm only going to Alaska to meet Dalton. I never said anything about marrying him." While that sounded good, Jenna did, in fact, expect to marry Dalton Gray.

Kim Roberts, her best friend, thought this plan of hers was wildly romantic, although she had some qualms. For that matter, so did Jenna. She wasn't stupid or naive, but her desire to escape her mundane, predictable life outweighed her usual caution.

Once Jenna knew Dalton a little better, she sincerely hoped their relationship would evolve into something permanent. However, she wasn't rushing into marriage, despite what Kim and her mother seemed to think.

"You're the executive assistant to the founder and president of Fulton Industries," her mother needlessly reminded her. "Do you realize how many women would give their eyeteeth to work for a man as rich and handsome as Brad Fulton?"

Jenna didn't want to discuss that. Yes, she had a good job and the pay was fabulous, but as far as she was concerned, it was a dead end. She'd fallen in love with Brad Fulton, but in the six years she'd been working with him, he'd never noticed her except as his assistant.

Competent, capable Ms. Campbell. Besides, she had no life. Correction, no dating life. At thirty-one she was unmarried and there wasn't a possibility in sight. Meeting a man on the Internet wasn't so unusual these days and it was perfect for someone like her. Jenna was shy, but when she sat in front of a computer screen, she found the confidence to assert her real personality. Dalton thought she was witty and he made her feel good about herself. Yes, this might be risky; however, Jenna didn't care. She was about to have the first real adventure of her life, and adventure was what she craved. Nothing was going to stop her now. Not her mother. Not Kim. No one!

"Say something," Chloe challenged.

"What would you like me to tell you, Mom? That I don't know what I'm doing and that in a few weeks I'll be flying home with a broken heart?" If that was the case, then so be it. At least she would've experienced life and had an escapade or two, which was all she wanted. Jenna had witnessed her mother's approach to marriage, and that certainly hadn't worked. So she was doing it her own way. Dalton might very well be her only chance. Another year at Fulton Industries and every feminine instinct would shrivel up and die. Brad Fulton's primary interest was his company. Jenna was convinced she could parade around the office naked and it would take him a week to notice.

"You know what they say about the men in Alaska," her mother muttered.

"Yes, Mom, I've heard all the jokes. Alaska—where the odds are good but the goods are odd."

Her mother chuckled. "I hope you pay close attention to that one."

"Alaska," Jenna said, her voice sarcastic, "where the men are men and so are the women."

Her mother giggled again.

"Dalton told me those, Mom. He wants me to be prepared."

"Did he happen to mention what the winters are like in Fairbanks? It's November, Jenna, and they have storms there, blizzards that last for days. You could freeze to death walking from the plane into the terminal. When I think of what could happen, I—"

"You don't need to worry, Mom. Dalton sent me books and it isn't

Fairbanks, it's Beesley. I'm flying into Fairbanks, where Dalton's meeting me."

"Did he pay for your airfare?"

"I wouldn't let him do that!" Jenna was surprised her mother would ask such a question. She had more sense than that and more pride too.

"Thank God for small favors."

"I'm not changing my mind, Mom."

"Jenna, oh, Jenna," her mother cried and slowed to twenty-five-miles an hour, which made even more cars blare their horns, not that her mother was aware of it. "Why couldn't you be like other daughters who cause their mothers grief and heartache from the ages of thirteen to thirty? It makes no sense that a daughter of mine would turn into this model of virtue." Chloe shook her head. "Why did you wait till thirty-one to shock me like this? I'm not used to worrying about you."

"I know, Mom."

"By your age I'd been married and divorced twice. You were twenty before you went out on your first date."

"I was not," Jenna protested, her cheeks heating. "I was eighteen."

"At ten you were more adult than I was."

"One of us had to be."

Her mother sighed, acknowledging the truth.

Jenna didn't understand Chloe's reaction. "I'd think you'd be pleased that I'm doing something exciting."

"But I'm not," her mother wailed. "Oh, Jenna," she sobbed, "what am I going to do without you?"

"Oh, Mom…"

"My divorce from Greg was final last month. You know how I get without a man in my life."

Jenna did know. Husband number five had bit the dust, but considering her mother, it wouldn't be long before she found the next man of her dreams. Dream man number six, no doubt a replica of the previous five. All of whom, Chloe had believed, would rescue her from the drudgery and hardships of life. Without a man she was lost. She preferred them rich and—Jenna hesitated to use the word stupid, but frankly her mother had yet to choose a husband with any common sense, let alone advanced brain power. If they did happen to have money, it never lasted for more than a few years.

Her mother frowned, shifting her eyes from the road to look at her daughter. "I can't go to Alaska, Jenna, I just can't. You know I have to be around sunshine. I could never take the cold."

"I know, Mom, but I'm not sure if I'll even be living there."

"You're leaving me," she murmured in a hurt little-girl voice. "You're going to marry Doug—"

"Dalton."

"All right, Dalton, and you're going to love Alaska." She said it with such finality that Jenna might as well be wearing a wedding band. Jenna pictured Dalton eagerly waiting for her at the Fairbanks Airport, with a diamond engagement ring in his pocket and a romantic proposal committed to memory. It wasn't a likely scenario, but Jenna figured she was allowed to dream.

This romantic fantasy had originally been intended for her boss, but if Brad hadn't even asked her out in six years, then it simply wasn't happening. Jenna was furious at herself for all that wasted time.

Her mother bit her lower lip. "Why can't I hold on to a man? I should've known better than to marry again. He's a crook."

"Greg isn't a crook, he's just, uh, creative when it comes to employment opportunities."

Her mother snickered and let the comment pass. "You'll phone me the moment you arrive in Fairbanks?" She turned and cast Jenna a pleading glance.

"Of course I will."

"What do you want me to tell Brad Fulton when he calls?"

Jenna stared out the passenger-side window. "Mr. Fulton isn't going to call you, Mom."

Her mother laughed. "Trust me, he'll call. He doesn't realize how valuable you are, otherwise he would never have let you go."

"Ms. Spencer is every bit as good an administrator as I am." In some ways, the middle-aged Gail Spencer was more efficient than Jenna because she wouldn't be tempted to fall in love with her boss.

After a long silence, Chloe murmured, "Just promise me you won't name any of your children after Dalton."

"Mom, you're making too much of this." Nonetheless, Jenna prayed the relationship would fulfill the promise of those countless e-mails. She'd stumbled across Dalton in a poetry chat room and they'd connected immediately. After two months of chatting daily, of quoting Emily Dickinson and discussing the Shakespearian sonnets, Dalton had wooed her with his own sensitive words. Eventually they'd exchanged snapshots. Jenna had studied Dalton's photograph, memorizing every feature. He stood stiffly by a nondescript building and stared into the camera. It was difficult to tell if he was handsome in the conventional sense because he had a full beard, but his deep blue eyes seemed sharp and intelligent. He wore a wool cap, a red plaid shirt and heavy boots; his arms were crossed over his chest as if to say he wasn't accustomed to having his photo taken. She'd sent him her photograph, too, although he'd insisted looks weren't important. Dalton said what was inside a person was all that counted. He possessed a poet's heart, although Jenna had a hard time equating this with the rough-looking figure in the workingman's clothes.

She sent her picture for practical reasons. He needed to be able to identify her when she stepped off the plane. She, too, stood facing the camera in her work uniform—a gray jacket and straight skirt. She'd worn her hair pulled away from her face, revealing features she'd always considered plain, although Kim called her looks "classic." Her hair was a mousy shade of brown that she detested and usually lightened, but it'd been due for a treatment just then. When Dalton had e-mailed back that his first look at her photo had stolen his breath—only he'd said it much more poetically—she knew he was the one.

The exit for L.A. International came into view, and her mother slowed. Irritated drivers honked their horns as the road narrowed to a single lane; cars were backed up all the way to the freeway.

"You have a place to stay?"

"Dalton's arranging that."

"You sincerely like this man?" Her mother's voice softened with the question.

"Yes, Mom, very much."

Her mother gave a shaky smile. "You've always been a good judge of character. But, Jenna, I'm going to miss you *so* much."

"I'm going to miss you, too." Unlike her own life, her mother's was never dull. Even now, as she entered her midfifties, Chloe "Moon Flower" Campbell Roper Haggard Sullivan Lyman was an attractive, desirable woman who never lacked for attention from the opposite sex.

Her mother followed the directions to the departure area and angled between two buses and a taxicab jockeying for position. From the way she'd parked, anyone might assume she intended to drive directly into the airport.

Leaping out of the car, her mother raced around to the passenger side and hugged Jenna hard before she could even unfasten her seat belt. The death grip around her neck made it impossible to climb out. "Mother," she protested.

"You can't go!"

"Mom, we've already been through this."

"I know, I know…I've begged you to loosen up for years and now when you do something crazy, as crazy as I would myself, I don't want you to."

"You have no choice, Mother. I'm leaving." Jenna finally managed to remove Chloe's arms from around her neck and got out of the car.

"For Dalton?" Her mother cringed as she said the name.

"For Dalton." For life and adventure and all the things she'd missed out on, being the responsible one from far too young an age.

Her mother stepped aside as Jenna pulled her large suitcase from the back seat.

They hugged, and Jenna entered the airport. Unable to resist, she turned back for one last look and noticed an airport security guard speaking to her mother. The two appeared to be arguing and the man withdrew a book from his hip pocket and started to write a ticket.

Jenna's first inclination was to race outside and rescue her mother as she had countless times. Instead, she gritted her teeth and forced herself to turn away. Her mother would have to cope without her.

Their lives were about to change. Jenna realized these adjustments were long overdue. For much of her life—except for brief periods during Chloe's marriages—she'd been the one taking care of her mother. She'd provided emotional support, handled practical details and kept track of their lives. No wonder she was so good at organizing her boss, she often thought.

The first part of her journey was uneventful and relaxing. She had a plane change in Seattle, where she boarded the flight for Fairbanks. She was assigned the window seat. The man sitting beside her had a beard similar to Dalton's. He was also dressed in a similar manner.

"Hello," she said, hoping to make polite conversation as a prelude to asking him a few questions.

He muttered something and stuffed his bag into the overhead compartment, then settled in the seat, taking more than his share of the arm space. She glanced around, hoping she could get another seat, but unfortunately the flight was full.

"Do you live in Alaska?"

He scowled at her and leaned back. Within seconds he was snoring. How rude!

Midway through the flight, she had to get up to use the rest room. He grumbled when he was forced to straighten so she could pass.

"Excuse me," she said as she exited the row.

He complained again when she returned, only louder.

Jenna frowned. Dalton had told her about men like this. They flew down to the lower forty-eight, squandered their money on women and booze, and then returned to Alaska hungover and broke.

Jenna tried to read but her eyes grew heavy; she closed her magazine and felt herself drift off. She'd been up late, too excited to go to bed, carefully selecting what she'd take with her. Dalton had been wonderful, offering suggestions and assuring her he'd be at the gate when she landed.

The next thing she knew, Jenna was jarred awake. Her head rested on something hard and unyielding, and the man's voice in her ear was— Man's voice? She jerked upright and to her dismay discovered that she'd pressed her head against her companion's shoulder.

"Sorry…" she whispered, too embarrassed to look at him.

"I wasn't complaining."

She stared out the window rather than face him.

"What's the matter? Did your own snoring wake you up?"

Jenna clenched her jaw. "I don't snore." *He* was the one with the problem, not her.

"Believe what you want, but you're right up there with my lumberjack friends."

She did look at him then, giving him a blistering stare. "Are you always so rude or is this strictly for my benefit?"

He grinned, apparently enjoying himself.

"For your information I do not snore."

"Whatever you say." Not bothering to hide his amusement, he crossed his arms.

Just her luck to sit next to this Neanderthal. This *large* Neanderthal.

Then, to Jenna's relief, the pilot announced that the flight was about to land. She reached for her purse and freshened her makeup, all the while conscious of her companion closely studying her. She ignored him as best she could, until the plane landed at the terminal.

As she left the plane, her heart racing with excitement, Jenna reflected that this was the moment she'd been waiting for all these months. At last she'd be meeting Dalton Gray. Dalton—strong and responsible yet sensitive, a rugged man of the outdoors who'd won her heart.

The cold air that blasted her as soon as she stepped into the jetway came as a shock. Dalton had warned her that the temperature often dipped below freezing in November. The cold actually brought tears to her eyes.

The airport's warmth was more than welcome. Walking inside, she looked around, a smile on her lips. Two feet past the secure area, she stopped, and then slowly, guardedly, moved forward. She surveyed the room, searching for Dalton. He'd said he'd be there to meet her. Promised he would. Nothing would keep him away, he'd told her. Gold could be found on his property, oil could spurt from the ground, but he'd be at the airport waiting for her.

Only he wasn't.

Chapter Two

Reid Jamison followed the blonde out of the airplane, wryly shaking his head. God save him from uppity women, and that one was about as uppity as a woman got. Uppity and a real Miss Priss.

She stood in the middle of the waiting area, obviously looking for someone. Reid strolled past her, headed for the baggage claim. He had another flight to go before he got home, and he hoped to fly out of Fairbanks before dark. First, however, he needed to collect his luggage and grab something to eat. With the airlines cutting back, one of the first casualties was the meals, not that they'd ever been that spectacular.

Unfortunately, his bag was one of the last to appear and he had to stand around and wait while all the passengers retrieved their suitcases and made a fast escape. His seatmate hung around, too, he noticed, although her bag had been one of the first to arrive. She looked anxiously about, then after a few minutes walked over to the phone. Whoever she called didn't have a lot to say, because she hung up shortly afterward.

The minute he had his bag, Reid hurried over to the cafeteria. The food wasn't great, and it was damned expensive, but he had few op-

tions. A couple of sandwiches from the airport restaurant would fill
his stomach until he got home.

"How you doin', Reid?" Billy asked when he'd placed the pre-
made, pre-wrapped sandwiches on his tray as well as a cup of coffee.

Reid spent enough time at the airport to be on a first-name basis
with a number of people. Billy was a good guy, retired from con-
struction, who worked part-time at the airport to make entertainment
money. Mostly he blew his wages on poker. Reid had played with him
a time or two, and had suggested Billy keep his day job. "Good to be
home." Almost home, he amended silently.

"Where you comin' back from this time?" Billy asked.

"Seattle." Reid sipped his coffee. It was hot enough to burn his
mouth, but he didn't care. "You wouldn't believe what those Seattle
folks are doing to ruin a good cup of coffee."

Billy chuckled and gave Reid his change. "You flyin' out tonight?"

Reid nodded, took his tray and sat down at the table by the window. His Cessna 182 was parked below. It was comforting to think
he'd be sleeping in his own bed tonight and not some too-soft mattress in an anonymous hotel room.

He ate the first turkey sandwich without stopping, then started on
the second.

His seatmate from the flight came into the cafeteria and scanned
the almost empty room. She seemed even more forlorn than she had
before. He watched as she took a tray, walking past all the food on
display. Then, as if she hadn't found a single thing to tempt her appetite, she simply poured herself a cup of coffee. She began talking
to Billy, and they were engaged in conversation for at least ten minutes.

"Reid, you're flyin' right over Beesley, aren't you?" Billy called
across the cafeteria. The two other customers, a pilot and a lumberjack, both grinned.

"Yeah."

"Do you mind givin' the little lady here a lift?"

Now this was downright interesting.

Miss Priss peered over her shoulder. When she saw him, she

jerked back and started talking animatedly to Billy. Billy shook his head repeatedly but apparently couldn't get a word in edgewise. It was enough to arouse Reid's curiosity. He couldn't imagine what he'd done that took five minutes to describe, complete with agitated gestures. He couldn't help it; he *had* to find out. He stood and walked over to the cashier just in time to hear Billy tell Miss Priss that Reid worked on the Alaska Pipeline and was a fine, upstanding citizen.

"You going to Beesley?" Reid asked the woman.

She raised her chin an extra notch. "How much will it cost for you to fly me there?"

"He's one of the best bush pilots around, miss," Billy rushed to assure her.

"Cost?" Reid shrugged. "I'm flying that way myself. It's no trouble to land and let you off."

She blinked as if she wasn't sure she should believe him. "You'd do that?"

"Folks in Alaska are neighborly," he said. "We lend a hand when we can."

She offered him a tentative smile, which transformed her features, made her seem softer, somehow. He was struck by what an attractive woman she was. All he'd noticed earlier had been the disapproving look in her eyes every time she happened to glance in his direction.

"You ready to leave now?"

She nodded. "That would be great. I have no idea what happened.... My friend was supposed to be here. I phoned his place, but apparently he's already left."

"Not to worry, I'll get you to Beesley."

"I can't thank you enough." She was all sweetness now, he thought wryly. Women were like that. Sweet as honey when they needed a man, and sour as lemons when they didn't. He'd dated but not much. There weren't any women in Snowbound. No single women, anyway. In fact, Snowbound was a one-woman town, and that one woman happened to be his younger sister. She'd tried to set him up with friends of hers from Fairbanks a few times, but nothing ever came of it.

"Thank you," she said to Billy as she began to follow Reid to his four-seater plane, which was tied down outside.

She half ran behind him. "My name is Jenna Campbell," she said. "Reid Jamison."

"Thank you so much," she said, hurrying to keep pace with him.

"You aren't in Beesley yet," he said. "You can thank me then."

While he did the preflight check, she prepared to climb inside the plane, but obviously had a problem figuring out how to do it.

He stared at her. "I take it you've never been in one of these before?"

She seemed a bit abashed to admit it. "No, I can't say I have."

"Use the wing," he said. "Climb on that and just scoot on in."

"Oh." She eyed it as though it was impossibly far off the ground, but she did as he suggested. He smiled at the inept way she maneuvered herself into the second seat. He had to give her credit, though, for not complaining.

As soon as he was inside, he put on the headphones and started talking to the tower. He handed her the second pair while he waited for clearance. She placed them over her head and clung to the door, closing her eyes as he roared down the runway for takeoff.

Once they were airborne, he circled the airport and headed north. "You can open your eyes now," he said, speaking into the small microphone.

Her eyes flew open. "Wow, that was incredible."

"It's even prettier when you're actually looking at it."

She smiled, and once again he was impressed by her beauty. He forced himself to turn away.

"How long before we reach Beesley?" she asked.

"About an hour."

"Oh." She couldn't quite conceal her disappointment. "I didn't realize it was that far from civilization. The distance between Fairbanks and Beesley was pretty small on the map."

He laughed. "What's in Beesley?" he asked. "Or should I say *who?*"

"I have a friend there—a man. The one I tried to call. He was supposed to meet me in Fairbanks but something must've happened. I'm actually kind of worried."

"How well do you know your...friend?"

She frowned. "Well...we've never met—technically, that is—but I feel I know him."

Reid didn't like the sound of this. Dalton Gray lived in Beesley and the man was lower than a swamp-crawling snake. "How long do you intend to stay?" he asked next.

"I...I'm not sure. I hope to find work in Beesley. I can support myself if that's what you're thinking."

"In Beesley?" Reid echoed. "Doing what?"

"I'm an executive assistant, or I was until recently."

He turned to look at her again, and wondered how much she really knew about the tiny Arctic community. "There's no one in Beesley who needs an executive anything."

"I heard otherwise." The prissy expression was back. "My friend assured me I wouldn't have any problem finding employment should I choose to do so."

The bad feeling he'd experienced earlier intensified. "And just who is your friend?"

"His name is Dalton Gray."

"Dalton Gray!" Reid shouted and cursed loudly. He should've suspected something like this. Damn fool that he was, he should've asked her before they departed.

Jenna yanked the headphones off and glared at him. "There is no need to use that kind of language and furthermore, shouting hurts my ears."

Reid muttered an apology, but there was nothing he could do now except fly her back to Fairbanks.

As the Cessna banked sharply to one side, Jenna let out a small cry and grabbed the bar across the top of the door.

"What are you *doing?*" she demanded, replacing the earphones.

"I'm taking you back to Fairbanks."

"You most certainly are not. You said you'd fly me into Beesley and I insist you follow through on your promise."

"By your own admission, you've never even met Dalton," he said. "One day you'll thank me."

"I'm fully capable of making my own decision about a person. Now I must ask you to fly me to Beesley per our agreement."

He couldn't help grinning at her business-speak. Did she think he was a CEO or something? Nonetheless he had his answer ready. "No way, lady."

She narrowed her eyes at him. "Who appointed *you* my guardian?"

Reid ignored her outrage. "You say you met him online?" This was becoming as interesting as it was scary. So Mr. Sleazebag was expanding his horizons, finding new prey through the miracle of modern technology.

She drew herself upright and folded her arms across her chest.

Reid's jaw tightened. This woman couldn't possibly understand what kind of man Dalton Gray was, and he knew he owed her an explanation. "Dalton isn't a man you can trust." That was putting it mildly.

"It seems to me you're the untrustworthy one."

"You don't believe me?"

"Damn straight I don't. Furthermore, I'm flying into Beesley whether you take me there or not. I'll find someone else."

This woman was starting to rile him. What was it about Dalton that turned sane, sensible women into gibbering idiots?

"If that's what you want, fine. Good luck finding another pilot, though, especially at this time of day." For enough money she could, despite the growing darkness, but most folks felt the same way about Dalton as he did. It was men like Dalton who gave Alaska a bad name.

"Tell me what's wrong with Dalton," she said after a while. "I'm not an unreasonable person, but you can't expect me to take the word of a stranger. Especially a stranger who happens to have a personal vendetta against the man I know in my heart to be decent and honorable."

"Decent and honorable? Dalton? We can't be talking about the same man."

"Yes, Dalton," she snapped. "Dalton Gray."

Chances were there might be another man named Dalton Gray somewhere in the world, but it was considerably less likely that this second man lived in Beesley, Alaska.

"If you won't tell me exactly what you mean, then all I can say is you're a coward."

"A what?" Reid exploded.

"A coward," she said without the least hesitation.

"And you're about to make the biggest mistake of your life."

"It's my life," she reminded him.

Reid shook his head. "I'm telling you here and now that Dalton Gray is bad news. He'll use you and when he's finished he'll discard you like yesterday's newspaper."

She raised her chin. "That's your opinion."

"No," he corrected. "It's my sister's. And it's the opinion of half a dozen other women I know. Gray is about as slimy as they come. He's a selfish, arrogant creep who takes advantage of women and—"

"I refuse to believe you."

"Would you believe someone else?"

Her certainty seemed to waver. "Possibly."

"So it's just me you don't trust?"

She didn't answer. This woman, this stubborn, idiotic woman, was about to make a first-class fool of herself. Worse, she'd be putting herself in danger. He could prove everything he'd said. Or he could take her to Fairbanks and let her discover this on her own.

Reid made his decision and banked steeply a second time.

"You're turning back?" she asked.

"Yes."

Her eyes revealed her astonishment. "Thank you for seeing this my way."

He didn't comment.

She held herself primly in the seat next to him and ceased conversation, which suited Reid just fine. He'd said everything he intended to.

An hour later, she glanced at her wrist. "I thought you said Beesley was an hour out. We've been in the air almost ninety minutes."

"I know."

She twisted around and looked over her shoulder. "Those lights we passed a while ago, could that be—" She paused and glared at him accusingly. "That was Beesley, wasn't it?"

"It was."

She gasped. "Where are you taking me?"

"Not to Beesley and not to Dalton Gray, if that's what you're wondering."

"You're—you're kidnapping me!"

"In a manner of speaking, I guess you could say that."

"I'll have you arrested!"

It was difficult to keep from laughing outright. "You could do that, too."

"I will. I plan to prosecute you to the full extent of the law."

"Good for you."

"And to think you said *Dalton* was arrogant."

She sat with her arms folded for the remainder of the flight. He landed in the tundra town of Snowbound and rolled to a stop on the gravel runway. The sense of home was immediate as he gazed out at the small hangar and the dark expanse beyond.

His ungrateful passenger sat there unmoving and unspeaking as he cut the engine. He studied her pursed lips and narrowed eyes— that disapproving look again—while he waited for the engine to wind down. As soon as it was safe, he unlatched the door and climbed out.

"You coming?" he asked.

"Reid!" His name came from somewhere in the night.

"Jim," he called back, recognizing the voice of his brother-in-law and best friend.

"Welcome home." Jim appeared under the single light outside the hangar door.

Leaving Jenna, Reid walked over to his friend and slapped him on the back.

His passenger was out of the plane and scrambling off the wing so fast he did a double-take. But then he'd suspected she would once she saw Jim's uniform.

"Officer! Officer!" she shouted, pointing to Reid. "Arrest this man. He's kidnapped me."

"You kidnapped her?" Jim asked.

Reid nodded. He'd explain later. Jim would understand; he'd had more than one run-in with Dalton Gray himself.

"Jim works for the Parks Department," Reid told her.

"Oh. Where am I?"

"Snowbound," he answered without further explanation. He didn't mention how small it was or that the only woman in town was his sister. Lucy would tell Miss Priss everything she needed to know about Dalton Gray and then some. Once Jenna Campbell learned the truth, she'd thank him, just as he'd predicted earlier.

"Come on," Reid said gruffly, "I haven't got all night."

She made an angry sound, which Reid ignored.

He walked away and left her standing next to the plane.

He noticed with some amusement that it didn't take her long to grab her suitcase and hurry after him.

Chapter Three

"I demand to know where you're taking me," Jenna panted, scurrying behind her kidnapper.

"Yeah, Reid, where are you taking her?" the other man asked.

They became involved in a lively discussion, most of which Jenna couldn't hear. What she did manage to discern depressed her. Apparently Reid had thought she could stay with Jim and his wife, Lucy. Lucy, if Jenna understood correctly, was also Reid's sister, but Lucy happened to be away at the moment. Oh, great!

Lugging her heavy suitcase, Jenna did her best to keep up with the two men. But hurrying after them in her pumps, concentrating on not tripping in the dirt, made listening nearly impossible. It was all she could do to keep Reid and his friend in sight.

They passed what some would consider the town's business district. Using the word *town* loosely, of course. There was a store of some sort, a café and then a row of houses. That was it. The entire town consisted of ten buildings without even a car.

Jim went in one direction and Reid turned in the other, past the small houses, glowing with light, to a scattering of cabins a little way past them. The suburbs of Snowbound, she supposed. Jenna paused, not knowing what to do.

Reid glanced over his shoulder. "Well, come on," he barked.

"Where are we going?" Jenna refused to move another step until she knew what his plans were.

"You'll be staying with me. I don't have any choice."

"I will not!"

"Fine. Park yourself in the street. Frankly, I don't care. I've had a long day and I'm tired."

He'd had a long day? *He* was tired?

Jenna hesitated and looked back to where Reid's friend had gone. Surely someone in this forsaken town would be willing to help her. She was considering her options when Reid turned to face her.

He shrugged in a resigned manner. "Listen, I apologize about this. Bringing you here wasn't the most brilliant idea I've ever had. I intended to have you stay with Lucy, but apparently she's in Fairbanks."

"I'll stay with another woman then."

"You can't—there isn't one."

"Lucy's the only woman in town?"

Reid nodded.

Surely he was joking. "In the *entire* town?"

He nodded again, marched back and took the suitcase out of her hand. "Come on. Everything will look better in the morning."

"Look better for whom?" she cried. This situation was horrible. Inconceivable. Like something out of a bad movie—or a worse dream. Dalton must be frantic worrying about her and she hadn't even contacted her mother yet. The only person in the entire world who knew where she'd gone was some cafeteria worker named Billy. This was what she got for listening to him. Apparently it was high praise that Reid Jamison didn't cheat at poker. She should've known better than to assume that made him reliable enough to keep his bargain with her.

"Isn't there anywhere else I can stay?" she pleaded. "Any other people?"

"There's Pete," Reid muttered. "He runs the store. He's sixty, but I wouldn't feel good about putting you in his home."

"Why not?"

Reid shook his head. "Just trust me on this one. He's a nice guy, but it's been a while since he spent any time with a woman and, well...you get the picture."

Jenna did.

"I don't know what I was thinking, bringing you here," Reid said as he opened the front door, which apparently wasn't locked. "I should have my head examined." He turned on the lights.

"In my opinion, you weren't thinking at all." Jenna followed him into what had to be the messiest quarters she'd ever seen in her life. Magazines and newspapers littered the furniture and floors. The kitchen was filled with dirty dishes. There appeared to be only one bedroom and through its wide-open door she could see an unmade bed and clothes strewn from one end to the other.

"I wasn't expecting company," Reid said, obviously a bit cha- grined. He put down her bag and his.

"So I gathered."

"You can have the bed," he said, gesturing toward the bedroom.

"Is there a lock?" Since there didn't appear to be one on the front door, she sincerely doubted it.

"Lock?" he repeated, then laughed sarcastically. "Don't worry. I have no intention of attacking you."

"You've already kidnapped me, so I don't exactly trust you, Mr. Jamison."

He flopped down on the sofa. "No, I don't suppose you do."

Jenna carried her suitcase into the bedroom and immediately set about creating order. She started by picking up the dirty clothes.

"Do you have a washing machine?" she asked.

Reid had apparently fallen asleep. Her question startled him and he bolted upright. He blinked in her direction. "What?"

"A laundry room?"

"Sorry, the architect forgot that."

"How do you wash your clothes then?"

"Lucy." He said it as though she should've figured it out herself.

"Fine." She dumped the pile in a corner of the living area and returned to the bedroom. Cringing, she peeled back the sheets. Lord only knew how long it'd been since they were last changed.

Back in the main room, she found him sitting upright and snoring. "Sheets," she demanded loudly. "I need clean sheets."

He opened his eyes, which widened as if he were seeing her for the first time. "I only have the one set."

Jenna was afraid of that. "I refuse to sleep on those." She pointed to the room behind her.

"Wait…" He struggled to his feet and walked over to a closet and brought out two sheets so new they were still in the package. "I nearly forgot. Lucy gave these to me last Christmas."

She didn't want to ask if he'd been sleeping in the same sheets all year, figuring it was better not to know.

"Happy now?" he asked.

"Ecstatic."

"Good. Can I go back to sleep?"

"By all means," she said sarcastically. "I'd hate to see you grouchy through lack of sleep."

Her comment earned her a hint of a smile.

"I believe every prisoner is entitled to one phone call and I'd like to make mine."

"Fine, you can call whoever you want as long as it isn't Dalton Gray, but you'll have to wait until morning."

"Why?"

"The only phone is over at Pete's."

"Pete who owns the store?"

"Right."

Oh, yes. Pete who hadn't seen a woman in years.

"*Now* will you go to bed?"

"Gladly." She marched into the bedroom and closed the door. Then, to be on the safe side, she stuck a chair beneath the door handle. It took her ten minutes to make the bed. After she'd stripped off the sheets, she flipped the mattress. This was done with some difficulty, but she managed it on her own and felt a sense of triumph when she succeeded.

"What the hell is going on in there?" Reid shouted from the other side of the door.

"I'm making the bed."

"Sounds like you're tearing down the walls."

It probably had sounded like that because she'd knocked over the lamp on the nightstand and the mattress had hit the wall with a solid thud.

"Go to sleep," she shouted back.

"I'm trying," he replied tersely.

Jenna smoothed a blanket over the mattress to serve as a mattress pad and put on the crisp, fresh-from-the-package sheets. Without a chair on which to lay her clothes, she folded them over the footboard and changed into flannel pajamas.

Jenna didn't expect to sleep well, and was shocked to wake seven hours later. She hadn't stirred once the entire night. As she dressed, she decided to confront Reid and demand that he take her either to Beesley or Fairbanks. If he agreed, she wouldn't press charges against him. If not, she'd be using the one and only phone in Snowbound, Alaska, to call a lawyer. *That* should tell Reid Jamison she was serious. He didn't look like the kind of man who'd take well to life inside a prison.

With a plan of action, she removed the chair and jerked open the door, prepared to confront her kidnapper.

To her dismay she discovered he was nowhere to be found. Nor had he bothered to leave her a note telling her where he was going. The man had some nerve!

However...

It could be that luck was with her. Jenna cheerfully packed her suitcase and left the house. As soon as she stepped outside, she saw two vehicles, both trucks and both parked in front of the café. That seemed like a good place to start.

Jenna walked over to the building and frowned at the display of elk horns above the doorway. The café consisted of five tables and a counter where two older men with thick gray beards sat eating hotcakes.

They turned and stared at her as if she were an alien species. To them, she probably was.

"Good morning," she said politely.

"You must be Jenna," the closer of the two said. He offered her an uncertain smile. "Reid said you'd be stopping by sooner or later."

"Sit down and make yourself at home," the man behind the counter instructed.

"Reid didn't say what a beauty she was," the first man whispered to the second in tones loud enough for her to hear.

"Jake Morgan here," the man behind the counter said. "And these two varmints are Addison Bush and Palmer Gentry."

Both men clambered to their feet and bowed at the waist. "Friends call me Addy," the taller one said.

"Hello, Addy."

"Most everyone just calls me Palmer."

"Palmer." She acknowledged him with a nod.

"Could I get you a cup of coffee?" Jake asked her.

"Please." She sat two stools down from her newfound friends, who continued to stare at her.

"Reid's down at the pump station."

She must have looked confused, because Jake added, "The pump station for the pipeline."

"Oh."

Jake brought her the coffee and she accepted it gratefully. "I'd like to hire someone to fly me to Beesley," she said, smiling at the two men.

Her three admirers put their heads together and immediately started mumbling among themselves.

"We only got two planes here in Snowbound," Addy explained. "Reid has one and Jim has the other."

"Jim left this morning to pick up Lucy," Palmer said.

"Yup. Lucy told him the only way she'd live up here was if Jim took her into Fairbanks every month so she'd be able to do woman things." All three men seemed to consider those things, whatever they were, a deep and incomprehensible mystery.

"Jim and Lucy will be back tomorrow," Addy told her.

So flying out with the other man was no longer an option. "Would it be possible to use the phone?" Jenna asked.

"The only phone here belongs to Pete," Jake replied.

So it was true and not just another lie of Jamison's. "Then I'll talk to Pete," she said, and took one last restorative sip of coffee before slipping off the stool.

"They got phones down at the pump station," Palmer said. "But that's a mile or so from here."

She thought of all the cell and car phones in L.A. that she took for granted. Her mother alone had six or seven phones: one in each car, a personal cell phone and four in the house. That number wasn't unusual among Jenna's friends, either.

All three men accompanied her to the grocery, which was a generous term for this place. Yes, there were shelves with grocery items—a few cans of this and a few cans of that. The shelves were sparsely stocked, to say the least. Under a glass countertop were several pieces of Alaskan art, scrimshaw and beaded jewelry, along with what appeared to be small chunks of gold.

A man who must be Pete walked out from behind a denim curtain and smiled broadly when he saw her.

"Well, hello, little lady. Let me personally welcome you to Snowbound." He looked her up and down, apparently enjoying the view. Then he reached for her hand and brought it to his lips.

"Pete's something of a ladies' man," Palmer explained from behind her.

"Manners and all," Jake added, whispering close to her ear.

"I understand you have a phone," Jenna said, ignoring the other three men. "I was wondering if I could use it. I have a phone card so I wouldn't be putting any long distances charges on your line."

"I would consider it an honor to be of service." He bent forward and kissed the back of her hand a second time. "But alas, the telephone is no longer in working order."

Jenna wanted to weep with frustration.

"I was afraid of that," Jake said sadly.

"Me, too," Addy and Palmer whispered in tandem.

"You aren't going to be mad, now are you?" Jake asked and re-treated a step. "Reid said you get downright testy when you're mad."

"I most certainly do not," she flared angrily. He'd accused her of snoring and now this! "How dare he say such things about me!"

The four men exchanged looks that suggested Reid knew what he was talking about and they'd be well advised to keep their distance.

"Where is Mr. Jamison, anyway?" Jenna demanded. "Perhaps it'd be best if you took me to him." She wasn't keen on the idea, but he was the one responsible for getting her into this mess, so he *had* to help her.

Her request was met with silence. Finally Pete ventured, "I'm afraid I can't do that, miss."

"Why not?"

"Reid said we shouldn't," Jake murmured.

Palmer agreed. "Said you'd caused him nothing but trouble from the moment he laid eyes on you. He didn't want that trouble follow-ing him to work."

Of all the unfair and untruthful statements the man had made, this exceeded everything. "Did he happen to tell you he kidnapped me?"

"Yes, miss."

"He said you came to Alaska to meet Dalton Gray."

"Dalton and I are friends," Jenna explained.

All four men frowned. "You don't want anything to do with Dal-ton," Pete said. "But if you're looking for a man, a real man, no need to search any farther. I might be sixty but I'm here to tell you I'd make a mighty fine lover."

"I beg your pardon?"

"Just an alternative, miss."

"An alternative that is of no interest to me."

Pete sighed resignedly. "You can't blame a man for trying."

Oh, yes, I can, Jenna thought. But all she said was, "When will Reid be back?"

"Can't say."

"No, can't say," Addy echoed.

"He doesn't keep regular hours?"

"He comes and goes as needed," Jake said importantly.

"Oh." Defeated, Jenna returned to Reid's cabin. There was nothing to do but wait for him and pray that in the light of day he'd be more reasonable.

The hours dragged. Jenna completed the crossword puzzle book she'd bought at the airport in Los Angeles and was halfway through the novel she'd started on the plane when the front door opened.

Reid came into the cabin, glowering when he saw her. What did he expect? It wasn't like she had anywhere else to go.

"I thought, being as fussy as you are, that you'd clean the place up a bit."

Jenna glared at him. What right did he have to assume she'd clean up after him? "I am not your housekeeper."

He held up his hand, warding off her outrage. "My mistake."

"Par for the course as far as you're concerned," she snapped.

Reid looked everywhere but at her.

"I want out of here."

He sighed. "Seems like you've got yourself riled up again."

"You could say that." Standing now, she planted her hands on her hips. "I insist you take me back to Fairbanks." She'd given up hope that he'd deliver her to Beesley.

"Believe me, your highness, I'd like nothing better."

"Good. Then we understand each other."

"Perfectly."

A face appeared in the window; Jenna caught a glimpse of it out of the corner of her eye and gasped.

"What?" Reid demanded.

"There's someone out there, peeking in the window."

Reid marched across the room, threw open the door and bellowed, "Addy...Palmer."

The two men crept around the side of the building, heads bowed, wool caps in hand. "What the hell are you doing listening in on a private conversation?"

"Sorry, Reid," Addy mumbled. "We were just curious."

"Yeah, Reid, we don't get much entertainment and we wanted to be here when you tell her."

"Tell me what?" Jenna asked.

Reid ignored her. "You two scat, and don't let me find you peeking in my windows again, you hear?"

"Yes, Reid."

"Sorry, Reid."

The two disappeared and Reid closed the door. "I apologize for that."

"What are you going to tell me?" she asked again.

"Now, listen," he said, stretching out his arm toward her. "You have every right to be upset, but a man can't be responsible for the weather."

"What the hell are you talking about?"

He shook his head. "If it was up to me, I'd have you back in Fairbanks in nothing flat."

"With an apology?"

He hesitated, then reluctantly nodded. "Okay, with an apology. You're a stubborn, rebellious woman, and if you're set on self-destruction, then it's none of my damn business. I was only trying to save you grief, but I'll admit I was wrong to bring you here."

"Exactly."

"I want you to know I've never done anything like this before."

"I should hope not."

"However," he went on, "it looks like you're going to be stuck here for the next two or three days."

"What?" Jenna exploded.

"There's a bad storm coming in."

Jenna studied him suspiciously. "And how do you know this?"

"There are weather-tracking devices down at the pump station. Now, listen, I don't like this any more than you do. I made a mistake and I apologize, much as it goes against my nature. I shouldn't have brought you to Snowbound. But we'll just have to make the best of it."

"I want to see this weather-tracking device for myself." She grabbed her coat, then flung open the door and stepped out of the cabin. She didn't know where she was going, only that she wasn't taking this man at his word. He'd already tricked her once and she refused to fall victim a second time.

Arms swinging at her sides, she marched in the direction of where she assumed the pump station must be. From her peripheral vision, she noticed Addy and Palmer, following her at a safe distance.

"Jenna!" Reid shouted.

She'd find that pump station if it was the last thing she did.

And it might *be* the last thing, she thought when a large black figure ambled out from between two houses. Jenna strangled a scream and froze.

It was a bear.

A huge black bear, and he was looking directly at her as if he'd just spotted dinner.

Jenna's heart was in her throat. Her mouth moved in a wobbly erratic manner, but no words came out.

The bear stopped and stood on his hind legs and seemed as tall as a California redwood. Jenna was so terrified that she feared she was about to lose consciousness.

"Blackie!" Reid shouted. "Get out of here. Shoo. Shoo." Reid came forward, waving his arms.

The bear thumped down on all fours, shook his massive head, and went casually on his way.

"That's Blackie," Reid said. "He generally doesn't cause a problem. Actually, it's pretty late in the year for him to be around."

Coherent speech remained beyond Jenna's capabilities. A bear had confronted her!

"You're all right, aren't you?" Reid asked, waggling a hand in front of her face.

She tried to move, but the shock and fear had incapacitated her.

Snow began to fall. Not thick flakes, but small icy ones.

"Here's your weather report," Reid said, glancing up at the sky. "Come on. We'd better get back to the cabin." He forged ahead, but came back for her a moment later, taking her elbow and gently steering her toward his cabin.

By the time they arrived, the snow was coming down fast. Having lived in Los Angeles most of her life, Jenna had only seen snow once before, on a vacation to Colorado. It had covered the ground and frosted the trees, but this was the first time in her life she'd seen it fall.

"It's beautiful," she said, pausing outside the door. She thrust out her hands and let the snow land on her palms.

"Yes, yes…" Reid seemed in a mighty big hurry to get her inside.

"How long did you say the storm would last?" she asked, thinking it would be so beautiful. The snow—not being trapped with Reid Jamison.

Reid hesitated. "Longer than either of us is going to like," he muttered, looking miserable.

Jenna was afraid of that.

Chapter Four

Brad Fulton stared at the woman standing in front of his desk and realized with a start that it wasn't his executive assistant. Where the hell was Jenna?

A couple of weeks earlier, before he'd left town to investigate a venture capital project, she'd made some threat about leaving. As he recalled, she'd even gone so far as to hand him a written notice. Not for a moment did Brad believe she'd really do it. He'd instructed Accounting to give her a twenty-percent raise and assumed that was the end of it.

"Where's Ms. Campbell?" he asked.

"Ms. Campbell's last day was Friday, Mr. Fulton."

"Who are you?" This was not the way he'd intended to begin his work week. He was a man accustomed to his comforts. He didn't like change and he liked surprises even less.

"I'm Gail Spencer, Ms. Campbell's replacement." She set a cup of coffee on his desk.

Brad glared at it. "I drink my coffee with cream."

"Sorry, sir, Ms. Campbell told me that, but I guess I forgot." She removed the coffee, was gone momentarily and returned with a fresh cup, complete with cream.

One look told Brad that she'd put in far more cream than he liked. "Where's my mail?"

"It's on the corner of your desk, sir."

"I prefer it in the center so it's the first thing I see in the morning."

"Sorry, sir, I'll make sure it's there tomorrow."

"It would be appreciated." He forced a smile, trying to reassure her, and waited until she was out of the office before he walked over to his small kitchen area, dumped a third of the coffee in the sink and added black coffee to the cup.

He sat back down at his desk and leafed through his mail.

Jenna had actually gone and done it, after six compatible and productive years as his right hand. It irritated him. No, in fact, it downright perturbed him. He'd given Jenna her start, offered her a position that assistants twenty years her senior would have envied, and *this* was the appreciation he got.

He didn't even know why she'd left. He pressed his buzzer.

"Yes, Mr. Fulton?" Ms. Spencer asked.

"Do you know if Ms. Campbell took another job?"

"I…I'm not sure, sir, but I believe she did."

Now he was more than perturbed. He was furious. The woman he had considered loyal and dedicated had defected to another firm.

"Do you know the name of the company, Ms. Spencer?"

"I'm not sure, Mr. Fulton. I was only with her for two days before she left. I recall her mentioning something about Dalton."

"Dalton Industries?"

"I really couldn't say, sir."

"Find out what you can about Dalton Industries and get back to me as quickly as possible."

"Right away, sir."

"Ms. Spencer?"

"Yes, sir?"

"Please don't call me sir."

"Yes, sir…I mean yes, Mr. Fulton."

Frowning darkly, Brad released the intercom button. He couldn't imagine what he'd done to warrant Jenna's leaving his employ. He liked her; they worked well together and there was a lot to be said for that. Brad realized he wasn't an easy man to work for. He knew there were times he could be demanding and impatient, but Jenna never got flustered. One of the things he appreciated most about her was that she was a sensible woman. She anticipated his needs and saw to his comforts. Last Christmas he'd had her buy all his Christmas gifts. She'd done a beautiful job. His mother had adored the porcelain figurine Jenna had chosen, and his father was pleasantly surprised by the autographed copy of the latest Tom Clancy techno-thriller. Brad didn't have a clue how she'd managed that.

It was this ability to pull off the impossible that he valued so much. She managed *everything,* and she did it with effortless calm. When Jenna was around, he could trust her to capably handle both his business and personal needs, from gift-buying to arranging for his suits to be cleaned. He depended on her and now she was gone.

Pressing down hard on the intercom button, he asked, "Ms. Spencer, what have you found out?"

"Sir—"

Brad cringed. He only had to tell Jenna something once and she remembered.

"I'm sorry, Mr. Fulton, I can't find any Dalton Industries."

"You're sure it was Dalton?"

"I—I think so, sir. It was just those two days."

The woman apparently couldn't remember from one minute to the next not to call him *sir.* It was highly unlikely she'd recall a conversation held last week. "Who would know?"

"I—I couldn't say. Did she mention anything in her letter of resignation?"

Now the woman was earning her pay. "Good idea. Bring it to me, please."

"Right away—Mr. Sir."

Brad paced the room until she entered his office five minutes later. Her hands were empty.

"I believe it might be somewhere on your desk, Mr. Fulton."

"Ah, yes—never mind, I'll find it."

"Very good." She backed out of the room as if she half expected him to demand something more of her.

As soon as the door closed, Brad tore into the stacks of files and memos piled on his desk. It took him thirty minutes to find Jenna's notice. He scanned it again, and wished he'd read it more carefully the first time.

Dear Mr. Fulton,

I would like to thank you for six wonderful years as your executive assistant.

It is with regret that I give you my two-weeks' notice. I've decided it's time to move on and seek adventure, which I'm sure I'll find in Beesley, Alaska. Who knows, I might even find a husband, too.

Sincerely,
Jenna Campbell

Alaska? Jenna was going to Alaska? Husband? Jenna wanted a husband? Never once had she said anything to him about marriage. Hell, Brad would marry her himself if it meant she'd continue to work as his assistant. Didn't she know how much he needed her? Clearly not.

"Ms. Spencer," he said, speaking into the intercom.

"Yes, Mr. Fulton?"

"Get me a phone number for Jenna Campbell. She's somewhere in Alaska—try a town called Beesley."

"Right away, sir."

Brad cringed; this sir business put his teeth on edge.

Another ten minutes passed and he was about to lose his patience. His intercom buzzed. "Yes?" he said, pen in hand.

"I'm afraid she didn't leave a forwarding phone number."

"Did you speak to anyone in Alaska?"

"I did. I checked with the only hotel in the town you mentioned, but she didn't check in there. The clerk suggested she might be visiting friends."

"I see. She didn't happen to mention any friends, did she?"

"Not that I can remember. But I may have misunderstood."

Brad wouldn't put it past her.

"I did find her mother's home number if you want that."

"No," he snapped, his blood pressure shooting up twenty points. The woman was to be avoided at all costs. "That won't be necessary."

So Jenna didn't want to be found. Well, there were ways around that. Brad Fulton wasn't a man easily dissuaded; he intended to find her and when he did, he'd make her an offer she couldn't refuse. One way or another, he was getting her back in his office—even if it meant he had to marry her.

Chapter Five

"Dammit," Dalton Gray shouted at the Alaska Airlines representative on Monday afternoon. "I've talked with my associate, and Jenna
Campbell was on Flight 232, leaving LAX on Sunday morning with
a plane change in Seattle. The flight landed in Fairbanks on schedule."

"I'm pleased you were able to confirm that." The woman behind the
counter displayed a decided lack of patience, which irritated him further.

"*And* she collected her luggage." He wasn't entirely sure of that,
though. The airlines had offered damn little help in locating Jenna.

"Yes." The woman's gaze dropped to the computer screen. "That's
the information I have as well."

Dalton did his best to maintain his composure. "Unfortunately, I
haven't been able to find any trace of her after she left the baggage
claim area." He'd spent almost twenty-four hours searching every
hotel in Fairbanks, looking for his Internet sweetheart. So far, all his
efforts had achieved was more frustration.

"Perhaps you should notify the authorities," the airline representative suggested.

"No, thanks," he muttered as he stepped away from the counter.

The "authorities" were the last people he wanted to visit. He'd been so anxious to meet Jenna, he'd arrived at the airport a full day early. With twenty-four hours to kill, he'd stopped for a beer at a local tavern. No need to sit around the airport and wait, Dalton had decided. That was his first mistake.

Sure enough, he'd met up with an old friend and one thing had led to another and before he knew it he was drunk. He might have made it back to the airport in time, but the waitress knew him and, well—what could he say? Dalton was weak when it came to women. He never could refuse a lady. Never had and probably never would.

Only now, his roving eye had caused him to miss Jenna's flight and he didn't have any idea where she was. Walking over to the pay phone, he dialed his office in Beesley.

Larry Forsyth answered. "Beesley Air Service."

"It's Dalton."

"You find your ladyfriend yet?" Larry asked.

"No. She didn't happen to show up there, did she?" He could always hope.

"I haven't seen hide nor hair of her. Just spoke to her the one time. You didn't tell me you had this woman flying in, Dalton. If I'd known, I would've told her you were on your way. She sounded anxious, too—said she was afraid something might've happened to you."

Dalton wanted to groan. He had a live one on the line, and due to his own foolishness he'd let her slip away.

Larry sure hadn't been much help. "The next time I'm not there and a woman phones for me, tell her where to reach me, okay?"

"You don't want me to do that," Larry told him. "Because you don't want certain women to know where you are—remember?"

Dalton ground his teeth. "You know what I mean!"

"You can't expect me to keep track of all your ladyfriends. Besides, it's your own damn fault for getting drunk."

Luckily he hadn't told Larry about his interlude with Trixie, the waitress. The woman was trouble—not only was she married, but she had a habit of clinging to him, especially when he needed to leave.

"I'll call back in a couple of hours. If Jenna phones again, find out where she is so I can get her."

"You looked outside recently?" Larry asked.

Dalton had been too busy canvassing the airlines and searching for Jenna to care about the weather. "No, why?"

"We got a storm coming in."

"What?" This situation was getting worse by the second.

"You're grounded."

Dalton ran his hand over his face. "How long?"

"Up to three days."

Dalton resisted the urge to stamp his foot. Damn, he didn't have any luck but bad.

"What you need to do," Larry suggested, "is think like a woman."

Dalton frowned. "Think like a woman?"

"Yeah. If you were this Jenna Campbell and you landed in Fairbanks and expected to be met and weren't—what would you do?"

Dalton thought about it. He didn't know. "I've already contacted every hotel in town. She isn't in any of them."

"Does she have friends in the area?"

"She said she didn't." This was helping, though. With so many frustrations getting in the way, he hadn't been thinking straight.

"Well, what else would she do?"

"If you were a woman in this kind of situation, what would *you* do?" Dalton asked.

"I'm not a woman."

"Dammit, Larry, don't get cute with me."

"If I were a woman," his friend said, elevating his voice to a squeaky, irritating pitch, "I'd be really, really upset."

Dalton let that sink in. "Yeah, I bet she's furious all right."

"Then I'd...I'd want to get even," Larry continued in his falsetto.

"Get even?"

"I'd want you to worry."

"I'm worried, I'm worried." Actually Dalton was more angry than worried. He'd already wasted two good days and now it looked like he was stuck in Fairbanks for three more. Normally that wouldn't be so bad, but Trixie's husband was due back this afternoon, if he could make it through the storm. Dalton wouldn't find any solace with her until his next visit, and only if his arrival happened to coincide with her husband's absence.

"How long have you known this new girl?" Larry asked, his voice returning to normal.

Dalton had to mull over the question. He'd been corresponding via the Internet with five or six women, but he'd chosen Jenna over the others. For some reason, he had an innate ability when it came to attracting the opposite sex. For him, it was all about conquest, about persuading a woman to fall in love with him. After the initial seduction he quickly lost interest.

The Internet had been a real boon. The word was out around town, but the Internet gave him a whole new field of operation. Women loved to weave unrealistic fantasies around Alaskan men. Dalton did his best to fulfill the role, dramatizing his life and adventures in the bush. They swooned over the fact that he was a pilot. He was equally good at playing the sensitive poetic type; a secondhand edition of *Bartlett's Quotations* had come in mighty handy there. That was the persona Jenna had preferred.

She was the third woman he'd convinced to visit Alaska. The first two had lasted less than a month. By the middle of the second week, Dalton was tired of them, anyway, and eager for them to leave.

"Dalton, you there?" Larry yelled.

"I'm here. I was just thinking about your question. I guess we've been e-mailing back and forth for three or four months now. Maybe longer."

"Three or four months?" Larry echoed. "But wasn't Megan Knoll with you then?"

"Yeah, and your point is?" Dalton figured Larry was jealous of his ability to attract women. He'd offered to give the other man lessons on the subtle art of seduction, but his business partner showed no talent for it.

"My point is…" Larry hesitated. "Never mind, you wouldn't understand."

Obviously not. "Hell, Larry, where could she be?"

"Is she like all the others?" Larry asked. "Or does this one have a brain?"

Dalton wasn't necessarily interested in that part of a woman's anatomy. "I suppose so, if talking about poetry means you have a brain."

"Could she have hired another pilot to fly her in?"

Dalton expelled his breath. "I thought of that. I've talked to everyone I know and a few I don't. As far as I can tell, she didn't connect with anyone here."

"Then I don't know what to tell you."

"Yeah, think like a woman," Dalton muttered sarcastically.

"Have you called the cops?"

Larry knew damn well he wanted nothing to do with the sheriff's department. He wasn't on friendly terms with Alaska's finest. No, sirree. He'd barely escaped jail time with his most recent scam and had no desire to further his acquaintance with the law.

"What're you going to do next?" Larry asked.

"Hell if I know." Damn fool woman should've stayed in one place. This was what he got for crediting her with common sense.

"You know—"

"What?" Dalton interrupted, anxious.

"Women like to talk," Larry said.

"Yeah." Dalton already knew that.

"Maybe she made friends with someone on the flight, chatting the way they do."

"Good idea, Lar."

"I was just thinking like a woman." The falsetto voice was back.

"I'll check with the airline right now."

"You do that, sweetheart," Larry purred.

Dalton ignored him. "I'll call back in a couple of hours. Maybe by then Jenna will have tried to reach me at the office."

"I won't tell her about us, darlin'."

"Cut it out, Larry." Dalton slammed down the receiver. He wasn't in the mood for jokes. However, Larry had given him a helluva good idea. He should've thought of it himself—Jenna meeting up with someone on the flight. When Dalton wasn't at the airport as planned, Jenna had probably accepted an invitation to stay with this newfound friend of hers. What didn't make sense was no contact since that time.

When he got to the Alaska Airlines counter, there was a long line of people waiting, hoping to escape before the full force of the storm hit. Thankfully he moved forward quickly as he waited his turn to talk to the airline representative. The same woman he'd spoken to twice before.

Her smile faded when she saw it was him. "How can I help you?" she asked.

"It's about my friend."

"Yes, I suspected it was. Have you been able to locate her?"

"Not yet." Dalton leaned closer to the desk. "I think that when I wasn't here to meet her, she went home with someone she met on the flight."

The middle-aged woman's expression didn't change.

"Do you think that might've happened?"

"It's a possibility."

"Yes, well, I'm short on those, so I was wondering if you'd be kind enough to let me see the names of everyone else on the flight."

She shrugged her shoulders ever so slightly. "I'm afraid I can't do that."

"And why not?"

"It's company policy. I can't hand over the passenger manifest simply because someone asked for it."

"But—"

"In these days of high security, you can't honestly expect me to give you sensitive material."

"Sensitive material?" he exploded.

"Perhaps you'd care to speak to my supervisor?"

Now that was more like it. "Yes, I would."

"I don't think it'll do any good," she added as she rang for someone else.

Dalton snorted. "We'll just see about that."

The woman had the nerve to look him full in the eye and say, "Yes, you will."

Chapter Six

Jenna had been thrilled at the first appearance of snow. It had seemed truly lovely and had brightened the whole landscape. The day had been overcast and bleak but an inch or two of snow had turned the world a pristine, sparkling white. Christmas was only six weeks away, and it seemed as if she'd stepped inside a holiday greeting card.

However, after several hours of continuous snowfall, she'd lost her fascination with it. It was still snowing, the wind so strong the flakes blew horizontally.

"Staring out the window isn't going to change anything." Reid spoke from behind her.

These were the first words either of them had uttered in ages. She didn't bother to respond.

"You can stand there and mope or we can make the best of this," he added.

"I am not moping." She whirled around to face him and discovered he'd brought out a deck of cards and was playing solitaire.

"I know Blackie frightened you."

Frightened her? It'd taken her pulse hours to recover from her encounter with the bear. "That isn't the half of it."

"You're over it now, aren't you?"

If she lived another hundred years, she would never forget the sight of that humongous bear rearing up on his two hind feet directly in front of her. The gleam in his eyes said she looked good enough to eat, and God help her, she couldn't have moved an inch if he *had* decided to make her his evening meal.

"Blackie's harmless," Reid insisted. "He comes into town to scrounge through the garbage, although I will admit he's generally down for the winter by now."

"I don't find that reassuring."

"This is Alaska, Jenna."

"Okay, fine. This is Alaska. I should've expected to meet a black bear on Main Street. Silly me." For emphasis she slapped her forehead with the palm of her hand.

"There's no need to be sarcastic."

She turned back and resumed staring out the window.

"Do you play cribbage?"

She didn't answer him.

"I was just trying to pass the time, but I can see you're determined to make us both miserable."

"It's what you deserve."

"Trust me, I'd have you out of here in a New York minute if I could. I don't need a woman messing up my life. In fact, I don't need anyone."

Turning back, she did a slow appraisal of his living quarters and then let her hard gaze rest on him. "I can tell."

He was angry now if his narrowed eyes were any indication. Slowly he rose to his feet. He opened his mouth as though to give her a verbal flaying, but before he could get out a word, there was a loud knock on the front door.

Jenna's gaze flew to the door. Maybe Dalton had found her and come to rescue her from this horrible man.

Reid stomped over to the door and threw it open. His brooding frown dissolved when Addy, Palmer and Pete marched inside. Pete carried a steaming cast-iron kettle.

"We brought you dinner," Addy announced.

"It's Jake's stew," Palmer said.

"Jake thought it might be just the thing to welcome Jenna to Snowbound, seeing that the town's living up to its name."

"How thoughtful." Jenna smiled at the three men. "I'll thank him when I can."

"Jake said there was plenty for four or five people." Addy eyed the pot suggestively.

"We figured you two might welcome company," Palmer said, glancing from Reid to Jenna and then back to Reid again.

A tense silence followed before Reid spoke. "Would you three care to join us?"

"Don't mind if I do," Addy leaped in.

"I suppose I could, since Addy's staying," Palmer said.

Pete shook his head. "I better get back. I only came to see if there was anything you needed from the store before the worst of the storm hits."

Jenna and Reid spoke at the same time.

"It's getting *worse?*" she muttered.

"We're fine," Reid assured the other man.

"How's it going?" she heard Pete ask Reid in a low whisper. The older man gave Reid a knowing poke in the ribs. "You going to score?"

"The only thing Reid is going to score is a black eye if he so much as comes within twenty feet of me." Jenna wanted every man in town to understand that right now. If Reid entertained any notion of a dalliance with her during the snowstorm, then he was in for more trouble than he'd know what to do with.

"I'd rather kiss a rattlesnake than *her,*" Reid retaliated, inclining his head in Jenna's direction as if there might be some other female in the vicinity.

Addy laughed and slapped his knee. "I'd like to see you try."

Palmer and Pete laughed heartily. As they'd mentioned earlier, there wasn't much entertainment in town, and they took their laughs where they could get them. Apparently they had a penchant for low comedy.

"So—we going to eat or not?" Addy asked.

"I'm starved." Palmer rubbed his palms together eagerly.

Pete stepped closer to the door. "See ya later."

"Be sure and thank Jake for me," Reid said.

"I will." The door opened and closed, and Pete was gone.

Addy and Palmer headed toward the pot of stew and waited impatiently while Reid washed four bowls and spoons.

Now that she thought about it, Jenna realized she was famished, too. It was dinnertime and she hadn't eaten all day.

Reid placed a ladle in the middle of the table, and Addy and Palmer both grabbed for it. Elbowing each other, they fought for the top bowl; Addy won and dug into the pot of simmering stew as if it was his last meal.

"Addy, Palmer," Reid barked.

The two older men froze, then glanced toward Reid.

"There's a lady present."

Addy scratched his beard and was about to argue, but changed his mind after Reid sent him a stern look.

"Ladies go first," Palmer said and reluctantly stepped aside.

"You help yourself," Reid instructed Jenna, stretching out his arms to hold back the two old geezers.

"Thank you," Jenna said, reaching for the third bowl.

"Don't be takin' all the meat, either," Addy grumbled.

"Addy," Reid said beneath his breath. "I can uninvite you."

Addy grumbled again, something she couldn't hear. Then he said, "You take as much of that tender meat as you want, Miss Campbell. Just remember, some people got real teeth."

"And some don't," Palmer added.

Jenna ladled a helping of stew into her bowl and picked up a spoon. As soon as she moved away, the two men landed on the stew like vultures on fresh kill.

The old men ate standing up. They kept their faces close to their bowls and slurped up the stew. There were only two chairs at the kitchen table and they'd insisted the lady have one and their host the other. Moments later Addy and Palmer had gulped down their meals.

"Good vittles." Addy nodded and placed his bowl in the sink.

"We hate to eat and run, but we better get home," Palmer said, following his friend.

"Goodbye, Addy, Palmer," Jenna said. "I hope I didn't take more than my fair share of the meat."

"It's all right," Addy told her kindly.

"You gonna stay in town after the storm?" Palmer asked.

"No," but it was Reid who answered instead of Jenna. "I'll have her out of here the first chance I get."

"I have no intention of staying a moment longer than necessary." She cast Reid a look that informed him she was capable of answering questions on her own.

"See ya," Addy said.

Palmer waved politely, put his wool cap back on his head and then the two of them were gone.

When the door banged shut, the ensuing silence seemed deafening.

Jenna finished her stew. Now that her stomach was full, she felt more relaxed, less irritated. She glanced at Reid and he immediately looked away.

"I'll do the dishes," she said, hoping he'd view her offer as a gesture of peace.

"No, I will," Reid snapped. "Far be it from me to ask anything of you."

"Then you do them." She was only trying to help.

"You were the one who made such a fuss about cleaning up earlier, remember? I'll take care of it myself."

"I wouldn't dream of destroying your sense of order." His housekeeping method consisted of accumulating piles of junk in every corner of the cabin.

"Good. That's the way I want it."

"Fine." She crossed her arms.

"Do you always have to have the last word?"

She shrugged.

He snorted.

She coughed.

He laughed.

While he did the dishes, Jenna picked up the deck of cards and shuffled them, then dealt out a game of solitaire. She pretended not to notice when he'd finished and momentarily left the room.

He came back carrying a thick paperback novel. He settled down in front of the fire with every appearance of comfort.

Jenna had read the courtroom drama several months earlier and been enthralled by its twists and turns, marveling at the author's ability to casually weave in elements that would later turn out to be of key importance. She'd read an interview with him recently and would have enjoyed discussing the book with Reid. His mood, however, didn't encourage conversation.

A half hour later, Reid went into the kitchen and she heard the coffeepot start to perk. He returned, standing behind her. She couldn't see him, but she felt his presence.

"Red jack on the black queen," he said.

"I saw that," she muttered, although she hadn't. She moved the cards around.

"Would you like a cup of coffee?"

"Please."

A few moments later, he brought her a mug.

When he set it down on the table next to her, she said, "To answer your earlier question, I do know how to play cribbage. My grandfather taught me—but it's been years since I played so I might be a little rusty."

"Are you saying you'd be willing to play?"

She rolled her eyes. "Yes."

"All right." He opened a drawer and brought out an exquisite hand-carved playing board.

Jenna picked it up and examined it, impressed by the fine workmanship.

"My father made that nearly thirty years ago," Reid told her.

"I don't think I've ever seen a more beautiful one."

An almost-smile flickered, then faded.

He shuffled and they cut for the deal. Reid easily won the first game. They decided to play a second one.

"How long have you lived in Alaska?" she asked as she gathered up her cards.

"Born here."

"In Snowbound?"

"No, Fairbanks."

He certainly wasn't forthcoming with details.

"There's just your sister and you?"

"Yup." They laid down their hands, counted back and forth, and each moved the pegs forward.

"I envy you having a sister," Jenna murmured. As an only child, she'd often dreamed of what it would be like to have a sibling. Her parents' marriage hadn't lasted long. Her father had moved on, re-married and apparently had other children. He'd never kept in touch with Jenna. It had just been Jenna and her mother—between mar-riages, of course!

"Then you can understand why I feel about Dalton the way I do. He used Lucy. She was young and naive and she fell right into his trap. He's a womanizer of the worst kind—seduce 'em and throw them away."

Jenna counted to ten before she spoke. "I think it would be best if we didn't discuss Dalton." She'd need to make her own judgments about the man. She would, once she'd met him for herself, but until then she'd go by what she knew of him from their Internet relation-ship.

Reid glared at her, then handed her the deck. "Your deal."

"Okay." She shuffled the cards and dealt. "My mother must be wor-ried sick. I told her I'd phone as soon as I landed."

"I saw you on the phone."

"I've already explained that I was calling the man we decided not to discuss."

"You phoned Dalton before your mother?"

"Why, yes. I was concerned. He said he'd be waiting for me and he wasn't. I didn't know what to think."

"Maybe his not showing up was a clue to the kind of man he is."

Jenna slapped the cards on the table. "We weren't going to discuss Dalton, remember?"

Reid cut the deck with such frenetic movements, it was a wonder the cards didn't go flying in every direction.

Jenna turned over the top card and flung it down. She hated being put in a situation in which she had to defend Dalton, but Reid refused to drop the matter. "Dalton Gray is one of the most intelligent, sensitive men I have ever known."

"He seduced my sister."

"So *you* say." When she had the opportunity, Jenna would speak to Lucy herself.

Reid stood forcefully as if he could no longer sit still. "I thought you didn't want to talk about Dalton."

"I don't. Now please sit down."

He hesitated before lowering himself into his chair. They finished their second game and played a third. Reid won all three. Jenna yawned. She was tired, upset and although she was trying to look on the bright side of her situation, it was difficult.

"I think I'll turn in for the night," she said.

"I will, too."

While Reid put the cribbage board away, Jenna stared out the window. It was still snowing hard and nothing was visible outside except swirling white. The wind howled and moaned with the pounding storm.

She closed the bedroom door, secured it with a chair and undressed. The room was bitterly cold; obviously the generator-run furnace couldn't keep pace with the falling temperature. She figured that once she was covered by the down comforter she'd be warm. Snuggling under it, she turned off the light on the bedstand.

Her mother drifted into her mind, and Jenna wished there was some way to reassure her. Then she remembered that Addy had mentioned a phone at the pump station. Turning on the light again, she climbed out of bed and opened the bedroom door. Reid glanced up from his chair, where he sat reading.

"There's a phone at the pump station?"

He looked at her a moment, then nodded.

"In the morning, I want to phone my mother."

"All right."

He'd surprised her; Jenna had expected him to argue.

"Thank you," she said, turning back to the bedroom.

"Jenna..."

She looked over her shoulder.

"It depends on the severity of the storm."

"I'm going to talk to my mother," she said with determination. Nothing was going to keep her from making that phone call.

"Let's not borrow trouble. I'll do everything within my power to get you there. You have my word on that."

He sounded sincere and she desperately wanted to believe him. "Thank you."

A half smile formed, one of regret. "I apologize for this. It was never my intention to keep you here for more than a few hours."

"I know." She didn't blame him entirely. Well, he'd had no right to kidnap her, but his reasons for doing it were obviously sincere; he'd wanted to protect her from whatever fate had befallen his sister, supposedly at Dalton's hands. Not that Jenna's life was any of his business... And she couldn't blame him for the storm. "I'll see you in the morning."

She started to close the door.

"If you get too cold, you can open the door and let some warm air in. I'm not going to attack you."

She pondered his words and shook her head. "I'll rest easier with it closed."

He grinned and she thought he said, "Me, too" but she wasn't sure.

Surprisingly, Jenna fell into a deep sleep soon after she settled back under the covers. She didn't know how long she slept before being startled awake by a loud booming noise. It sounded like an explosion of some sort or something huge crashing down. The cabin shook with the reverberation.

Bolting upright, she screamed.

It happened a second time, closer, louder. Terrified, Jenna screamed again.

"Jenna! Jenna!"

She heard Reid on the other side of the door, which was secured by the chair. The door rattled and just when she'd managed to find the lamp and turn it on, the door splintered, falling open.

Reid stumbled into the room. "What's wrong?"

She stared at him, hardly able to believe her eyes. He wore long underwear and his hair was disheveled.

"What's wrong?" he repeated.

"Something fell on the cabin!" Surely he'd heard the racket himself.

Reid placed his hands on his hips. "You mean to tell me I broke down my own bedroom door because you're afraid of a little thunder?"

"That was *thunder?*" In the middle of a snowstorm? Jenna had never heard of such a thing.

"And lightning. It occasionally happens in snowstorms."

"I…I didn't know that was possible."

"It happens," he insisted.

Jenna was in no position to argue. "I didn't know what it was." Now she felt like a fool.

Grumbling under his breath, Reid examined his shattered bedroom door.

"Sorry," she whispered. "The thunder woke me out of a sound sleep."

"Your screaming woke *me*. Scared ten years off my life. I didn't know what to think."

"All I can do is apologize."

Reid paused and wiped a hand across his face. "Want a glass of whiskey to settle your nerves? Personally I could use one." He leaned over and picked up the two pieces of the broken door and set them aside.

Jenna had never been much of a drinking woman, but as Reid had said, there were times a person needed something to settle the nerves.

"I think it might do us both good."

Chapter Seven

Reid hurriedly pulled on jeans and a shirt. Next he took two shot glasses from the kitchen cupboard, plus a bottle of his finest single malt Scotch. After the fright Jenna had given him, he needed a stiff drink. He wasn't sure liquor would help, but he needed *something,* and from the look on Jenna's face, so did she. Silently Reid cursed himself for ever having brought her to Snowbound. If he came out of this unscathed, it would be a miracle, he thought grimly. But on the other hand, he refused to deliver her or any woman to Dalton Gray.

He poured them each a finger's worth and carried both glasses into the living room. Jenna sat at one end of the sofa, her feet on the cushion's edge, chin resting on her bent knees. She looked small and shaken. A surge of guilt shot through him. He wanted to apologize again, but restrained himself; there were only so many times he could admit he'd been wrong.

"Thanks," she whispered when he handed her the drink.

Reid sat at the opposite end of the sofa and stared straight ahead. He wasn't good in this kind of situation. If he'd been able to think of some reassuring words, he would've said them. "Lightning during a snowstorm is rare, but like I told you, it does happen." That was the best he could do. Reid glanced in her direction and saw her squint as she swallowed her first sip of Scotch.

"You do this often?" she asked.

"Drink or hijack women?"

A slight smile played across her lips. "Both."

"You're the first woman I've ever brought here." The last one, too. He'd learned his lesson.

"I don't mean to be disagreeable, but I'm not flattered."

Reid wasn't sure if it was the whiskey or the fight she'd given him, but he found that amusing.

"You're actually quite nice-looking when you smile." Jenna cocked her head to one side and stared at him. "At least I think you are. It's difficult to tell with your beard."

Reid's hand went to his face. His beard was so much a part of him he didn't ever think about it. On the tundra, a beard was protection against the elements, as much protection as his hat or gloves. He explained that.

She took another sip, shuddering dramatically. "You *like* this stuff?" she asked.

"I'm not much of a drinker, and I don't often touch hard liquor," he said. "But there are occasions that call for it."

"Occasions such as having ten years shaved off your life?"

"Exactly."

She stared down at the shot glass as if she had no idea what to say next. Reid spent a great deal of his time alone and readily acknowledged that he wasn't much of a conversationalist. He found himself puzzled by the fact that he wanted to know more about Jenna. He couldn't understand why a woman who, from all outward appearances, was savvy and intelligent would link up with a rat like Dalton Gray. It didn't make sense. But sure as hell, the moment he mentioned the other man's name, Jenna would leap to Dalton's defense.

"Are you enjoying the novel?"

Reid's gaze fell on the thriller he was currently reading. "Very much."

"I read it a while back. The ending will surprise you."

Reid held up his hand. "Don't tell me."

"I wouldn't dream of ruining it for you, but I definitely predict you're going to be surprised."

"Did you figure it out?" he asked. He didn't mean to be smug, but he'd pegged the killer from the fourth chapter, and all the evidence since that point confirmed his insight. The novel was a courtroom drama in which one attorney's skill was tested against that of another. The case had gone to the jury, and the man being tried was clearly innocent. "Jones did it," Reid said.

"Jones?" Jenna had the audacity to laugh at him. "He's the prosecuting attorney."

"I know who he is. No wonder he's working so hard to convict Adam Johnson."

"Oh, puleeze."

"That's what all the evidence tells me. Why else would Jones be covering his tracks the way he has?"

She shook her head. "To be fair, I thought it was him, too. At first…"

"You mean it isn't?"

She pantomimed zipping her lips closed.

Reid wanted to reach for the book and turn to the last page to prove her wrong, but that would've been childish. Besides, having already read the story, she was in a position to know.

"Look at you," she said, sounding absolutely delighted.

"What?"

"You're trying to figure out who else it might be."

She was right. That was exactly what he'd been doing.

"Tell me about Addy and Palmer," Jenna said.

They were a thorn in his side and—at the same time—two of his greatest friends. "Addy and Palmer both came up to work on the pipeline a hundred years ago, made big money, blew their wad and then stayed in the state. Pretty soon, they were drifting from town to town. They settled here because they knew Jake and he gave them enough work to keep them occupied and out of trouble."

"They seem harmless enough."

Reid nodded. "They are certainly characters."

Jenna laughed softly. "Did you see the look on Addy's face when I scooped up a ladle full of stew? I thought his eyes were going to bug out of his head."

"That was just his way of warning you not to take more than your fair share."

"So I assumed."

"Anybody else you want to know about?"

"Tell me about Jim and Lucy." They were the only married couple in town. She'd seen a few men wandering around before the storm hit. Since then, everyone seemed to have hunkered down to wait it out.

"Well, you already met Jim."

"You wanted me to stay with him and your sister, didn't you?"

Reid shrugged. So much for the best-laid plans. "Yeah, but Lucy was in Fairbanks and now Jim's there, too. What would you like to know about them?"

She looked unsure. "Addy told me Lucy agreed to marry Jim and live here only if she could return to Fairbanks every so often."

"That's true. Lucy says it's because she's the only woman in Snowbound."

A one-woman town. "She must be lonely."

"Nah, Addy and Palmer are company for her—"

"Addy and Palmer," Jenna repeated, sounding incredulous. "They're *men*."

Reid couldn't see why that made any difference. "I'm here, too." She ignored that.

"Lucy must crave female companionship. She's way up here, completely isolated from her friends and everything that's convenient and familiar. I don't know how she does it."

Reid hadn't thought of it that way.

"No wonder she flies into Fairbanks every chance she gets."

"She only goes about once a month. She might fly in more often now that she's pregnant."

"She's *pregnant?*"

"Only a few months. She's got Jim flying in all kinds of equipment for that baby. I had no idea babies needed that much stuff." Actually Reid was thrilled for his sister and her husband.

"I haven't met Lucy yet, but already I admire her," Jenna said solemnly.

Now that he considered it, his sister did deserve a lot of credit. Moving to Snowbound couldn't have been easy for her. Lucy invited him to dinner once a week, but he'd never realized how lonely she must be for female friends.

"She obviously loves Jim very much." Jenna said this with unmistakable awe.

"She does." The conversation was growing a bit uncomfortable for Reid. He didn't understand women, not even his sister. Romance had never played a large role in his life. Most women seemed mysterious and temperamental—as much a mystery to him as the novel he was reading. Still, he *liked* women; he adored Lucy and he had several female friends, including Susan Webster in Fairbanks, whom he met for dinner every once in a while. Even his one semi-serious relationship had ended without pain or suffering on either side.

And Reid had to admit he enjoyed talking to Jenna; when they managed to avoid the subject of Dalton, they were able to find common ground without difficulty.

"Care to play another game of cribbage?" he asked. Now that he was awake, he wasn't the least bit sleepy.

"No, thanks. I think I'll go back to bed."

He didn't let his disappointment show. "I'll put the door in place for you."

She took another sip of the liquor and blinked away tears.

Reid found it difficult not to smile.

"I am sorry about the door," she said carefully as she took her empty glass to the tiny kitchen.

"I was the one who tore it down."

"Yes, I know, but I shouldn't have put a chair under the doorknob. Other than holding me captive, you seem to be an honorable man."

"Except for that one minor detail."

"Right." But she was smiling when she said it.

The oddest sensation came over him. It was as though Jenna's smile had traveled all the way through his body. He actually *felt* it. He wasn't the most intuitive of men, but he sensed that this smile offered his absolution. A forgiveness of sorts…an understanding.

He didn't want their night to end. He didn't want her to go to bed, to leave him alone with his thoughts—and his yearnings. Unfortunately he couldn't think of any way to stop her.

"Don't bother about the door," Jenna said. "Since it's in two pieces."

She had a point. "I don't suppose it would help much if someone wanted to break in. Not that anyone's going to." He hoped to convey that she was perfectly safe with him.

"Night, Reid."

He lingered in the doorway with his hands in his pockets. "Night." As he turned away, he heard the mattress shift and realized she was already back in bed. His bed. He tried not to think about that—her hair spread out on his pillow, his blankets covering her…. Reluctantly he returned to his makeshift bed on the sofa, which was less than comfortable. Lying down, he tucked his hands behind his head and closed his eyes.

Try as he might, he couldn't sleep. He kept thinking about Jenna and the way her smile had affected him. It was a small thing—and yet it wasn't. Maybe he was going soft in the head. He recalled when Jim and his sister had first met. His friend walked around town wearing a funny grin, and flew into Fairbanks so often people began to wonder how he could still manage his job. Then before Reid understood what was happening, Jim had asked Lucy to be his wife, and his sister was living in Snowbound.

A sleepless hour passed and then he heard Jenna climb out of bed. The mattress squeaked, followed by the sound of her feet shuffling on the floor.

"Jenna?" he called in a loud whisper.

She didn't respond for a moment. "I didn't wake you, did I?"

"No," he said. "I can't get back to sleep."

"Me, neither." She padded into the darkened room. "Don't turn on the lights, all right?"

He frowned. "Why not?"

Again she hesitated. "I don't know… It's more…relaxed with them off."

"Okay." He sat up.

"Do you mind if we talk for a few minutes?"

Mind? Of course he didn't mind. "What do you want to talk about?"

She sat on the corner of the sofa in the same position she'd assumed earlier, feet up, knees bent. "I want to ask you something."

Reid hoped it wouldn't be a personal question; he wasn't good at answering those. "Fire away," he muttered.

She didn't speak immediately, and when she did, her question took him by surprise. "Why do you live up here so isolated from the world?"

"You mean in Alaska or in Snowbound?"

"Snowbound."

That was easy enough. "I work here."

"Monitoring the pump station for the pipeline?"

"Yes." It was a good job and he enjoyed his work.

"What exactly do you do?"

"For eight hours every day, I'm at the station monitoring the flow of crude oil. It might not sound involved, but it actually is."

"Do you have a lot of free time?"

"Some." He didn't elaborate.

"How do you spend it? Doing what?"

Reid paused. She was right; talking in the dark was more relaxed, but even in the anonymity of the night, there were certain subjects that left him uneasy.

"Is that such a difficult question?" she asked, a smile in her voice.

"No, it's just that I never told anyone—none of my family or friends."

"It's a secret?"

"Not exactly, but it's private." He wished he knew how to turn the conversation in a different direction, but verbal maneuvers had never been his forte.

Jenna's voice rose with enthusiasm. "Now I'm fascinated."

"Tell me something about you first."

"Me? No fair. We're discussing you."

"Tell me a secret. Something few people know about you."

"I don't have any secrets," she insisted.

"You do. Everyone has secrets."

"All right." She sighed, and Reid could see she wasn't happy about this. "I bit my nails until I was sixteen."

"Now *that's* shocking."

She slapped playfully at him and managed to graze his elbow.

Reid chuckled. "You really are an innocent, aren't you?"

"It's men," she said, speaking in a whisper. "I don't have what it takes to attract them."

"How do you mean?"

"Oh, I don't know. Look at me—I'm thirty-one and the only successful relationship I've ever had was over the Internet. I think there must be something seriously wrong with me."

Oh, boy. Reid was stumbling into territory he had no desire to explore. It did explain why she'd sought out Dalton Gray, though. She was getting desperate and afraid, and a man, especially one she'd met online, must have seemed safe. Little did she know she was about to tangle with a tundra rat.

"I'm like everyone else. I want a husband and family but I just don't know how to attract a man."

"And that's why you're in Alaska."

She didn't confirm or deny the statement. The words fell between them, and then she seemed to gather herself emotionally, reminding him it was his turn. "What's *your* deep, dark secret?"

Reid wasn't ready to drop the matter. "Why, Jenna? I don't understand it. You're a beautiful, desirable woman." It probably wasn't good manners to admit that, especially while they were sitting in the dark, both of them a little tipsy.

"I'd rather not discuss me anymore, okay?"

That was a problem, because Reid wasn't eager to drag his private life into the open, either. "I need another drink."

"Me, too," she said. As he got up to refill their glasses, she added, "Don't think you're going to escape from telling me your secret."

He returned a couple of minutes later and they sat beside each other on the sofa, so close their shoulders touched.

"Does it have to do with being spurned by a woman?" she asked in a low voice. "Or did you commit a crime? Or—"

His nervousness made him laugh. "Not exactly. Okay, here's my secret. You asked me what I do with my free time. Well, I draw. I'm—"

"What?" she demanded, outraged.

"I said I like to draw. Especially landscapes. I—"

"You mean to say being an *artist* is your deep, dark secret?" She set aside her drink and got to her feet. "I should've known you'd pull something like this. I spill my guts, tell you how hopeless I am with men and you—you tell me you like to draw."

Reid stood, too. "Well, I'm sorry, but that really is my biggest secret."

"You're making fun of me."

He caught her by the shoulders. "I'm not. I swear I'm not. I've had a knack since I was a kid, but I never did anything with it and now... I guess I'm not ready to tell anyone because I'm not sure I'm any good, beyond having a...superficial facility, I suppose you could say." He shrugged. "I'm not ready to have my work judged."

He ran his hands over the curve of her shoulders. With all his heart he wanted her to understand he wasn't teasing her. "I draw, Jenna, and that's the honest-to-God truth."

"This is baring your soul?"

"I've never told anyone about it before." He'd fumbled this whole conversation.

"No one else in Snowbound knows? Not even your sister?"

"No one."

"Oh." Her response was the merest whisper.

His fingers relaxed against her shoulders. She felt so small and soft and utterly feminine. His pulse started to react to her nearness—the first sign he was in trouble—but he didn't break away from her. He knew he should drop his hands and back off before he did something they'd both regret. Instead he drew her closer. He refused to listen to common sense, which was ordering him to stop. Ignoring all caution, Reid lowered his mouth to hers.

Jenna leaned into him. A tiny sound came from her just before their lips touched, but for the life of him Reid didn't know if it was a sigh of welcome or a groan of protest. Either way, she was in his arms and she seemed willing enough to be there. He fully intended to follow through with this.

The instant their mouths connected, Reid swore he felt something explode inside him. Jenna must have felt it, too, because the next thing he knew, they were both sitting on the sofa again, their arms locked around each other. His fingers were in her hair, and hers were tugging at his shirt collar. It took him far longer than he wanted to collect his wits and move away.

Breathing hard, Jenna hung her head.

Reid was having a difficult time recovering his own breath. He thought she might want an apology, but it simply wasn't in him to find any regret.

"That shouldn't have happened," she said sternly.

Unable to speak, he simply nodded.

"That kind of...physical contact is asking for trouble."

"Right." Thankfully one of them was smart enough to recognize that. "Do you want me to apologize?" he asked warily.

She thought about it, then shook her head. "I was as much at fault as you."

Reid reached for his drink. He needed it, even more than he had the first one. As he'd told her, she'd taken ten years off his life, frightening him the way she had, and now he'd easily subtracted another ten by kissing her. If he spent much more time with Jenna Campbell, he'd be dead inside a week.

"I think the best thing I can do is go back to the bedroom. In the morning we'll both forget about this...indiscretion. Agreed?"

"Agreed." He was grateful, too, although he didn't say so.

She stood. "Um…I probably shouldn't tell you this—and my experience is pretty limited—but you're a very good kisser."

Reid didn't know if it would be proper etiquette to thank her, so again he said nothing.

She rubbed her finger across her upper lip and he realized his beard had probably grazed her tender skin. "I didn't hurt you, did I?"

"No, your mustache tickled me. That's all."

"Sorry."

"Good night, Reid."

"Good night. The storm probably won't be so bad in the morning and you can make that phone call to your mother."

"I'd appreciate it."

Just before she went into the bedroom, she stopped. "Is your artwork at the pump station?"

"Some of it."

"Would you mind showing me your pictures?"

He hesitated, then figured he might as well. "Sure."

"Thank you."

"I'll talk to you in the morning." He waited until she disappeared into the darkness of the bedroom before he lay down on the sofa. This time when he closed his eyes all he could see, feel and taste was Jenna.

Chapter Eight

Jenna woke at first light and memory came flooding back. Not only had she revealed her deepest fears to Reid Jamison, she'd welcomed his kisses. Even more damning, she'd *enjoyed* them. She'd read about people in instances such as this—instances in which captives fell in love with their captors. It was called the Stockholm syndrome. Except that Reid appeared to be as regretful over these unfortunate circumstances as she was.

She could hear him moving about the cabin and the smell of freshly brewed coffee wafted in from the other room. Jenna hurriedly dressed and combed her hair.

"Good morning," she said, entering the small kitchen.

"Morning." He kept his back to her. "Would you like a cup of coffee?"

"Please." Something wasn't right. Reid seemed to make a point of not facing her. "Reid?"

He turned then and she saw that he'd shaved off his beard. "When did you do that?" she asked, although the real question was *why.* He was the one who'd stressed the importance of a beard for an Alaskan male.

"This morning," he barked.

"There's no need to snap at me." He was in a horrible mood, and she'd done nothing more than walk from one room to the next. "Why'd you do it?"

"Hell if I know. And it wasn't for you, if that's what you're thinking." He slapped a mug of coffee down on the table, half of it sloshing over the sides.

"Did someone get up on the wrong side of the bed this morning?" she asked in a singsong voice.

"I didn't sleep in a bed, as I might remind you."

"And why is that?" she asked sweetly. "Could it be because you offered your one and only bed to your kidnap victim?"

He scowled at her. "The storm's still raging, but we'll head out anyway."

"Can I drink my coffee first?"

"Fine," he said gruffly, stomping out of the room. He reached for his coat and shoved his arms into the sleeves. It took him another five minutes to lace up his boots and add the extra protective gear. "I'll be back in a few minutes. Be ready to go when I return."

"Yes, sir." She saluted him smartly.

He paused to glare at her. "Don't get cute with me, Jenna. I'm not in the mood for it."

"Now, just one minute." Jenna had endured enough of his temper tantrum. "I don't know what's wrong with you this morning, but I suggest you get over it. If anyone has the right to be annoyed, it's me. I'm not holding *you* hostage."

"You're not a hostage! Trust me, if I knew how to get you safely out of here, I'd do it."

"And I'd go, partying all the way."

He snorted loudly and threw open the door.

A blast of cold air enveloped her, sending a chill up her spine and spraying the room with fresh snow. Snuggling under her blankets, all warm in bed, she'd fantasized about Reid and their kisses. The charm of those few moments had been a fluke and any lingering pleasure had best be forgotten. He slammed the door, which only seemed to emphasize her decision.

Between tentative sips of hot coffee, she hurriedly dressed in her warmest clothes before Reid had any reason to change his mind about that phone call. No sooner was she finished than he came back into the cabin.

"You ready?"

"Ready," she said, echoing his clipped tone.

Reid hesitated. "Addy and Palmer saw me warming up the snowmobile." He glanced at her. "It seems Jake and Pete and the two of them plan to come over here for dinner tonight."

"I hope you don't expect me to do the cooking."

"No," he said, disgruntled. "I'll cook, but I wanted you to be aware of what they were planning."

"All right." Frankly she'd welcome the company. It would certainly be preferable to another evening trapped inside the cabin with Mr. Personality.

"Addy intends to bring his musical saw and Palmer plays the harmonica—and well, they're probably all going to want to dance with you. I just thought I should give you fair warning."

"I've been duly and properly warned."

"Good." He paused before opening the door. "You'd better take my arm. I know you'd rather not, but for safety reasons you should. Technically it isn't a blizzard anymore, since the wind's down to thirty-one miles an hour, but it's still damn strong."

She slipped her arm through his and once outside, was grateful she had. Blizzard or not, the snow was thick and falling fast. The road was barely recognizable and drifts had formed against the sides of the house, stretching up toward the roofline.

"You okay?" Reid asked as they approached the snowmobile.

"I'm fine."

The pump station seemed to be half a world away. Driving slowly and carefully they made it, but Jenna could feel the tension in Reid. She didn't reveal her own apprehensions.

Inside the station, Reid led her into his office. The man was a constant source of contradictions. His house was an environmental disaster area, but his office couldn't be neater. It didn't stop there, either. He was unreasonable, demanding, bad-tempered and yet he'd kissed her with a gentleness that had practically melted her bones. He barked at her as if he was angry and then risked everything to get her to a phone so she could reassure her mother.

The telephone line was bad. Jenna heard heavy static as she waited anxiously for the number to connect to her mother's cell phone in California. When the first ring came, Jenna relaxed.

"Hello," the familiar voice said.

"Mom, it's Jenna."

"Jenna! Hello, honey! I was wondering when I'd hear from you. How's Alaska?"

"It's great, Mom." No need to worry her, Jenna decided.

"Why didn't you call earlier? Still, I'm glad you called now. I'm having a pedicure and you know how boring it is just to sit here." Jenna heard a little snuffling sound and realized her mother must be baby-sitting Bam-Bam, her neighbor's Pomeranian. Chloe found this the perfect way to have a pet—the benefits of companionship without the responsibilities of meals, vets or training.

"Well, honey," she said. "Tell me what's been going on."

Jenna hardly knew where to start.

"That Dalton friend of yours phoned," her mother announced before Jenna could tell her anything.

"Dalton called for me?" Her heart pounded crazily.

"He sounded worried."

"When was that?" Jenna pressed the phone hard against her ear, straining to make out every word.

"Oh, dear," her mother said, sighing. "I can't remember. You know how bad I am with details like that."

"Mom, I'm in Snowbound, Alaska. If Dalton phones again, tell him that right away." She glared at Reid, defying him to challenge her. She'd find her own way out of here, since she obviously couldn't depend on him.

"Snowbound, Alaska," her mother echoed. "Oh, that sounds romantic."

"Tell me everything Dalton said," Jenna insisted. He might be her only chance of escape.

"Let me think." Jenna could hear her mother tapping her fingernail against her teeth. "Well, I don't remember all of it, only that he was in Fairbanks and you weren't. We talked for a few minutes. He's very concerned about you."

"I'm with a man called Reid Jamison, Mom. If Dalton calls again, you tell him that, all right?" Reid stared at her, but he said nothing.

"Sure, honey. I'll do that. Are you having fun?"

"Yeah, Mom. Lots of fun. I just didn't want you to worry."

"Worry? Jenna, why would I do that? Well, okay, I was a *little* worried. But you're perfectly capable of taking care of yourself."

How Jenna wished that was true.

The line faded in and out. "Mom…Mom?"

"I'm here. Oh, before I forget, Brad Fulton's new secretary called asking about you, too."

"Brad phoned?" Jenna was hardly able to take it all in. "What did he say?" she asked eagerly.

"Not Brad," her mother said. "His new secretary who, if you don't mind my saying so, isn't worth a hill of beans compared to you. She's the one who phoned."

"What did Ms. Spencer want?"

"Apparently Mr. Fulton's looking for you."

"Brad's looking for me?"

"According to Ms. Spencer, he wants you back."

Jenna bit her lower lip. She had no idea what to think—or say.

"Is there anything you want me to tell him?" her mother asked. "Because I'm sure he'll be contacting me himself."

"Oh, Mom, I don't know." Jenna had wasted years being infatuated with her boss. In all that time, Brad hadn't seen her as anything other than an efficient and capable assistant, and she suspected that wasn't going to change now. Brad viewed her the same way he would a comfortable pair of shoes. As soon as he broke in a new pair, he'd forget about her. Besides, Brad was married to his job. He didn't need or want a wife.

The connection started to fade. "Mom?" she shouted. "Mom?"

"I can't hear you. Jenna? Jenna? You're fading out."

"Mom, I'm here."

"Oh, good, that's better," her mother said. "Okay, now what should I tell Dalton if he phones again? Oh, heavens, what was the name of that town?"

"Snowbound."

"And you're with some other man?"

"Yes, Reid Jamison."

"My goodness, Jenna, Alaska must be some kind of state. You haven't been there three days, and already you've got two men on the line. Maybe I should come up and check it out myself."

"Mom…no, don't do that."

The line went dead. Emotionally drained, Jenna replaced the receiver.

Reid stepped back and crossed his arms over his chest. "Who's Brad?"

Jenna frowned at him. "Although it's none of your business, Mr. Fulton is my former boss."

He let that information sink in. "Now I know why you hooked up with Dalton," he muttered.

She raised her eyes to meet his. "Why?"

"You're in love with your boss."

Chapter Nine

Chloe Lyman shook her cell phone in a desperate effort to hear her daughter. "Jenna. Jenna?"

Alas, there was nothing but static and then a droning sound that confirmed the connection had been severed. "Oh, drat!" Chloe pushed the button to turn off her cell. Tucking the Pomeranian more securely under her arm, she tossed the phone inside her huge purse and sat back, trying to relax. Bam-Bam snuggled close to her side.

"Everything all right?" Dolly, her nail tech, asked, coming into the spa room.

"That was Jenna."

"Oh, you heard from her?"

"I'm telling you, Dolly, I don't know what's come over that girl. It's like she hit thirty-one and decided to dive into the deep end of the pool without any swimming lessons."

"Jenna? I don't think you need to worry. She has a good head on her shoulders."

"Had," Chloe corrected.

Dolly lifted Chloe's foot out of the swirling water and wrapped it in a fluffy white towel, propping it in her lap.

"She hasn't been in Alaska three days and already she's involved with two men."

Dolly looked up, astonished. "Jenna?"

"Not only that." Chloe dropped her voice, so none of the other women in the salon would overhear. "Brad Fulton wants her back. Apparently he's lost without her."

"He never appreciated everything she did."

"You're absolutely right!" Chloe had been saying as much for years. Jenna had refused to listen to her suggestions for luring her boss into a romantic liaison. Unlike Jenna, Chloe had never had a problem enticing men into her bed. But then again, Jenna hadn't gone through two husbands by age thirty.

"Did she meet up with the man she's been talking to on the Internet?"

Chloe frowned as she mentally reviewed their all-too-short conversation. "No, she's with some other guy in a town with a funny name—something like Snowdrift. For the life of me, I can't remember what it was."

"Jenna's already got two men. Wow. Alaska must be something else."

Chloe's smile was slow and thoughtful. "Three men," she reminded Dolly. "Remember Brad Fulton."

Dolly dried Chloe's foot. "I think the competition will do him good."

Chloe nodded. "You're right. As soon as I'm done here, I'm going to visit Mr. Fulton."

"I thought you were banned from the building."

Chloe sighed gustily. "That was an unfortunate misunderstanding. Trust me," she said, leaning back in the comfortable chair. "He'll be more than happy to see me—this time."

"Two men," Dolly said in a dreamy voice. "I wonder if Jenna knows what to do with two men."

Chloe giggled. "If she's anything like her mother, she'll figure it out."

An hour later, dressed in her skimpy high heels with cotton balls between her freshly painted red toenails and the Pomeranian under her arm, Chloe Lyman clip-clopped her way through the executive lobby on the seventy-seventh floor of the Fulton Industries building.

"I'm here to see Mr. Fulton," she announced to the receptionist.

"I'm sorry, we have a no-animal policy in this office building."

"Oh," Chloe said, hating the other woman's superior attitude. "Next time I'll leave Bam-Bam at home with his mommy. But I believe Mr. Fulton will make an exception this once, especially when he learns why I'm here."

The woman frowned. "And your name is?"

"Chloe Lyman." She paused for effect. "I'm Jenna Campbell's mother."

The woman's attitude change was instantaneous. "Oh, hello..."

"Hello," Chloe smiled sweetly, letting her know there were no hard feelings despite her lack of welcome earlier.

The receptionist looked around, then lowered her voice. "Everyone misses Jenna. I do hope she's coming back soon."

Chloe played dumb. "I wouldn't know about that. Do you think Mr. Fulton would be willing to see me?"

"I'll find out right away." She pushed a button and spoke to Brad Fulton's new executive assistant.

No more than a minute later, the large double oak doors opened and an older woman bustled through. "Ms. Lyman, I believe we spoke earlier."

"We did," Chloe confirmed.

"Mr. Fulton only has a couple of minutes, but he said he'd see you."

Chloe hadn't thought for an instant that he'd turn her away. "I knew he would." She trotted after Ms. Spencer. As soon as she entered the inner sanctum, Bam-Bam growled.

"Shh." Chloe hushed the dog, who'd apparently taken an immediate dislike to Jenna's former boss.

"Ms. Lyman." Brad stood up behind his massive desk as she entered his office. "It's, uh, good to see you."

"You, too," she responded although it was a lie. She'd never cared for this man, who appeared to be utterly blind when it came to her daughter.

"I understand you have some information regarding Jenna."

"I do." She sat down in the leather chair reserved for visitors and crossed her long legs. Bam-Bam settled nicely in her lap but kept his eyes on the evil man.

"Is she in Alaska?"

"Yes."

"Did she mention where?"

"Oh, yes. It's just a small town. I bought a map and looked it up before I stopped by." She'd checked all the places beginning with "snow," which made it easy to find. "Did you know Alaska has more than three million lakes?"

"No," he returned impatiently.

"Well, it's true," she said with a little nod.

As though he recognized that he wasn't going to extract the information easily, Brad Fulton sank into his chair. He steepled his fingers beneath his chin and waited.

This was more like it. Chloe enjoyed being the center of attention and she intended to take advantage of it.

"Why Alaska?" Fulton asked.

Chloe shrugged while she dug a dog cookie out of her purse and fed it to Bam-Bam. "It might have something to do with the men there."

"Men?"

"My daughter is like most women her age. She wants a husband and family. She chose a state where she'd have any number of eligible men vying for her affections."

Fulton frowned. "Are you saying she's involved with more than one?"

"Apparently that's the case. She's already mentioned two who are interested in her." It was gratifying to see him clench his jaw.

"I see."

Chloe sighed expressively. "I don't know if she's chosen one over the other. We only spoke briefly."

Fulton stood. "Are you going to tell me where Jenna is or not?"

Chloe fed Bam-Bam a second cookie. The Pomeranian gobbled it down, all the while keeping his gaze fixed on Fulton. "Ask and you shall receive."

"I'm asking."

Chloe smiled mysteriously…and let him wait. "Jenna's in a little town called Snowbound," she finally said. "Isn't that something? Snowbound, Alaska."

Brad Fulton pressed the button for his secretary. "Ms. Spencer," he thundered. "Have my private jet readied for me."

"Right away, sir," the secretary's faint voice returned.

"You're going after her?" Chloe was too excited to hide her feelings.

"I need Jenna."

It was all she could do to keep from clapping with delight. "Bring her home, Mr. Fulton, bring my daughter home."

For the first time since she'd entered his office, Brad Fulton smiled. "I plan to do exactly that."

"Good." With her mission accomplished, Chloe got to her feet. "Then I'll leave you to your task." She cuddled Bam-Bam in her arms and headed out the doors. Suddenly remembering, she said. "Oh—I believe she's with a man named Reid Jamison."

Fulton wrote that down. "I'll have her home within a couple of days."

"Thank you." Chloe let him know how grateful she was. "You won't be sorry."

He had that determined look about him. The last time she'd seen it, he'd had her escorted from his office. That happened the week he'd hired Jenna, but Chloe recognized it even after all these years.

"You're aware of what Jenna wants?" She probably shouldn't force the issue, but Chloe wanted it understood that her daughter's demands had to be met. If he didn't accept Jenna's terms, then he'd be wasting his time. "My daughter is looking for a husband."

"Yes." He wasn't happy about it, but he seemed willing to comply.

Chloe smiled and petted Bam-Bam's head. "Don't worry. You don't need to call me Mom."

Fulton scowled. "I have no intention of calling you anything other than Ms. Lyman."

She didn't let this bother her. "Whatever makes you comfortable...Brad."

Judging by the way his lip rose in a snarl, it might be a good idea for Chloe to make her exit. "I'll see you soon."

He muttered something about anytime being much too soon, but Chloe let it pass. Fulton was going to bring Jenna home, and that was what mattered. By Christmas she'd be mother-in-law to one of the richest men in America.

"Have a good day," she said cordially to Gail Spencer as she tripped out of the office.

"Oh, yes. Thank you so much for stopping by."

In the elevator, Chloe realized she couldn't allow her daughter to make the most important decision of her life without her mother there to guide her. She toyed with the idea of asking Brad Fulton to take her with him. But common sense prevailed. The man had never been fond of her and he wouldn't agree to fly her to Alaska. Especially if it meant they'd be in the same plane.

No, Chloe was going to have to find her own way to Snowbound. Well, she could do that. She wasn't as helpless as her five husbands— and even her daughter—assumed.

Chloe was about to show them all.

Chapter Ten

Jenna kept her hand on the telephone receiver for a moment after the connection was broken. Away from her mother for three days, and already she missed her terribly.

"You okay?" Reid asked, sounding genuinely concerned. His bad temper had disappeared the same mysterious way it'd appeared that morning.

"I'm fine... It was just so good to speak to my mother." She turned away, fearing she might embarrass them both by bursting into tears. Alaska was nothing like she'd expected. The snow didn't bother her; in fact, there was a certain beauty in that. Even the blizzard hadn't disturbed her too much. Blackie had, but she'd lived to recount the tale of her encounter with the bear.

The isolation was a shock. Dalton hadn't prepared her for that aspect of life in the forty-ninth state—the isolation and the vastness.

All her dreams of Alaska had been wrapped up in her fantasies about Dalton. They'd exchanged messages every day, and she'd let herself believe he was everything he'd claimed to be. She was beginning to suspect he wasn't, but she refused to admit that to Reid.

This was what she got for being so desperate for—what? for *love*— that she was willing to risk her whole future, just like that. Could she have been any more naive?

"You ready to go back?" Reid asked.

Jenna nodded.

Reid gave her his arm and they headed into the storm. The wind and the snow stung her face. Jenna closed her eyes and allowed Reid to lead her to the hangar, where he'd parked the snowmobile. It wasn't until she was safely inside that Reid broached the subject of her former boss.

"When you said you had trouble attracting men, you were talking about your old boss, weren't you?"

She stared outside at the swirling snow and didn't answer.

"It's fairly obvious."

"Listen, Reid, it isn't the middle of the night and we aren't sitting in the dark, drinking Scotch and sharing secrets."

"Now look who's testy."

"I have a right," she flared.

"Okay, okay, sorry I asked."

He should be.

They rode in silence all the way back to Reid's cabin. As soon as they'd pulled into the enclosure, he got off and plugged the snowmobile into the heating element. As if by magic, Addy and Palmer appeared. They were both dressed in heavy coats and hats with earflaps hanging loose.

"'Morning, Jenna," Addy said as he helped her climb off the snowmobile.

Palmer stood directly behind him. "You cooking tonight or is Reid?"

"I am," Reid barked.

"Spaghetti for sure," Addy said with a disgruntled expression. "It's the only thing he knows how to cook."

"Are you makin' it with moose meat again?"

"I'll cook with whatever is in the freezer."

"Moose," Addy and Palmer said simultaneously.

Jenna wouldn't have minded cooking for the guys, but she didn't want Reid to assume she'd willingly take over all domestic tasks.

"I'll play you a game of cribbage," she told Reid. "Loser does the cooking."

"If I win, you cook?"

Jenna nodded.

He grinned, and without his mustache and beard blocking the view, she realized he had a very nice smile. "You're on."

Addy and Palmer instantly crowded around Reid, leaving Jenna to trudge to the house alone. Reid hurried around to meet her, Addy and Palmer close behind.

"There are ways to cheat so she won't know what you're doing," Addy murmured under his breath.

"Boys." Reid whirled around to face them. "Dinner's at six. We'll see you then. Understand?"

Addy's and Palmer's mouths gaped open. "You saying you don't want us around?" Palmer asked.

"You might need our help. We watched last month when Pete beat you at cribbage. This is too important, Reid! You can't lose this time."

"Yeah, Reid," Palmer said in a pleading voice. "This is important. You can't lose."

Reid slapped them each on the back in a good-natured way. "I'm saying let Jenna and me work this out for ourselves. Whatever happens, you're going to be served a mighty fine dinner."

This seemed to appease the two men. "Can't ask for more than that," Addy told his friend.

"You want us to tell Pete and Jake to come here at six?"

"Good idea."

On a mission now, both men hightailed it over to the café.

Reid helped Jenna through the snowdrifts to the cabin door. "The guys don't mean any harm," he said as soon as they were inside.

"I know. They must be tired of their own cooking."

"I don't think either of them knows how. They eat everything out of tin cans," he explained.

The image that took shape in Jenna's mind produced an instant smile. She found Reid watching her, grinning, too. She *wanted* to be angry with him for ruining her plans, but she'd discovered it was impossible to maintain her irritation for very long.

Once they'd removed their coats, hats and gloves, Reid set up the cribbage board while Jenna made fresh coffee and poured it.

"Everything's ready," he said when she brought their coffee to the table.

Jenna pulled out a chair and sat down, sipping from her mug as she surveyed the board. "Are you planning to cheat?"

"Don't need to. I beat the socks off you the last time we played."

Jenna scoffed at him. "Nothing but a fluke, my friend."

Reid pushed the cards to her side of the table. "Deal 'em and weep."

She wasn't sure how Reid managed it, but she had one terrible hand after another. He was well on his way to winning before she'd rounded the last turn.

He didn't say anything as he triumphantly planted his peg over the finish line.

Jenna muttered under her breath. "Want to play two out of three?"

"That wasn't our bargain."

"What if I said I'm not all that great a cook?"

Reid leaned back in his chair and crossed his arms over his chest. "I wouldn't believe you."

"And why not?"

He didn't hesitate. "I may only have known you a short while, but in that time I've learned something about you."

This Jenna wanted to hear. "What's that?"

Reid wore a smug look, the same look that had annoyed her earlier but now amused her. "You'd never offer to do something you weren't qualified for."

He was right.

"Do you want to check out the freezer?" he asked.

"Looks like I don't have any choice." She pretended to be disgruntled about this turn of events, but she wasn't. In truth, cooking the evening meal for practically the entire Snowbound community gave her a genuine sense of purpose.

Reid settled down with his novel while she flipped through the only cookbook he had on the shelf. It must have belonged to his mother because it was nearly thirty years old. Sorting through the recipes, she found several that looked appetizing.

The freezer had an abundant supply of seafood, and she took out clams, shrimp, crab and scallops, plus several loaves of frozen French bread. She laid everything out on the kitchen counter to thaw.

"What are you making, or is that another one of your secrets?" He lowered his book.

"Dinner," she said.

"Very funny."

"I'm glad you're amused."

He raised his book again. "You really do have to have the last word, don't you?" he muttered.

Jenna had never realized that about herself, but suspected he was right. From this point forward, she determined that she'd make an effort to respond to any unpleasant or teasing conversation with dignity.

That decided, she set to work. She tucked a dish towel into the waist of her jeans and rolled up her shirtsleeves. She collected the rest of the ingredients, impressed by Reid's well-stocked cupboards. Onions, chopped garlic in a jar, a choice of pastas, dried herbs... The next time she looked up, she found him napping.

What a complex person Reid Jamison was, Jenna mused, studying him. Rarely had any man made her so angry. Nor had anyone ever frustrated her more. He could be arrested for what he'd done, but she'd never press charges. Despite her frequent annoyance with him, she actually *liked* Reid and enjoyed his company.

Unfortunately, his companionship wasn't the only thing she enjoyed, but she absolutely refused to dwell on their kisses. They were both eager to admit it had been a mistake, something best ignored. And forgotten. Jenna, however, had been unable to put it out of her mind. Try as she might, the memory resurfaced at the most inappropriate times.

Concentrating on dinner, Jenna had everything cut up and ready to go, plus she'd cleaned up the cabin a bit. Nothing major. As she'd explained to Reid, she wasn't about to become his maid, but his friends were arriving and pride demanded that there be a degree of order and cleanliness. When she'd finished, it was late afternoon.

Reid watched her bustle about, which unsettled Jenna when she noticed.

"Need anything?" he asked, slowly emerging from his chair.

"Cooking wine."

He shrugged. "Any wine I have is for drinking."

"That will do."

"How much do you need?"

Jenna checked the recipe. "Just a cup."

Reid rummaged in the room's one closet and came out with a bottle of white wine. "It seems a shame to open it, then let it go to waste. Would you like some?"

"Please." Jenna was far more accustomed to wine than whiskey.

Reid poured them each a glass of the chardonnay and gave her the rest of the bottle.

"I thought we'd have a salad," she said. "Do you think Pete would have lettuce at his store?"

"Not in the wintertime, unfortunately. Fresh fruit and vegetables are almost unheard of up here for most of the year. Supplies are shipped in once during the summer and other than that, we get everything either canned or frozen with a few exceptions."

"I found onions and potatoes in the pantry."

"Those are the exceptions."

"That's too bad." Their meal wouldn't be quite the same without a Caesar salad.

"Lucy makes a nice salad from frozen veggies. You could ask her when she returns."

Reid would be flying her back to Fairbanks at the first opportunity, but Jenna sincerely hoped there'd be a chance to meet Lucy.

"You're looking thoughtful," Reid commented.

"I was thinking about Lucy and how much I'd like to talk to her."

"The storm could be over as soon as tomorrow afternoon. Do you want to wait until Lucy and Jim get home before we take off?"

She nodded immediately. "I'd like that."

"Good, because Lucy would probably have my hide if you left before she got back."

Jenna sipped her wine and as she did, another thought came to her. "Do you have any rum?"

"Rum? Do you think I run a liquor store here?"

"Sorry, I should've asked for it when I requested the wine, but it just occurred to me. My third stepfather liked rum cake and Mom used to bake one or two a month. I thought it would be a real treat for Addy and Palmer. I know the recipe by heart, but it would help if I used real rum."

Shaking his head, he returned to the closet and ransacked it noisily. Eventually he pulled out a dusty bottle, handing it over.

"I don't know how old this is," he muttered. "But it's the good stuff."

"Thanks. I'm sure it will do nicely."

She set about mixing the cake batter, using his supplies of flour, sugar and liquid eggs. Working efficiently, Jenna was surprised by how contented she felt. When she glanced up, she saw Reid watching her with a pad and pencil in his hand.

"What are you drawing?"

"You."

Jenna wasn't sure how she felt about that. "Can I see?"

He shook his head. "Not yet."

"You were supposed to show me your drawings when we were at the pump station," she reminded him.

"I forgot." He moved the pencil quickly across the page, then hesitated when he realized she'd stopped her work to stare at him. "Don't let me distract you."

"You're not," she said, but he had. She wasn't one who rushed to have her picture taken; in fact, she avoided it whenever possible. A lot of people felt the camera didn't do them justice, but in Jenna's case it was true. Photographs seemed to sharpen her features and make her skin look sallow. Every shot ever taken of her was unflattering.

"By the way, what are we having for dinner?" he asked.

"Spaghetti."

"Addy and Palmer won't be happy."

"Seafood spaghetti, with an olive oil and wine base. I use lots of garlic and basil."

"This is beginning to sound interesting."

"You're going to *love* it." She brought her fingertips to her lips and gave them a noisy kiss.

His gaze lingered on her lips for an embarrassingly long moment. As though both were aware that this could lead to danger, they studiously ignored each other.

Ten minutes later, Reid said, "Are you ready to look at my drawing? Keep in mind it's just a quick sketch."

Jenna set the cake into the preheated oven and walked over to Reid's chair by the fireplace. She stood behind it and peered over his shoulder.

"Ready?"

"Ready."

Reid turned the tablet and there she was. Only it wasn't her. Not the way she saw herself in the mirror, or even the way cameras revealed her. The woman in his drawing was soft and gracious...and beautiful.

"Well?" he asked, watching her expectantly.

"It's very nice." She left abruptly and went into the bathroom and closed the door.

As soon as she was alone, she stared at herself in the mirror. Could that really be her in the drawing? She felt like weeping—and that was even more ridiculous than racing out of the room like a frightened rabbit.

Soaking a washcloth, she pressed it to her face and took a few moments to compose herself before she faced Reid again. Heaven only knew what excuse she was going to give him.

With her hand on the doorknob, she inhaled deeply in an effort to appear calm. She'd walk back into the living room, apologize and tell him how talented he was, and indeed that was true.

She didn't get the chance. Reid was waiting for her on the other side of the door.

"What did I do wrong?" he demanded.

"You didn't do anything wrong."

"Then why did you turn tail and run?"

"Because I'm an idiot."

Reid rejected that immediately, shaking his head with vehemence.

She had nothing left to tell him except the truth. "Okay, if you must know, when you sketched me, you made me look the way I've always wanted...the way I always *hoped* to look and never have."

"You are exactly the way I drew you. I didn't make this up, you know. I draw what I see."

Nothing she said would make him understand. She began to walk away.

Reid caught her hand and pulled her back, staring at her intently. "If you want to find fault with my technique, fine, but don't criticize my eye."

"You see me as...as soft and feminine?"

"You are soft and feminine," he countered.

"Oh, Reid." She only meant to hug him in thanks, and then, without another word on the subject, walk away. But their friendly embrace quickly became more.

Reid's mouth sought hers and she turned to him, trusting and open. Their exchange the night before was only a foretaste of what awaited them now. Their kisses deepened until Jenna's head swam and her heart pounded in her ears.

"I thought you said this was a bad idea," Reid said, dragging his mouth from hers and nibbling on her lower lip.

"It's a terrible idea," she moaned as she slipped her arms securely around his neck.

"It's only going to lead to trouble." He groaned between kisses.

"Big trouble," she agreed.

He lowered his head and kissed her jaw while Jenna ran her hands along his back. This was so wonderful. She didn't want it to stop.

All at once, with an abruptness that left her reeling, Reid pulled away. He braced his hands against the wall on either side of her, and hung his head, his eyes closed. His breathing was ragged.

She reached up to touch her lips to his.

"Jenna, stop…"

"Okay," she said. "In a minute." She slid her moist lips across his and seconds later, their mouths and tongues became involved in an erotic foray that was gentle and slow and inexpressibly tender.

"You must enjoy tormenting me," he said, and his voice was unsteady.

"Do you trust me, Reid?" she whispered, outlining his lips with the tip of her tongue.

"Yes…yes."

"Then tell me about her."

Everything ceased. He instantly straightened and nearly lost his balance. "What?"

"You didn't isolate yourself on the tundra without a reason."

"Since when did you turn into Sigmund Freud?" His eyes narrowed.

"Come on, I'm not completely naive. There was a woman in your past. One who really hurt you. Otherwise you wouldn't be living such an isolated life."

"You're so far off-base, it's unbelievable." With that he marched into the living room.

"Really?" She followed him.

"This is what I don't understand about women," Reid said, throwing himself in the chair and grabbing his novel. "One kiss, and you suddenly think you have access to my soul."

"So she did hurt you?"

"No, Jenna, she didn't. It was a mutual parting of the ways. And it wasn't exactly a life-changing relationship. Now that's all I'm going to say about it. You got that?"

"All right," she said mildly. "Don't—"

A knock sounded at the door, interrupting her. "Anyone home?" Pete let himself in, followed by Addy and Palmer.

"We aren't too early, are we?" Pete asked anxiously. "I'm gettin' kind of hungry."

Jenna checked her watch. It was barely five, and she had yet to start the seafood spaghetti.

"We'll go ahead and set up our instruments," Palmer said, placing an antique washboard and wooden spoon alongside his harmonica on the sofa.

"What you got in the oven?" Addy asked. He leaned his saw against the wall.

"Smells like she's cooking rum to me," Palmer said. He looked at Jenna and added, "We've had liquor for dinner before, and we like food better."

"So, we too early or not?" Pete persisted.

"Don't worry about it," Reid said, glaring at Jenna. "I'd say you arrived in the nick of time."

Chapter Eleven

Addy slurped up the remains of his seafood spaghetti with a large piece of bread, then wiped the back of his hand across his mouth. He got up to look around the table, but the large bowl was empty and Palmer had already snatched the last slice of buttery French bread.

Sighing loudly, Addy sat down in his chair again, resting his hands on his stomach. They'd rearranged the living room and were seated in a circle. The table held the food, which they'd dished up buffet-style.

"Excellent dinner," Pete added. "Thanks to both of you."

"You ever decide to set up shop, you'd put me out of business," Jake told them. Unlike the others, he'd shown up at the appointed time.

Reid gestured in Jenna's direction. "The credit all goes to Ms. Campbell. The only thing you should thank me for is my cribbage skills. Otherwise, you'd be eating moose-meat sauce with your spaghetti."

The men stared at her with something akin to awe. Uncomfortable with their scrutiny, Jenna blushed. "You guys are easy to please."

Jake scoffed at that. "Well, maybe Addy and Palmer's tastes aren't as discerning as mine, but this meal would impress royalty."

"The company wasn't bad, either," Pete added, charming her with his smile. "Snowbound needs more women. Sure wish you'd stay until Christmas. We do it big up here—the whole community gets together. You'd be very welcome."

"I'll wash the dishes." Reid leapt to his feet.

"What's the matter, Reid? Don't you agree?" Jake pressed.

"We don't need any more women in town than the one we've already got."

"Who says?" Pete demanded.

"I do." Reid carried his plate to the sink.

"What would it take to convince you to stay?" Jake asked, looking at Jenna.

"She's leaving the minute this storm lets up," Reid insisted. He jerked Addy's plate from beneath his nose.

"Let's not be hasty about flying Jenna out of here," Pete said. "Let's listen to what the little lady has to say."

Jenna was enjoying the conversation. Imagine—four men eagerly seeking her company. If only her mother was there to see it. But Chloe was several thousand miles away in Los Angeles.

"Tell them how fast you want to get out of here," Reid said, crossing his arms. He seemed mighty confident that she'd set the record straight.

"Well, I was hoping to meet Lucy before I left."

"She wants to meet Lucy," Addy repeated, sounding righteous. "That could take a day or two, and there's no telling what might happen once the women get together. Jenna could be here for a month. Or longer."

"You think Lucy could convince Jenna to stay?" Palmer asked his friend in a whisper loud enough for everyone to hear.

"Can't say, but there's always hope."

"She's leaving," Reid said again, whipping Palmer's plate away before the older man had a chance to protest. "Remember, she's off to meet Lover Boy."

This remark about her meeting Dalton appeared to please Addy and Palmer. "You'll be back," Palmer said, nodding vigorously. Addy only grinned.

Jenna stood, prepared to take her wineglass to the kitchen. "What makes you think that?" she asked.

"Dalton's got a reputation with the ladies," Jake explained. "A *bad* reputation."

Pete looked over his shoulder at Reid and lowered his voice. "He's the love 'em and leave 'em type. If you do meet up with him, just remember that."

"I'm sure you've confused Dalton with some other man." She said that to get a rise out of Reid, and it did. He glowered at her and she sensed that he found it a struggle not to comment.

"I think it's time to start up the music," Jake said quickly to his friends.

"What about the cake?" Addy's attention had been on the rum cake from the moment Jenna took it out of the oven.

"I thought we'd save that for later," she said, still full from dinner.

"How much later?" Palmer asked.

"Soon," Jenna promised, which seemed to appease the two older men.

It wasn't long before the small band had assembled. Addy played the saw, with Palmer as backup on washboard with wooden spoon. Pete had a fiddle. Addy started alone, holding the saw between his legs and vibrating it over his knee, creating an eerie sound. He played "Amazing Grace" so hauntingly that it sent chills down Jenna's spine. Pete's fiddle joined in, followed by Palmer's rich melodic voice as he lifted his face toward the heavens, closing his eyes. If she hadn't seen and heard it for herself, Jenna would never have believed this unusual trio could put on such a stunning performance.

When the hymn was finished, she applauded enthusiastically. "That was lovely."

"Thank you." Addy nodded once. He set the saw aside. "Now it's time for real dancing music. You ready, Pete?"

"Ready." Pete lifted the fiddle to his chin and began a lively folk tune—music that made her think of hoedowns and barn dances, not that she'd ever been to any.

Addy stepped over to Jenna, and bowed low from the waist. "Might I have the pleasure of this dance?"

Jenna smiled and gave him her hand. Addy led her to the center of the room while Jake, Palmer and Reid pushed back the furniture. When the area was clear, Addy spun her around until she was so dizzy she could barely stand upright.

Palmer stood in one corner, rhythmically stamping his foot while playing his harmonica. Soon he was the one partnering her and then Addy was dancing with Jake. Reid clapped along with the old-time country music.

Jenna found herself passed from one man to the next, until their faces started to blur.

"Enough," she cried, laughing. Bending over, hands on her knees she labored to catch her breath.

"Are we wearing you out?" Jake asked.

"Only a little." She rested for a few minutes, and then she was back, kicking up her feet with the rest of them and loving it.

Pete went from one lively song to another with barely a pause in between. Jake and Palmer taught her a country two-step, an Irish jig and several other dances. Jenna picked them up quickly, grateful for her years in ballet class. She couldn't remember the last time she'd enjoyed herself this much.

"I'm exhausted," she finally said.

"Let her take a break." Reid held her gently by the shoulders and led her to a chair.

"We didn't overdo it, did we?" Addy asked, looking genuinely concerned.

"No...not at all." Sitting down, she stretched her legs in front of her.

"You're a fine dancer," Addy said.

"Mighty fine," Palmer agreed.

"How about that cake?" Jake asked. "I've worked up an appetite."

"You sit," Reid ordered Jenna when she started to get up. "I'll get it."

"You'll need help," Addy insisted and hurried after him, Jake on his heels.

"You did say that was rum cake, didn't you?" Palmer asked, and then with only the slightest hesitation, rushed after the other men. That left Jenna and Pete alone in the room.

"You play very well," Jenna told him.

Pete sat on the sofa across from her and set the fiddle on his lap. "Music's good for the soul," he said simply.

Jenna nodded in agreement but her eyes followed Reid in the kitchen. When she looked away, she noticed Pete studying her.

"So you've taken a liking to Reid?" Pete didn't sound surprised by this.

Jenna wasn't sure how to respond. Reid had kidnapped her, claiming it was for her own good. And yet...maybe he'd done her a favor, strange as that was to admit. There was convincing evidence that Dalton wasn't what he'd seemed; not only that, she *liked* Reid. She longed to know more about him. "Reid is an interesting man."

"Yup," Pete said. "Sure is."

"What happened to him?"

"Happened?" Pete asked, frowning.

"Why isn't Reid married?" It wasn't any of her business, but she couldn't help thinking there was heartbreak in his past.

"I don't think there's any big reason, if that's what you mean. In fact, I think Reid has the same problem we all do. He hasn't met anyone who's willing to live up here."

That answer didn't satisfy her. Reid was a determined man; if he wanted to be married, he'd do whatever was necessary to bring a woman into his life.

"You're saying a woman *hasn't* hurt him?" she asked dubiously.

Pete scratched his beard. "I can't rightly say, but I doubt it. If any woman affected him negatively, I'd say it was his mother. She abandoned Reid and his dad when Reid was ten and his sister was six. I gather she died quite a few years ago."

"Why did she abandon her family?"

"Apparently she hated it up here. Reid's dad never got over it. She was from somewhere in Texas, I think, and she couldn't handle the cold or the isolation. Reid's father always warned him about getting involved with women from the lower forty-eight." Pete sighed mournfully. "He died last year. Reid and Lucy took it hard."

"I'm sorry about his death," she murmured.

"I think he's got a girl," Pete announced in a sudden change of subject.

This was a shock to Jenna and information she didn't take kindly to hearing. "I beg your pardon?"

"Well, Reid flies into Fairbanks every few months and he's in real good spirits when he gets back. Reid's the kind of guy who keeps his cards close to his vest, if you know what I mean."

Jenna did indeed. So there was every likelihood that Reid had a girlfriend. And what about his trip to Seattle? Did he have a woman there, too?

"Want a piece of cake?" Reid asked, carrying two plates into the living room.

"Looks mighty good," Pete said, accepting one plate.

"I'll pass," she said, scowling at Reid, jealousy burning in her eyes.

Reid's head reared back as if he'd been slapped. He scowled at her in return.

Jenna purposely looked away.

"If you ain't interested, I could do with a second piece," Addy said, rushing across the room.

"You already had two pieces." Palmer elbowed his friend out of the way. "I'll take Jenna's piece if she don't want it."

"She might change her mind later," Reid said, taking the plate back to the kitchen.

Pete rubbed his beard again and looked regretful. "I shouldn't have said anything. Besides, I could be misreading the situation entirely. I'd hate you being upset with him because of me."

Jenna ignored the comment. "Do you know her name?"

Pete hesitated. "No, can't say I do. Maybe you should ask him yourself."

She was overreacting and knew it. But being irritated with Reid helped her control the attraction that was beginning to gain momentum between them. She *wanted* to believe he had a girlfriend hidden away somewhere. It would make leaving him a whole lot easier if she could convince herself he wasn't trustworthy.

"I'm ready for more dancing," Addy said, leaping into the center of the room. Crossing his arms over his chest, he squatted down and kicked out his left foot.

Palmer grabbed for the washboard, and Pete his fiddle.

"Addy," Reid said, his voice low and full of warning. "The last time you tried this, your back went out."

"Play!" Addy instructed, thrusting his right arm into the air like a Russian folk dancer.

Pete set the fiddle beneath his chin and started slow and easy, the tempo gradually building as Jenna, Jake and Reid clapped to the music. Addy kicked out his legs one at a time.

When the song ended, Palmer and Jake helped Addy to his feet.

Jenna applauded loudly. "Addy, my goodness! That was incredible. Where did you learn how to dance like this?"

Addy blushed with pleasure at her praise. "When I worked on the Aleutians—lots of Russians there." He wobbled for a moment. "In the old days, I did this pretty often, but my knees ain't what they used to be."

"He only does it now when he wants to impress someone," Palmer said in a whisper.

"If I was staying longer, I'd bake you your very own rum cake." Jenna kissed Addy's cheek.

"Hey, what about me and my fiddle?" Pete said. "Don't we deserve a kiss?"

"Sure you do." She kissed his cheek, too. Then Palmer's and finally Jake's.

"Don't I get a kiss?" Reid asked.

She gave him her sweetest smile and took delight in refusing him. Reid Jamison had gotten all the kisses from her that he was going to get. "No," she said sweetly.

Addy and Palmer loved it, slapping their knees and laughing with glee.

"What's so funny?" Reid demanded.

"You," Addy told him.

Grumbling under his breath, Reid glanced at his watch. "Isn't it time for you to go home?"

"It's not even nine," Addy protested. He propped his hand against the small of his back. "Then again, maybe we should."

Palmer helped Addy on with his coat.

"You might have to take the top bunk tonight," Addy told his friend.

Palmer frowned in confusion. "I get the top bunk every night."

Addy chuckled. "Oh, yes, I guess you do."

"I think we should pack up and head out," Jake said. "Mighty fine dinner, Jenna."

"Best meal I've had in months," Pete muttered as he filed past, his fiddle back in its case. "If you change your mind about staying in Snowbound, you can always move in with me." He jiggled his eyebrows suggestively.

"Jenna's leaving as soon as the storm dies down," Reid said from behind her. His voice was as cold as the air that blew in through the open door.

"Can't blame a man for trying," Pete said with a shrug. "The winters are long and lonely in Alaska."

"Longer and lonelier for some than others," Jenna added with meaning.

"'Night," Jake said.

As soon as the last man was gone, Reid closed the door. He turned to look at Jenna. "What was *that* all about?" he asked.

"What?" she asked, putting on an air of innocence.

"That last comment, for one thing."

"Oh, you mean about long, lonely nights?"

"You know damn well what I mean." Reid stared at her as if he'd never seen her before. "What the hell is the matter with you?"

"I think the question should be reversed. *You're* the one who enjoys misleading people."

"I've never misled you."

She gave a short, mirthless laugh. "I'm going to bed."

"Go right ahead," he snapped. He pointed toward the bedroom with its cracked door. "Be my guest."

"I have been your guest for three miserable days."

"Well, you don't need to worry, because we're out of here the minute it stops snowing."

Angry now, Jenna stormed into the bedroom. Just so he'd know how upset she was, she slammed the door, which was a mistake. Reid had repaired it earlier, but it wasn't up to this kind of abuse. The instant the door hit the jamb, it came apart and fell inward in two pieces.

She gasped and leaped out of the way to avoid being hit.

Reid rushed in and stared at the door in horror. "You're a crazy woman."

"Then you'd do well to be rid of me."

"Yes, I would," he said, stepping over the broken wood and marching into the other room.

A sick feeling attacked her stomach. She was being ridiculous, and all because she was jealous of some unknown woman. Reid was right—there *was* something wrong with her!

Chapter Twelve

Dalton staggered into his hotel room and fumbled for the light switch. The storm had been raging for nearly two full days, and the only solace he'd found had been in the hotel's cocktail lounge. He was charging the booze to the company, although it wasn't official business. His bar tab was likely to be higher than the bill for his room, but he didn't care. It wasn't as if Larry was going to fire him, since Dalton was half owner, anyway.

The light came on with an irritating brightness. Dalton squinted and rubbed a hand down his face. He saw that the red light on his phone was flashing. Sitting on the edge of the bed, he searched for the message button and listened.

"Dalton, it's Larry. You're gonna want to call me back. I got news on that ladyfriend of yours. The one you've been looking for."

Dalton replaced the receiver. "Ladyfriend?" he said aloud and then remembered that all his troubles could be attributed to one Jenna Campbell. She was the reason he was trapped in Fairbanks—although he'd been stuck in worse places.

Dalton had done his utmost to find her, to no avail. The airlines hadn't been any help, since he wasn't a relative. With security as tight as it was, even in Alaska, he hadn't gotten a word of information out of them. In his frustration he'd turned to alcohol, and that had seen him through the worst of the storm.

He squinted at the bedside clock and dialed Larry's home number. Larry answered, sounding groggy. "Hello."

"What did you find out?" Dalton asked.

"That's a fine way to greet me after dragging me out of bed."

"As you might've guessed, I'm anxious to find out what I can about Jenna."

"Worried, are you?" Larry pressed.

He wasn't—in fact, he was ready to forget the whole Jenna Campbell mess—but his partner didn't know that. "Of course I am."

"Her mother called."

"Her mother?" This wasn't news Dalton wanted to hear.

"Yes. Apparently she heard from Jenna."

"You mean Jenna phoned her mother and not me?" This could be a problem. Jenna was turning out to be way more of a headache than she was worth.

"Aren't you curious about what she had to say?"

He was more than curious and frankly a little concerned. He didn't like the mothers of his women friends having access to him. That might cause serious trouble later on. Mothers tended to protect their little darlings.

"Dalton, have you been drinking again?"

"What else is there to do in the middle of a blizzard?" Dalton demanded. "I'm stuck here, you know."

"All right, all right."

"Just tell me what mommy had to say."

"She's on her way up to Fairbanks."

"What?" This had to be a joke. "Jenna's mother?"

"Yes, like I said, she heard from her daughter and—"

"Where the hell is Jenna anyway?"

An uncomfortable pause followed. "You're not going to like this."

Nothing was working out the way he'd planned. Just how hard was it to figure out what to do when he was a few minutes late picking her up at the airport? Couldn't she wait? "Tell me," he growled.

"Remember how you suspected Jenna might've met up with someone on the plane?"

"Yeah." He'd done everything he could think of and hadn't managed to get that information.

"Well, she did."

"Who?" He breathed the question.

"Reid Jamison."

Dalton slammed his fist against the wall, shaking his fingers to lessen the pain. He couldn't believe that of all the people in the entire state of Alaska, Jenna would link up with the one man who'd do anything to thwart him.

"Where are they?"

"At his place in Snowbound."

"He took her *home* with him?"

"Yes, and damned if I know why."

Dalton knew. He'd have done the same thing had the situation been reversed. "So Reid was on her flight?"

"I don't know, but that's my guess. A friend of mine said he goes down to Seattle every so often."

Dalton released an expletive that was best not repeated.

"Either that or—"

"She hired Jamison to fly her into Beesley," Dalton said, finishing the thought. When he was late, Jenna had immediately taken matters into her own hands. Dammit, you just couldn't count on a woman.

"Why's her mother flying up?"

"I didn't get around to asking. The lady's something of a talker, if you catch my drift."

"From what Jenna said, her mother wasn't keen on the idea of her coming up here."

"Yes, well, she didn't sound all that upset when I spoke to her."

"Really?"

"No, in fact she sounded downright excited." Larry himself

sounded puzzled. "I don't know what Jenna told her, but she said she's landing in Fairbanks in the morning."

"She's coming here?"

"Yes, and I told her she should connect with you."

"Why?"

"Well, because she needs someone to fly her into Snowbound."

So Jenna's mother wanted a ride to Snowbound. This might work out, after all. Jenna was with Reid, who had as much finesse with the ladies as a bull moose. Jenna was probably more than ready to leave the isolated town, and if he were to arrive with her mother, he wouldn't have any difficulty in getting her to leave with him.

"Did she give you her flight information?" Dalton asked.

"She did."

"Good," Dalton said, searching for a pen to write it down. Yes sir, this could be very interesting indeed, he thought, wincing as he clutched it with his sore fingers. He'd sweep Jenna off her feet, and if he was lucky, he could have a fling with her mother, too. That way, potential problems became a bonus instead.

Reid was too angry to sleep. He hadn't heard a sound from the bedroom since Jenna had destroyed the door for the second time. Okay, technically he was responsible for the original break, but she was the reason the door had gotten busted in the first place.

With nervous energy, he started picking up clutter in the house, making as much noise as possible. For the life of him, he didn't know what had gotten into her. They were all having fun and then, out of the blue, she'd turned on him. He couldn't understand it.

Filling the sink with hot water and soap, he washed the dishes and set them on the counter.

"You have a lot of nerve," Jenna said from behind him.

Reid glanced over his shoulder and was gratified to see her looking furious. Her hands were on her hips, her stance was aggressive and her eyes glittered dangerously.

"What's wrong now, Your Highness? Is there a pea under your mattress?"

"You kissed me!"

"Big mistake."

"You're telling me."

"No, actually you were telling me." He did his best to sound bored, when in reality he'd lost his sense of annoyance and was fast becoming amused. "Instead of throwing insults at me, why don't you just say what's wrong and be done with it?"

"I am not insulting you."

"Okay, you're not insulting me." He could tell his being agreeable irritated her even more.

"You're the one who's insulting *me.*"

Reid reached for a kitchen towel and dried his hands. "Forgive me for being dense, but would you kindly explain how I managed that?"

"I already did. You kissed me like you really meant it."

The flicker of pain he saw in her eyes surprised him. "I did mean it, Jenna. It wasn't the right thing to do, but—"

Her only response was a groan of frustration.

"You're still upset about that kiss? You kissed me, too, remember?"

"Yes—but that was before I knew about your woman friend."

"What?" All at once everything was making sense. He sighed. "Who told you that?"

"Pete, but don't blame him. I asked."

"He tell you anything else?"

"He mentioned that your mother left your father when you were a child."

Reid frowned. "Pete's got a big mouth."

"He saved me from acting like more of an idiot than I already have. I...it mortifies me now to think of the way I confided in you."

"If it keeps you away from Dalton Gray, I can only be grateful."

"That's just fine and dandy. Go ahead and have your fun. You must find me a joke—a diversion between your sojourns in Fairbanks. And Seattle."

"Come on, Jenna."

"You keep telling me what a creep Dalton is, but you're no better." She marched back to the bedroom.

A knot formed in Reid's gut. He'd never viewed Jenna as vulnerable and insecure, but he realized she was. He hadn't meant to hurt her.

The room was dark when he strolled past. "Jenna," he called from the doorway. His eyes adjusted to the lack of light, and he found her sitting on the side of his bed. She ignored him.

"Listen," he said, "Susan's an old friend. Nothing more. We have dinner when I'm in town on business, but that's it, I swear."

A pause and then, "Does she know you're an artist?"

"Like I said earlier, no one knows about that—other than you."

"Oh."

She might as well hear it all. "I don't make a habit of kissing a lot of women, either, if that's what you're thinking."

"What about your trip to Seattle? Why did you go there if not to meet a woman?"

"If you must know, I took a week-long art course."

"Oh," she said again, her expression rather sheepish.

A moment later, she said, "You didn't tell me about your mother."

He wasn't ready to delve into that. "You didn't tell me very much about yours, either, although you've mentioned several stepfathers. If you want to know about mine, I don't really have all that much to tell you. She died when I was sixteen. A car accident in Houston."

"She left your father, though—and she left you and Lucy."

"Yes, but that has nothing to do with you and me."

"Oh...you're probably right," she whispered.

He waited a moment and then asked, "Friends?"

"Friends," she repeated. After a short hesitation, she said, "I feel like even more of an idiot, if that's possible."

"You're not. If I heard there was a man you were serious about, I'd wonder, too—considering the way you kissed me."

"I think I should just leave.... I'm not good with relationships. I mess them up every time. I apologize. You must think I'm insecure and silly and...worse. Good night, Reid."

He wasn't sure he wanted the conversation to end here, but if they continued, he was afraid they'd just end up kissing again. Which wouldn't be a good thing, since this was not a relationship with a future. "Good night, Jenna."

He made up his bed on the sofa and lay down with his head on the pillow. A half hour must have passed. He thought he heard Jenna tossing and turning, and called out in a husky whisper, "Are you awake?"

"Yeah."

"What are you thinking?"

"I'm so embarrassed."

Reid chuckled. "Actually I'm flattered. You were jealous and I loved it."

"I feel a whole lot better now," she muttered sarcastically.

He nestled his head against the sofa arm and closed his eyes. The attempt to sleep didn't last long. "Are you still set on meeting Dalton Gray?" He suspected he wasn't going to approve of the answer.

"Yes."

"I thought so." He closed his eyes again but the images that came to mind distressed him. His eyes flew open. "Is there anything I can do to persuade you not to?"

"Probably not."

At least she was honest. "Then I won't try."

A few more minutes passed.

"Reid, the picture you drew of me, can I have it?"

"I don't think so. I'd prefer to keep it myself."

"Why?"

He didn't have an answer, at least not one he was willing to share. All he knew was that he wasn't giving it up.

"I checked with the weather people," he told her. "The storm will be gone by morning."

"How early will you be flying me out?"

She didn't say anything about Lucy, and because of everything that had happened, he wasn't going to use his sister as an excuse to delay their departure. "Addy and Palmer will have the runway cleared by first light. We'll leave soon after that."

Chapter Thirteen

Jenna was up and dressed before dawn. She dreaded leaving Snow-bound. Her short time here had been the best adventure of her life, which was exactly the reason she'd left Fulton Industries. In this brief period, she'd come to consider Addy, Palmer, Pete and Jake friends. Reid, too—only she'd made such a fool of herself with him, the only sensible option was to escape as quickly as possible.

She had coffee brewed by the time Reid woke. He sat up on the sofa and stared at her as if he couldn't remember who she was.

"Coffee's ready," she said.

"Thanks." He rubbed his eyes and made a growling sound that a few days earlier would have irritated her.

"How long have you been up?" he asked.

"Not long." She brought him a steaming mug.

Reid sipped the hot coffee. "Did you sleep well?"

She hadn't, but vanity insisted he not know that. "Fine. How about you?"

"All right, I guess."

"You can have your own bed tonight."

"Right." But he didn't sound too pleased and for that matter, she wasn't either.

"The snow's stopped," she informed him, making conversation and unable to think of anything else.

He nodded. "I figured it would."

Jenna set her empty mug in the sink and carried her suitcase out to the living room. "I'm ready anytime you are."

"Why the hurry?" he asked with a frown.

"I—no reason."

"Good. If you don't have any objections I'd like to linger over my morning coffee."

Jenna murmured a response, then returned to the kitchen and sat at the table. She felt Reid studying her, which made her self-conscious. Her emotions were more confused than they'd ever been in her life.

A knock at the door startled her. Reid answered it, his blanket draped around him. Addy stood on the other side, wearing a wide grin. "Jim and Lucy just landed."

Reid turned to ask Jenna, "Do you still want to meet my sister?"

"Sure." Jenna looked away. "I don't suppose an extra hour or so would matter."

Reid turned back to Addy. "Tell Lucy I'll be bringing Jenna by in about ten minutes."

"Okay," Addy said and leaned around Reid to find Jenna. "I already told Lucy all about you and how she should try to talk you into staying. We sure did enjoy having you."

"Thank you, Addy," she said and she meant it. "Thank you for everything."

"I'll go tell Lucy," Addy said and was off.

Reid disappeared into the bathroom and reappeared a few minutes later, completely dressed. His expression was somber and cheerless as he reached for his coat. Jenna looked around the cabin one last time before Reid opened the door.

The world outside was a pristine, sparkling white and so lovely that Jenna paused for a moment to take it all in. The landscape stretched endlessly around them, punctuated by only a few stunted but sturdy trees now flocked with snow.

Addy and Palmer had been busy shoveling a pathway between the two houses, which touched Jenna's heart. No sooner were they out the door than Lucy stepped outside to meet them.

Reid's sister was short, with long dark hair and eyes that flashed with welcome and warmth. She held out both arms.

"You must be Jenna," she said, giving her a hug. "I couldn't believe it when Jim told me what Reid had done." She admonished Reid with a scolding look that grew into a smile. "Shame on you, big brother, but thank you for bringing me a friend."

"I'm afraid I'm flying Jenna out this morning," Reid informed her briskly.

"Not before we've had a chance to chat," Lucy insisted, ushering Jenna inside. Although the cabins were relatively similar in size, the difference between Jim's and Reid's was striking. Whereas Reid's place was utilitarian and almost stark, Lucy had turned hers into a real home, with feminine touches everywhere.

"I've already made tea," Lucy said, leading Jenna into the kitchen. "Now, tell me, are you completely disgusted with Alaska? I'm going to give Reid hell for doing such a crazy thing—kidnapping you! Rest assured he's never done anything like this before."

"Lucy, honestly, it wasn't so bad. He was planning to have me stay with you, but then you were gone and there wasn't much he could do but take me home with him. Addy and Palmer did their best to make me feel welcome and last night Reid and I had everyone over for dinner."

"Those guys are such scoundrels! They manipulated you into cooking for them?"

"Yes, but I enjoyed it. I lost the cribbage game to Reid, so I agreed to do the cooking."

"That Reid. I don't suppose he told you he's a champion cribbage player?"

"Actually, it was fine. We had a wonderful evening."

"Knowing Addy and Palmer, they probably danced your feet off."

"I didn't mind," Jenna said. "We all had a great time."

"What about Reid? I certainly hope my brother was a gentleman."

Jenna looked down at the kitchen table with its colorful woven mats. "Reid was…wonderful."

Lucy sat across from her. "*How* wonderful?" she asked in a low voice.

Jenna didn't answer right away. "Well, you can imagine how I felt at first. I was furious."

"And rightly so."

"Then the storm hit, and there was nothing to do but make the best of it. He…wasn't so bad once I got to know him."

"My brother isn't someone who freely shares a lot about himself."

Jenna nodded. She barely knew Lucy, but she desperately needed a friend she could confide in. "Oh, Lucy, I'm afraid I made a complete fool of myself."

Her declaration was met with silence, a comforting pat on the hand and a question. "Do you want to tell me about it?"

"Oh…this is almost too embarrassing."

Lucy jumped to her feet, fists on her hips. "Reid didn't seduce you, did he?"

"No, no! It was nothing like that, but we did…kiss, and then later Pete told me that Reid flies down to Fairbanks to visit a woman and I assumed—"

"I can imagine what you assumed."

"Well, then I was jealous and silly and I confronted him as if it were my business, which it isn't. He could have six women stashed away, but it's none of my concern."

"He doesn't. If you're talking about Susan Webster, I can assure you she's just a friend of ours. There's no romantic relationship with her or anyone else. If there was, I'd know about it."

"If he's so private about his affairs, how would you?"

"He's my brother and if his heart was involved, he'd either leave to be with the woman in question or—more likely—find a way to convince her to join him here. Jim did. I would never have considered living in such an isolated location. Jim offered to move to Fairbanks, but I knew how much he cares about his job. Still, I didn't arrive with the best attitude." She paused, meeting Jenna's eyes. "Over the last year I've come to love it in Snowbound."

Jenna could understand that. In this brief time, she'd grown to appreciate Reid and the tiny tundra community.

"Addy, Palmer and the rest treat me like a queen," Lucy continued. "Now that I'm pregnant, they're more protective than ever. I can only imagine how spoiled this baby's going to be with five honorary uncles."

Jenna smiled. "They want me to stay, too."

"I know. If I thought I could convince you, I'd certainly try."

It was now or never and Jenna had to ask. "Will you tell me about Dalton Gray?"

Lucy looked down, but not before Jenna saw the flash of pain in her eyes. "It's probably better if I don't."

"Why?"

Lucy sighed audibly. "You've got to form your own opinion of Dalton and you can't do that until you meet him for yourself."

Jenna had expected a scathing report on the other man. But Lucy refused to say one ugly word about him, despite her obvious distress. "You're right. I should at least meet him."

Lucy nodded. "You're an intelligent woman. You can come to your own conclusions—but be cautious. Dalton can seem very persuasive. That's all I'm going to say."

"Now," Jenna said, eager to learn more about Lucy, "How did you meet Jim?"

The sweetest smile lit her face. "Reid thinks he introduced us, but we actually met before that. I was living in Fairbanks and was at the library with a friend. Arlene caught sight of Jim and said he looked more interesting than any book we were likely to find."

Jenna smiled.

"He did, too, but when it came to meeting decent men, I didn't have much of a track record."

"I don't either," Jenna muttered.

"Well, anyway, I urged Arlene to go ahead and talk to him, but she'd just met this really wonderful guy and wasn't interested."

"So you went up and introduced yourself?" Jenna would never have had the courage, but she was sure that was what Lucy must've done.

"No," Lucy said, shaking her head. "I couldn't, although I wanted to in the worst way."

"Jim came up and introduced himself?"

"No." Lucy giggled. "I told Arlene that if I was supposed to meet him, then I would. I believe that things happen for a reason, I really do. Anyway, Arlene and I left the library. She had her bike and I drove, but when I went out to the car, the engine wouldn't start."

"And Jim rescued you?"

"I wish. No, some other guy did as Jim walked blindly past me. Of course, I imagined he was on his way to meet a girl. I could see it all in my mind, which made me feel like a fool after he was gone. I'd let a golden opportunity slip through my fingers and wanted to kick myself."

"But you did meet him eventually." That much was obvious.

"Yes, but it was weeks later. I kept thinking about him. I didn't know his name so I thought of him as 'the guy from the library.' I made countless trips back, hoping I'd run into him and of course I didn't, because I was trying to *make* it happen."

Jenna supposed she was doing something similar with this Alaskan adventure—trying to shape her future…and perhaps trying too hard. But her seat on the flight from Seattle had been beside Reid's, so maybe things did happen for a reason, as Lucy said. Granted, she'd wasted all those years being infatuated with Brad Fulton, but that was behind her now.

"Then I got angry with myself for not having the courage to talk to Jim when I'd had the chance," Lucy went on. "Here I was, pining after a guy I'd never even met. But I'd had that glimpse of him and felt—I don't know how to explain what I felt."

"A sense of connection?" Jenna suggested.

"Yes. I did, Jenna, I really did, and then…nothing. I didn't see him anywhere. I didn't dare tell anyone, because it sounded like I'd lost my mind. I gave up. It seems crazy now when I think about it, but I sort of figured I was never going to find the right guy."

Jenna nodded, feeling much the same way. She was falling for Reid, although any hope of a relationship seemed unrealistic. And Dalton—well, she'd certainly learned enough about him, all of it bad.

"Go on," she told Lucy.

"Then one day," Lucy continued, "I was grocery shopping. I was outside in the parking lot when Jim drove past me in his car. I nearly dropped everything. He was in a vehicle that identified him as an Alaska Park Ranger. When he saw me, he stopped, put the truck in Reverse and drove back to where I stood. He rolled down his window and just looked at me."

"No!" Jenna burst out delightedly.

"I swear it's true. Then he grinned the biggest grin I'd ever seen and said he knew he'd eventually find me."

"Find you? You mean he'd been looking for you, too?"

"Yes! Oh, Jenna, it was the most magical, wonderful moment of my life."

"He remembered you from the library?"

"Yes, and he was furious with himself for not talking to me then. He had a second chance when he left the library and saw the other guy helping me with my car. He told me in the parking lot that he'd already let two chances go by and wasn't going to lose a third opportunity, which was why he stopped."

"You started dating then?"

"Yes, but we knew we were meant to be together. That was the scary part. Jim had just gotten stationed in Snowbound, and that was where Reid was. My brother had told me he wanted me to meet his friend, and I'd made all kinds of excuses. But Reid didn't pressure me, and besides, Jim hadn't been all that interested in meeting me, either."

"You mean to say that all along it was Jim he wanted you to meet?"

Lucy nodded. "It didn't take us long to figure that out, and then we decided we should just go along with Reid's plan to introduce us and let him think he was responsible for getting the two of us together."

"How long was it before you realized you were in love with Jim?"

Lucy blushed. "A month. I knew from the beginning that I could fall in love with him, but after one month together, I was sure of my feelings for him. Very sure."

"You left everything familiar and moved to a town where you'd be the only woman."

"Yes. At first, after Jim and I decided to marry, I didn't think about anything except being with him, but closer to the wedding I felt terrified. It isn't like I can call and get an appointment for a haircut up here. Or run to the library." They both smiled. "The most mundane activities often require weeks of planning. Then there's the fact that I live twenty-four/seven with a group of burly men who don't have much appreciation for the niceties of life."

That would give Jenna pause, too. "But in the end you decided marrying Jim was worth it."

"Yes, and it has been. I got over my resentment—and my fear—about living so far from anywhere and now I absolutely love it. Snowbound's my home."

"Don't you get lonely?"

"Dreadfully. I miss my friends, but we made certain agreements before the wedding."

Addy and Palmer had explained that to Jenna. "Once a month you visit civilization."

"Yes, and I return a happy woman. Now that I'm expecting a baby, I'll probably make the trip every two weeks or so."

It was difficult to tell that Lucy was pregnant except for the happiness she sensed in the other woman. Given the opportunity, Jenna knew she could be good friends with Lucy. Unfortunately she was about to leave.

"Will you keep in touch?" Lucy asked. "No matter what happens with Dalton—or Reid?"

"Of course."

"If you need anything or just want to talk, you know where to find me."

"Oh, Lucy, what a warm, generous soul you are."

The other woman sighed. "I wish we had an entire day together. Are you *sure* you want to go? You'd be welcome to stay with Jim and me if you wanted. I'd love it, and it might give you time to clear your head."

Jenna was tempted, but she declined. Clearing her head was important, but she couldn't do that unless she got away from Reid.

"Do you want my advice?"

Jenna grinned. "You've already given me good advice—by example."

"What?"

"I'm going to take a hands-off approach the way you did."

"This could be very interesting," Lucy said, obviously satisfied at the prospect. "Very interesting indeed."

"I've decided that whatever *should* happen *will* happen," Jenna told her. "Just like it did for you."

Chapter Fourteen

Chloe stepped out of the jetway and into the interior of the Fairbanks airport. The trip had been long and gruelling, and she was badly in need of sleep and something edible, since airline food wasn't. She could only hope that Jenna appreciated the sacrifice she was making on her behalf.

The information she'd gotten from Brad Fulton's secretary assured Chloe that she could reach Jenna before Brad did, but she'd had to catch the red-eye out of LAX. It was imperative that she talk to her daughter before Jenna's former boss arrived.

Jenna needed motherly advice, and after five failed marriages, no one was better qualified to advise her than Chloe.

Slinging her purse over her shoulder, she looked around. She hadn't spoken directly to Dalton Gray, but his partner, Larry Forsyth, had promised her Dalton would be at the airport to pick her up. Since he'd already abandoned Jenna, Chloe didn't hold out much hope of Dalton's showing up.

"Are you Jenna's mother?" A tall, lean man with bloodshot, blue eyes approached her.

Well, speak of the devil. He must be over forty. This man would never do for her daughter; Chloe recognized that in a flash. "Chloe Lyman," she said sweetly, extending her hand, "and you must be Dalton Gray."

Dalton seized her fingers and raised them to his lips. "At your service."

"Exactly where is this place called Snowbound?" Chloe demanded, unimpressed by his hokey charm and fake gentility.

"About a ninety-minute flight from here."

"I need sustenance. Maybe, oh, a yogurt or a chai tea or something."

"I thought you wanted me to fly you into Snowbound?" Dalton said testily.

"I do, but first I *must* have food. They don't serve anything decent on planes these days."

"Okay, fine," Dalton agreed, muttering.

"Where's the closest restaurant?"

"Restaurant? You're joking, right? All we have open at this time of the morning is the cafeteria."

"A cafeteria?" Chloe shuddered at the thought

"That's the only place available, but from what I hear, the food's edible."

"You don't eat there yourself?"

"Not if I can help it," he said.

Chloe sighed. He led her to the baggage claim area, and she stood back and let him collect her five bags.

"Five suitcases," he whined. "Just how long were you intending to visit?" He tucked the smallest of the cases beneath his arm.

"Be careful with that," she snapped, "I've got my yoga tapes in there." In an effort to be helpful, she took her cosmetics bag.

"You aren't going to find a yoga class in Snowbound," he muttered.

"Don't talk down to me. I'm sure they have a VCR. After the trip I've had, I need peace and serenity."

He started to mutter something else, but Chloe wasn't interested. She was hungry, had gone without her morning chai and had taken an instant dislike to the man her daughter hoped to marry.

While Dalton took care of her luggage, Chloe followed the signs directing her to the cafeteria. It went without saying they wouldn't have soy milk, and, she soon discovered, no chai or yogurt either.

She slid the orange plastic tray along the steel bars and looked through the pitiful display, choosing a brownish banana, decaffeinated coffee and a bran muffin. The cashier added up her total, which came to a ridiculous amount, although Chloe didn't bother to complain. It wouldn't do any good.

"Have a nice day," the gentleman said pleasantly.

"Thank you." This was the first cordial greeting she'd received in Alaska.

She sat close to the entry, so Dalton would see her when he returned. No sooner had she found a table and added skim milk to her coffee than he was back.

"Dalton Gray," the cashier called. "Did you ever find your friend?"

Dalton turned to the other man. "How'd you know I was looking for someone?"

"Because she was in here asking about you."

"You spoke with my daughter?" Chloe was instantly on her feet. "When was that?"

The older man contemplated the question. "Oh, it must've been three or four days ago now. I hooked her up with Reid Jamison, who agreed to fly her into Beesley."

"My poor baby." Chloe scowled at Dalton. She felt like hitting that…that low-rent Romeo over the head with her purse. He had some nerve luring Jenna to Alaska and then abandoning her.

"You sure about this, Billy?" Dalton demanded.

"Positive. She came in here looking lost and asked me if I knew you. I told her I did, but that I hadn't seen you around in a while. I suggested she get a hotel room for the night and search for you in the morning, but she didn't want to do that."

"Why not?" Dalton cried. "It would've saved me a lot of grief if she had."

"Well, she was afraid she wouldn't know where to look, which is true. She had your address in Beesley and said if she could find a way north, you'd eventually show up there."

"Jenna is too smart for her own good," Chloe muttered. "That sounds just like her. My daughter wouldn't rest until she achieved her goal."

"So you're the one who hooked her up with Reid Jamison," Dalton said in a low growl. "Thanks a lot."

"Yes," the other man returned. "She seemed a little hesitant about going with him, but I convinced her she didn't have anything to worry about. Reid's a good guy."

"And I'm not?" Dalton protested.

"I wouldn't know about that," Billy fired back, "but I've heard plenty."

"Lies," Dalton insisted. "Are you ready, Ms. Lyman? I don't think we should delay. Jenna needs us."

"Jenna can take care of herself," Chloe assured him. "At least until I've finished my coffee." She could see this didn't please Dalton, but she really didn't care.

Fifteen minutes later, Dalton escorted Chloe to the tarmac where his plane was parked. Never in all her years would Chloe have believed she'd voluntarily fly in such a contraption. Somehow she managed to climb onto the wing and into the seat. This feat, she was convinced, could only be attributed to practicing yoga.

Once she was belted into place, she waited for Dalton to finish loading her suitcases. Chloe couldn't imagine what Jenna had been thinking when she flew up to meet this dreadful man.

As soon as Dalton was inside the plane, he put on a headset and handed her one, then began talking to the control tower.

Chloe waited until he was finished. "Can I speak to my daughter through this?" she asked him.

"No."

Well, fine.

"Not to worry, Ms. Lyman, we're going to rescue Jenna. If Reid Jamison has so much as touched a hair on her head, I'll personally beat the hell out of him."

It wasn't what Reid Jamison had done to Jenna that he needed to worry about, Chloe mused. It was what *she* intended to do to *him*— after he'd safely delivered her to her daughter, of course. She didn't know yet what punishment she could bestow but she'd think of something. One thing was certain; he had a snowball's chance in hell of getting within thirty feet of Jenna.

Reid glanced toward the house, where Lucy and Jenna had been sequestered for the last hour.

"What could two women who'd never met before today have to talk about?" he asked Jim.

"Don't have any idea," Jim muttered. He leaned back in his chair inside the park station office and Reid felt his friend's scrutiny. "So," Jim said, "how'd it go?"

Reid lowered his eyes. "All right, I guess. We didn't murder each other."

"No. In fact, since the last time I saw you, there seems to be a big change of attitude on both your parts."

Reid didn't confirm or deny his friend's assessment.

"The two of you were holed up together for how long?"

"Long enough," Reid said.

"Long enough for what? For you to start liking her—or more?"

Reid wasn't willing to discuss his feelings with Jim. The other man was a good friend, but Reid had yet to define what he felt for Jenna. That would take time he didn't have. In a little while, he was flying her back to Fairbanks, and what she did after that was none of his business. Or so he reminded himself.

"Addy said the two of you had the whole gang over for dinner."

"We didn't actually have much of a choice," Reid said with a grin.

"Invited themselves, did they?"

Reid nodded. "As I recall, you've had more than one of those impromptu parties yourself." He looked out over the runway where his Cessna 182 sat, fueled and ready for takeoff.

"It seems to me you don't want her to go," Jim said quietly.

Reid tensed. "Am I that transparent?"

"Not to everyone. I know because I felt the same way myself whenever I had to leave Lucy. The question is, what are you going to do about it?"

Reid had spent most of the night reflecting on his situation. "What *can* I do?"

"You could ask her to stay."

"Why would she stay?" Reid asked.

"Because of you," Jim said. "Give her the option, at least."

Slowly, Reid shook his head. "She came here to meet Dalton, and she's determined to do it."

"Then let her. We both know what he's like. It won't take Jenna long to get the lay of the land when it comes to Gray. You need to make sure you're around afterward, though."

This was something else Reid had thought about during the night. "In other words, I'm supposed to hang around Fairbanks or Beesley, and hope she'll come to me once she's recognized Dalton for the rat he is?"

Jim considered that, then shrugged. "More or less."

"But I work *here*."

"You're saying she has to come to you?"

Reid didn't like it, but that was the truth.

"In that case, she might just go back to California."

Reid didn't like that, either, but it could be the best solution all around. "She might."

Jim shook his head. "That doesn't bother you?"

"She's better off in California."

Jim's eyebrows shot up. "Really?"

"She'd be away from Dalton."

"But she'd be away from you, too."

It didn't help to have Jim point out the obvious. "Her boss is the reason she came to Alaska in the first place," Reid muttered. "Now that she's gone, he might've had a sudden change of heart." In fact, Reid had heard evidence of that very thing, during Jenna's phone call with her mother.

"He might," Jim agreed. "But that doesn't answer my question."

It was a question Reid didn't want to answer. "She's safer outside Alaska," he finally said.

"Safer from whom? Dalton or you?"

Reid chuckled. "Both of us."

"Let me offer a second scenario," Jim said, leaning forward. "You fly Jenna back to Fairbanks and wait there until Dalton comes to get her."

Reid frowned. He couldn't see handing Jenna over to that bastard, but he was willing to listen to what Jim had to say, since he was completely out of ideas himself.

"You with me so far?" Jim asked.

"So far."

"When Dalton arrives, you make it plain how you feel about him."

Reid had every intention of doing that. "She already knows how I feel about Dalton." He wasn't aware of clenching and unclenching his fists until Jim's gaze dropped to his hands.

"Then you tell Jenna you'll come back for her any time, day or night."

He nodded.

"The hardest part will be walking away."

Reid didn't know if he could. "What do I do after that? Sit around and twiddle my thumbs?"

"Give her time. A day, two at the most. If she's half as smart as you seem to believe, she'll contact you. Still, I expect she'll want to return to California." There was a weighty pause. "For a while, anyhow."

That was the way Reid figured it, too. "I should let her go, don't you think?"

"That's up to you. But whatever happens, you should give her a reason to come back."

Reid sighed. This was harder than he'd realized. "How?"

Jim stood and slapped him on the back. "You'll know what to say."

"I will?" Reid wasn't nearly as confident as his friend. Living way up here, he didn't have much experience with women.

Jim looked out the window and stood. "Here they come now."

Reid's heart fell. He didn't like this one damn bit, but he was powerless to change anything. Wasn't he?

Jim and Lucy walked with them onto the snowcovered runway.

While Reid placed Jenna's suitcase in the storage area behind the rear seat, Lucy and Jenna hugged as if they were the closest of friends.

"You'll keep in touch, won't you?" Lucy asked.

"I will," Jenna promised, and then the two women parted.

"You ready?" Reid asked, doing his best to keep any emotion from his voice.

"Ready," she said, taking a moment to look around the town one last time.

When Reid had helped her inside, he boarded. Once he'd finished the preflight check, he taxied away from the hangar.

Before he had a chance to change his mind, he removed his earphones and set them in his lap.

Jenna stared at him. "What's wrong?"

"Nothing," he said, "I have something to say and I'm not sure I can do this right. First, I'm sorry for bringing you here. Like I said a few days ago, it wasn't the most brilliant idea I've ever had, although I want you to know my intentions were good." He paused. "If you wanted, you could probably have me arrested and—well, that's up to you."

"I'm not pressing charges, Reid."

"Thank you," he said solemnly. "I have to tell you that it goes against everything in me to take you back to Fairbanks when I know you're going to link up with a no-account bastard like Dalton Gray."

"Reid—"

"I know, I shouldn't have said that, but it's how I feel." He replaced the earphones and was taxiing toward the end of the runway, when there was an unexpected transmission. Abruptly he cut the engine and returned to the hangar.

"What is it?" Jenna asked.

"I should just take off and be done with it," he muttered.

"Be done with me?" she challenged.

"No," he countered. "Another plane's about to land."

"Here?"

He nodded.

He watched as understanding dawned. "Dalton?"

He nodded again. "He's got a passenger."

"A passenger? Who?"

"Apparently, it's your mother."

Chapter Fifteen

"My mother!" Jenna repeated in shock. "What's she doing here?"

Reid expelled his breath. "How would I know?"

"There's no need to snap at me."

He didn't respond.

"Dalton's flying her in?" Jenna wanted to be sure she was clear on this.

"That was him on the radio," Reid said. "Apparently Lover Boy's coming to collect you."

"Stop calling him that."

"Yes, Your Highness."

"You're deliberately trying to irritate me and I refuse to let you."

Once again, he didn't respond, which was just as well. Although she claimed he hadn't upset her, it wasn't true. She was furious with him, and by all indications, the feeling was mutual—although she didn't know why. Reid didn't have a single thing to be angry about. Okay, he didn't like Dalton, but surely Dalton was more her problem than his? And in addition to the Arctic gigolo, she had to deal with her lunatic if loving mother.

Reid taxied back to where the plane had originally been parked. Jim was outside to greet him, wearing a puzzled expression when Reid turned off the engine and climbed out.

Jenna didn't wait for him to come around to help her, knowing that in his present frame of mind he was just as likely to leave her sitting in the cockpit.

"What's wrong?" Jim asked.

"We've got company of the unwelcome variety," Reid told his friend.

"Dalton?"

Reid nodded.

"My mother's with him," Jenna inserted.

"Your mother!" Jim repeated and looked at Reid who shrugged.

The three of them stood there staring south as a speck appeared in the sky and slowly advanced toward them. Jenna's heart thundered. This was the moment she'd been waiting for all these weeks and months, but she experienced none of the anticipation she had when she'd first arrived in Alaska. Instead, a growing sense of dread filled her. And the fact that her mother was accompanying Dalton complicated everything.

The Cessna began its descent and attracted the attention of the others in town.

"Who's that?" Jake asked, coming out from his café.

"Any other women?" Pete demanded, stepping up next to Jenna.

"My mother," she whispered, and then she remembered how interested Pete had been in her when she'd landed in Snowbound. "Hands off, understand?" She narrowed her eyes at him, letting it be known that she wouldn't approve of any flirting with Chloe.

Pete sighed forlornly. "Why is it," he muttered, "that there's a hands-off policy for every woman who comes here?"

"Depends on the hands," Palmer guffawed.

Jenna gave him a stern look. "Mom isn't staying long," she told Pete.

"Why not?" Addy asked, sidling up to Jenna. "We don't get much company in these parts."

"We could have another party," Palmer suggested.

"I think we've had all the partying we can take," Reid gruffly informed the pair, who grumbled something unintelligible.

The entire town had gathered at the airstrip by the time the Cessna landed. Jenna held her breath as the wheels touched down on the hard-packed snow. The two-seater plane came to a stop within eight feet of where Reid had parked his own Cessna.

Jenna's mother waved at her as though she were a beauty queen on parade.

Before anyone could stop him, Pete rushed toward the passenger side and held out his arm, offering her mother assistance as soon as she unlatched the door. With what appeared to be real delight, Chloe slid effortlessly into Pete's waiting embrace.

He released her with obvious reluctance.

"Jenna," her mother cried, hurrying toward her.

"Hello, Mom."

Her mother threw both arms around Jenna, clinging tight.

"What are you doing here?" Jenna asked. Showing up in Alaska was the last thing she'd expected her mother to do.

"What does it look like? I've come to save you."

Save her? From what? "I don't need to be saved."

Her mother laughed. "Oh, Jenna, so much has happened. We must talk. I have lots to tell you."

"In a moment," she told her, looking over at Dalton Gray. Jenna broke away from her mother and steeled herself for the introduction. This man was the reason she'd traveled to Alaska. She'd longed to meet him, to know him and deep in her heart, she'd hoped to marry him. But that was before...

"Jenna," Dalton said reverently as he walked toward her. He held out both arms.

Jenna's stomach tensed and she watched Reid's face harden. It seemed for an instant that he was about to stop Dalton, but Jim placed his hand on Reid's shoulder, detaining him.

Before she could react, Dalton hugged her. "I have waited for this moment for three long months."

She returned his hug, but with little enthusiasm. There was no question that this man was not what he'd purported to be. She had that on good authority, and she suspected it wouldn't take him long to prove Reid and the others right.

"Tell me you're as glad to find me as I am to find you." He reached for her hand and raised it to his lips. "I've lived in horror of what might have happened to you in the last few days."

She snatched her gloved hand away. "I've been fine. Where were you?" He had to realize that if he'd been at the airport as he'd promised, none of this would've happened. Yet he offered not a word of explanation or apology.

"I'll tell you everything later, when we can be alone." He slipped his arm around her waist, and then turned to face Reid as though flaunting her.

Jenna wrenched free from his grasp.

Dalton's face darkened with a frown. "What's wrong?"

"Nothing, but I think it's more important that I deal with my mother right now."

"Come on, everyone," Jake called. "Let's get out of the cold. I've got coffee brewing, and if anyone's hungry there's sourdough hotcakes."

While the others headed for Jake's Café, Pete unloaded Chloe's five suitcases from Dalton's plane and, with Addy's help, lugged them toward town. Out of the corner of her eye, Jenna saw him deposit the luggage at his store but didn't have the opportunity to ask why or to stop him.

Once inside Jake's place, sitting beside Palmer, Jenna realized that Reid hadn't joined them. He remained outside, talking to Jim, although Lucy was in the café, coffeepot in hand.

"It seems you're destined to stay in Snowbound," Lucy whispered as she slid past Jenna and set coffee mugs upright on the long counter. "I sometimes come over to help Jake out," she explained.

Before Jenna could respond, Dalton edged Palmer away from her. He grabbed hold of Jenna's hand with both of his. When he noticed Lucy, he hesitated, leaned close and then whispered, "I hope you didn't listen to anything Lucy had to say about me."

Jenna glared at him. "What makes you think she said anything?"

Dalton sighed as though burdened by his discomfort. "Reid and I have had troubles in the past. Lucy and I were once an item, but I broke it off, and big brother didn't take kindly to that. All I can do is hope you'll listen to my side of the story."

Out of fairness she would, but her sympathy inclined sharply toward Lucy instead of Dalton.

"Jenna," her mother whispered, sitting on the stool on her other side. "Tell me about that gorgeous man who helped me out of the plane."

"Mother," Jenna cried. "You don't want to get involved with Pete."

"Why not?" Chloe protested. "No man's been that sweet to me in years. Did you see the way he took my luggage directly to his store? I think he's attracted to me."

"Mom," Jenna said with a groan, "he's been stuck up here for months without seeing any women. He'd be attracted to—"

"Now don't insult me," her mother warned.

"I'm not insulting you, I'm worried about you."

"Don't be," Chloe said. "Besides I think he's cute in a caveman sort of way."

Jenna could see she was fast losing this argument. "I thought you wanted to talk to me."

"I do," her mother assured her, "but it doesn't have to be this very minute, does it?"

"I think we should speak privately," Dalton, who sat on the other stool, whispered. "Let's get out of here."

Jenna felt like a rubber band, being stretched and pulled from both sides. She looked out at the snowy street, where Reid was still talking to Jim. If he cared about her at all, he'd do or say *something* to dissuade her from going with Dalton. Instead he was out there chatting with Jim as if he didn't have a concern in the world.

"Let me take you to my home," Dalton pressed. "Once we're there, I'll prove how much I love you. I want to take care of you, spoil you. But first we have to get away from all these people."

"I can't do that," she said. She longed for Reid to ask her to stay in Snowbound. Instead, he appeared willing to stand aside and allow Dalton to steal her away.

"Why can't you come?" Dalton asked, sounding hurt. "Let me make up for failing you earlier. I promise when we're through you won't have a thing to complain about. I know how to make a woman happy." What was presumably supposed to be a charming, sexy smile seemed more like a leer.

"I refuse to leave without my mother," Jenna insisted.

"Why not? She seems perfectly capable of looking after herself."

"She isn't, and I'm not deserting her for a…a rendezvous with you."

"You're angry," he said, his tone suggesting he was the injured party.

"Not angry—but you have to understand that none of this is turning out the way I anticipated."

Addy edged between their stools, and with several well-placed jabs against Dalton's ribs, managed to squeeze into the narrow space. "You want me to take Mr. Gray here outside and teach him a lesson or two?" he asked eagerly.

The thought of the older man tangling with Dalton wasn't an appealing one. "Thanks, but that won't be necessary," Jenna said, although she appreciated his eagerness to come to her defense. It was more than Reid seemed willing to do.

"You don't need to worry about me getting hurt," Addy said, dropping his voice to a whisper. "Palmer and I can handle him." He jiggled his eyebrows, as though to imply that they had their own methods of dealing with a tundra rat.

"I'm sure you can."

"Listen, old man," Dalton said, shoving Addy out of the way. "Isn't it time for your nap?"

"Dalton!" Jenna said, outraged at his treatment of Addy. "This is my *friend.*"

"Then I think you should analyze exactly who your friends are."

"Maybe I should," she said, disgusted by his selfish attitude toward her mother and now Addy.

Dalton exhaled sharply. "Jenna, please, I don't want to argue. We've barely had a chance to get to know each other. This isn't right! All I want is some time with you without a bunch of hangers-on. Surely you can appreciate that?"

"What I'd appreciate is the opportunity to deal with this situation as I see fit." Jenna didn't know what to do. Already her mother was deep in conversation with Pete. Their heads were close together and they were gazing into each other's eyes. This didn't bode well. Not only did she have to put up with Dalton, but she had to find a way to keep her mother and Pete apart.

"Leave with me now," Dalton urged, "and I'll fly back for your mother."

"I am not leaving my mother in Snowbound," Jenna said, a resolve strengthened when she viewed the lovelorn looks Chloe and Pete were exchanging.

She watched as Pete reached for her mother's hand.

"I need to get her out of here," Jenna muttered. Since Dalton only had room for two in his plane, she had no choice but to turn to Reid for help.

"Are you going to talk to her?" Jim asked Reid as they stood in the cold while Reid debated his next course of action.

"Talk to her about what?" Reid demanded impatiently. It'd taken every bit of self-control he possessed not to drag Dalton away from Jenna. For an intelligent woman, she sure seemed blind when it came to the other man. He hated the way Dalton had cozied up to her in the café, whispering in her ear. He didn't need much imagination to guess what that creep was saying, either. Apparently Addy had tried to step in, but nothing had come of it. Dalton seemed to be getting what he wanted.

If he'd left even ten minutes earlier, they would have missed Dalton entirely. Their planes would've passed each other in the skies. Now he was trapped here, watching Jenna get friendly with that…that sleazebag. Worse, Reid was forced to pretend he wasn't affected.

"Jenna's not stupid, you know," Jim said. "She'll see through him in no time."

Reid grunted noncommittally.

"Talk to her," Jim advised again.

"About what?" Reid asked, just as he had earlier.

A disgusted look came over his friend's face. "I can tell you what to do but not what to say. That's got to come from you."

Great. What *could* he say to Jenna? He'd tried before takeoff, but it hadn't made any difference.

Reid wasn't going to beg Jenna to give him and Snowbound a second chance. He'd already said as much as he felt capable of saying. He'd told her how difficult it was to take her into Fairbanks, knowing he'd be delivering her to Dalton. What he *hadn't* said was how badly he wanted her to stay in town. He hadn't realized it himself until he taxied down the runway. The dread had built up inside him until he didn't know how he could stand to leave her in Fairbanks. With Dalton. But then Dalton had come here instead....

The café door opened and Jenna walked outside.

"Looks like the decision's been taken out of your hands," Jim said. Reid wasn't amused.

"Can we talk a moment?" Jenna asked him.

"Sure." His heart felt as if it had lodged in his throat.

The café door slammed, and Reid glanced up to see Dalton Gray following in Jenna's wake.

Reid stepped forward to meet them both.

"I want to talk to you," Dalton shouted, pointing a thick finger at Reid's chest.

Reid wished he could shove the guy's teeth down his throat.

"Got a problem, Dalton?" he asked.

"No, I do," Jenna said, moving between them. "Dalton's plane will only take one passenger, and I can't leave my mother behind."

"So you're going with him?" Reid had hoped she'd be sensible enough to recognize what kind of man Dalton was. Sadly, that didn't appear to be the case.

"Of course she's going with me," Dalton said, and slid his arm around Jenna's shoulder.

Jenna tried to shake it off, but Dalton's arm tightened.

"It seems to me Jenna would rather not have your arm around her," Reid said between gritted teeth.

"Are you afraid she prefers me to you?" Dalton smiled.

Reid bit down hard to keep from letting the other man know how much he'd enjoy seeing him in pain.

Jenna managed to shrug off Dalton's arm. "Would you two stop it? I'm ready to go, but I won't unless my mother's with me."

All right, if that was what she wanted, then Reid wasn't going to refuse her. But he had no intention of delivering Jenna to Beesley. He hadn't been willing to do it earlier and he wasn't willing now. Mother or no mother. "I'll fly you back to Fairbanks."

"Jenna's flying with me," Dalton insisted.

That was fine by him, but Reid wanted no part of it. "Then the deal's off."

"Reid," she pleaded. "I can't leave my mother here."

"Then don't go." There, he'd said it.

"You're being ridiculous. I can't stay here, and neither can my mother."

"If anyone flies Jenna out of here, it'll be me," Dalton said again.

Reid's gaze locked with Dalton's.

"She wouldn't be in this predicament if you hadn't dragged her here against her will." Dalton took one step closer to Reid.

"You want to make something of it?" he said, his voice low and menacing, fists clenched.

"You bet I would."

"For the last time, would you stop this nonsense?" Jenna shouted. Her right hand was planted against Reid's chest and her left against Dalton's as she strained to keep them apart. "This is idiotic! All I want is to get my mother back to Fairbanks."

Reid removed her hand. "I'll be more than happy to fly you both. I'm the one with the four-seater plane."

"The hell you will," Dalton shouted. He skirted around Jenna to take a wild swing at Reid.

It was sad to see Dalton's attempt go so far off the mark. Reid had been waiting for this moment too long to be denied, and immediately retaliated. His aim was far more direct and his fist made instant contact with Dalton's jaw. The other man reeled from the force of the impact and stumbled back several steps. Reid's hand hurt like hell, but that was a small sacrifice for the satisfaction of seeing Dalton Gray land on his ass in the snow.

"Now look what you've done," Jenna cried, dropping to her knees beside Dalton. Her eyes were full of tender concern. "Are you all right?"

"He's fine," Reid answered for him.

"That was despicable." Jenna focused her gaze on Reid with such intensity, he felt it burn straight through him.

All he'd done was defend himself. Dalton had thrown the first punch. It wasn't his fault the man was so inept.

"He sucker-punched me," Dalton accused, still in a sitting position and rubbing his jaw.

"No way. You swung first." Jim moved forward and offered Dalton his hand. "Seems to me you got what you deserved."

Standing, Dalton continued to massage his jaw, and his eyes narrowed on Reid. "You're going to pay for this. Come on, Jenna, let's get out of here."

Jenna stared at the sky, and when she spoke her voice was quiet and controlled. "Not without my mother."

"Unfortunately," Lucy said, joining them, "your mother is currently occupied."

"With Pete?" Jenna cried. She closed her eyes. "I had a feeling this was going to happen."

"Why don't you come back to the house with me," Lucy invited, "and leave the men to settle this among themselves."

Reid sincerely hoped she'd agree to that, and with his sister doing the talking, maybe they'd all listen to reason.

"All right," Jenna said, although she sounded reluctant. "But I've got to check on my mother first." She started walking backward, holding Reid's gaze. "Don't hurt Dalton, understand?"

Dalton took exception to that comment. "I can take care of myself," he snarled.

"Don't worry about Dalton," Reid said.

"This is something of a predicament," Jim murmured after the women had left.

"It wouldn't be if Reid hadn't kidnapped my woman."

Reid felt his temperature rise. "Jenna might be a lot of things, but 'your woman' isn't one of them. She doesn't belong to you."

"She will soon enough," Dalton said with confidence.

"I wouldn't count on it."

"She's a woman, isn't she?" His smile struck Reid as coldly reptilian. "Women like me. Lucy certainly did." Now it was Jim who advanced on him, and Dalton quickly got in a second dig. "She couldn't keep her hands to herself. Couldn't get enough of me."

"Keep Lucy out of this," Reid shouted.

"My turn," Jim said, and stepping forward, raised his fists. Dalton swung and Jim easily stepped aside. Apparently Dalton hadn't learned his lesson the first time and took a punch square in the stomach. Eyes wide with disbelief, he doubled over.

Jim shook the pain out of his hand. "Damn, that felt good."

"Jenna's mine," Dalton managed to choke out. "It'll give me even more pleasure to take her to bed, knowing you're sweet on her—and knowing she chose me over you."

Reid wasn't going to respond to his taunts. The man seemed to be looking for a fight; given his experience of the past few minutes, Reid couldn't figure out why.

"I suggest you drop this now," Jim said to Dalton, coming between the two of them.

"Don't worry," Reid assured his friend. "If he wants Jenna so badly, he's welcome to her."

"You lose!" Dalton's voice was smug. "Because Jenna wants me. Why else would she uproot her entire life to come to Alaska? Do you think she'd do anything so drastic if she wasn't serious about me? It's me she came to meet and it's me she'll fly out of here with." His face showed his contempt. "Get used to it, Jamison. You're a loser. You always have been and you always will be." With that he sauntered away.

Jim waited until Dalton was out of earshot, staring at Reid as though he couldn't believe what he'd heard. "You don't mean that about Dalton being welcome to Jenna."

"I do," Reid said. "If she can't see the truth by now, then she never will. Or at least not until it's too late."

"Have faith in her," Jim urged.

Reid wished he could.

Chapter Sixteen

"Are you comfortable?" Pete asked Chloe as he brought her a fresh cup of tea.

"Oh, yes." Chloe sank into the large chair, resting her feet on the ottoman. He'd placed a blanket over her lap and seemed intent on pampering her. They'd come here, to his residence at the back of his quaint little store, to talk privately, which was impossible at the café with everyone pestering them.

"I don't understand why my daughter's in such a hurry to leave," Chloe complained. "I just got here."

"Exactly." Pete lowered himself into the chair across from her. "Tell me about yourself."

Chloe believed in getting the bad news over with first. "I've been married five times," she said abruptly.

"*Five* times?"

"I just can't seem to get it right."

"Perhaps you haven't found a man who'll love you the way you deserve to be loved," Pete suggested.

She could have kissed him for that remark alone. "No, it's my own fault. I keep marrying the wrong man."

"Maybe it's time you found the right one."

Good idea, but Chloe seemed to have difficulty making the distinction. "They're not as easy to find as you might think."

Pete got up and perched on the ottoman, gazing up at her. "Perhaps you've been looking in the wrong places," he said.

Seeing him there, his face so full of adoration and concern, Chloe was beginning to think he might have a point. "Tell me about you," she said, sorry now that she'd brought up the subject of her five failed marriages. "How did you end up in Alaska?"

"I was working on the pipeline, same as Addy and Palmer."

"But that was finished twenty years ago."

"Even longer now, but I liked Alaska and I drifted around from town to town, seeking a little corner of my own. A friend of mine had this store and wanted out. He made me an offer I couldn't refuse and I'm happy here—except for one thing."

"Yes?" she breathed softly.

"I need someone to share it with."

"Oh?"

Pete leaned closer to her. "Now, I realize we haven't known each other long...."

Chloe checked her watch. "We've been together all of forty minutes."

"That's long enough for me. I'm positive you and I could make each other happy. *Very* happy."

"Oh, Pete." Chloe's hand fluttered to her throat. "You don't even know me."

"I know you're a good mother."

"I try, but Jenna's actually the capable one."

"Reid's in love with her."

Her daughter had more men than she could handle, it seemed. "Reid, that big burly man who stood outside and ignored her?"

"That's him."

"Oh, dear, and how does Jenna feel about him?"

Pete shrugged. "Can't say. I don't know her nearly as well as I do Reid, but they spent three days together and...well, she seems smitten."

"This could be a problem."

"Why? It seems to me you'd be more inclined to stay in Snowbound if your daughter was here."

"Stay in Snowbound?" Chloe repeated, shocked by what he was saying.

"I can't let you go, Chloe. Not yet."

Her heart melted. "You're very sweet, and I have to admit that after my divorce from Greg, I'm feeling low and unloved. But you can't *possibly* expect me to live so far from civilization."

"You have to stay, because I think I'd shrivel up and die if you left me now."

That was one of the most romantic things anyone had ever said to her. Chloe smiled softly. She was flattered... and tempted...but she needed more than such a tiny town had to offer. And how could she cope with all this snow and cold? She was a California girl!

"You don't believe me, do you?"

"It isn't that. Let me be honest, Pete. This isn't the right place for me. And you and I..." She shook her head. "After a while we'd get on each other's nerves. I'm speaking from experience here."

"If you stay with me, I'd make it worth your while," he said eagerly.

Chloe couldn't help being curious. "Exactly how do you intend to do that?"

He gave her a smile that warmed her from the inside out. "Let me show you," he murmured in a sexy voice.

Whew. Chloe sipped her tea, and thought it best to change the subject before she succumbed to his undeniable charms. "I'm worried about Jenna. You don't really think she'll leave with that Dalton idiot, do you?"

"I doubt it."

"Good." But Chloe did have doubts. Over the years she'd experienced more than one lapse in good judgment. Until now, Jenna had been sane and sensible, but this flight to Alaska was completely out of character. She seemed to be following in Chloe's footsteps, which was a frightening prospect. Especially for Chloe.

"More tea?" Pete asked.

"No, thanks. I've had enough."

"I haven't." Pete knelt and once more stared up at her with adoring eyes. Slowly, sadly, he shook his head. "You *must* stay. I don't think I can bear it if you leave now."

Chloe giggled with sheer delight. It'd been so long since a man had given her this much attention. And oh, how she needed it.

"You think I'm just flirting."

"Of course you are."

"Don't be so sure…my love."

Chloe blushed. "I should go and see what's happening with Jenna."

"Now? Do you have to?"

"I'm afraid so. My daughter might need me."

"What about *my* need for you?" Pete asked.

Chloe smiled and on impulse leaned forward and kissed his cheek.

Pete's hand went instantly to his jaw. "I won't wash my face for a week."

Chloe smiled again. She'd been doing a lot of smiling in the last hour.

"Allow me to escort you to your daughter, then," Pete said. He offered her his hand and helped her up from the chair.

Arm in arm, they left the store and walked into what remained of the daylight. "It'll be dark in a couple of hours," he told her.

"That soon?"

"In Alaska we have very long nights."

"That would bother me," Chloe interjected.

"Not if you had someone to cuddle with. Then you'd barely notice."

This man made her feel sexy again—sexy and alluring. She dared not listen to his flattery, though; otherwise she'd fall into his bed and, worse, his life. That was a mistake she'd already made five times.

"I wonder where Jenna went," she muttered, glancing around.

"I'll check the café." Pete bounded next door, returning a few minutes later. "She's not there."

"Is Dalton?"

"Yes, and he doesn't seem to be in the best frame of mind."

That was good news, anyway.

"Could anyone tell you about Jenna?"

"Not to worry, she can't be far." Pete guided Chloe toward the ranger station.

Jim stepped out from his office. "We've got another plane coming in."

"Another?" Pete asked. "Who?"

"I can answer that," Chloe said confidently. This was the moment she'd been waiting for since her arrival.

"You know who's coming?" The question came from Reid, who'd joined Jim.

"Brad Fulton," Chloe announced joyfully.

"The business tycoon?" Jim looked as if he had trouble believing this.

"Her former boss?" Reid asked.

Chloe nodded, resisting the urge to crow in triumph. "It's Brad, all right. He's going to ask Jenna to marry him."

Chapter Seventeen

"Did you *see* that?" Jenna cried as she followed Lucy into the cabin. "Reid actually punched out Dalton. Of all the stupid things to do!"

Lucy giggled. "I wasn't there for the full show, but it did seem to me that Dalton swung first."

"He did." Jenna blew out an exasperated breath. "But Reid should've ignored him. Dalton wasn't even close. In fact, his swing was downright pitiful."

"Dalton got what he deserved," Lucy said, grinning, hands on her hips.

"I suspect you're right," Jenna muttered. "Do you, by any chance, still have feelings for Dalton?"

"No way." Lucy shook her head. "I'm so over him you wouldn't believe it. I learned a harsh lesson because of him. I can honestly tell you that when I look at Dalton Gray I don't feel anything but contempt." She chewed on her bottom lip for a moment. "I've said more than I intended. You need to make up your own mind about him."

Jenna mulled over what she'd seen. "Reid was looking for an excuse to fight."

"Yes, I know and I apologize for that," Lucy said.

"The animosity between them has nothing to do with me. Or rather, I'm just the latest…object of contention."

Lucy turned around to face her, leaning back against the kitchen counter. "True, but it doesn't discount the fact that my brother and Dalton both want you."

"Sure they do—as a trophy." Jenna was under no illusions about this.

"It's much more than that," Lucy said with quiet certainty. "At least for Reid."

Suddenly exhausted, Jenna sat down. This hostility between Reid and Dalton was bad enough, but she had other problems. "Do you happen to know where my mother is?"

"She's with Pete at his store."

Jenna groaned. "That's not good news."

"What are you worried about? Pete's an old darling."

"That, my friend, doesn't reassure me," Jenna said. Her mother had a weakness for men. In fact, she seemed to be addicted to them—addicted to male attention and to that first, giddy flush of being "in love." Which meant she and Pete were both craving what they thought the other could provide. "I'd better find her," she said grimly.

"Let them be," Lucy advised. "You've got enough on your plate without worrying about your mother."

"*Someone* has to," Jenna insisted. "And who other than me."

"Find her then, and bring her here for tea."

Jenna was halfway to the door when she hesitated. "No, you're right. If Mom hasn't figured out men and marriage by this point in her life, nothing I do is going to save her." For far too long, Jenna had been in the business of rescuing her mother, only this time, she had troubles of her own.

Lucy carried the teapot over to the table and Jenna sat down.

"So," Lucy said, pouring them each a cup. "This hasn't turned out the way you planned, has it?"

Jenna sagged against the back of her chair. "Not at all." Even now, this was a little difficult to admit. "The fact is, I don't like Dalton. I thought I knew him. When I agreed to meet him, I thought we shared something special. But I can see that we don't." So much for her illusions. She gave a resigned shrug. "I believed he was sensitive and artistic and—" She was interrupted by an indelicate snort from Lucy.

There was a brief silence.

"How long did you and Dalton e-mail each other?" Lucy asked.

"Four months."

"And on that basis you decided to quit your job and come to Alaska?"

Jenna lowered her eyes. "It sounds ridiculous, doesn't it?" As she looked back on the decision, she realized this was something her mother might have done. In fact, Chloe had said so in no uncertain terms. Jenna had always viewed herself as different from Chloe—more practical, anyway—but she was forced to acknowledge that they were more alike than she would've believed possible.

"Not ridiculous exactly," Lucy said thoughtfully. "I don't know you very well yet, but this doesn't seem typical of you."

"It was—it *is* crazy. I knew it even when I made the decision to move."

"So why *did* you? Aside from Dalton, I mean."

"I felt like I had to get away from Los Angeles and—" She paused to stare down at her tea. "I was turning into a frump."

"A frump?" Lucy repeated as though she'd never heard the word before.

"My entire life revolved around my job with Fulton Industries and Brad Fulton. I was his executive assistant, and for a long time I was in love with him. Naturally I would've died rather than let him know that."

"Was he married?" Lucy sounded worried.

"In a manner of speaking. Brad's married to Fulton Industries. I finally figured out that if he hadn't noticed me in all those years, he probably never would. I was afraid I'd end up dedicating my entire life to him, and later I'd be some pathetic spinster who's always carried a torch for her boss. I want a husband and children. A family. It seemed I was constantly taking care of Brad and my mother, and there just wasn't anything left for me."

"But if you're looking for a husband, why choose to meet a man over the Internet?"

"I didn't. That just sort of happened."

Lucy frowned.

"I met Dalton in a poetry chat room."

"Dalton reads poetry?" Lucy's eyes widened with disbelief.

"Somehow, I doubt it. That was all part of his deception." In retrospect, Jenna could see that he'd been lurking at the site, seeking someone naive and trusting. Like a true predator, Dalton had recognized her weakness and gone in for the kill.

Heaven only knew what might have happened if she hadn't run into Reid.

"What are you going to do now?" Lucy asked.

"I...don't know."

Lucy leapt up, throwing both arms around her. "I do. Stay here! Make Snowbound a two-woman town."

"But what kind of work could I do?"

"Oh, I think we can come up with something. If you're as valuable an employee as I suspect, Fulton will keep you on. You could work for him via the Internet."

The idea appealed to Jenna, although she wasn't sure she could ask Brad Fulton for any favors. "There aren't any jobs here?"

"Sure there are. Jake would like to take a day off now and then, and you could work for him. I help him out occasionally. No reason you shouldn't do that, too."

Jenna would need more income than part-time work could provide; still, she was tempted. "Where would I live?"

"At first you could stay here with Jim and me."

Jenna dismissed that out of hand. Jim and Lucy were recently married and expecting a baby, and Jenna refused to intrude on their lives.

"Just for a few days," Lucy said. "You'd be our houseguest, and once everything died down, we'd wait for Reid."

"*Wait* for your brother?"

Lucy grinned. "You'll see what I mean soon enough."

Jenna had a fairly good idea of what Lucy was talking about. She wanted Jenna to hang around town until Reid made up his mind about her. Forget it. Jenna wasn't about to put herself in a situation where she'd be dependent on the whim of a man. Any man. Especially after years of watching her mother do exactly that.

"No," Jenna said, "I'm returning to California."

"But you can't!" Lucy told her. "You just can't."

"I don't see any other alternative. Dalton's a waste of time and Reid—" What could she say about Reid? She felt weak and disoriented just thinking about him. They'd only met a few days ago; they were essentially strangers. No, she couldn't stay in Snowbound and she had nowhere to go except back to the life she'd always known.

"Reid isn't the type to chase after a woman," Lucy warned her.

Jenna had already guessed that. "No, I don't suppose he is."

Lucy began to pace in agitation. "This isn't right! It just isn't right. You and Reid should have a chance to see if you want to be together. And I need a friend. I'm not letting you go, and that's all there is to it."

Jenna loved the determination she saw in Lucy's eyes, but it didn't solve her problems. Her bags were packed and once she retrieved her mother, she'd send Dalton on his way. As soon as he was gone, Jenna would ask Reid to fly her and Chloe back to Fairbanks. From there, the two of them could book the earliest flight home.

Home, she repeated. The word echoed in her mind, hollow and meaningless. Home to her boring, mundane life. Back to being a spectator on the sidelines of life when she so desperately yearned for love and adventure.

"Where are you going?" Lucy asked when Jenna started toward the door.

"To talk to Dalton." She offered her friend a brave smile. "It's time I told him to get out of here."

"Good riddance," Lucy said, giving her a thumbs-up.

Jenna returned the gesture.

"After that, you're going to talk to Reid?" Her look was hopeful.

Jenna nodded, but the subject of her talk with Reid wouldn't be what Lucy assumed. She opened the door and stepped outside. A buzzing noise attracted her attention, and she shaded her eyes against the sunlight as she stared into the skies. She wasn't the only one watching the approaching plane.

"I wonder who that is?" Lucy said, joining her. She, too, shaded her eyes. "Good grief, I can't remember the last time we had this much traffic."

As the plane drew near, Jenna recognized the logo and gasped. Her legs nearly went out from under her. In an effort to keep her balance, she grabbed hold of Lucy's arm. "No," she breathed, hardly able to trust her eyes.

"You know who it is?" Lucy asked.

Incapable of speaking, Jenna merely nodded.

"Am I supposed to guess?"

"It's Brad Fulton."

"Your former boss? The one you said you were in love with?"

Again Jenna nodded.

"Oh, boy," Lucy muttered, sounding depressed. "I guess I'd better get used to the idea that you're leaving Snowbound."

"Who's that?" Palmer asked Addy.

Both men stood outside Jake's Café and studied the plane. "No idea," Addy said. Life in this town had turned mighty interesting ever since Reid brought Jenna here. For many years, Addy hadn't had much use for women. Snowbound had done just fine without 'em. Then Jim had to go and get married; Addy had figured that would ruin everything. He'd been against it and tried, with Palmer's backing, to talk the park ranger out of getting hitched. Jim, however, wouldn't hear of it. Reid wasn't any help, either, seeing that the intended bride was his sister.

The day Jim brought Lucy to live in Snowbound, Addy was convinced their way of life was over, but he'd been wrong. It took a big man to admit he'd made a mistake, but Addy was willing to own up to his. Unfortunately, that was a weakness of Palmer's, who'd jump into a lake full of ice before he'd confess he'd been wrong.

But even Palmer had to admit that Lucy's arrival had been a boon to them all. She didn't say a word about how often they bathed. Nor had she asked questions that were none of her business. Women he'd been with in the past—the distant past—were notorious for wanting to know everything about him. Lucy hadn't pried into his private affairs and he appreciated that.

What she did was invite him and Palmer to dinner, and he appreciated that even more. She was a mighty fine cook, too.

"There's something written on the plane," Palmer commented, squinting up at the sky. "Can you read it?"

"You know I don't see good without my glasses."

"Then why don't you wear them?"

"Why don't you wear yours?"

"'Cause I don't."

"Well, I don't either." Palmer could be real irritating at times.

"If you wore your glasses, you could read Jake's menu." Palmer went on, refusing to drop the matter.

"Now why would I need to do that?" Addy demanded. It was a good thing he was a patient man, because there weren't many who could tolerate Palmer's annoying questions. Darn it, he was worse than the women Addy used to know. "Jake hasn't changed the menu in ten years. We both have it memorized."

"That's true," Palmer muttered. He continued to squint. "Fulton Industries," he cried triumphantly. "That's what it says on the plane."

"Fulton Industries," Addy repeated, then asked, "When was the last time we had two planes land here within an hour of each other?"

Palmer shrugged. "Never."

"That's what I thought." A promising idea was beginning to take shape in Addy's mind. Excitement coursed through him and he raised his arms in the air and shouted, "We've been discovered!"

Palmer stared at him. "What?"

"All of a sudden, Snowbound is on the map. It's turning into a tourist destination."

Frowning, Palmer scratched the side of his head.

"Don't you see?" Addy said urgently. "People are coming here in *droves*."

"We got two planes, Addy."

"Still, that's two planes more than we had a week ago. It wouldn't surprise me if people started flying in here off of those cruise ships."

Palmer looked confused. "We're a long ways from any cruise ships."

"It's what they call an excursion. The cruise ship sends 'em to Fairbanks by train."

"Yeah," Palmer agreed readily enough. "But we're a long ways from Fairbanks, too."

"Don't you get it?" he said. He didn't know how Palmer could deny the evidence when it was right before his eyes.

"Get what?"

"That people have a hankering to visit the tundra."

"Maybe," Palmer said slowly. "But what's that got to do with us?"

"You and I are going to start a tour business. That's what."

"Touring where, Addy?"

"Here. The tundra." Sometimes his friend could be downright obtuse. "People want to see it."

Palmer scratched his head again. "There isn't anything to see out there."

"Yeah, but the tourists don't know that."

Palmer agreed with him but still seemed puzzled.

Addy was getting tired of explaining the obvious. "Do you want to be my partner or not?"

Palmer hesitated. "I think we should talk to Reid first."

Addy shook his head. Reid had a habit of squelching their ideas. The last time he'd thought of a way to make their fortunes, Reid had talked him out of it. Okay, so maybe selling genuine tundra snow wasn't his most brilliant plan, but he kept thinking about the guy who came up with pet rocks.

"Reid's smart about these things."

"I don't have time to wait on Reid," Addy insisted, marching into the cabin he shared with his best friend.

"What are you doing?"

Addy found a piece of cardboard, then got a black felt-tip pen from the kitchen drawer. "What does it look like I'm doing?"

"Making a sign," Palmer suggested tentatively.

"Yup."

"What's it gonna say?"

Addy groaned in despair. "Just find me a two-by-four, would ya?"

"Sure, Addy."

A few moments later he could hear his partner rummaging about in the cabin's one closet. Palmer returned just about the time Addy had finished with the sign.

"Can't find one," Palmer said. "What about one of the pickets off that old fence down by the airfield?"

"Now you're thinking."

"You won't tell Jim I was the one who took it, will you?"

"Nah," Addy promised, although it wouldn't take Jim long to realize where that missing picket had gone.

Addy found a hammer and nail and attached his sign to the weathered picket. When he finished, he decided his effort looked surprisingly good.

"Where you gonna put it?" Palmer asked.

"Right outside our office," Addy told him.

"We've got an office?"

"We sure do, and it's right here." He walked outside and set up the picket directly in front of the cabin. Anyone who happened by would read the sign that said: TOURIST INFORMATION. TUNDRA TOURS ARANGED. WELLCOME TO ALASKA!

Palmer joined him and they stood straight and tall with their sign between them. Now all they had to do was wait for the tourists to start arriving.

Chapter Eighteen

Reid viewed the approaching plane with a feeling of unease. Brad Fulton had come for Jenna. He couldn't prove that—yet—but why else would a powerful industrialist fly into Snowbound? He obviously wanted Jenna, and from what Reid could tell, she wanted him, too. So much for any romantic notions *he'd* entertained.

The Learjet landed, its wide body taking up every inch of the airstrip. The entire town had come out in the fading light of the short November afternoon to see what was happening. Everyone lined up along the edge of the strip, including Addy and Palmer, who carried some kind of ridiculous sign. Everyone except Pete. Reid frowned suddenly. Correction, everyone except Pete and Jenna's mother.

The plane door opened, and a set of stairs appeared. The business tycoon stepped forward, his face peering out. He looked around, and when his gaze landed on Jenna, he smiled.

He climbed down the stairs.

Addy and Palmer rushed toward him and planted themselves directly in his path, holding up their sign. Fulton ignored them and walked over to Jenna. Reid wanted to groan out loud when Dalton slipped into place beside her and put his arm possessively around her shoulders.

Reid would have turned and walked away then, but he wanted to know what Jenna was going to do. Jenna had confessed that she was in love with her boss and now Fulton had arrived to claim her. He felt an immediate sense of loss.

"What are you doing here?" Jenna asked. To her credit, she'd skillfully removed Dalton's arm from her shoulders.

"I came for you," Fulton said, as though that was a foregone conclusion.

No surprise there, Reid thought.

Addy and Palmer stood a respectable two feet behind Brad Fulton, holding their sign as high as they could manage.

"Is there someplace we can go to talk?" Fulton asked. "Someplace private?"

"The café," Jenna suggested.

Fulton glanced past her to the café and sighed. "Perhaps we could talk in the jet?"

"I don't think so," Dalton said.

"Stay out of this, Dalton," Jenna snapped.

Fulton regarded Dalton with a look of disgust, and asked, "Who is this man?"

Jenna waved her hand between them. "Brad Fulton, meet Dalton Gray."

The two eyed each other suspiciously.

"We need to talk," Fulton said again, leveling his gaze on Jenna.

"Before you do, I have something to say," Dalton insisted. He reached for Jenna's hand, got down on one knee and stared longingly into her eyes.

It was all Reid could do not to gag.

"You're the midnight sun to me," Dalton began. "You're the mysterious moon and the stars in the night sky." He waited, apparently gauging the effect of his words. When she stared at him open-mouthed, he brought in the pièce de résistance. "Marry me," he declaimed.

"I beg your pardon?" Jenna said, leaning closer.

Reid held his breath. If she accepted Dalton's proposal, he wasn't sure what he'd do. It wasn't a prospect he wanted to consider.

"Marry me," Dalton repeated. "I've loved you from the moment we first shared our thoughts on the Internet. I know why Mr. Big Shot is here, and that's to steal you away from me. I'm not going to let that happen."

"I don't believe you have a lot of say in the matter," Fulton said coldly. "The choice is hers."

"I'm not interested in marrying you, Dalton." Jenna didn't hesitate, and Reid had to restrain himself from cheering out loud. She did have the common sense he'd credited her with. Relief filled him, quickly followed by despair. If Jenna rejected Dalton, that was one thing, but if she left with Fulton that was another.

Fulton sent Gray a victorious smile. "You have your answer."

Dalton glared back at the other man, then turned to Jenna, his face suffused with sincerity as he got to his feet. "I refuse to take no for an answer. At least hear me out."

"There's nothing to hear," Jenna told him. "I don't mean to be cruel, but I'm not interested in any kind of relationship with you. I came to Alaska to meet you, I have, and that's all there is to it."

Like a bad actor, Dalton struck his forehead, obviously intending to signify his grief and shock at her heartlessness.

No one appeared to notice.

"If Jenna marries anyone, it'll be me," Fulton announced.

Reid knew that was coming, but he hadn't expected the other man to propose in front of the entire community.

"Marry you?" Jenna said.

"Surely this can't be a surprise," Fulton said with a good-natured chuckle.

"I was your assistant for six years. Why are you asking me to marry you *now?*"

"I need you, Jenna," Fulton murmured. "Nothing's right without you. I want you back."

"As your assistant?"

"Yes…no. I want you, period. I didn't realize how empty my life would be without you. You've been with me nearly every day for the last six years and all of a sudden, you weren't there anymore. That was when I realized what I should always have known. I need you in my life." He looked a bit embarrassed to be declaring his feelings in front of all these strangers.

Jenna seemed on the verge of tears, and Reid strained to hear her response.

"I was in love with you for years," she whispered.

Dalton shook his head angrily. "You might've said something to me," he spat. "Take her," he muttered as if this were his decision alone. "I'm getting out of this pathetic little burg." With that, he stalked toward the airfield.

Addy and Palmer followed him, holding up their sign. As soon as Dalton got in his plane, the two old men returned to stand behind Fulton, patiently waiting for the tycoon to acknowledge them.

"Then it's settled," Fulton said. "You'll marry me."

Reid could no longer remain silent. "Congratulations, Jenna," he said, approaching the couple.

"Congratulations?" She looked at him in a daze.

"Who's *this?*" Fulton asked.

Reid offered the other man his hand. "Reid Jamison."

Jenna gestured toward him. "Reid…flew me into Snowbound."

Fulton nodded as though that explained everything. "I see."

"For a woman who claims to have trouble with relationships, you seem to be doing all right for yourself," Reid said. "I doubt many women can claim to have received two marriage proposals within five minutes. That's quite a feat, isn't it?"

"Yes…I suppose it is," she replied distractedly.

"Congratulations, Fulton," Reid said, shaking the other man's hand. Fulton shook his head. "She hasn't accepted my proposal yet."

Everyone looked at Jenna, anticipating, no doubt, a resounding *yes.* When she did speak, she hardly sounded like herself at all. "Where's my mother?"

"She's still at Pete's," Jim told her.

For reasons Reid couldn't explain, she turned to face him. "I need to talk to my mother."

Fulton frowned heavily. "You're asking your *mother* for marital advice?"

Jenna nodded, although, in fact, she had other compelling reasons for finding Chloe. Like getting her away from Pete—and onto a plane home.

"Do they serve anything stronger than coffee over at that café?" he asked Reid.

"Sure do," Jake said, steering the other man toward his establishment. "We got beer and wine."

Fulton marched off to the café, with Addy and Palmer directly behind him, still holding up their sign.

"I'll help you find your mother," Reid volunteered.

Jenna nodded. "Did you hear?" she said, her voice awed. "Brad asked me to marry him."

"I heard." It was difficult to conceal his antagonism, but he managed. "You'd be a fool to turn him down."

"Why?"

"Why?" Reid echoed in disbelief. "You're in love with him. You said so yourself. This is your dream come true."

"I used to think it was," Jenna said slowly. "What if I said I wasn't sure I wanted to marry Brad?"

Reid shook his head. "Why wouldn't you? He's perfect. The two of you have worked together for years. He knows you, and you know him. Besides, he's so rich you could have whatever you want."

"Money isn't everything," Jenna informed him primly.

"Maybe not everything," he agreed, "but it's a good ninety percent."

She dismissed his comment with a shake of her head. "So you think I should marry him."

"I didn't say that," he was quick to tell her.

Her face turned red, which Reid recognized as barely controlled anger. He'd seen this same look a dozen times in the last three days.

"Let me see if I've got this straight…" she began.

"You don't want to talk to me about this," Reid interrupted. "Let's find your mother."

"Right," she agreed with a sigh. "My mother's been married five times. I'm sure she'll have a simple solution to this."

In his opinion, there weren't any simple solutions, but he wasn't going to tell her that. He led the way to Pete's store, which had a closed sign in the front window. He ignored that and walked inside. "Pete?" he shouted.

Almost immediately he heard a rustling sound from Pete's living quarters in the rear of the shop. "Are you in the back?" Reid called.

"Out in a minute," Pete returned gruffly.

His words were followed by the distinct sound of a female giggle.

"Mother!" Jenna charged ahead and tore open the curtain that separated the store from Pete's private quarters.

Reid charged after her and stopped abruptly at the sight before him. Pete, wearing the most incredulously happy grin, sat up in the sofa bed. Jenna's mother sat next to him. She was clearly naked, clutching a sheet against her breasts.

"You *slept* with him?" Jenna was aghast.

"Now, sweetheart, it isn't what it looks like," her mother protested.

"The two of you are naked in bed together!" Jenna shouted. "What else could you possibly be doing?"

"Pete was just demonstrating why I should stay in Snowbound."

"He took you to bed for that? If you'd been smart enough to ask, I would've told you all he wanted was sex."

"Well, yes, I realize that, but it's really wonderful sex." Her mother blushed as she said it. "I mean…well, sweetheart, if you were more experienced, you'd know what I'm talking about. There are men and there are *men,* and well, I don't suppose there's a genteel way of saying this—but Pete is one hell of a man." She sighed expressively and rested her head against his bare shoulder.

Pete beamed with pride.

"This might not be the best time for a heart-to-heart with your mother," Reid suggested. Taking Jenna by the hand, he steered her out of the room.

Jenna pointed back at the closed curtain. "My mother went to bed with a total stranger."

"Pete's a good guy."

"He just slept with my mother!"

"I didn't say he was perfect."

Chapter Nineteen

Life had certainly taken an unexpected turn. Jenna had left Los Angeles, hoping for love and adventure in Alaska, and she'd found them—but not with the man she'd intended to meet. Now she was about to return to California. When she boarded Brad's Learjet, she would leave both her mother and her heart behind.

"You're sure this is what you want?" Lucy asked, walking out to the airstrip with her.

It wasn't, but Jenna didn't feel she had any choice. "It's what has to happen."

"I'll keep an eye on your mother," Lucy promised and hugged her, looking forlorn.

Jim slipped his arm around Lucy's shoulders.

"You're really leaving?" Palmer asked. He removed his hat with the dangling earflaps and stared down at the frozen snow as solemnly as if he were attending a funeral.

"I have to," Jenna said. She couldn't stay in Snowbound, much as she wanted to. She needed a reason and the one person who had the power to give her that had remained silent.

"I'm going to miss you," Addy said in a low voice. He, too, had removed his hat and stared down at his muddy boots. "It isn't going to be the same without you here."

Palmer agreed with a nod of his head. "Never had seafood spaghetti that tasted better than what you cooked for us that one night."

"Me, neither," Addy said.

"Thank you." Jenna kissed Addy's forehead.

"Doesn't feel right having you leave like this… We were just getting to know you," Palmer whispered.

"I know," Jenna said and kissed the other man's stubbled cheek.

"Are you ready?" Brad asked.

Jenna gave the town a final look before she boarded the plane. She hadn't said goodbye to Reid, who'd mysteriously disappeared. The moment she'd announced she was returning to California with Brad Fulton, he'd vanished. She'd hoped he'd ask her to stay, but he hadn't. That hope refused to die, though, and she'd held out until the last possible moment.

She'd just started up the steps when Reid shouted her name. She turned to see him, her heart pounding with a mixture of dread and excitement. Hurrying toward him, she didn't bother to disguise how pleased she was.

He took both her hands in his. "I can't let you go without saying goodbye." He glanced at the plane. "Fulton will be a good husband."

"Perhaps." Jenna wasn't convinced she would marry Brad. He didn't truly love her. He was accustomed to working with her, to seeing her five or six days a week. He enjoyed the ease she brought to his professional and private lives. That wasn't a firm enough foundation on which to establish her future.

"You *aren't* going to marry him?" Reid asked, frowning.

She hesitated, then explained. "I've agreed to come back to work for him."

His frown deepened. "But eventually you'll marry him." He made it sound like an immutable law of nature—like something that couldn't possibly *not* happen.

"I don't know." She hesitated, hoping Reid would say the words she longed to hear. When he didn't, she hung her head, defeated.

"Right," he said abruptly. "Well…"

"Jenna," Brad called impatiently from the plane's opening.

"I have to leave. Thank you," she said, putting on a brave front. "You know, when we first met, I thought you were horrible."

His grin was sheepish. "I *was* pretty detestable."

"No," she whispered and ran her index finger tenderly along his shaved upper lip. "You were wonderful. I might have made the biggest mistake of my life if not for you."

Reid dismissed that, shaking his head. "You would've seen through Dalton in five minutes. You're a lot more savvy than you realize. I should never have brought you here," he said and then with meaning added, "but I'm glad I did."

"I'm glad you did, too." Impulsively she hugged him and, for just a moment, closed her eyes and savored the feel of Reid's arms around her. It broke her heart that she might never experience this again. She waited, her heart in her throat, for some sign that he wanted her to stay.

"Goodbye, Jenna." He stepped away from her.

"Watch out for my mother?"

He nodded, grinning. "She seems a little preoccupied."

Jenna rolled her eyes and he laughed. She took in the dear, sweet faces of her friends, then walked purposefully toward the plane.

"Jenna! Jenna!" Her mother shouted from the distance as she raced toward the plane. Pete was with her. Judging by their open coats and flapping scarves, the two had dressed quickly in an effort to catch the plane.

"Mom…" Jenna narrowed her eyes at Pete. She began to warn her mother about staying with such a man, but then changed her mind. As she'd told Lucy, Chloe was old enough to make her own decisions and live with the consequences. Jenna was through rescuing her.

"You're really leaving?" Her mother apparently hadn't believed her earlier.

"I told you I was."

Pete stood next to her, his hand at the back of her neck and his gaze, as always, adoring.

"I'm staying." They exchanged a long glance, obviously drunk on love. The only thing wrong with that, Jenna thought wryly, was the nasty hangover that came later.

"All right, Mother, stay," she said in an even voice.

"I *can't* leave," Chloe whispered, her gaze not wavering from Pete's. "I've never known this kind of happiness."

"Yes, Mother."

Chloe looked away. "I mean it, Jenna."

Jenna was sure she did. "I don't doubt you, Mom. It's just that I've heard this all before." Still, she wasn't going to list her mother's failed marriages now. More than likely, Pete didn't know a thing about any of the previous men. That was her mother's habit. She didn't see any reason to compromise a new relationship with a small thing like the truth.

"I've discovered my soul mate," her mother said dreamily.

"Of course you have."

"I mean it," she insisted. "When you fall in love, you won't be so skeptical."

That was true enough, she supposed. "You'll call me, won't you?" Jenna urged.

"She can use the phone in the office," Reid assured her.

"Thank you." Jenna offered him a grateful smile. She'd give her mother a week, two at the outside, and then Chloe would return to California, disillusioned, miserable—and cold. For two or three weeks afterward, she'd be an emotional wreck, waking Jenna at all hours of the day or night. Then, miraculously, Chloe would snap out of it and everything would go back to normal until the next man. And the next, and the man after that.

"Jenna," Brad called to her a second time. "We need to leave."

She nodded and gave each of her friends one final hug before racing up the stairs, blinded by tears.

Pete's store was closed for an entire week. Everyone in town was ready to complain, but on the seventh day after Jenna flew out of

Snowbound, the sign stated OPEN. Apparently Pete was back in business.

Reid had to admit he was curious. Who wouldn't be? No more than half an hour after the sign appeared, everyone in Snowbound found an excuse to visit. Reid wasn't the first customer of the day. Jake had beaten him by a good ten minutes. Pete was totaling up the other man's purchases when Reid entered the store.

"'Morning," Pete said, sounding more jovial than Reid had ever heard him.

Reid acknowledged the greeting with a nod.

"Anything I can help you find?" Jenna's mother asked, stepping out from behind the curtain. She looked mighty chipper herself, Reid mused.

"I was thinking of making myself a pot of chili," he said, taken aback by her bright smile.

"He'll want kidney beans and a packet of spices," Pete told her. "And add a package of toilet paper. I figure he must be nearly out." Pete had an uncanny ability to keep track of all his customers' household supplies.

"Right away." Chloe scurried behind the counter and assembled Reid's groceries.

"Chloe's agreed to be my partner," Pete explained.

"Do you want me to put this on your tab?" she asked Reid before he could ask what Pete meant. Business partner? Marriage? Or the living-together kind of partner? He wondered what Jenna would think of *that*.

"Please."

She nodded, and Pete smiled benevolently in her direction.

"So," Reid said, hoping the "partners" might give him a few more details. "How's it going with you two?"

"Fabulous," Chloe assured him.

Pete pulled her into an embrace. "Life couldn't be better."

Reid could only hope it lasted. "Do you want to phone Jenna this afternoon?" It was an innocent enough question, but he wasn't just being neighborly. He hadn't been able to get the woman out of his mind. At the end of the day, his cabin felt empty. *He* felt empty. He didn't know what he could've said or done to persuade her to remain in Snowbound. He had nothing to give her, nothing except his heart, and that wasn't enough. He couldn't compete with everything Brad Fulton had to offer.

"I probably should call Jenna," Chloe said. "She worries, you know."

"I'll drive you out to the station on the snowmobile," Pete murmured.

"See you both later, then," Reid said, and taking his purchases with him, he left. He returned to the cabin long enough to put the ingredients for his dinner in the crock pot, then hopped on his snowmobile and drove out to the pump station.

Chloe and Pete showed up early in the afternoon. He found it difficult to be around them, constantly reminded as he was of their overwhelming happiness. Reid hadn't considered his own existence bleak or dull until he saw Pete with Chloe. He felt like a man who didn't realize he was hungry until he stumbled upon a table sumptuously set for dinner.

"Would you dial for me?" Chloe asked, handing him a scrap of paper with the number.

Reid dialed and waited for the connection, then passed the phone to Jenna's mother.

"Don't you want to talk to her?" Chloe asked, not taking the receiver.

Reid did, more than he cared to admit.

"Hello?"

Her voice made him weak with longing. "Jenna?"

"Reid? Oh, Reid, it's so good to hear from you! Is everything all right with my mother?"

"Everything's fine. She's here now. Do you want to talk to her?"

"Of course, but…I'd like to talk to you, too."

"Okay. I'll give you to your mother first." He passed the phone to Chloe. It occurred to him that from the moment she'd left Snowbound, he'd been waiting for the sound of her voice. He just hadn't known it....

Absorbed by his thoughts, Reid didn't hear anything Chloe was saying. When he did start paying attention, Jenna's mother was making plans to collect her things in California and move to Alaska permanently. Apparently Jenna was objecting and the conversation wasn't going well.

"Here," Chloe muttered, handing him back the receiver. "*You* reason with her."

Reid preferred not to be caught between mother and daughter, but he was so anxious to talk to Jenna, he disregarded his better judgment. "What's going on?" he asked.

"Mom and Pete want to get married."

"I see." Pete was holding Chloe and she'd buried her head in his shoulder, weeping quietly.

"This would be her sixth marriage," Jenna said.

"I guess practice makes perfect," he said frivolously, immediately sorry when his remark was greeted by disapproving silence.

"They've barely known each other a week." Jenna was definitely aghast. "A week! Reid, you've got to *do* something."

Reid felt at a complete loss. "I don't see how I can. They're both adults and they certainly seem compatible."

"That's an understatement if I've ever heard one," Jenna agreed with heavy sarcasm. "Besides, when my mother gets like this, it's impossible to reason with her. I'll do my best to talk her out of it when she flies down to get her things."

"Worth a try if you feel that strongly about it."

"It's the best I can do for now," Jenna muttered. "How are you?"

"Fine," he told her heartily. "What about you?"

"Good," she said after a moment.

"Are you working for Fulton Industries?"

"Yes."

She didn't sound happy or excited, and selfish as it was, Reid felt downright glad.

"How's Lucy?" she asked, changing the subject.

"Doing well." Reid hadn't talked to his sister much. Lucy and Jim were in love, and their relationship, like Pete and Chloe's, emphasized how alone he was. At this point, Reid didn't want to think about that.

"Addy and Palmer? Have they come up with any more business ventures lately?"

"Not yet."

"Oh."

"Give them time, it's only been a week."

"A week? That's all?" she asked.

"It seems longer to me, too."

The line went quiet, and Reid discovered that he'd admitted more than he wanted to. "I guess I'd better go," he said briskly, as though he had a dozen other things he needed to be doing, when all he really cared about was talking to Jenna.

"Yeah, me, too. You'll call again?"

"If you'd like." He didn't want to appear too eager.

"Only if it's convenient," she said.

"Okay."

"Bye."

"Bye." Reid replaced the receiver and kept his hand on it for an extra moment before he realized that Chloe and Pete were watching. He cleared his throat and straightened. "It was good to talk to Jenna," he said.

Pete and Chloe exchanged glances. "So it seems," Chloe said with a knowing smile.

Chapter Twenty

Jenna received three letters from Snowbound on the same day. The first was from her mother, the second from Lucy and the third, the shortest of the three, from Reid. Jenna opened her mother's letter first.

My Darling Jenna,
I know you're upset with me, but please don't be. I'm insanely, deliriously happy. Pete is a wonderful, wonderful man. For the first time in my life, a man sincerely and utterly loves me. Because of your objections, we've decided to wait a month before applying for a wedding license. That should please you.

You assumed I'd be home by now, I know you did. I thought I'd miss California, but I don't. This is *love,* my darling daughter. Love as I've never known it with five previous husbands. I don't expect you to understand, although I'd appreciate it if you'd try. You didn't expect me to last a week in Alaska, knowing how I thrive in the sun, but I've discovered I could be happy living in a desert as long as Pete and I were together.

I can hear all your arguments. I agree with you, it *is* too soon.

You think Pete and I don't know that? You see, my sensible daughter, I've wasted almost forty years on men who were wrong for me. I knew the first time Pete took me in his arms that we were meant to be together. Scoff if you want. I can't say I'd do anything different if the situation were reversed. But in my heart I know Pete's the one and only man for me.

Everyone asks about you. Addy and Palmer are such dears, aren't they? When they heard Pete and I wanted to get married, they decided to turn their cabin into a wedding chapel. They're still trying to get a minister, though.

I'm planning on making a trip back to Los Angeles in the near future. I need to pack my things and put the house on the market. I know you're living there right now, which I appreciate, but I hope you won't mind finding a new place. With your salary increase from Brad Fulton, it shouldn't be hard.

Write me soon, and please, Jenna, try to understand. For the first time in my life, I'm truly happy.

Mom

Jenna went through the letter a second time, attempting to read between the lines to be sure Chloe hadn't backed herself into a corner and was afraid to admit she'd made a mistake. Her decision to sell the house was a shock. Throughout her five marriages, she'd maintained her own home, a gift from her parents, refusing to give it up. Now she wanted to put it on the market. If anything, this convinced Jenna that her mother was telling the truth—she was in love.

Lucy's letter confirmed it. Her friend wrote about Christmas preparations in the town, about Addy and Palmer's wedding chapel and how everyone was amazed at the changes in Pete since Chloe's arrival. Most days the store didn't open until noon and the two of them seemed passionately involved with each other. She concluded with a discussion of the names she and Jim were considering for the baby.

Jenna purposely saved Reid's letter for last. His was a single page, written in his slanted scrawl. He, too, mentioned her mother and Pete. They appeared to be the main attraction in Snowbound. He asked about her job and told her the cribbage board was gathering dust. In the end, he said he'd be happy to hear from her. Very little of what he'd written was personal, but he added a series of comical pencil sketches in the letter's margins, depicting Addy and Palmer holding up their Tourist Information sign and decorating their wedding chapel.

Jenna searched for any hint that he missed her or was thinking about her. Well, perhaps the comment about the cribbage board. If she wanted, she could attach a lot of significance to that—which was something she couldn't afford to do.

She wrote everyone back the same day.

The next week, she wrote again and included small gifts. A shop apron for her mother, a baby blanket for Jim and Lucy and for Reid, she enclosed a new deck of cards.

Almost right away, she got two letters from Reid and learned that mail was delivered only twice a week in Snowbound. Her mother sent word that she was coming home on December tenth to make arrangements for the house. Jenna was dying to talk to Chloe, dying to learn about her friends, but mostly she wanted to ask about Reid. She treasured his letters and read them often, sharing bits with her friend Kim, seeking her advice. Even when she knew she wasn't likely to receive a letter, she hurried home to check her mailbox.

Her mother was due to land early in the afternoon, and Jenna had agreed to meet her at the house directly after work.

"Is something bothering you?" Brad asked her at the end of the day.

They'd quickly fallen into their old routine. He hadn't brought up the subject of marriage again, and really, why should he? She was in his office the way she'd been for the past six years. Nothing had changed, except that she had a substantial raise.

"Sit down, Jenna," Brad said, motioning to the chair across from his desk.

She didn't want to get home late, not today, when she was so eager to see her mother.

"This will only take a moment," he assured her.

"All right." Pen and pad in hand, she positioned herself in the comfortable leather chair across from his massive desk.

His eyes grew serious. "You're not happy, are you?"

She opened her mouth to deny it, and then decided that would be a lie. "I miss Alaska."

"Alaska?" he repeated. "Or Reid Jamison?"

She dropped her gaze. "Both."

Brad didn't say anything for a long moment. "I thought so. You're in love with him, aren't you?"

She nodded, not trusting herself to speak.

"You haven't been the same person since you returned."

"I hope my work's still satisfactory." She hadn't been as scrupulous about details and sincerely hoped she hadn't disappointed her employer.

Brad dismissed her worries with a shake of his head. "I could see it when I flew into Snowbound. I assumed if I brought you back here you'd eventually forget him. That hasn't happened, has it?"

"I tried to put him out of my mind," she admitted. She'd tried to convince herself that her feelings for him had dwindled, but then the letters had started coming and her heart had refused to maintain the pretense.

"What are you planning to do about it?" Brad asked next.

Jenna knew the answer, although she'd delayed facing the truth. "I'm going back with my mother. I'm sorry, Brad. I'm letting you down, but this isn't working."

To her amazement, he grinned. "I know, Jenna. Don't feel guilty about it. Go, with my blessing."

Jenna leaped to her feet. Dropping the pad and pen, she blinked back tears. Until he'd pressured her for an answer, she hadn't realized how lonely she was for her friends, her mother and—above all— for Reid.

She understood now what her mother had tried so hard to tell her in letters and phone calls. Chloe had indeed found her soul mate in the unlikeliest of places, and so had Jenna. But Jenna didn't have the courage or the faith in her own judgment to follow the dictates of her heart, to believe in her feelings. Not anymore. She knew she loved Reid and as soon as she could, was telling him exactly that.

"Go," Brad said again. "I know you're in a hurry to leave. Don't worry about giving me your two weeks' notice. And wish your mother much happiness, all right?"

"My *mother?* You want me to give my mother your best wishes?"

"Sure do." Brad chuckled. "I've let bygones be bygones." He gave her a quick, affectionate glance. "Keep in touch, Jenna. And send me an invite to your wedding."

Jenna hurriedly, joyfully, gathered up her personal effects and was out the door. She drove to her mother's house, which was in a friendly neighborhood of row houses constructed in the early 1950s. Signs of Christmas were everywhere. Lights glittered from rooftops and brightly colored bulbs dangled from trees and bushes. A Santa and reindeer were propped on the roof across the street. She saw that the front door to the house was open.

Jenna parked in the driveway and hurried inside. "Mom?"

But it wasn't her mother who came to greet her. Instead, Reid walked out of the kitchen.

"Reid?" She felt as if someone had knocked the breath from her lungs. "What are *you* doing here? Where's my mother?" Then it occurred to her that none of those answers mattered. What did matter was seeing him. She tossed her purse aside and ran into his outstretched arms.

Reid lifted her from the ground, and their mouths met in an urgent, hungry kiss. A kiss that held back nothing, gave everything.

Jenna was weak and breathless when they finished. Her legs would barely hold her upright. Reid's large hands framed her face as his eyes devoured her in the same way his mouth had.

"Your mother's with Pete," he murmured, his voice husky.

"In Snowbound?"

"No, here. They went out to get boxes."

"Pete came with her?"

He nodded. "They couldn't bear to be apart, so he left Addy and Palmer to run the store."

"You came, too?"

He smiled, and Jenna swore it was the most beautiful smile she'd ever seen. Then he kissed her again, and finally, reluctantly, eased his mouth from hers. With what appeared to be a huge effort, he clasped her shoulders and stepped back. "Let's talk, all right?"

"Sure." There wasn't a chance in hell that she'd object.

Reid led the way into the kitchen, where they sat side by side at the small table. "I got a phone call from Brad Fulton last week."

"Brad phoned you?" This was a shock. "Why?"

"Frankly, I wondered the same thing."

"What did he want?"

Reid held her gaze. "He asked me if I was in love with you."

Her heart stopped, then started again at an accelerated pace. "What...what did you tell him?"

Reid shook his head. "It irritated me, if you want to know the truth."

Jenna bit her lower lip and looked down, trying to hide her disappointment.

"I asked if he'd called to gloat," Reid said with a humorless chuckle. "But Fulton said I'd won. You're in love with me."

"He told you that?" Jenna cried.

"Is it true?"

When she hesitated, he added, "Your mother said it, too."

"And if I am?"

"Then I think Addy and Palmer might be on to something."

"What do Addy and Palmer have to do with this?"

"Well, you know they've opened a wedding chapel. I'd like to give them some business."

Jenna stared at Reid. Unlike her mother, Jenna intended to marry only once in her life—and she wanted it all. She wanted the romance *and* the companionship, the laughter *and* the heartfelt declaration of love. She needed the sure knowledge that this man would move heaven and earth to make her his.

"Are you asking me to marry you, Reid?"

"Yes." Then he quickly said, "You came to Alaska for adventure and romance. I want to give you both, but I want our marriage to last longer than a vacation. What I need is forever." He took her hand in his and gazed into her eyes. "I love you, Jenna. I don't have anything to offer you but my heart— and an entire community that loves you and wants you back. Please say you'll marry me. Be my snow bride."

With tears blurring her eyes, she nodded.

Reid kissed the inside of her palm. "I hope you don't believe in long engagements."

"No."

"Good. Because I propose a Christmas wedding."

She was in his arms then, and Jenna knew that was exactly where she was meant to be.

Epilogue

Jenna and Reid were getting married in Snowbound on Christmas Eve. The ceremony would take place in Jake's Café, with Addy and Palmer serving as wedding consultants. Their own cabin was far too small for the expected number of guests, so they'd agreed to the restaurant instead. Thankfully Lucy and Chloe offered the two entrepreneurs lots of assistance with all the arrangements. In fact, the entire community was caught up in the wedding plans.

A couple of hours before the ceremony, Jenna stepped into the brightly lit café to look around. She was astonished by the transformation the rather mundane café had undergone. The tables had been set against the wall, covered with white tablecloths. Orderly rows of chairs had been arranged in a churchlike setting, with an aisle wide enough for Pete to escort her down. Poinsettias lined the front of the room, where a square table held a large candle, as yet unlit, and a Bible.

"I wondered if I'd find you here," Reid said from behind her.

Everyone in town was preparing for the wedding. The only two who seemed to be at loose ends were Jenna and Reid.

"It all looks so beautiful," she whispered, glancing around the room, feeling the love of her friends in every detail. Even Brad Fulton, who wasn't able to attend, had sent two cases of the best champagne and his very good wishes.

"Who's there?" Jake called, sticking his head out from the kitchen. "Hey," he muttered, wearing a cantankerous frown, "the groom isn't supposed to see the bride before the wedding."

Reid was having none of that as he gave Jenna a quick hug. "I didn't know you were so conversant with wedding etiquette."

Jake shook his head. "If I wasn't so busy, I'd chase you out of here, but I'm rolling meatballs for the reception and I don't have time for you."

"Good." Reid shared a sexy grin with Jenna.

Still mumbling under his breath, Jake returned to the kitchen.

"How are you holding up?" she asked, sliding her arm around his middle. She'd been in town a week, and was living with her mother and Pete—who'd been married, much to Addy's and Palmer's consternation, while visiting California.

"I'm doing okay," he muttered, which told Jenna he wasn't.

"Honestly?"

"No," he confessed, and leaned down to kiss the bridge of her nose. "I want you with me. Every minute we're apart is torture."

Although Jenna loved hearing it, she had to point out that her situation these past few days hadn't been any easier. "I don't think I've ever seen my mother this much…in love. Those two—I can't believe it." She shook her head. "Oh, Reid, they're just crazy about each other."

"I'm crazy about you," Reid whispered. "My snow bride."

Jenna basked in his words. "I love you, too." She giggled, adding, "My snow man."

"I can't believe you're actually willing to marry me."

"It took you long enough to ask," she said sternly, reminding him that he'd made no effort to stop her from leaving Snowbound.

"You flew out of here and it was as if my whole world went dark."

"It *is* dark in Alaska," Jenna said, "especially in winter." In December there was barely an hour of daylight before night descended on them again.

"That's not what I mean and you know it," Reid said. "I let you leave, thinking I was better off without you, but I was wrong."

Reid couldn't come up with poetic lines the way Dalton could, but he possessed so many more of the qualities she considered important. "I felt pretty dreadful, too."

"The only reason I let you go was that I assumed you'd marry Fulton, and really, why shouldn't I think that? One of the richest men in the country came chasing after you."

"Why shouldn't you think that?" Jenna echoed. "Because, my soon-to-be husband, I'm in love with *you*."

Reid pulled her into his arms and held her close. "Do you mind saying that again? I can't seem to hear it often enough."

The door opened, and Kim and Lucy entered. Both came far enough into the café to notice Reid and Jenna with their arms entwined and stopped cold.

"What are you two doing here?" Lucy cried.

"Together?" Kim added.

Jenna exchanged a look of longing with Reid, a look that reminded him that within a few hours they'd be together. Forever.

"Everyone was hustling and bustling about," Reid confessed. "I was only in the way."

"Me, too," Jenna told her friends.

The café door opened a second time, and Addy and Palmer hurried in, each carrying a small wicker basket filled with what Jenna assumed were wedding favors. She didn't think it would be a good idea to examine those too closely.

"You're early," Addy commented, and rubbed the side of his neatly trimmed beard. He wore his heavy boots and hat with dangling earflaps; his nose was red from the cold.

"You aren't dressed proper, either," Palmer complained, glaring at Reid. "If I'm going to wear a suit, *you* should have to."

"You're wearing a suit?" This Jenna had to see.

"He looks good, too," Addy said, nodding proudly in his friend's direction.

"It's a bit tight." Palmer reluctantly removed his heavy winter jacket. "I can't remember the last time I tried it on, but I think it'll do. As soon as the preacher finishes, I'll take off the jacket."

The suit, a bold green-and-blue plaid, looked like something out of a fifties clown catalog. Jenna managed to squelch a laugh when she realized how hard her friends had tried to make her wedding as beautiful as possible.

"Oh, Palmer," Lucy whispered.

"He looks dapper, doesn't he?" Addy said, as if to claim credit.

"Quit talking about me," Palmer insisted. "I don't want to grab any attention away from the bride. Jenna's the one people should admire, you know." He sent Jenna an apologetic glance. "Sorry, Jenna, I didn't mean to steal your thunder. This is your big day, yours and Reid's. If you want me to change, I will," he said hopefully.

"Oh, no, Palmer, you wear your suit. I'll take my chances."

Reid reached for her hand and squeezed her fingers, letting her know he appreciated her patience with his friends.

"You're going to be a beautiful bride," Kim whispered.

"She is," Lucy agreed.

Despite herself, Jenna blushed.

"Now scoot," Lucy said, ushering Jenna out the door. "The wedding's in a couple of hours and we want to have everything ready."

"I think we have our marching orders," Reid said.

"It seems that way."

Before Jenna had a chance to object, Kim and Lucy whisked her out the door and away from Reid. She shrugged and cast him a resigned smile before the door closed.

Two hours later, with the entire population of Snowbound in attendance, Pete escorted Jenna down the aisle to the makeshift altar, where Reid waited. She wore a white dress that was elegant and traditional at the same time—the perfect garb for a snow bride. Chloe stood off to the right, in the front row, weeping decorously. Loud sniffling came from Palmer and Addy, who sat on the other side. Kim and Lucy were serving as maids of honor, while Reid had asked Jim to be his best man.

The flame on the candle danced and cheered as "Silent Night" played softly in the background.

Reid held out his hand. With tears of happiness blurring her eyes, Jenna stepped toward him, ready to link her life with his.